THE DEAD

MARK OLDFIELD was born in
Sheffield, and now lives in Kent.
He holds a PhD in criminology.

By the same author

THE SENTINEL

THE EXILE

THE DEAD

MARK OLDFIELD

HEAD of ZEUS

First published in the UK in 2017 by Head of Zeus Ltd

9 7 5 3 1 2 4 6 8

A catalogue record for this book is available from
the British Library.

ISBN (HB) 9781781851692
ISBN (XTPB) 9781781851708
ISBN (E) 9781781851722

Typeset by Adrian McLaughlin

Printed and bound in in Great Britain by
CPI Group (UK) Ltd, Croydon CR0 4YY

Head of Zeus Ltd
First Floor East
5–8 Hardwick Street
London EC1R 4RG

WWW.HEADOFZEUS.COM

For Viv

Only the dead have seen the end of war.
George Santayana

I think the dead care little if they sleep or rise again.
Aeschylus

The living know that they will die,
but the dead know nothing; they have no further
reward for the memory of them is forgotten.
Ecclesiastes 9:5

Men should either be treated generously or destroyed,
because they take revenge for slight injuries –
for heavy ones, they cannot.
Niccolò Machiavelli

Once again, the women return. Older now, the years of sorrow etched deep on faces that resemble those of the crucified Christ in the nearby church where tomorrow a few of them will take mass. Most will not. Faith is so often a casualty of these events. That and truth, of course.

Each year they gather on this date, their numbers diminished by the inevitable attrition of age and sickness. But those who can will make their way once more to this isolated hotel, noting its slow decline without comment, perhaps sensing that the deterioration of the building mirrors their own.

The women keep to themselves in the small garden, quietly watching the grey waves break along the shoreline below. The past lies across their lives, a dark monument to cruelty, its presence still raw and immediate. No amount of talk can alter that and so they say little. Perhaps there is comfort in the silence, a hope that someone might say something that would, in some unimaginable way, alleviate their inexhaustible grief. No one ever does.

At the end of the second day, as taxis arrive outside, their engines grumbling in the heat, the hotel manager appears on the terrace, stooping, as if he bears the accumulated weight of the women's pain. This year, he is obliged to walk with the aid of a walking frame and it takes quite some time to get down the steps to lay the bouquet of flowers on their table as he always has. The women wait in silence until he is back inside the hotel. Then they rise, take the flowers and throw them to the ground before trampling them into a fragrant mulch.

1

She opened her eyes and stared into the darkness, wondering how long she had been here. Wherever here was. She remembered being in her apartment, watching flickering images of her father's murder projected on to a wall. His casual wave as he started the engine. The car pulling away from the kerb. The explosion. Oily smoke rising into the spring air.

Then waking to this.

When she first regained consciousness, she had panicked, thrashing and twisting, trying to loosen the grip of the thick leather straps that kept her spread-eagled against the rough wooden board, condemned to this blind, timeless suffering. But her efforts were futile and the Barcelona shirt she wore as a nightdress was soon soaked with sweat from her exertions. With a groan, she let her head fall back, shivering violently.

Hours passed. Hours of lying immobile in the dark and the cold. Each attempt at movement generated new complexities of pain. She could move her head, twist her body slightly, but no more. She fought to stay calm, hearing only the drip of water somewhere in the darkness, the sound of her frantic breathing, her existence reduced now to a nightmare of enforced anticipation.

A door creaked open. She tensed as she heard muffled footsteps coming towards her. Two people, one walking quickly, the other more slowly. She lifted her head, straining to see.

Suddenly, the world burned with white light, dazzling and painful after so long in the dark. Slowly, she looked up at the man standing over her and felt all hope drain away. She hadn't expected this.

'Pleased to see me, babe?' Sancho chuckled as he lit a cigarette. As her eyes became accustomed to the light, she saw clusters of chains and pulleys hanging above her, ropes with hooks on the end. Some sort of warehouse perhaps, though the equipment looked as if it could be put to other uses.

Sancho came closer and sat on the edge of the pallet, humming to himself. Trying to intimidate her, she guessed. It was working.

The slow footsteps came nearer, the sound of laboured breathing. She raised her head and watched as a tall elderly man emerged from the shadows.

'Look who's come to meet you, Ana,' Sancho laughed. 'Meet *Comandante* Guzmán. He's going to ask you some questions.' He leaned closer and gripped her chin, forcing her face towards the newcomer. 'You've been wanting to meet him, haven't you?'

Her eyes widened as she thought of the hours she'd spent documenting Guzmán's bloody work as Franco's assassin. She had never expected to encounter him in the flesh.

She saw the old man's expression as he looked at her. It was not pleasant. He moved away, outside her limited range of vision. A moment later, she heard noises at the foot of the pallet. The sounds of tools being taken from a case. Metal parts being screwed together. Unable to see, she could only imagine what he was doing. Beads of sweat trickled from her hair.

'I've got a meeting in an hour, so I want this over as quickly as possible.' Guzmán's voice was sharp. 'Push this against her leg,' he said, handing something to Sancho.

She swallowed, desperate to look, afraid of what she might see. Then looked anyway.

Sancho was holding a metal rod connected by a wire to a box on the floor. She flinched as he came closer. His stale wine breath, the sour odour of nicotine.

'Fuck you.' It was the best she could think of.

Something cold touched her left calf. As she struggled to see what was happening, Sancho put the metal probe against her leg a few centimetres above the knee. She started to insult him in a

3

desperate gesture of defiance but her words were cut short by a firestorm of pain as the electricity surged through her. A terrible blinding pain, as though her limbs were being ripped from their sockets, her back arched as if pulled upwards by an invisible cord. She heard a voice begging them to stop. Her voice.

Abruptly, the pain stopped and she slumped back against the pallet, gasping for breath. When she opened her eyes, she saw Sancho watching her. He was smiling.

'You fucking tattooed, pierced freak.'

He grinned. 'Ana's been rude to me, *Comandante*. What do we do about that?'

Guzmán ignored him. 'Ready for a few questions, señorita?'

She glared back defiantly, though she kept quiet.

'Each time we give you another shock,' Guzmán said, 'I'm going to raise the strength of the charge. At those levels, it's not unusual for bones to break or joints to be dislocated.'

'That should be interesting,' Sancho laughed.

'The pain will be considerable. Unbearable, in fact,' Guzmán said as he picked up the electrode. 'Shall we proceed or are you going to answer my questions?'

Galíndez let her head fall back onto the pallet, trying to prepare herself for the pain. Judas thoughts raced through her head: *Tell them something. Anything.*

She flinched, startled as Sancho took the metal rod from her thigh. 'Come on, Ana, tell us what we want to know.'

'She will, eventually,' Guzmán said. 'They always do.'

'Wait.' Galíndez raised her head as far as she could. 'What is it you want to know?'

'You can begin by explaining why you started investigating my activities,' Guzmán said. 'And if you don't I'll show you what pain really is. Understood?'

'Yes.'

'You mean, "Yes, *Comandante*."'

She swallowed. 'Yes, *Comandante*.'

'That's better. Now, answer my question.'

This time, Galíndez didn't hesitate. She began with the drive out to an old mine in the sierra where fifteen desiccated bodies had lain hidden since the fifties. Described how she met Profesora Ordoñez who revealed the killer's name to her: Guzmán.

'But you found no real proof?' Guzmán asked. 'Nothing tangible?'

'Oh yes we did.' Behind her, she heard Sancho taking a drink from a plastic bottle of water. She licked her cracked lips, tempted to beg him for a drink. Instead, she continued, recounting how she'd dug several bullets from Guzmán's Browning out of the ditch where the execution took place. And then later, she'd discovered a map at the university showing a hiding place in Guzmán's old *comisaría*.

'A map you stole from Profesora Ordoñez,' Sancho chipped in. 'You can't trust anyone these days, even prissy cops like you, *Anita*.'

'Don't call me that.'

A bleak laugh. 'Why don't you stop me?'

Guzmán pushed the electrode against her leg, prompting her to continue. Galíndez hurriedly explained how she and Natalia broke into his abandoned police station in search of his hidden secrets.

The last part was the hardest, telling him how she'd discovered Guzmán's hiding place only to be attacked by Natalia, the woman she loved. The woman she thought loved her, though Natalia was a thief, employed by the *Centinelas*.

'The *Centinelas*? You're sure it was us who hired her?'

'That's what she said,' Galíndez said. 'Just before she fractured my skull.'

'That must have taken some doing.' Sancho laughed.

'How much do you know about the *Centinelas*?' Guzmán asked. The electrode pressed against her ankle and her breathing grew faster, anticipating the pain.

'Not much. I found documents signed by someone called Xerxes. That's the code name for their leader.'

'Our leader.' Guzmán nodded. 'What else?'

She closed her eyes, trying to remember. 'The documents

showed they were involved in the attempted coup in 1982. They were angry because it had been carried out too soon. A memo said that they should wait until the time was right.'

'Oh we're very good at waiting,' Guzmán muttered.

Galíndez lifted her head. 'You were mentioned in those documents.'

'Do tell.' Guzmán's voice was almost gentle. 'If you don't, I'll make you scream like a pig in the slaughterhouse.'

'I saw a memo that said that all communications had to go through you. And there was a comment that some people thought you were unreliable.'

'Was there any mention of the Western Vault?'

She narrowed her eyes. 'What's that?'

'The name doesn't mean anything to you?'

'No. I've never heard of it.' If he asked another question, she decided to make something up. Anything to defer the pain.

'Tell me about the sword,' Guzmán said.

That came as a surprise. Her mind raced, wondering if he already knew it was at *guardia* HQ, wondering how much pain she could stand if he guessed she was lying. Then again, he might already know she had it, in which case there would be more pain.

'It's at *guardia* HQ,' she said, cursing herself for giving in. 'In the evidence store.'

'Good girl,' Guzmán said. 'I'm sure you were tempted to lie. It's a good job you didn't or Sancho would be scraping you off the roof now.' He turned away and put the electrode on one of the packing cases. 'We're done,' he said to Sancho. 'She's worthless.'

Sancho sounded disappointed. 'Give her a few more shocks, she might be holding something back.'

'If she knew anything, she'd have told me, I can assure you,' Guzmán said. 'I'll leave her to you, now, you know what to do.'

Galíndez's eyes darted from one man to the other. 'What are you going to do?'

'Where's the Bulgarian?' Guzmán asked, ignoring her.

'Waiting next door.' Sancho laughed. 'He's keen to get started.'

6

'Make sure he does a good job,' Guzmán said. 'Destroy all the evidence afterwards.'

Galíndez struggled frantically against the leather straps. 'What are you going to do?'

'Nothing,' Sancho grinned. 'That's why we have the Bulgarian. He's good: you'll be dead before you know it.'

'I wouldn't count on that,' Guzmán chuckled.

MADRID, M-607, TRES CANTOS

Isabel Morente pressed the accelerator, glad to be free of the thick city traffic. As she drove, she lifted her phone and dialled a number. The phone rang a couple of times before someone answered.

'Colegio de la Virgen, how can I help you?'

'Good morning,' Isabel said. 'I'm picking up my friend's daughter this lunchtime, I just wanted to know what time you break for lunch?'

'One o'clock, señora.'

Isabel cut the call and turned the radio back on. As she'd guessed, the main topic was Galíndez's disappearance. A variety of speakers gave their opinions, most opted for kidnapping, probably terrorist related. Isabel sighed as a psychic called in to give her explanation of what might have happened. It was clear no one had a clue, not the *guardia*, not the police and certainly not the radio station. After twenty minutes she'd had enough and reached out to switch off the radio just as the presenter revealed that the search for the missing civil guard was now focusing on a stretch of the river Manzanares, near Arganzuela.

COLMENAR VIEJO 2010, COLEGIO DE LA VIRGEN

The school yard echoed as a knot of children poured out of the school doors, desperate for lunch. Inés Fuentes wandered towards the gate with a friend, both with their eyes on their phones. She groaned. 'Oh no, Mum's going to be ten minutes late picking me up. Can you believe it? She can be so selfish.'

Her friend smiled. 'I'd wait with you but I'm going to the dentist this afternoon.'

Inés shrugged. 'I'll live.'

'See you later then. Text me?'

'I will. See you, Blanca.'

As Blanca disappeared out of the school gate, Inés returned to checking her messages. Engrossed in reading them, she didn't notice the woman coming towards her.

'Are you Inés Fuentes?'

Inés looked up and saw a dark-haired woman, vaguely familiar. She was beautiful, big eyes, a soft smiling mouth. 'Don't I know you?' Inés asked.

'You might, I'm a reporter,' the woman said. 'My name's Isabel Morente.'

'You used to be on the radio, didn't you?'

'And on TV before that.'

'I'd like to be on TV one day. Are you here to interview someone?'

'I want to talk to you about Ana María,' Isabel said. 'You remember her, don't you?'

Inés gave her a brief nod, suddenly uncomfortable.

Isabel looked her in the eye. 'Want to tell me why you made up those lies about her?'

A sudden silence. Inés looked down. 'It was all true,' she muttered.

'You took a photo of her when she came out the shower,' Isabel said. 'Ana didn't know you'd taken it, did she?'

Inez shook her head, irritated. 'I told my papa what happened.'

'Your papa believes you because he thinks he brought you up to tell the truth,' Isabel snapped. 'But you lied to him about that photo. Do you really want Ana to go to prison? To be picked on every day, to be beaten up, maybe even killed, because she's a cop?'

Inés tossed her hair from her face, anxiously. 'She told me off and I got mad.'

'And you thought a few years in prison would teach her a lesson?'

'I didn't mean for it to happen,' Inés sighed. 'I came into the room just as she came out of the shower. She had her back to me and I took a picture while she was getting a towel. It was only a bit of fun. I didn't know Mamá would see it. But then she went nuts and so did Papa. After that, I didn't say anything because I knew they'd be angry.'

Isabel heard the sound of heels behind her and turned. A woman was coming towards her, her face flushed with anger.

'What's going on? What have you been saying to my daughter to make her so upset?'

'You must be Inés's mother?' Isabel said. 'I'm a friend of Ana María.'

'How dare you talk to my daughter about the case. This will make things much worse when Ana goes to court.'

'Oh, I don't think Ana will be going to court. Do you, Inés?'

Inés shuffled. She said nothing.

Isabel raised an eyebrow. 'Two minutes ago you told me you took that photo without Ana María knowing.'

'No,' Inés muttered. 'I didn't, Mamá. Honest.'

'This is outrageous,' Mercedes Fuentes said. 'I'm going to call my husband. I wouldn't be surprised if you get arrested for this.'

'I doubt that will happen,' Isabel said, taking her phone from her pocket. 'You can use my phone to call your husband if you like. I've got some nice apps on it.'

'What do I care about apps? You're harassing my daughter.'

Isabel shrugged and pressed the button on her phone. 'This is my favourite app of all.'

'I took a picture while she was getting a towel. It was only a bit of fun. I didn't know Mamá would see it. But she did and then she went nuts and so did Papa. After that, I didn't say anything because I knew they'd be angry.'

9

Isabel stopped the playback and put the phone back in her pocket. 'I'm done harassing your daughter, Señora Fuentes. But I suggest you and your husband start worrying about the lawsuit that's going to be coming your way.'

Isabel started to walk off but after a few steps she came storming back, her face rigid with fury. 'Incidentally, Ana María fought off several armed attackers and saved both your daughters' lives when your house was attacked and you never even thanked her. And now she's been kidnapped.' Her voice cracked with emotion. 'You couldn't care less.'

Angrily, Isabel walked back to her car. She got behind the wheel and switched on the radio. The news was just beginning and she listened as the newscaster announced the breaking news. The search for missing civil guard Ana María Galíndez was over. Her body had been recovered from the River Manzanares earlier that morning. A statement from General Ramiro Ortiz of the *guardia civil* was expected within the hour.

MADRID 2010

'You're going to be headline news, señorita,' Guzmán said, looming over her. 'This will send out a very strong message.'

Galíndez frowned. 'To who?'

'The people it's intended for.' He reached for his briefcase. 'I'll be off, Sancho.'

'OK. I'll take care of the cleaning up after.'

'After what?' Her voice was tight.

'Sancho will tell you.' Guzmán turned and walked away into the shadows.

She listened as his footsteps faded. A door opened and closed. Then silence.

'You know, you're in real trouble,' Sancho said.

'Let me go now and I'll see to it that you get a discount off your sentence.'

A mocking laugh. 'Did they teach you to beg at the Dark Moon dojo?'

'How do you know I trained there?'

'Because the only person I know who'd teach you to fight like you do worked at the Dark Moon. A tall black girl called María Cristina Mendez.' He prodded her in her side with the toe of his boot. 'Am I right?'

She looked away, wondering how he knew so much about her. And why. 'Who's this Bulgarian?' There was no hiding the anxiety in her voice now.

'He's a Bulgarian, how do you think he got the name? He kills people for a living.'

'I'll fight you,' Galíndez said quietly. 'Just you and me.'

'That's very generous but no.' Sancho sighed, exasperated. 'It's your own fault. You've stuck your nose into things that are none of your fucking business without ever thinking about the consequences. You had a chance to back off but you never took it. And because of that, you're about to be on the receiving end of the worst our resident East European psycho has to offer.' He shook his head. 'You had a chance. You should have taken it because that was the only chance you're going to get.'

'How was I to know that?' Galíndez snapped.

'Ignorance is no excuse.' He grunted. 'I thought you were a Legions of Death fan?'

'Legions? They were the worst band in the world.'

'One of the kids at the Fuentes place said you liked them.'

Somewhere in the shadows, she heard a door open.

'I only said that to be polite because Inés had one of their albums.'

The door closed. Her breathing grew faster as she heard footsteps coming towards her.

'You remember their last album?' Sancho said. 'There was a track written just for you, "Death is for Losers". That's what you are, a loser.'

'Fight me then. I'm not scared of you.'

'Too late to get feisty now, babe. You've got an appointment with the Bulgarian.' He gave her a contemptuous look. 'Look at you: your pants are showing.' He bent and pulled the hem of her football shirt lower. 'There, you don't want Mr Bulgaria getting ideas, do you?'

Galíndez turned her head away, hiding her anger.

'Speak of the devil.' Sancho sniggered.

She saw a figure emerge from the darkness. A squat man with dark cropped hair above a sallow vicious face. He licked his lips. 'This her?'

'No, it's my sister, come to visit me for Easter. What do you think, Ygor?'

'My name not Ygor, is Stefan.'

'Stefan is spelled Ygor in Spanish,' Sancho said. 'Didn't you learn that in prison?'

'I don't understand you sometimes, man.'

'That's because you're stupid. Just do your job and we'll all be happy.'

The Bulgarian smirked. 'She don't look too happy.'

'Nah, she can't wait for you to get started, Ygor.'

'Is not Ygor, boss, is Stefan, I keep telling you.'

'And I look like I care, do I?'

Galíndez strained against the straps, her mind reeling.

'You know where to do it?' asked Sancho. 'Take her through that door over there, turn right and there's a cell at the end of the corridor. Do her in there. I've put down some plastic sheets and newspapers. Wrap her body in plastic and clean up when you've finished.'

'No problem,' Stefan said. 'Just give me a hand to get her up.'

As they began to unfasten the restraints on her wrists and ankles, Galíndez tensed, determined to take advantage of this unexpected opportunity. She had a plan: once she was on her feet, she would drive her finger into Sancho's eye, putting him out of action while she dealt with the Bulgarian. *One chance?* She'd show him.

There was a flaw in her plan. She realised that as soon as the straps were unfastened and the blood began circulating painfully through her cramped limbs. Her legs gave way and she fell heavily, moaning with frustration.

'I forgot to say, it might hurt for a bit.' Sancho laughed as he dragged her to her feet. 'Come on, Ygor, get the cuffs on her. That's it, hold your hands out, there's a good girl.'

She slumped against him, letting him take her weight as he snapped the handcuffs around her wrists, cuffing her hands in front of her.

'You really are a loser, Galíndez.' Sancho took a step back and slapped her across the face. The blow snapped her head back, sending her falling into the Bulgarian.

The Bulgarian gripped her by the shoulders. 'You coming to watch, Sancho?'

'I've got more important things than her to worry about. What's up, can't you do it on your own? What kind of Transylvanian pussy are you? She's had it, look.' He grabbed a handful of Galíndez's hair and yanked her head back. She closed her eyes against the glare of the overhead lights. 'Helpless as a kitten.' He rolled her head from side to side. 'See? She's finished.'

'She's not finished till I'm done with her.' Stefan grinned.

'Take her away then, Prince Charming, she's yours.'

Galíndez walked slowly, the stone floor icy against her bare feet, obeying the Bulgarian's directions as he steered her across the chamber and through a door into a low passageway that stank of damp. A solitary light bulb dangled from the arched ceiling.

As they walked, Stefan took the opportunity to torment her, explaining in detail what he was going to do before she died. She tried to stay calm, remembering the things Mendez taught her at the dojo. But dealing with this situation was far harder than listening to the instructor in a gym, ten years ago. Her first instinct was to fight back against the Bulgarian's roaming hands. But if she tried to fight him now, he would win: her limbs were still too stiff after being restrained for so long. She needed to wait, seize her chance. That meant being patient. Meekly, she kept her head lowered, a picture of defeat.

As they came to another door, she raised her head a little, looking for something that might give her an advantage. She needed to focus, but concentrating was difficult with Stefan pawing her. Despite her revulsion, she let herself fall against him once more, forcing him to hold her steady, confirming her helplessness.

'Stay on your feet, bitch,' Stefan muttered, pushing her against the wall. She leaned against it, her head lolling from one side to the other. 'Stay here, OK? I got to undo the bolt.' He stepped back, hands raised ready to catch her if she fell. Satisfied she was able to stand unaided, he turned to open the door.

As he turned away, Galíndez tossed her hair from her face and saw the door in front of her, the door to the cell where he was going to kill her. Rusty bolts, at the top and bottom. Her arms were dead weights as she raised her hands, taking care not to let the chain between the cuffs make a sound. Sweat dribbled down her forehead and she blinked it away, watching intently as Stefan knelt and began struggling with the bolt. Now was the time to take him, while he was on his knees. But then she heard the dry scraping of the bolt as it opened and the moment was gone. As Stefan got to his feet, tears stung her eyes. Sancho was right after all: *One chance.* She'd missed it.

Stefan reached for the bolt at the top of the door. Being short, he had to stretch, clutching at the bolt with both hands, his head tilting back as he tried to move the rusty metal. A sudden guttural laugh as the bolt loosened. The laugh of a man happy in his work.

Galíndez hurled herself forward and looped the handcuffs over the Bulgarian's head, dragging the chain against his throat as she wrapped her legs around his, unbalancing him.

Stefan teetered, on the verge of falling, he threw himself backwards, slamming her into the wall, the pain shimmering through her ribs like fire. Winded, she hung on as he struggled, trying to get his fingers under the chain cutting into his throat. When that failed, he smashed her into the wall again. The pain was worse this time: if he kept this up, she was finished. She had to take the offensive.

As he struggled, trying to pound her against the wall again, she sank her teeth into his ear, biting deep, feeling the crunch of flesh and cartilage as she threw herself sideways, her legs still wrapped round his. He fell with his weight on top of her, though she kept his legs pinioned as she dragged the chain tighter around his throat. The metal cuffs cut deep into her wrists but she clung on, sensing a change in his movements. Sudden desperate noises, his hands scrabbling at his throat, feet flailing helplessly. And then his struggles grew weaker and she heard the rattling in his throat, felt the sudden convulsions as he died.

For a moment, she lay beneath him, gasping for breath. Somewhere along the passageway a door slammed. Frantically, she squirmed out from under the dead man and searched his pockets, holding her breath against the growing stench of his shit until she found the key to the handcuffs. As she removed them, she bit her lip to stop herself crying out as blood dripped from the raw circles where the metal cuffs had cut deep into her flesh.

She staggered back down the corridor, fighting the urge to run, for fear of attracting Sancho's attention. Rising ahead of her, she saw a steep flight of stone steps. As she stumbled towards them, she heard Sancho's voice, booming from the chamber, asking what the Bulgarian was doing. She was in no shape to take Sancho on right now, and she hurried up the steps.

At the top of the steps, she saw a large wooden door with a rusty key in the lock. Quickly, she tried to open the door. The key didn't move. Down the passageway Sancho was asking what the fuck was taking Stefan so long. Desperate now, she gripped the key in both hands, grunting in pain as the rough metal chafed her hands. Sancho heard the noise and shouted again, thinking she was Stefan. When he got no reply, he started to come down the passage, his slow, cautious footsteps echoing along the damp walls.

Galíndez felt the panic rising, her breath coming in ragged gasps. Gripping the key tight, she put what was left of her strength into a last desperate attempt. Slowly, the key began to turn, the grating of metal agonisingly loud in the shadows. She grabbed the door handle and pulled but the door stayed put.

'That you, Ygor?' Sancho's voice, low and threatening.

She put her foot on the wall at the side of the door, grasped the handle and then brought her entire weight to bear on it. The door gave a grudging creak, though it didn't move.

'Ygor?' Sancho's footsteps stopped.

Galíndez heaved again and the door swung open, almost sending her sprawling on the landing. As she picked herself up, she heard Sancho's heavy footsteps coming up the stairs. She dashed through the door and staggered out, blinking as she found herself looking across a busy street. Without looking back, she ran across the road, making for a grocery on the far side.

As Galíndez entered the shop, the people queuing at the counter moved away from her. A glimpse in a mirror behind the counter told her why: wild, tousled hair, dark-ringed eyes stark in her pale face, the Barcelona shirt torn and soaked with sweat and blood.

Someone muttered about an escaped mental patient. Another said she looked like the missing woman they'd been talking about on TV. And then an authoritative voice cut through the speculation, telling them to dial 062 and get the *guardia*, for fuck's sake. A familiar voice: it was hers.

As the adrenalin left her body, she slumped against the wall, shivering, vaguely aware of someone putting a jacket round her shoulders. After that, things blurred into a vague sequence that ended when she woke up in hospital: the siren of the ambulance as it arrived, a brief argument with the paramedics before Galíndez reluctantly allowed them to put her on a stretcher. One of the customers saying they'd heard on the radio she was dead. Another onlooker seemed vaguely disappointed that she seemed much taller in the photo they'd used on TV. There was no pleasing some people, she thought as the ambulance pulled away from the kerb. Safe now, she let her head fall back on the pillow. A moment later, she was asleep.

Once the ambulance had driven off, the small crowd gathered on the pavement began to disperse. One man stayed at the kerbside for a little longer, watching as the ambulance gave a quick blast of its siren to force its way into the heavy traffic. A light drizzle was falling and the piercings in the man's face glinted as he walked over to a parked car and got behind the wheel. He lit a cigarette, listening to the siren fading. As the first green and white vehicles of the *guardia civil* screeched to a halt outside the grocery, he started the car and swung out into the traffic, heading for Puente de Toledo.

CHAPTER 2

MADRID, OCTOBER 1982, SEVILLA–MADRID EXPRESS

The dissonant metallic rhythm of the train pounded through his head with the precision of carefully inflicted torture. That comparison was based on professional opinion. Though Guzmán knew little of trains, in the other matter he was vastly more experienced.

It was just after nine in the morning and he already bristled with an incipient rage, provoked by six hours of sitting in a smoky first-class compartment that was anything but first-class. He looked round at worn seats with grimy headrests and scowled as he recalled just how much a first-class ticket cost. Not that he'd paid for his.

The conductor's voice suddenly interrupted his angry reverie. 'I told you before, señor, you can't travel in this coach without a ticket.'

Glad of the distraction, Guzmán turned from the window and stared at the conductor. 'And as I told you before, fuck off.'

'I'll have the police on you when we get to Madrid.'

'I am the police, you cretin.' Guzmán sighed as he pulled his identity card from his pocket and held it up. That had an immediate effect, since the movement caused his jacket to fall open, revealing the Browning nestling in its holster under his left arm.

The conductor's face grew pale. 'Are you travelling on official business, señor?'

At least some people still maintained a proper respect for the forces of law and order, Guzmán thought, sensing a climb-down. He gave a conspiratorial nod.

'That's all right then,' the conductor muttered, hurrying away into the next carriage.

Thirty minutes later, the train pulled into Atocha station beneath the great arched iron and glass roof. By then, Guzmán was standing by the door with his suitcase, waiting impatiently. As he pushed through the milling crowd towards the taxi rank, he promised himself he would never use a train again. If it had been down to him, he would have driven here. But circumstances prevented that and the thought of those circumstances angered him still further.

He left the shadowy confines of the station and went out into the damp morning. It had rained during the night and a strange haze in the sky rendered the city vague and unfamiliar. Clucking streams of water filled the gutters and dark odours rose from the drains. Some things never changed.

A taxi pulled up. The driver had a tobacco-coloured face, pitted with acne scars. It gave him the appearance of an orange someone had tossed into the gutter.

'Waiting for a taxi, señor?'

'No, I'm admiring your tyres.' Guzmán wrenched open the door and climbed in. He sat back, noticing the driver's sullen face staring at him from the licence photo fixed to the back of his seat. Remarkably, the photograph succeeded in making the man even uglier than he was in the flesh.

In front of him, in a plastic dispenser, he saw various cards advertising accommodation in the city. One, El Paraíso on Calle del Carmen, seemed reasonably priced and he slipped the card into his top pocket. With a name like The Paradise, it ought to be comfortable enough. Leaning forward, he gave the address to the driver.

The cab grew warmer, pervaded by a smell of tobacco and other people's sweat. A familiar odour, or at least it had been once. People didn't smell like they used to. Apart from the ones he threw in the cells. They always stank. And if they didn't when they went in, they did when they came out.

Guzmán watched the city pass by with a critical eye, noting familiar sights with approval, scowling whenever he detected changes in the names of shops or some big store or hotel. Some changes were more drastic: blocks of new flats and expensive-looking shops where once he remembered slums and ruined buildings shattered by the war. Maybe change was inevitable, as the politicians said. That didn't mean he had to like it.

The driver cut in and out of the heavy traffic, enraged by the sight of motor vehicles and pedestrians alike, muttering a litany of expletives as his anger grew. 'Look at them wandering across the road. Fuck's sake, get out of the way, you stupid old goats.' He gave an emphatic blast of the horn as he sped past the two women, cursing them through the open window. 'Fucking jaywalkers. You'll get somebody killed.'

Guzmán thought the man's reaction to two nuns trying to negotiate a pedestrian crossing a little extreme. But if he complained, the driver might argue, obliging Guzmán to drag him from the cab and beat him senseless. That would make him late for his appointment and he had no intention of missing that.

'Christ, look at the arse on her, will you?' the driver spluttered, taking his hands from the wheel to gesticulate at a woman on the far pavement.

Guzmán turned to look, though too late. Another disappointment.

The taxi slowed as it approached the Plaza del Callao. At the far end of the square was Calle del Carmen and Guzmán told the driver to pull over. Because of the man's tardy information about the woman on the pavement, Guzmán declined to tip him. The next time the driver saw an arse worth commenting on, he would be well advised to inform his passenger in good time.

MADRID, OCTOBER 1982, PENSIÓN PARAÍSO, CALLE DEL CARMEN

Guzmán's humour was rapidly fading as he searched for the *pensión*. Finally, he came to a series of shabby buildings a couple of hundred metres from where the street opened out into the plaza. The shabbiest building in the row was narrow, with a flight of steps leading up to a dilapidated entrance that had seen better days, though none of them recently. Above the door was a sign, the painted letters faded and barely legible: Pensión Paraíso. Never had a hotel had a less appropriate name: it looked far from paradise and even further from the photograph on the card he'd taken from the taxi.

He hurried up the stairs into a spartan reception area with a long wooden desk by the wall. A window on the far side of the room overlooked an alley. Beside the window was a cane chair piled with magazines in various languages, though none of them Spanish. Clearly this fleapit was aimed at foreigners willing to part with their money in return for a stay in what looked like a bankrupt whorehouse. He hit the tarnished brass bell on the reception desk and waited for someone to attend him.

As he glanced round, he saw a staircase with a sign: *Habitaciones 1–4, Comedor.* The cheaper rooms, he guessed, exposed to the noise of the street and the smell from the dining room. He decided to ask for something quiet on an upper floor.

Behind the desk, he saw a doorway, covered by a curtain of coloured glass beads, through which he heard the continuous blare of a television. He brought his fist down on the bell again, harder this time. Despite that, the noise of the TV continued unabated, competing with the drone of traffic outside.

A sudden rattle of footsteps as a young woman came hurrying down the stairs, her high heels tapping out a staccato rhythm on the worn tiles as she went behind the reception desk.

Sixteen or seventeen, he guessed, with an unruly froth of dark red curls and bright attentive eyes. An attractive little thing, although he was troubled by the large tears in the knees of her jeans and the sleeveless basketball shirt that displayed her shoulders in a manner that would once have been thought shocking. Another sign of the times.

'What can I do for you, señor?'

'Can't you guess? And don't use *tú* when you speak to me. Have some manners.'

'Did the gentleman get out of bed on the wrong side today?'

'The gentleman got the early-morning train from Sevilla and would like a room without having to answer questions from a receptionist about his temperament.'

'You want to stay here?' She gave him an amused look. 'Really?'

'Unless I've wandered into a garage by mistake.'

'Not at all, we do have a room available.' The girl reached under the counter and pulled out a battered leather register. 'I'll need your details for the police, of course.'

'Naturally.' Guzmán took out his *documento nacional de identidad* and slid it across the desk. 'What happened to the sleeves on your shirt?'

She glanced up from her examination of his identity card, amused. 'It's supposed to be like this. Hasn't the gentleman seen one before?' Her smile carried a hint of pity for his lack of fashion sense. 'They're really cool.'

'I hope you got a discount for the lack of sleeves,' Guzmán muttered.

'I must say, the gentleman's very sharp. He should be careful he doesn't cut himself.' Turning to the board behind her, she reached for a key. 'I'll put you in room three, señor...' she glanced again at his ID, 'Ramirez.'

'Actually, I'd prefer a room on one of the upper floors.'

The corners of her mouth twitched. 'There are no upper floors. My father could barely afford this one when he set up the *pensión* after the war.'

'He's a veteran?' That was good, it meant a discount for a fellow ex-soldier.

'He's in a wheelchair. The beatings in prison damaged his spine. That's him you can hear, watching kids' TV. It's all he does these days.'

Guzmán's voice stiffened with professional animosity. 'He fought for the Republic?'

'I take it you were on the other side, from that look you're giving me?'

'I was.' Guzmán scowled. 'And I'm not ashamed to say so.'

'Well, the war's long over, isn't it? We've got democracy and it's here to stay.'

He decided to ignore that attempt at provocation. 'Can I see the room now?'

'It might be a good idea, before any money changes hands. You wouldn't be the first to walk out once you've seen what's on offer.'

He followed her up the stairs and along a narrow corridor. At the end, he saw a small room with several small tables, each with a single place setting. On the wall, a faded poster advertised the appearance of some long-dead matador.

'This is the dining room,' the girl said. 'If you're staying for a while I'll set a table aside just for you. You'll have your own napkin, a little bottle of oil and everything.'

'What about drink?'

'I'll get you a bottle of wine and draw a line on the label when you've finished your dinner so you know you're not being cheated.'

'No need. I don't leave bottles half empty.'

Guzmán waited while she opened the door to room number three. 'This one overlooks the alley, so there's a bit of noise, I'm afraid.'

Noise was the least of his problems, Guzmán thought as he looked around the dingy room with its scuffed wooden floor, a wardrobe that must have come from a funeral sale and a nightstand with a ragged Bible and a smeared glass. Over the bed, a cheap carving of an agonised Christ hung precariously from a nail. The bed looked rather frail, too. He doubted it would survive an encounter with an enthusiastic whore. Assuming he could afford one. Enthusiasm always came at a price.

'Not very big is it?' he grunted.

'Perhaps the gentleman thought the sign outside said "The Ritz"?'

'Never mind, I'll take it.'

She reached down and tried to lift his case onto the bed. 'What's in here? Bricks?'

'A couple of Uzis and some ammunition,' Guzmán said, taking the case from her.

She laughed. 'You're a real joker, I must say, señor. I'm Daniela Argüello, by the way. That's my father Alejandro behind the curtain downstairs.' She paused by the door. 'Welcome to the Paradise Pensión, Señor Ramirez.'

When the door closed, Guzmán went over to the dirt-encrusted window and looked down at the alley, its pavements lined with bulging refuse sacks. Bored with the view, he cast a baleful eye over his room. He'd stayed in worse places, he was sure, though it was difficult to remember when. Near the door, a light switch hung from a ragged piece of wire. Surprisingly, the switch worked, though the single bulb barely illuminated the room with its insipid pallor. In the walls, he heard the muffled sounds of the building, the intermittent murmur of water pipes, soft indistinct voices and the ever present rumble of traffic competing with several televisions, each tuned to a different station.

Out of habit, he searched the room, finding nothing but a few antiquated hangers in the wardrobe, dangling from a sagging wire. Sliding the chamber pot aside, he took a knife from his pocket and used it to lift a couple of the floorboards beneath the bed before transferring the oilcloth bags holding the Uzis into their new hiding place. He pressed the floorboards back carefully. No use making things easy for unwanted visitors.

For a few minutes, he lay back on the bed, staring at the cracked ceiling. With a sigh, he reached into his holdall and pulled out a bottle of Carlos Primero. He took a swig and then hid the bottle in the wardrobe. He felt a sudden urge to go out on the town and get drunk. But there was only half an hour until his meeting and he needed to be sober for that.

MADRID, OCTOBER 1982, BRIGADA ESPECIAL HEADQUARTERS, CALLE DEL DOCE DE OCTUBRE

Resentfully sober, Guzmán took a taxi to Calle del Alcalde Sáinz de Baranda. At the end of the street, he paused to admire the autumn colours in the Retiro park. His aesthetic interlude over, he turned into Doce de Octubre, a quiet, narrow street lined with apartments, warehouses and a few shops and offices. He walked slowly, checking the numbers of the buildings until he came to a large though rather bland red-brick office, with a broad flight of steps leading up to ornate double doors. A metal sign over the door: BE LTD. The *Brigada Especial*'s new headquarters was certainly a step up from his old *comisaría* in Calle Robles. Guzmán hated it at first sight.

To his surprise, Gutiérrez himself opened the door. He looked old, his face was pallid and drawn and there were dark shadows under his eyes. It was not the look of a well man. That cheered Guzmán considerably.

Gutiérrez started talking before Guzmán was inside the door. 'I'm glad you're here, *Comandante*. The politicians are talking about investigating our activities. Can you imagine? We knew the shit might hit the fan once Franco died, but why now, of all times? *Joder* just when—'

'I'm very well, thanks for asking,' Guzmán said as he took a seat in a leather armchair by the window, waiting with growing impatience for Gutiérrez to pour him a brandy. On the wall, he saw a faded photograph of Franco. 'Time you threw that out, isn't it? He's been dead seven years.'

Gutiérrez shrugged. 'It hides the wall safe.'

'At least he's finally doing something useful.' Guzmán took the brandy Gutiérrez offered and raised it to his lips. 'This isn't Carlos Primero.' He drank it in one swallow and glared at the empty glass. 'It's like piss, where's the good stuff?'

Reluctantly, Gutiérrez opened a drawer and brought out a bottle of Carlos Primero. 'This stuff is so expensive,' he grumbled, half filling Guzmán's glass. Guzmán kept the glass extended until he took the hint and filled it.

'Let's get down to business,' Guzmán said. 'I suggest you start by explaining why I haven't been paid for months, or do you want me to starve to death in front of you to make the point?'

'The government is auditing the *Brigada Especial*'s accounts, *Comandante*. They want to know if we give value for money.'

'Value for money?' Guzmán spluttered. 'For fuck's sake, they can't do without us.' He stared at Gutiérrez, hard. 'Can they?'

'We won't know until they've done the audit.' Unhappily, Gutiérrez watched Guzmán help himself to more drink. 'There's no more after that bottle's finished. We can't afford it.'

'Don't worry, I'll buy my own with the money you owe me.'

'Until they unfreeze the bank accounts, there is no money,' Gutiérrez sighed.

Guzmán glanced at the elaborate ostentation of the office. Filigreed alcoves, Regency chairs, expensive flock wallpaper and a couple of oil paintings Guzmán found despicable. All of it bought with money that by rights should have been in his bank account. 'You could sell this furniture, it looks like something from a brothel.'

'I wouldn't know about that, *Comandante*.'

'Of course, I was forgetting you've led a sheltered life.' Guzmán leaned towards him, suddenly threatening. 'There's got to be something you can do to free up some cash?'

'Like what? They've got accountants going over everything with a fine-tooth comb.'

'I thought you always ran a tight ship as far as finances went?'

'We're a secret department, Guzmán. The money's been hidden all over the place. When we hire someone to do a hit or steal secrets from a friendly embassy, we don't save the receipts for the taxman. Franco understood those kind of nuances. These new politicians think differently. They're more like grocers than statesmen.'

Guzmán reached for the brandy and filled his glass again. 'So we're fucked, is that what you're saying?'

'There's still hope,' Gutiérrez said. 'At least they haven't disbanded us.'

'You mean they were considering it? Why didn't you tell me this sooner?'

An evasive shrug. 'They talked about incorporating us into the

Secret Service but then the top brass decided against it, because of the things you did. They don't want their new Secret Service sullied by the Francoist past.'

'You mean *because of what we did*,' Guzmán growled. 'You gave the orders.' He took an angry swallow of brandy. 'Christ, since the nineteen sixties I've been travelling the country knocking off foreign spies and suspected terrorists and no one in government has ever complained about my track record.' His eyes narrowed as he sniffed his glass. 'Did you forget to put the cork back in the bottle last time you opened this?'

'For God's sake, never mind the brandy. You know what's going to happen later this month, don't you?'

'Of course. There's going to be an election. I'm looking forward to voting. In fact, I may vote twice to make up for lost time.'

'The polls suggest we'll end up with a Socialist government. Hard to believe, isn't it?'

'Isn't it just,' Guzmán agreed. 'When Suarez became prime minister, I thought we'd have ten years at least before we had to worry about any of this. I never thought the bastard would sell us out overnight.'

'A man who'd had almost every job in the Falange from top to bottom.' Gutiérrez sighed. 'We all thought he'd be a safe pair of hands.'

'His parents even named him Adolfo after Hitler. And then the bastard legalised the Communist Party. Christ knows what the Socialists will do once they take power.'

'There are even bigger problems than them,' Gutiérrez said. 'The *Centinelas* for one.'

'Those old lunatics? A bunch of cavalry officers who formed a secret bodyguard for Franco, that's all they were. In any case, most of them must be dead by now.'

'Not all.' Gutiérrez stifled a wheeze. 'They brought in younger men during the sixties and seventies when they started moving into politics.'

'Those bastards have worse records than mine,' Guzmán scoffed. 'Who'd elect them?'

'The *Centinelas* don't want to be elected, they want power. Everywhere you look, in government, the civil service, the armed forces and the police, even industry and commerce, there are influential people who owe their positions to the *Centinelas*. And all of them fiercely loyal to the men at the top who form their central council.'

'What keeps them so loyal?'

'Money, of course. That and the fact that anyone crossing them is liable to be killed.'

'How the fuck did they get to be so powerful?'

'I blame Carrero Blanco. When he became prime minister, he opened the doors to them, thinking they'd support him. But once the *Centinelas* had settled in, they followed their own agenda, using their resources to buy up politicians. And if the politicians didn't honour their debts, the *Centinelas* could take away all the privileges of office very quickly. They've been expanding ever since.'

'Why didn't the spineless bastards stand up to them?'

'Despite appearances to the contrary, Guzmán, politicians aren't stupid, they know once they've taken the *Centinelas'* money, there's no getting out.'

Guzmán shook his head slowly. 'If things got tricky with them, that would be a war we couldn't win. We haven't got the resources. But that's not my problem. I'm going to take my back pay and sit on a beach with all those Scandinavian girls.'

'I thought you of all people would have the stomach for a fight, *Comandante*.'

'I think my record shows I've done my share of fighting.'

'Even so, you haven't reached retirement age yet.'

'That doesn't matter. My contract says I can leave at any time.'

'Just to sit on a beach all day? You'd be bored within a couple of hours.'

Guzmán smiled. 'I doubt that, those foreign women are shameless. I reckon all the decent whores will be out of business in another year. Free love, they call it.'

'Protestants.' Gutiérrez sighed. 'Dreadful.'

'I wouldn't put it quite so strongly.' Guzmán took his hat from the table. 'I'll leave this card with the address of my *pensión*. You can send my money there.'

Gutiérrez took the card and glanced at it. 'Why are you always Señor Ramirez?'

'It always takes too long to get new documents forged.'

'Don't people ever recognise you?'

'Sometimes, though they usually regret it.' Guzmán got to his feet. 'I'll expect my money in the next couple of days.'

'Wait, I haven't finished yet,' Gutiérrez said. 'Even if you leave the *Brigada* now, what's to stop the Socialists arresting you once they're elected next week?'

'The Amnesty Law of 1977 protects us from prosecution,' Guzmán said. 'I know my rights.'

'Laws can be repealed, Guzmán. You could spend years in prison. We both could.'

Reluctantly, Guzmán sat down. 'So, what do you suggest?'

'I've found a way to make sure we're not held accountable for what we did in the past *and* pull the rug out from under the *Centinelas* at the same time.'

Guzmán finished his brandy and looked round in search of the bottle. 'Keep going.'

'You remember how many records the regime kept? All those membership lists of trade unions, the Communist Party and Freemasons?'

'Very useful they were too. We could never have shot so many Reds without them.'

'But that's why they could incriminate us,' Gutiérrez wheezed. 'Imagine if a Socialist government got their hands on those files. They'd find the names of all the people we killed or tortured. If all that was made public, the government would need scapegoats and they wouldn't have to look far. Your name crops up time after time in those files.'

Guzmán frowned. '*Our* names. You signed the orders.'

'Of course, it's only a hypothesis, *Comandante*. It might not happen.' Gutiérrez reached down for the bottle of Carlos Primero hidden at the side of his chair. 'A little more?'

'A lot more. Fill it up.' Guzmán took a long swig of brandy. 'You might have a point about the Socialists,' he said. 'If they get their hands on those records, we could end up in front of a firing squad. Those Reds never forget anything.'

'Exactly.'

'But then the same is true for the *Centinelas*, surely? Their leaders were staunch Francoists: they've got as much blood on their hands as us.' He stopped, seeing Gutiérrez's expression. 'What's so funny?'

Gutiérrez took out an inhaler and sprayed a fine mist into his mouth. 'If we can get hold of those files, we can destroy them before the Socialists are elected. Wipe the slate clean, so to speak.'

'That's a big if.'

'I haven't finished. Suppose we also got our hands on the material relating to the *Centinelas'* leaders? Imagine the reaction if we gave copies of that to the press. If their leaders were revealed to have taken part in atrocities and massacres, the *Centinelas'* political support would vanish overnight.'

'And all the records of what we did?' Guzmán almost smiled. 'Would go up in smoke, *Comandante*.'

Guzmán refilled his glass. 'Trouble is, that material is stored all over the place. It would take years to collect.' He frowned. 'What the fuck are you smiling at now?'

'Franco had those records catalogued. There are only two copies of the catalogue and strangely, one of those is in my possession. I've already located the archives containing the most damaging material.'

'In that case, fuck off and collect it. The exercise would do you good.'

'I can't do it on my own. But you'd have no problem. I can arrange for some men to help you. It would only take a week or so. Less if you work hard.'

'Don't I always?' Guzmán snapped. 'Unfortunately, hard work doesn't always bring the promised reward.'

'Nonsense. When haven't you been rewarded for your work?'

'Alicante.' Guzmán exhaled the word in a cloud of smoke.

The atmosphere in the room changed.

'For God's sake, that was years ago. You surely don't still hold a grudge?'

'I have a great capacity for grudge holding, so yes, I fucking do.'

'I can arrange payment for your services,' Gutiérrez said hastily. 'The auditors won't be working on the accounts for ever. They could be finished in a few weeks.'

'I want out as soon as possible.' Guzmán poured the last of the brandy into his glass. 'You owe me several months' back pay and I'm entitled to a pay-off. It's in my contract.'

'I'm afraid not. The contracts were changed following Franco's death.'

Gutiérrez was shaken by another bout of coughing and Guzmán waited until he'd finished before taking out a packet of Ducados. 'Here, have a smoke, it'll clear your chest.' He pushed the cigarettes towards him. 'Come on, take one, I can't stand listening to you gasping like that. You sound like a geriatric whore.'

'I can't smoke,' Gutiérrez complained. 'And I'd rather you didn't. It upsets my chest.'

Guzmán took out his Zippo and lit his cigarette. 'Franco didn't smoke either.' He took a long drag and slowly exhaled a cloud of smoke in Gutiérrez's direction, provoking another protracted spasm of coughing.

'I don't know why you're so reticent, *Comandante*,' Gutiérrez said, once he'd finished coughing. 'You're more than capable of carrying out an operation like this.'

'Reticent? I'm fucking angry,' Guzmán snapped. 'All these years you've relied on me to risk my neck doing your dirty work and now it's time to settle the bill, you can't pay. It's always been the same: Please, Guzmán, kill Trujillo's son while he's in Madrid and make it look like a traffic accident, blow up Carrero Blanco's car and blame it on ETA, cover up the *Yanqui* plane crash that polluted our beaches with radiation...'

Gutiérrez looked at him, appalled. 'You agreed never to talk about those things.'

'That was when I was paid to keep quiet. That agreement's over.' 'You need me, Guzmán, just as I need you. You've no money and I need help to get hold of those records before the Socialists are elected.'

Guzmán smiled. 'I've got a plan of my own. Remember Operation Begging Bowl? Back in the day, when we were short of cash, I'd visit a few of Franco's oldest, most affluent supporters and tap them for funds for some bogus operation to protect Franco's reputation. I'd explain that it was a secret operation – so secret that we couldn't fund it through normal channels. Most were only too happy to chip in. And then, since it was all a lie, I'd pocket the cash. It worked very well.' He took a sheet of paper from his jacket. 'I drew up a list of candidates on the train.' He extended his hand, palm upward. 'Give me your car keys.'

'I'd rather you didn't take my car. You have a history with motor vehicles.'

'I'll bring it back later.' Guzmán plucked the keys from his hand. 'What make is it?'

'A grey Dodge Dart GT. It's parked across the road.'

'That's an adventurous set of wheels for you, isn't it?' Guzmán laughed.

'Don't you want to hear the details of my plan before you go?'

Guzmán paused by the door. 'I listened to you in Alicante and look what happened.'

'Be reasonable: you're ignoring an opportunity to start again with a clean slate.'

'I know,' Guzmán laughed as he opened the door. 'I'm my own worst enemy.' The door slammed behind him.

A few moments later, Gutiérrez heard the sound of an engine being revved overenthusiastically. He winced as he heard the meshing gears and the screech of tyres as the car roared off. 'No you're not,' he muttered. 'Not by a long chalk.'

A brooding sky was darkening into night as the man made his way up the cliff road. Fifty metres below, the sea gleamed with the last rays of the setting sun. Slowed by the heavy briefcase, he paused for a moment to catch his breath, watching the contours of the headland turn to shadow. The road levelled out and he saw an old wooden sign, pointing inland along a steep track. He rummaged in his pocket for a torch and shone the light up the slope, its pale beam roving over the rocks and dark branches. Further up the track, he heard the deep muffled throb of an engine, the grinding of tyres on parched soil as a vehicle came down the slope.

As the vehicle approached, he lifted the heavy briefcase into the beam of its headlights. The vehicle slowed and lumbered to a halt. As the front door opened with a mechanical sigh, he saw the driver, his hands resting on the wheel. A woman stepped down onto the platform, a battered ticket machine slung round her neck.

'Señor Guzmán?'

As the man's hand left the pocket of his raincoat, she realised what was about to happen and threw herself back into the aisle just as he started shooting. As a result of her agility, the driver was the first to die.

He was not the last.

CHAPTER 3

MADRID, OCTOBER 1982, AVENIDA DE SALAMANCA

Guzmán's footsteps echoed on the ceramic tiles as he followed the servant down the elegant hall. The expensive vases and paintings around him brought back happy memories of looting during the war. The servant opened the door to the library and ushered him in. 'The *marqués* will join you directly, *Comandante*.'

The Marqués del Castillo was famed for his library and rightly, Guzmán thought, running his eye over the elegant shelves filled with rare first editions and ancient leather-bound tomes, trying to guess how much the collection would fetch on the open market.

His thoughts were interrupted as the door opened and a rotund gentleman entered, moving with a strange, ceremonious air, as if worried that walking faster would disturb the long, carefully cultivated strip of hair that failed miserably to hide his balding pate.

Nor did the *marqués's* eccentricity end with his coiffure. The English tweed suit was combined with a yellow waistcoat which clashed violently with a tie in the tartan of some obscure Scottish clan who, family legend had it, slaughtered his shipwrecked ancestors when they were washed up on the coast after the battle of Trafalgar. It was a tale he had told many times and Guzmán sincerely hoped he wouldn't tell it again today.

'Guzmán, old sport.' The *marqués* grabbed Guzmán's hand and pumped it vigorously. 'How long has it been?'

Guzmán had to think for a moment. 'Franco's funeral.'

'God, that was a splendid day out, wasn't it? I was blind drunk as I recall. Must have been the grief. Was it you who threw up?'

'I think everybody did,' Guzmán said, remembering what a good time they'd had.

'Speaking of which, would you care for a drink?'

'If you twist my arm.' He'd taken his time getting round to it, Guzmán thought.

The *marqués* bustled over to a painted wooden globe and lifted the top, revealing a well-stocked drinks cabinet. He selected a bottle of Carlos Primero and poured two glasses.

'This must be what you taste when you arrive in heaven,' Guzmán said, sipping the brandy appreciatively.

'Better enjoy it while you can then, Leo, because we'll be going in the other direction once we're gone, don't you think?'

'Do you know why I'm here?' Guzmán asked, annoyed the *marqués* had introduced death into their conversation. Clearly the rotund bastard hadn't spent enough time in the company of gypsies. Even setting aside the *marqués's* lack of respect for the evil eye, Guzmán was fucked if he was going to discuss theological matters with a man dressed like Toad of Toad Hall.

'You want cash for some secret operation, I imagine. Killing commies, I hope?'

'It's a top-secret operation.' Guzmán nodded. 'Vital to prevent the memory of the *caudillo* being stained for ever.'

'Really? My God, did the old chap do something awful?'

'The usual, though at least it was with a woman.'

'Ah, someone's trying to blackmail the family are they?'

'Exactly. I'm going to meet them and give them the money.'

'And then you shoot them, eh? Good man.' The *marqués* let his smile slip. 'Thing is, I'm a bit short on funds. Those damned tax people are all over me at the moment.'

'I'm sure you'll convince them you're beyond suspicion.' Guzmán's tone was suddenly less friendly than before.

The *marqués* shook his head, careful not to dislodge the strange length of hair arranged across his scalp. 'That's the problem: their suspicions are correct. I've been filtering cash from my estates for years and stashing it in Switzerland. It seemed a good idea at the time, but the tax boys have got on to me now and they've got me by the sensitive parts.'

'It's not an expensive operation,' Guzmán said, much less friendly now.

'You saw that chap who showed you in, my butler? Had to fire him. Can't afford his wages. He's working out his notice, and then he'll have to go and beg or something, I haven't asked. Best to preserve his dignity and all that.'

'We need the money to buy weapons,' Guzmán said, returning to the point.

'I can let you have ten thousand, but that's it. I really am broke.'

Guzmán shrugged. 'That will have to do.'

'I won't be a minute.' As the *marqués* hurried out of the room, Guzmán took the opportunity to help himself to another brandy. The *marqués* returned a few minutes later and pressed a large wad of banknotes into his hand. 'Here we are. I had to borrow it off Cook.'

'Pesetas?' Guzmán scoffed, staring at the bills. 'I thought you meant dollars.'

'No chance of that, I'm afraid. It's all she had. Still, it's an ill wind: she won't be able to retire now, so at least I won't starve.'

Guzmán put the money in his pocket. He could use it to buy a shirt.

'Good to see you again, old chap.' The *marqués* stood in the doorway, waving as Guzmán went down the steps to his car. '*Viva España.*'

Guzmán didn't reply. That time was over. It was every man for himself now.

MADRID, OCTOBER 1982, CALLE SERRANO

'Time is money, Señor Guzmán, so make it quick, will you?'

It was the first time Guzmán had met Guillermo Masias and it was an encounter he could have done without. 'Señor Masias, your father was one of Franco's most loyal supporters. He was always happy to contribute to the cause when necessary.'

Guillermo Masias was slumped in a round chair made of orange plastic that strangely mirrored the artificial tan smeared over his heavy face. The rest of the room was decorated in similar colours apart from a large painting on one wall, which, Guzmán thought, resembled something used by opticians. Masias noticed his interest. 'Bridget Riley.' He smirked. 'Cost a fortune and it'll fetch a hell of a lot more when I sell it.'

Bragging about money brought a brief smile to Masias's face but the smile slipped now, returning his face to its previous leaden hostility. 'That's what I do, *Comandante*, I buy and sell things and I make a great deal of money doing it, just like my father before me. And now you come along and ask me to part with my hard-earned cash to stop someone smearing Franco's name? *Joder*, if you want to beg, why don't you bring a tin cup with you and have done? I didn't make a fortune to give handouts to Franco's old gunmen. I'm not as free with my money as my father.' He glared at Guzmán. 'You're finished, you and your sort. No more eating for free in restaurants or taking someone else's table by waving your ID card. If you want money, try getting a job – if you can. You have to see the world in a different way these days.'

'You're right.' Guzmán certainly saw Masias in a different way: a cluster of potential targets, nose, teeth, belly, crotch, knees, each with its own distinctive level of pain when damaged.

'What am I right about, exactly?' Masias sneered.

'That you're not like your father,' Guzmán said. 'He made his fortune from hard work whereas you're a spoiled brat who inherited a lot of money far too young, so don't lecture me about your fucking wealth because you didn't earn a peseta of it.'

'You talk as if my father was a saint,' Masias snarled. 'The old bastard had his fatal heart attack in a whorehouse, for Christ's sake.'

Guzmán shrugged. 'We should all be so lucky. And, since you

might be going through that window in a minute, I'd say your father got the better deal.'

Masias glared furiously at him. 'You've got a fucking nerve, threatening me. First you try to con me out of my money and now you try to intimidate me? Get out, before I throw you out.'

Guzmán smiled. 'Why don't you try?'

'I expected you'd try something like this,' Masias said. 'That's why I asked some of my associates along.' He raised his voice. 'Come in, gentlemen.'

A door on the far side of the room opened and two men stepped in. One was a gypsy with greasy shoulder-length hair. The other man was heavier with a pudgy blank face and a nose that had been broken more than once.

'These gentlemen work for a friend of mine, Eduardo Ricci,' Masias said.

Guzmán didn't bother asking who that was.

'You're leaving, boss,' the gypsy said. A mocking emphasis on the last word.

'You heard him, did you? Better go while you can still walk,' Masias said. 'Why not take a holiday if you can afford it? Maybe you could visit the Valle de los Caídos and see Franco's tomb?'

Best not to overreact, Guzmán thought. This was business, after all.

'If you don't go we'll have to give you a hand,' the fat man said, moving towards him.

Guzmán noticed his reluctant stance, the sheen of sweat on his jowls. The nervous flicker of his tongue over his lips. The body language of fear. 'Don't worry, I'm going.'

'Very sensible, *amigo*.' The fat man sounded relieved.

Guzmán went to the door and reached for the handle.

'And don't come back,' Masias called. 'Other people are running Madrid now. People like Eduardo Ricci and me.'

Guzmán's hand closed on the door handle. It was well made in hand-crafted metal, almost a work of art. He doubted he could afford a door handle like that. As his hand tightened on it, he realised Masias's taunt had touched on a universal truth: like it or not, things had changed. Not so long ago, no one would have dared speak to Guzmán the way Masias just had.

He let go of the door handle and turned. Saw the looks on their faces. All three of them laughing. Then they saw the Browning and the laughter stopped.

Out of professional courtesy, he started with the gypsy.

The shot was loud and unexpected. One minute the gypsy was sneering at Guzmán, the next he was flailing on the floor, the blood from what was left of his knee ruining the pattern of Señor Masias's carpet.

Masias stared at the gypsy in horrified fascination. So fascinated, he failed to see Guzmán coming towards him until the butt of the Browning smashed into his face, knocking him from the plastic chair onto the carpet alongside the gypsy. He lay, dazed, trying to stop the bleeding caused by the loss of his front teeth.

'That just leaves you,' Guzmán said, staring at the fat man.

The man's jowls trembled. 'I don't want no trouble, *jefe*.'

Guzmán snorted as he slid the Browning back into its holster. 'You don't know what trouble is.' He looked down contemptuously at Masias who was still lying on the floor, pressing a handkerchief to his bloody mouth. 'I've always liked men who underestimate me, Señor Masias, it amuses me when I go to their funerals.'

'You'll be sorry, you bastard,' Masias spluttered. 'I'm protected.'

'Not from me, you're not,' Guzmán said. 'Don't get up, I'll see myself out.'

MADRID, OCTOBER 1982, CALLE COLUMELA

'*Comandante*.' Count Noguera hoisted himself out of his chair and came across the thick carpet to shake hands, blinking at Guzmán through his thick spectacles. The elderly aristocrat hadn't changed much over the years, though his hair was white now and reached down to his collar, giving him the appearance of an elderly dowager in need of a hairdresser. Guzmán doubted the count would object to that comparison.

'You're looking well, Leo, as far as I can tell, anyway. With my eyesight, I can't be sure.' He shuffled over to the cocktail cabinet. 'Carlos Primero's your drink, isn't it?'

Guzmán took the glass of brandy from him and made himself comfortable in a chair he guessed was at least a hundred years old, like most of the count's furniture. That was why rich people had so much money, he supposed: they put their cash in the bank and used their grandparents' tables and chairs.

'It's hard to believe, but no one's offered to help fund this operation,' he said. 'Then I remembered how often you supported the Cause in the past. Unlike some.'

The count sighed. 'A lot of those people who used to contribute aren't around any more. There are new faces everywhere.'

'Things have certainly changed since Franco died,' Guzmán agreed.

'Haven't they just? Though I don't know if you appreciate just how much.'

Guzmán gave him a dark look. 'What does that mean?'

'It means I keep an eye on what's happening, Leo. I've got influential friends who keep me informed.'

'That's surprising for a man like you.'

The count gave him a world-weary smile. 'For an elderly *maricón*, you mean?'

'Exactly. You'd have done ten years' hard labour if I hadn't let you bribe me.'

'That was 1962. I've been showing my appreciation for a long time.'

'And you never complained once,' Guzmán said. 'You didn't plead for mercy, you just asked how much it would cost to get the charges dropped. I like straightforward people.'

'Then I'll be straightforward now, Leo. There's a number of people who'd like you and Gutiérrez gone. You know where the bodies are buried, so to speak.'

'I should, since I helped bury most of them.'

The count gave a long, nostalgic sigh. 'You and the *Brigada Especial* used to run this city. But there's only one player in Madrid now and that's the *Centinelas*. Since they got involved with organised crime, they've become a law unto themselves. You don't want to mess with them.'

'I've been away from Madrid for a long time. What's this about organised crime?'

'After Franco died, the power vacuum created by his death created new opportunities,' Noguera said. 'Everyone was too busy worrying about what would happen next to notice the flood of criminals pouring into the country.'

'We had other things to worry about back then,' Guzmán recalled. 'Like trying to prevent the spread of democracy.' He took a gulp of brandy. 'Though we didn't make a very good job of it.'

'Exactly. And while you and the police were putting all your energy into clubbing demonstrators, the foreigners were importing huge amounts of drugs, trafficking women and robbing banks. You name a crime and they're involved in it, these days. And a large share of the profit goes to the *Centinelas*.'

'It's not my job to sort out foreign gangsters,' Guzmán said, lighting a cigarette. 'There's no point messing with those people, it would take years to get them under control.'

'You've messed with some of them already.' The count reached out and put his hand on Guzmán's knee, by way of emphasis or perhaps solidarity. Whatever his reason, he saw Guzmán's expression and hurriedly took his hand away. 'I understand you had a run-in with Guillermo Masias earlier?'

'You really are well informed, aren't you? That only happened an hour ago.'

'Masias phoned to warn me you might come here, Leo. You should be careful, he's acquainted with some very unpleasant people in the Madrid underworld.'

'I can imagine. Even his choice of furniture was criminal.'

'I'm serious, Leo. Masias is a friend of Eduardo Ricci. You know what they call him? "Eduardo Bastardo", though not to his face. You need to steer clear of him.'

'All I need is the money to fund my operation,' Guzmán said, impatiently.

With some difficulty, Count Noguera raised himself from his chair. 'I'll give you the money, Leo. For old times' sake. How much do you want?'

'How much have you got?'

'How does two million pesetas sound?'

It was better than nothing, Guzmán thought. The price of a car. 'In cash?'

'Of course, I'm sure you don't want a cheque. Have another drink, while I get the money from the safe.'

Once the count had ambled off upstairs, Guzmán went to the window and looked out at the street. Dazzling shards of light reflected off the windows across the road, forcing him to look away. His gaze settled on the entrance to a tailor's a few doors down, where a man was standing under the shade of the awning, reading a newspaper.

Or rather, he was pretending to read it: even at this distance, Guzmán could see the paper was upside down. Casually, the man glanced up at the window from where Guzmán was watching him. A professional glance, quick but thorough. So, the count was under observation? More than that: the man's repeated glances along the street suggested he was expecting company.

Five minutes passed. Count Noguera was taking his time getting the money. Guzmán finished his drink and walked quietly to the stairs, listening for the sound of Noguera bagging up the cash. He heard nothing. The apartment was drenched in a thick funereal silence as he climbed the stairs, his footsteps muffled by the opulent carpet. From the walls above, portraits of the count's ancestors looked down on him, grim-faced. *Maricónes* the lot of them, Guzmán was certain.

The pale light at the top of the stairs shimmered with motes of dust. Silently, Guzmán crossed the landing towards a half-open bedroom door. In the bedroom, Noguera was talking to someone on the phone. Not talking, whispering. Asking them to hurry.

By the door, a pair of ornate brass candlesticks stood on an elaborately carved wooden plinth. Guzmán lifted one and hefted it speculatively. In the bedroom, the count was just finishing his conversation. He put down the phone, careful not to make a noise, and got up slowly, grunting at the pain in his knees. On the bed was a leather holdall and, next to it, a pile of banknotes, still in the teller's wrappers. Noguera scooped the money into the holdall and zipped it. Behind him, a floorboard creaked. Slowly, he turned towards the door.

Guzmán was standing in the doorway, gripping the big candlestick in his right hand.

'Ah.' Noguera swallowed with difficulty. 'This is rather awkward, Leo.'

'Who did you just call?' Guzmán asked, stony-faced.

'Guillermo Masias. He told me to let him know if you came here. He's frightening, Leo, and I'm not a brave man.' The count took off his thick spectacles and rubbed them with his handkerchief. 'I'm in trouble, aren't I?'

'We're all in trouble sooner or later,' Guzmán said, moving closer. 'Turn around and face the wall.'

'Bullet in the head then?' The count's voice trembled as he turned. 'Shall I kneel?'

'Yes.' It would have been kinder to shoot the old queer, but the noise of the shot would alert the men outside. 'Close your eyes.'

Slowly, Noguera knelt, clasping his hands together in prayer.

As Guzmán moved towards him, raising the heavy candlestick, the count began to pray. '*Hail Mary, full of grace, the Lord is with Thee, blessed art thou—*'

Guzmán was in a hurry. He cut the prayer short.

Once he had rinsed the blood from his hands in the bathroom, Guzmán replaced the candlestick next to its twin on the plinth before hurrying downstairs with the money. The far side of the road was washed in bright sunlight and as he stepped out into the street, he felt damp heat rising from the cobbles. From the upper floor of one of the buildings he heard the murmur of a radio. Further away, the low rumble of traffic from the main road. Cautiously, he went towards the grey Dodge, keeping a tight grip on the holdall. The street was quiet and still, the windows shuttered for siesta. So quiet and still, he could sense them watching. To his right, he saw movement in a doorway, subtle and fast. More than one, then. He'd expected that.

He opened the driver's door, and tossed the holdall onto the seat. Glancing round, he reached into the car and put the key in the ignition. Before he could get behind the wheel, he heard a shout as two men wielding baseball bats came running from a doorway a few metres away, one coming at him along the pavement, the other from the road.

Guzmán drew the Browning and aimed at the man in the road. The harsh report echoed along the street, the shell case tinkling on the cobbles as the man crumpled to the ground and lay still. Guzmán spun round as he heard the second attacker tugging at the handle of the driver's door, trying to wrench it open. On the seat was the holdall, stuffed with his money.

He stepped forward, rested his arm on the roof of the car and fired. The shot sent the man staggering back into the metal shutter behind him. For a moment, he struggled, trying to stay on his feet. The second shot sent him sliding to the ground, leaving a long smear of blood down the shutter as he went.

Guzmán got behind the wheel, gunned the engine and accelerated. Behind him, he saw a red SEAT Fura pull out from the line of parked cars, following as he headed towards the city centre. Ahead, the traffic was slowing as the lights changed to red. In the mirror, he saw the Fura closing, expecting him to slow as he joined the vehicles waiting for the green light.

Guzmán floored the pedal and the car hurtled through the lights, provoking a sudden outraged chorus of horns as oncoming vehicles swerved to avoid him. Behind him, the red Fura briefly mounted the pavement, sending pedestrians flying before it regained the road and sped after him, trying to close the gap as Guzmán raced down Calle Lagasca.

He cursed as he saw the thick line of traffic at the end of the road, crawling along the side of the Retiro Park heading for the roundabout of Puerta de Alcalá. To join that, he would need to slow to a crawl and wait to filter in. That would be a slow process and he didn't have the time to wait.

In the mirror, he saw a motorcyclist weaving through the traffic, the rider steering one-handed, keeping his other hand low. Even in the constricted view of the mirror, Guzmán could still see the pistol in the man's hand. The man on the bike had the advantage. Caught up in the stationary traffic, Guzmán would be a sitting target.

As the vehicles ahead patiently waited their turn to merge into Calle de Alcalá, Guzmán accelerated violently, weaving through a gap in the traffic, ignoring the sounds of grating metal and breaking glass behind him as the Dodge mounted the pavement and smashed into the stone wall by the park gate. Grabbing the holdall, he jumped out, hearing enraged shouts from the drivers of the damaged vehicles littered across the road as he ran to the park entrance. Behind him, he heard the roar of the motorbike as it weaved through the stalled traffic in pursuit.

As Guzmán reached the entrance to the park, the rider raised his pistol and fired. Fragments of pulverised stone stung his face as a bullet impacted on the wall above his head. Moving quickly, he took cover behind the trees near the public toilets and waited, guessing the rider would follow. He was wrong: no one followed him through the gate.

It was time to make himself scarce and Guzmán set off down the tree-lined avenue of the Paseo de Colombia. From there, he planned to cut across the park to Menéndez Pelayo and be at the *Brigada Especial's* HQ within ten minutes. After a few hundred metres he turned and looked back. There was still no one following him and he slowed to catch his breath.

The park was quiet. A few metres from the path, several children were playing football on the grass, their excited shouts ringing through the trees. Further along, a young couple sat kissing on a bench, oblivious to the children's laughter and the sudden impact of their ball against the trees.

Guzmán paused, sensing a sudden subtle shift in the day. Around him, the intermittent drone of the city, distant sirens. And something else: the children had stopped shouting. He peered through the trees to where the kids had been playing only a few moments before. They were still there, though now they were standing open-mouthed, watching three men coming across the grass, each holding a pistol.

Guzmán raised the Browning and opened fire. At this range it was unlikely he would hit them but the effect was immediate as the men dived for cover.

Their response came in a rattling burst of gunfire that tore into the trees, spattering Guzmán with shredded bark and leaves. He fired again and once more, three handguns fired back, forcing him to keep low as the bullets hammered into the trees around him.

Outgunned and with no hope of backup, the sensible thing was to put some distance between him and his attackers. But with the lake behind him, his escape routes were limited. And then, before he could consider other options, the men broke cover and came forward, firing as they ran. He aimed at the nearest and pulled the trigger. A dull metallic click as the hammer hit the empty chamber: he was out of ammunition.

Escape was the only sensible option now and he ran, making for the fence alongside the lake. A bullet hissed through the trees, its sibilant whine followed by a muffled thud as it struck a tree. Running at full tilt, Guzmán's foot caught an exposed root, sending him flying onto the sharp gravel path. As he scrambled to his feet, he saw the holdall lying on the grass a couple of metres away and wondered about trying to reach it before the men saw him. His answer came in a sudden flurry of shots that kicked up dust around him, driving him away from the path towards the lake.

The men's shooting was inaccurate so far, but if he stayed put, it was only a matter of time before one of them got lucky. As another bullet whined past his head, Guzmán vaulted the fence onto the grass bank surrounding the lake and sprinted into the cover of the big equestrian statue of Alfonso XII. Sheltered by the monument, he waited, expecting another burst of gunfire. There was no further shooting and he soon realised why. On the far side of the lake, a group of brown-uniformed *policía nacionales* were hurrying across the park, attracted by the pall of smoke rising from the wrecked car over on Calle Alcalá.

When he glanced round, there was no sign of his attackers and he cautiously made his way back to the spot where he'd dropped the holdall. As he expected, the holdall was gone. The park was bathed in a profound silence now, broken only by the shrill ringing in his ears. A sudden murderous thought: he'd been robbed in his own city. There was nothing he could do about that now, and he walked away, heading for the gate on Calle Menéndez Pelayo.

MADRID, OCTOBER 1982, BRIGADA ESPECIAL HEADQUARTERS, CALLE DEL DOCE DE OCTUBRE

Gutiérrez sat at his desk, a glass of Scotch in front of him. Slowly, he lifted his cigarette to his lips. After a couple of drags, he stubbed out the cigarette and spent the next few minutes coughing. When the spasm had subsided, he went to the window and peered out into the street. 'I'll be going in a minute, Captain Utrera.' He opened a desk drawer, took out a pistol and slipped it into a holster under his jacket. 'Anyone hanging about out there?'

Utrera opened the door and went out onto the steps. 'Looks clear to me, sir.' He glanced along the road in the direction of the Retiro park. 'Should I call a taxi?'

'I'll be fine,' Gutiérrez said. 'Ask the *comandante* to leave my car across the road when he gets back, will you?'

'I think that's him coming up the road now,' Utrera said, pointing.

Gutiérrez stared as Guzmán came towards the building. He was limping, there was a cut down one cheek and the skin was raw on the knuckles of one of his hands.

'Where's my car?' Gutiérrez asked as Guzmán came up the steps.

'Still burning, I expect.' Guzmán met his eye. 'Have you got any brandy?'

Before Gutiérrez could answer, Guzmán pushed past him into the office and flopped into a chair, watching as Gutiérrez reluctantly took a bottle from his filing cabinet. 'Make it a large one.'

'This was for medicinal purposes only, *Comandante*.'

Guzmán took the brandy and emptied the glass in one greedy swallow before gesturing for Gutiérrez to sit down.

'We're going to need a small squad, all complete unknowns,' Guzmán said. 'They have to be volunteers: no hired gunmen and no one from the military above the rank of *teniente*. We act fast. We go in, get the files and get straight out. And we need to make sure the *Centinelas* know nothing about what we're doing until it's too late for them to stop us.'

Gutiérrez frowned. 'What does all that mean, exactly?'

'It means I'm in,' Guzmán said. 'So you'd better fill me in on the rest of your plan before I change my mind.'

'You won't regret this, *Comandante*,' Gutiérrez said, suddenly cheered. He picked up the bottle of Carlos Primero and filled Guzmán's glass to the brim.

'I'm already regretting it,' Guzmán said.

CHAPTER 4

MADRID 2010, HOSPITAL GREGORIO MARAÑÓN

'Come on, you've got to stop crying. It's over now.'

Galíndez wriggled, trying to make herself comfortable though it wasn't easy with Isabel sprawled across her hospital bed. 'I mean it, Izzy,' Galíndez said. 'Let me up, you're crushing my legs.'

'I thought you were dead,' Isabel sniffed, wiping her eyes with a tissue. 'I heard it on the car radio.'

'But it wasn't me, was it?' Galíndez took a packet of tissues from the nightstand. 'Here, use these or you'll get mascara on the sheets.' She glanced round the small room. 'Where are my clothes?'

'In that wardrobe,' Isabel said. 'Are you sure you shouldn't stay here a bit longer?'

'No, I'm just a bit shaken, that's all.'

The door opened and a young man in a white coat came in. 'All your tests were fine, Ana María. You can leave whenever you like.'

'Thanks, Dr Flores.' Galíndez swung her legs out from under the sheets. As she got to her feet, she winced.

'You'll be sore for a while,' Flores said. 'I can prescribe some painkillers if you like?'

Isabel started to speak but Galíndez cut across her. 'That would be great, thank you.'

'I'll leave your prescription at the desk,' Flores said as he went out the door.

'Should you be taking painkillers, Ana?' Isabel frowned. 'I found a tube of them in the office other day. You must have dropped them.'

Galíndez was rummaging through the clothes Isabel had brought from her flat. 'Have you still got them?'

'They're in my bag. But you won't need them if the doctor's going to give you a prescription, will you?'

'Just give me them, will you?' Galíndez snapped.

Isabel reached into her bag and gave her the yellow plastic tube. 'I still think—'

'Tell you what, just get me out of here. We can do the thinking later.' Galíndez opened the plastic tube, shook two tablets into the palm of her hand and swallowed them.

Traffic was heavy and Galíndez leaned back in her seat, trying – unsuccessfully – to be patient. 'I'm glad you're driving,' she said as the traffic ground to a standstill again.

'While we're not moving, maybe you could tell me what happened?' Isabel said. 'If you feel up to it, that is?'

Galíndez shrugged. 'All I remember is that I was in my flat watching an old film I found in Corporal Ochoa's apartment.'

Isabel frowned. 'You didn't tell me about that.'

'It was on a reel of eight-millimetre film,' Galíndez went on. 'I didn't have anything to play it on so I bought a projector from Amazon. When I got home on Friday night, it had just been delivered. I took a shower and then set up the projector and watched the film.'

'And what was it, a home movie?

'Not at all. It was filmed from inside a car and showed my father coming out of our house with me.' Agitated, she twisted a strand of hair in her fingers. 'It was the day he was killed. They filmed him getting into the car and then, as he drove off, the bomb exploded. What was so horrible was that they kept the camera on my face as I watched his car burning.'

'ETA always were callous bastards,' Isabel said. 'They must have wanted to use the film for propaganda.'

'But if it was ETA, why did Corporal Ochoa have the film hidden under his kitchen floor?' Galíndez said. 'Now he's dead, I suppose we'll never know.'

'So what happened after you watched the film?' Isabel asked as the traffic started to move again.

'I had one of my seizures and passed out. When I came round, I was in a cellar, tied to a board.'

'My God.' Isabel gave her a horrified look. 'Who did that?'

'Sancho.' Galíndez tried to keep her voice natural. 'Worse still, Guzmán was there.'

Isabel stamped on the brake, narrowly avoiding shunting into the car in front. 'Jesus Christ, he's alive?'

'He certainly is.' Galíndez's eyes grew darker. 'He and Sancho tortured me. Luckily, I managed to escape.' She glanced at her watch. 'Shit, I'm supposed to see the director general at twelve thirty. We're never going to make it in this traffic. Tell you what, I'll get out and walk. I really need to talk to him about my suspension.'

Isabel smiled. 'I don't think you need worry about that. Inés Fuentes admitted she took the photo of you without you knowing.'

'She decided to tell the truth, then?'

'Not really. I recorded her admitting it and then played it back to her mother.'

Galíndez leaned over and kissed her on the cheek. 'You're a star, Izzy.' She opened the door and got out. 'I'll call you later.'

'Dr Galíndez, *mi General.*' As the adjutant showed her in, Ramiro leaped up from his desk and wrapped his arms around her. The adjutant hurried away, unsettled by such an overt display of emotion.

'Take it easy, Uncle Ram, you're crushing me,' Galíndez said, squirming out from Ramiro's bear hug. 'I'm already battered and bruised.'

'We'll soon remedy that.' Ramiro waved her towards an opulent leather chair. 'Drink? A drop of medicinal brandy perhaps?'

'Just water, please.' Galíndez smiled. 'Brandy doesn't mix with—'
She stopped and corrected herself. 'I'm still delicate, I mean.'

'Of course.' Ramiro fetched her a bottle of mineral water. He sat
down and looked at her intently. 'So how are you?'

'Everything hurts right now, but the doctor said it should wear
off in a few days.'

'I was so worried about you.' Ramiro's voice was thick with
emotion.

'Don't, Uncle Ram, I'm safe now.' She leaned forward and patted
his hand.

He took a deep breath and composed himself. 'Teresa and I
suffered a terrible loss years ago – I won't go into detail – but it
made me realise that if anything happened to you...' His voice
faltered.

Unused to such a display of emotion from her uncle, Galíndez
went quiet, struggling to deal with it. 'I'm OK,' she said, finally.
'I've written a report for you on what happened so let's talk about
something more pleasant, shall we?' She opened the bottle of
water and drank half of it in one swallow.

'Christ, you look like you haven't had a drink in weeks, girl.'

'I'm a bit dehydrated, according to the medics. It could have
been worse.'

'It certainly could. You were lucky to survive, Ana.'

'Don't start, Uncle Ram. I'm fine.' She gulped down the last of
the water. 'So, do I have to guess why you sent for me?'

'There's a couple of things I want to speak to you about,' Ramiro
said. 'First is the matter of the photograph of you on the Fuentes
girl's phone. Naturally, the charges have been dropped now she's
admitted she took it without your knowledge.'

'I've got Isabel to thank for that. She got Inés to admit she was
lying and taped her confession.'

'Journalists, eh?' Ramiro said. 'They're a cunning bunch,
though I'm sure Señorita Morente is perfectly charming.'

'She's very nice,' Galíndez agreed, 'and a good worker too. Why
are you smiling?'

'She often appears in the magazines your Aunt Teresa reads,' Ramiro said. 'I was wondering...'

Galíndez's face lit up. 'Do you want her autograph, Uncle?'

'If it's no trouble. It's for *Tía* Teresa, of course, not me.'

'You're not the first to ask,' Galíndez laughed. 'Izzy keeps a pile of photos in her desk at the research centre. I'll ask her to sign one for you.'

'Your aunt will treasure it.' The smile suddenly left his face. 'Let's talk about you for a moment, shall we? You know it's going to be difficult to go back to Forensics after what's happened.'

'I know. Though since I didn't do anything wrong, it seems unfair.'

'Life often is,' Ramiro sighed. 'That's why I'm about to make you an offer you can't refuse. How would you like a transfer to Profiling?'

Galíndez looked at him, her mouth open. 'Really?'

'It's what you always wanted, isn't it?' He reached across his desk and picked up a file. Galíndez saw her name on the cover as he started reading. '"I'm passionate about developing profiling systems that will contribute to greater effectiveness in law enforcement across a wide range of criminal activities."'

'That's my application to join the Profiling Unit,' Galíndez said, remembering. 'I wrote it two years ago and I still haven't heard from them. There's a waiting list a mile long.'

'What if I was to move you to the head of the queue?'

'You can't do that, Uncle Ram. It wouldn't be right.'

'At least take a look at the set-up there. I'll have Coronel Mascarell show you round.'

She thought about it for a moment. 'OK, it can't hurt, can it?'

'Of course it can't. And I'd be much happier if you were working in a safe environment.'

Galíndez was still trying to work out what he meant by that when Ramiro got to his feet, signalling their meeting was over. She gave him a peck on the cheek and hurried off down the corridor to the lift before he started making his usual remarks about her appearance to his adjutant.

MADRID 2010, GUARDIA CIVIL HEADQUARTERS, DEPARTMENT OF
FORENSIC INVESTIGATION

The lift stopped at the fourth floor and Galíndez got out, suddenly apprehensive. This had been her base for almost three years and it hurt to think about the reason she was leaving. She paused in front of the door to the Forensics department, angry as she recalled how she'd been accused of something she hadn't done. Angry because her colleagues had thought she was guilty.

She knew what she'd see as she opened the door: Capitán Fuentes in his small glass-walled office, surrounded by piles of paper, the admin staff, Belén and Elena, at their desks, fingers rattling over their keyboards, their work only interrupted when they reached for another biscuit or slice of cake. And in the centre of it all would be Sargento Mendez, calmly doing three jobs at once, pausing from time to time to write a message on a post-it note which she'd add to the cluster on Galíndez's computer screen. Most were brief updates on cases, others would be bits of advice or jokes. Not so long ago, Galíndez used to look forward to reading them. Not any more.

She took a deep breath and opened the door.

'Surprise.' The sudden chorus of voices stopped her in her tracks.

Galíndez stared at the profusion of coloured balloons and ribbons hanging from the ceiling. A big banner hung over the door to Capitán Fuentes' office, a child's writing in coloured paint: We're Sorry, Ana María!!! And emerging from their father's office, the two Fuentes girls, little Clari, stumbling as usual, and Inés, looking younger than her thirteen years, hesitant as she came out of the office, followed by her mother, Mercedes.

'There you are.' Mendez came towards her, intent on giving her a welcoming hug.

'Don't touch me,' Galíndez said, backing away. 'What's all this?'

Señora Fuentes gave her a nervous smile. 'Ana, we realise how badly we behaved towards you and we want to apologise. Especially Inés, don't you, darling?'

Inés nodded shyly. 'I want us to be friends like we were before.'

'Really?' Galíndez narrowed her eyes. 'And I want world peace. That doesn't mean it's going to happen.'

'Girls?' Mercedes said. 'I think Ana's probably feeling a little angry. Perhaps we should give her a moment to herself?' She gave Galíndez a pleading look.

'You know why I'm angry,' Galíndez said. 'Your daughter told a lie that could have sent me to prison and you backed her. You think I'm going to forget that in return for a slice of cake and a paper cup of fizzy orange? Forget it.'

Capitán Fuentes raised his hands in a conciliatory gesture. 'We know how you're feeling, Ana. That's understandable, but—'

'*You* understand how *I'm* feeling?' Galíndez shouted. 'You understand nothing. How can you? I saved your children's lives and you never even said thank you.' She turned and went to her desk. 'Fucking unbelievable.'

'Language,' Mendez said in a low voice. 'The children.'

'The children need to know that everything has a consequence.' Galíndez picked up a large cardboard box, tugged open the drawers on her desk and began shoving the contents into the box. When she'd emptied the drawer, she turned her attention to the small clump of yellow post-it notes on the top of her monitor. The latest bore a brief message from Mendez. *Glad to have you back. Mx.* With an angry sweep of her hand, Galíndez tore the notes from the monitor and tossed them into the waste bin.

After a moment she looked up, aware of the silence around her.

Clari was sitting on the floor, staring at her wide-eyed, Inés was dabbing her eyes with a crumpled tissue and Capitán Fuentes and his wife were standing grim-faced, at a loss as to how to handle things.

'Ana?' Mercedes said. 'Please let Inés apologise. We've always taught her to say sorry when she's done wrong.'

'It's a pity you didn't teach her not to do wrong in the first place,' Galíndez snapped, intent on opening the last drawer of her desk. Making no progress by conventional means, she yanked the drawer from its rollers and tipped the contents into the box. 'That's me done.' She picked up the box and headed for the door. 'By the way,' she said to Capitán Fuentes, 'you'll be getting a letter from my lawyer. My union rep is handling it but it's only fair to warn you that your daughter's actions are going to cost you a great deal of money.'

'I'm supposed to be your union rep, Ana,' Mendez said.

'Not any more; I want someone who's on my side.' Galíndez stormed out into the corridor. As the door closed behind her, she heard someone crying.

MADRID 2010, GUARDIA CIVIL, SECCIÓN DE ANÁLISIS DE COMPORTAMIENTO DELICTIVO

Galíndez swore as she saw the time: she was ten minutes late already. Even worse, as she crossed reception, she saw the director of the Profiling Unit waiting for her by the desk, looking pointedly at the big clock on the wall.

Coronel Mascarell was a tall woman in her early forties. She gave Galíndez a powerful handshake before escorting her down a long corridor into the depths of the building. The place had an antiseptic atmosphere, as if it was scrubbed regularly throughout the day. For some reason, she found that depressing.

'You come well recommended,' Coronel Mascarell said. 'General Ortiz was most insistent that you're just what we're looking for.'

'The general gets a bit carried away sometimes.'

'I wouldn't let him hear you saying that,' Mascarell said, icily. 'Doesn't make the best of impressions, criticising the man at the top.'

Galíndez bit her lip. It was like being back at school.

'The thing is,' said Mascarell, 'General Ortiz isn't very knowledgeable about profiling.' She looked at Galíndez hard. 'And to be frank, neither are you.'

'Just a minute,' Galíndez protested. 'I did my PhD in—'

'I know. I've got your CV here.' The *coronel*'s tone suggested she was about to throw it out of the window. 'We also have a copy of your PhD thesis that you sent with your application. A run-of-the-mill work on profiling property crime, I thought.'

'I was awarded my doctorate *cum laude*,' Galíndez said. 'Anything else?'

'Since you ask, yes. I'm not impressed by your service record either.'

Galíndez blinked, taken aback. 'What's wrong with it?'

'Where to start? Since you joined the *guardia*, you seem to have indulged yourself by chasing some long-dead Francoist gunman, working with a minimum of supervision. I get the impression that you're a disaster waiting to happen. You need to change your ways, that's my opinion.' She gave Galíndez a thin smile. 'You know what the Japanese say? "The stake that stands out gets hammered down."'

'My superiors were satisfied with the way I handled things.'

'Since your uncle's the most powerful man in the *guardia*, that's hardly surprising.'

Galíndez felt her face burn with anger. 'I've never asked for preferential treatment from General Ortiz and he's never offered any.'

'If you say so. But we're an elite unit, I have to know my staff are able to take orders.'

'I can take orders.'

'You'd have no choice if you worked here, Ana, because all our staff work under extremely close supervision.' Mascarell set off down the corridor towards a glass-paned door, clicking her fingers to hurry Galíndez along.

'This is where you'd be working.' Mascarell pointed to a spartan room with large glass windows on three sides, each offering different views of the car park and the M-30. Several women were working at long tables, hammering away at their computer keyboards with furious concentration. None looked up until Mascarell introduced Galíndez to them. The women gave her a few words of greeting and then went back to work.

Galíndez sensed something familiar about the women as the

colonel led her away. She'd seen that same dull expression before: a weary look of resignation when faced with a series of mind-numbing tasks. Her own expression, reflected in the windows of the university library when she was completing her PhD.

With the tour over, Coronel Mascarell escorted her back to the entrance, promising she'd be in touch in the near future. 'I may sound firm,' Mascarell said, 'but I always get the best out of my staff.' She gave Galíndez a chilly smile. 'You'd be a challenge, Ana. But I'm sure given six months, I could shape you into an excellent member of staff. I'll tell General Ortiz that.'

Galíndez muttered a few words of thanks and went back to her car.

The motorway traffic was heavy and slowed to a halt almost as soon as she joined it. She sat, drumming her fingers on the wheel, nursing her anger at Coronel Mascarell's demolition of her career. *A disaster waiting to happen?* The sudden blast of a horn startled her as she began to drift into the outside lane. She tried to put the criticism out of her mind. It wasn't easy: she had a nagging feeling Coronel Mascarell might have been right.

MADRID 2010, GUARDIA CIVIL RESEARCH CENTRE, UNIVERSIDAD COMPLUTENSE

Isabel looked up from her laptop as Galíndez came through the door. 'Where have you been?'

'Job interview,' Galíndez headed for the coffee pot, 'in the Profiling Unit.'

'Oh yes?'

'What does that mean exactly, Izzy?'

'I mean "oh yes" as in why didn't you tell me you were going for an interview? After all, if you leave, that's the research centre finished and I'm out of work.'

Galíndez held up her hands. 'You're right, I should have told you. Sorry.'

'It's not like it's the first time, Ana. You never keep me up to speed on anything.'

'Well, you're the first to know that I won't be working in Profiling. And don't worry about your job, we've still got four years' funding for this centre.'

'I thought profiling was the job you always wanted?'

'So did I,' Galíndez said. 'But the director is some sort of head-mistress from hell and as for the office where I'd be working...' She shook her head as if trying to erase the memory. 'There were these five women I'd be working with. It would be awful.'

'What was wrong with them?'

'They were all like me. Like I used to be, anyway. Studious, utterly involved in the work, not taking lunch breaks and working flat out on data all day.'

'And you think you're not like that?' Isabel laughed. 'But if you're not leaving, what's the focus of our investigation going to be?'

'Guzmán,' Galíndez said. 'So far, we've only collected infor-mation about the crimes he committed in the past, but everything's changed now we know he's alive. Instead of cataloguing his old crimes, we're going after the man himself.'

Isabel shook her head. 'He'd be covered by the 1977 Amnesty Law, surely?'

'For crimes committed during the dictatorship, he would,' Galíndez agreed. 'But not for kidnapping and torturing me. That will keep him in prison for the rest of his life.'

'It sounds a challenge. So why the long face, Ana?'

Galíndez went over to Isabel's desk and sat down next to her. 'Can you keep a secret?'

'Of course.'

Galíndez took a deep breath before she started talking. 'I found out Uncle Ramiro adopted a baby girl in 1970. Her birth certificate showed she was one of the children stolen from hospitals during the dictatorship. Not only that, the birth certificate was signed by Guzmán.'

'Have you asked Ramiro about it?'

59

'I can't, it's too sensitive. When the girl was twelve, Ramiro's wife gave birth to a baby boy. A few months later, Ramiro and Teresa went out, leaving the girl to babysit. Izzy, she pulled a boiler pipe from the wall and asphyxiated them both.'

Isabel looked at her, open-mouthed. 'And it was definitely Guzmán who authorised the birth certificate?'

'Apparently, he must have been involved with the people at the hospital. It would have been easy money for him, I suppose,' Galíndez said. 'Ramiro never talks about it to anyone. Too traumatic, I guess.'

'And the girl was definitely a stolen child?'

'It looks that way, though I can't be certain. I just wish I could find out one way or the other to set my mind at rest.'

'But it's ancient history, Ana María, why are you getting so worked up?'

Galíndez sighed. 'Being an amnesiac, I get paranoid when I realise there are things I still don't know about my family.' Her voice cracked with emotion. Impatiently, she waved away Isabel's attempt to comfort her. 'I just want to know, that's all. I want to know who my family are, who they were and who I am. Normal stuff, like everyone else.'

'So what are you going to do?'

'I can't ask Ramiro about it, can I? It would look like I was prying into his private life.' Galíndez slumped against her. 'He's been so good to me over the years, I couldn't do anything to harm him or his career.'

Isabel put an arm round her shoulders. 'Maybe you should just leave well alone?'

Galíndez turned to look at her. 'A DNA test would show if the girl was Ramiro's biological daughter or not. I could do that without him knowing and spare his feelings.'

'So how easy is it to do a DNA test?'

'Very easy. I'll just take a glass Ramiro's used and swab it.'

'But how long has the girl been dead?'

Galíndez thought for a moment. 'Nearly thirty years.'

'Can you get a DNA sample from her after all this time?'

'I can,' Galíndez said, hesitantly, 'but that's where I could use your help.'

'To do what?'

Galíndez gave her a weak smile. 'I need you to help me break into the crypt.'

CHAPTER 5

MADRID, OCTOBER 1982, PENSIÓN PARAÍSO,
CALLE DEL CARMEN

Guzmán rose early. After he had showered and shaved, he selected a suit before taking his seat in the cramped dining room. The fact that it was empty pleased him. He had no wish to make small talk at this time in the morning.

Downstairs he heard voices and the rattle of cutlery. That was encouraging, it sounded as if the staff were preparing breakfast. But time passed and nothing appeared that even vaguely resembled breakfast. Finally, he went down into reception in search of food.

Daniela was standing at the desk talking to a woman. A rather attractive dark-haired woman, Guzmán noticed, so much so that he decided to dispense with the broadside on the lack of service he'd been about to deliver.

'*Buenos días*, Señor Ramírez.' Daniela gestured towards the other woman. 'This is my cousin, Luisa Ordoñez. Luisa's just completed her doctorate at the university. Isn't that something?'

'It certainly is.' Guzmán nodded, giving Luisa a casual appraisal. Disappointingly, his interest was not reciprocated. Undeterred, he held out his hand. 'Leo Ramírez.' When they shook hands, hers was cool and limp and she pulled it away quickly.

'I'd like my breakfast as soon as possible,' Guzmán told Daniela. 'I have an appointment this morning.'

'Breakfast?' Daniela took a deep breath. 'That might be a problem.'

'What kind of problem?'

'We've no food and Dad's pension hasn't arrived.'

62

Guzmán reached for his wallet. 'I'll pay you in advance for my room, how's that?'

'Great.' Daniela scooped up the banknotes he laid on the desk. 'Keep Señor Ramirez company for a moment, will you, Luisa? He's a veteran, so perhaps he'd like to take part in your research?'

Luisa's expression brightened, though not much. 'That would be helpful.'

'What research?' Guzmán asked, ogling Luisa's breasts as discreetly as possible.

'We're interviewing people about the war,' Luisa said. 'Building up a collection of accounts for future generations about the experience of the war and the dictatorship.'

'And you'd want to interview me?'

'Yes, although it won't be me who does the interview, I'm managing the project.' She saw the lack of interest in his expression. 'It's very important work, Señor Ramirez. We'd ask you about what it was like to fight, what you recall most vividly and of course what it was like to suffer such a terrible defeat at the hands of the fascists.'

He gave her a fierce stare. 'I didn't suffer a defeat.'

Her smile suggested he was simple. 'I don't mean in battle, I mean the war itself.'

'So do I,' Guzmán said. 'My side didn't lose the war.'

There was an embarrassed silence. Finally, Luisa regained her composure. 'Perhaps you'd contribute anyway?'

'Perhaps,' Guzmán grunted.

'I'll ask one of my researchers to call in and see you.' Suddenly aware of the real focus of his attention she quickly fastened the top button of her shirt. 'He's an Irish student who's working with us. He speaks excellent Spanish.'

Across the street, Guzmán saw Daniela returning with the food. 'Fine,' he said, no longer interested. 'Send him along. I'll tell him exactly what it was like.'

'Thanks.' Luisa went to the door, pausing to exchange a few words with Daniela as they passed on the stairs.

'Your cousin's an attractive woman,' Guzmán said as Daniela came through the door.

She laughed. 'You won't get far with Luisa. She's gay.' She saw his expression. 'You know, a lesbian?'

'I know what they are, thanks,' Guzmán said. 'Though I wouldn't have guessed.'

'You know what, Señor Ramirez? "Oft expectation fails, and most oft where most it promises."' Her shy smile reminded him of someone he'd once known.

'Who said that?' Guzmán's preferred quotations were usually by military men, preferably dead ones.

'An English playwright,' Daniela said. 'We studied him in school.'

'You'd be better off learning how to sew.' Her expression made him change the subject. 'What did you get for breakfast?'

'Ham, eggs, tomatoes – all the things you said you liked. Take a seat in the dining room. It won't take very long.' She hurried away to the kitchen.

As Guzmán reached into his jacket for his cigarettes, he had a feeling of being watched. Behind the reception desk, he saw a faint movement behind the curtain of glass beads. Quietly, he went behind the desk and pushed through into a large windowless room. A bed was pushed against the far wall and a sink and stove were crammed into the corner near the door. In the centre of the room, an old TV set stood on a rickety wooden stand.

A man was sitting in a wheelchair in front of the flickering television. A thin, sallow face, an unkempt air and clothes that were easily thirty years out of date. He had the shrunken appearance of someone who had not moved in a long time. A shave wouldn't have hurt either, Guzmán thought.

The man in the wheelchair spoke first. 'You must be the fascist.'

'Actually, I'm a paying guest, so watch your mouth.'

'Lucky you.'

'Been hiding in here since the war, have you?' Guzmán asked, casting a baleful eye over the miserable room.

'You'd like that, wouldn't you? Then you could turn me in. I must still be on someone's list.'

'I'm a police officer,' Guzmán said in a low voice. 'And if you'd been on one of my lists, you'd be a few dry bones in a ditch by now.' He paused, hearing Daniela call to tell him his breakfast was ready. He looked scornfully at the TV screen. 'I'll leave you to your wildlife safari, señor.'

In the dining room, Guzmán beamed as Daniela set down the plate of ham, eggs and tomato in front of him. He speared a piece of ham with his fork. 'This looks good. Aren't you having any?'

Her eyes flickered for a moment. 'I'll get a sandwich at college later.'

'By the way, I met your father just now.'

'Oh dear. How did you get on?'

He smiled. 'Like a house on fire.'

MADRID, OCTOBER 1982, GUARDIA CIVIL HEADQUARTERS

Footsteps echoed in the cool morning air as the two men walked across the courtyard. An orderly opened the door and pointed down the corridor. 'Straight ahead, señores.'

They crossed a small patio and went into a waiting room with a row of khaki chairs lined up along one wall. On the far wall was a door with a light bulb mounted above it.

'Not exactly welcoming,' Guzmán grumbled.

The door on the far wall opened and a corporal came in to greet them. 'Brigadier General Gutiérrez and Comandante Guzmán, would you follow me?' Guzmán led the way, knowing it would annoy Gutiérrez.

The interview room was spartan. A large Spanish flag hung on the wall behind a desk. On one side of the desk, next to the phone, Guzmán noticed a metal panel fitted with several coloured buttons.

'If the gentlemen require anything I'll be outside,' the corporal said.

'We'll have coffee,' Guzmán called after him. He settled into the chair behind the desk and tested it for comfort, finding it sadly lacking. Idly, he watched Gutiérrez as he struggled to get one of the chairs across the room. Finally, with a great effort, he wrestled it into place and slumped into it, gasping for breath.

'You know, you're in bad shape,' Guzmán said. 'You were fit once.'

'You don't have to tell me that,' Gutiérrez wheezed.

'Now you know how I felt after Alicante.'

Gutiérrez took a packet of Ducados from his jacket pocket and toyed with them.

'Do you want a light or are you just going to play with those?' Guzmán asked, irritated. Gutiérrez offered him the packet and Guzmán plucked a cigarette from it. He lit it and then leaned across the desk to give the brigadier general a light.

Gutiérrez started coughing just as the corporal returned with their coffee. Guzmán let the corporal pour and then dismissed him. 'You can go now,' he said, 'though I might call you back to shoot my colleague if his cough gets any worse.' The corporal gave Guzmán a conspiratorial smirk as he left the room.

'I'm ill,' Gutiérrez gasped. 'And don't start again with that shit about Alicante.'

'It wasn't shit to me,' Guzmán said, immediately angry. 'And it was your fault.'

'You blame me for everything.'

'That's because everything that goes wrong usually is your fault.' He blew a stream of smoke across the table and watched Gutiérrez convulse in another fit of coughing.

Gutiérrez's bronchial spasms finally calmed enough for him to speak normally. 'There's a meeting tomorrow between the *Centinelas* and various heads of government departments. General Ortiz thinks it would be a good idea if you're there as well.'

'You want me to sit at a table with those bastards?'

'No, it's a covert observation. The general likes to keep an eye on the enemy.'

'So what sort of activities are the *Centinelas* involved in that need formal meetings?'

'Policy direction,' Gutiérrez wheezed. 'They give an indication of what's going to happen in the next month and how they expect certain departments to respond. Minimising customs surveillance around certain ports, for example.'

'So they can smuggle in drugs?'

'Drugs, guns, explosives, women. All manner of things, as long as they're profitable.'

'Just like we used to,' Guzmán muttered, 'apart from the women.'

'The things you were involved in were just perks, Guzmán. They were never on the scale of the *Centinelas*' operation.'

Guzmán frowned. 'Do they give *you* orders?'

'We're too small and specialist for them to bother with, though that could change.'

'I'm surprised General Ortiz tolerates them at all. He should take a squad of civil guards along and shoot the bastards. That's what I'd do.'

'General Ortiz is the only person who's dared to stand up to them,' Gutiérrez said. 'So far he's managed to keep them from infiltrating the *guardia civil*. He's a brave man, because no one else is prepared to support him.'

'I take it that includes you?'

'I prefer to work behind the scenes, *Comandante*.'

'Action,' Guzmán snorted, 'that's what's needed. If they're all together in a meeting room, one man with a machine gun could take them out.'

'That's why I'm glad you're only going along to observe tomorrow.' Gutiérrez's words were lost in a burst of coughing. 'We don't want to start some sort of war.' He began coughing again and reached for his handkerchief.

Guzmán waited impatiently until the coughing died down. 'Did you bring the list of archives we're going to steal the files from?'

Gutiérrez took a map from his briefcase and smoothed it on the desk. 'These are the sites where the most incriminating material is housed. I've prepared lists of the file reference numbers for you.' He put another sheet of paper on the table. 'There's a list for each site we need to visit.'

'*I* need to visit,' Guzmán corrected.

'Some of the sites with less sensitive information aren't guarded,' Gutiérrez said. 'I suggest you do them first.' He continued, outlining the various locations of the archives and the numbers of men guarding them, all the practical information Guzmán would need, delivered with the Germanic precision he'd acquired there during the war. There was only one thing that differed from the Gutiérrez of old, Guzmán thought: he looked as if he was dying.

'This is good stuff,' Guzmán said, skimming through the briefing papers. 'Assuming the men we're borrowing from the *guardia* are up to the job, I'll get started at once.'

Gutiérrez fumbled with the straps of his briefcase, as if he lacked the strength to fasten them. 'How much money did you raise yesterday?'

'If you're after a loan you're out of luck,' Guzmán growled. 'Count Noguera made a generous contribution but I lost that in the Retiro when I was ambushed.'

'Not to mention my car.'

'I wasn't going to mention it.' Guzmán's face darkened. 'At least I'm alive.'

'While we're on the subject of death,' Gutiérrez said casually, 'Count Noguera's housekeeper found his body late last night. The victim of a violent burglary, it seems.'

'That old queer didn't have the brains to go playing a dangerous game like that.'

'That's an understatement, Guzmán, since his brains were all over the room.'

Guzmán watched impassively as Gutiérrez struggled to his feet, panting with exertion. 'I must go. I've got a meeting with the director general of CESID in an hour.'

'Really? Well, when you see the head of the Intelligence Service, make sure the first item on the agenda is a large cheque made out to Leopoldo Guzmán, will you?'

'I told you, you'll be paid in full,' Gutiérrez gasped as he opened the door. 'Just make sure you complete this job successfully.'

Guzmán's dark eyes narrowed. 'And when haven't I done that, Brigadier General?'

'You know very well,' Gutiérrez said. 'Alicante.'

After the door closed, Guzmán stared at it for a long time. When he had calmed down, he lit a cigarette and then put the papers Gutiérrez had given him back into their cardboard folder. Someone knocked at the door and he bellowed for them to come in. As the door opened, he jumped to his feet as he saw who his visitor was.

The man strode across the room, tall, steely-haired, the breast of his uniform jacket glittering with the numerous decorations Franco had bestowed on him.

'General Ortiz,' Guzmán said as they shook hands. 'You look very well.'

'Guzmán, you old bastard. How long has it been?'

'A long time, *mí General*. Just after they nicknamed you "Iron Hand", I think.'

The general's booming laugh filled the room. 'You know that was because of the number of people I had shot when we captured Santander? I always thought it made me sound like a boxer.'

Guzmán gestured to the chair Gutiérrez had just vacated. 'Have a seat.'

Ortiz sat down and laid his riding crop on the table. 'How are you keeping?'

'Still adjusting to democracy,' Guzmán said. His expression said much more.

Ortiz's face twitched with anger. 'I know what you mean. I'm glad I'm only two years off retirement, otherwise I'd be fronting up to these politicians and the cretins who surround them. We should have cleared the deck when we had the chance, before the *Centinelas* moved in. And now, it looks like the Socialists will form the next government. It makes me sick, all this talk of change.'

'They say we all have to adapt now and again.'

'Bullshit. You don't believe that any more than I do, Guzmán. Leopards and spots.'

Guzmán pushed a sheet of paper across the desk. 'I've been looking at the men you've seconded. Is this Ramiro Ortiz junior a relation, by any chance?'

The general bellowed with laughter. 'He's my son. I thought it would do him good to get some experience with one of the best.'

'Very kind. What's he like?'

Ortiz frowned. 'He's not a born leader, that's for sure.'

'He doesn't take after you then?'

Ortiz's face looked as if it might burst into flames. 'No, he fucking doesn't. I don't know where he gets it from.'

'Gets what?'

'Another time.' Ortiz waved his hand, brushing away the thought. 'You know about his accident, I suppose?'

Guzmán shook his head. 'First I've heard.'

'Don't say anything to him, for Christ's sake. It took months for him to pull himself together.'

'Car accident, was it?'

'Worse: his children,' Ortiz said in a heavy voice. 'When they got married, I bought Ramiro and his wife Teresa a chalet out at San Sebastián de los Reyes. They wanted to start a family, but nature didn't take its course, so in 1970, they adopted a little girl, Estrella Lucia. Bought her from a single mother from some hospital or other, you know how it works, they get someone in authority to sign off the paperwork.'

Guzmán nodded as he lit a cigarette. 'People can make a lot of money out of that. In fact, I've signed quite a few myself. The hospital paid me for every hundred I signed. Only fair to take their money really, since they were making so much.'

'Anyway, out of the blue,' Ortiz continued, 'at the end of last year, Ramiro and Teresa had a baby.'

'Often happens,' Guzmán said, struggling to maintain interest in the Ortiz family tree.

'They left Estrella looking after the baby,' Ortiz went on. 'I don't blame them, I mean, she was twelve, that's old enough to know how to look after a baby, for Christ's sake. In any case, they only popped out for a short time. But when they got back, the children were dead. It was a boiler accident. They died from carbon monoxide poisoning.'

A familiar story, Guzmán knew. Stoves weren't connected correctly, pipes sprang a leak. It had happened all the time after the war.

'Ramiro nearly fell apart.' Ortiz saw the look on Guzmán's face. 'He's fine now though, Leo.'

'You don't have to convince me,' Guzmán said, discreetly pencilling a question mark against Ramiro Junior's name.

Ortiz snorted. 'It's me I'm trying to convince. If he doesn't pull his weight, I want to be the first to know, understand? Praise when it's due and a boot up the arse when it's not.'

'That's always been my approach, General.'

Ortiz looked at his watch. 'Fuck, look at the time. I'd better get off, I'm seeing the minister of defence in half an hour. By the way, there's a café, El León, just across the street from the main gate. The officers meet in there most evenings. Call in, it gets quite lively.'

'I will,' Guzmán said. 'I understand we're attending a meeting tomorrow?'

'My adjutant will give you the details.' Ortiz took his riding crop and got to his feet. 'You know, these lads I'm loaning you don't have much experience, but they're willing. I also got hold of that corporal you asked for. Miserable bastard, isn't he?'

'He's an expert in misery,' Guzmán agreed. 'But he's reliable.' He got up to see the general out. 'Before you go, I have to ask, what are these buttons on the desk?'

Ortiz grinned. 'New technology, Guzmán. You'll have fun with those. Press the green button and the light over the door goes on to tell the next interviewee to come in.'

Guzmán tried it. 'What about this yellow one?'

'That's my favourite.' The general chuckled. 'Watch, you're going to love this.'

A firm knock at the door, as if someone had punched it. Guzmán looked up and saw a tall, well-built man with sharp cheekbones and dark sullen eyes. His uniform was immaculate and his patent-leather hat gleamed from hours of polishing.

'Miguel Galíndez, *a sus órdenes.*' He reached for a chair.

'Don't sit down,' Guzmán said sharply. 'You're not stopping.'

Galíndez straightened to attention.

'You're a big bastard,' Guzmán said. 'Can you handle yourself?'

'I box from time to time, *Comandante.*'

'This job isn't all about scrapping. I need brains as well as brawn.'

Galíndez stared straight ahead at the flag. 'I've got those, sir, don't worry.'

'I see you've applied for a transfer to the *antidisturbios*,' Guzmán said, looking down at his papers. 'Why do you want to join the riot police?'

'I like a bit of action, sir. With all these lefties coming out of the woodwork since Franco died, it sometimes seems we're in a different country. I want to crack some heads, stop the Reds from taking over the streets.'

'The correct answer was "to serve my King and country",' said Guzmán. 'There'll be no cracking heads and no shooting unless I authorise it. We don't want to draw attention to what we're doing, understand? Because if you fuck up, it won't just be your job you lose: you'll be singing soprano in the *guardia* choir.'

'All I want is to get on, sir. I'd like to climb the ranks as high as I can.'

'Good for you.' Guzmán put a tick next to Galíndez's name. 'Now get out.'

Once Galíndez had gone, Guzmán pushed the yellow button on the panel.

A sudden hiss of static. 'I said I want to crack heads and he says crack all you want, Miguel, you're my kind of man. I reckon him and me will get on fine.'

Guzmán smiled as he pushed the button again, cutting off Galíndez's bragging. He pressed the green button and looked up as the next man came in. 'Name?'

'Teniente Ramiro Ortiz. *A sus órdenes, mí Comandante.*'

Guzmán narrowed his eyes. 'Where did you learn to salute like that?'

'In the *guardia* of course, *Comandante.*'

'No you didn't. Otherwise you'd do it properly. Do it again.'

Ramiro made another attempt. 'That's enough: life's too short,' Guzmán sighed. 'Your father says you'll do your best, that's good enough for me.' He narrowed his eyes. 'But it had better be your best.'

'I won't let you down, sir, I promise.'

'I judge men by their actions, not their promises,' Guzmán said menacingly. 'You look miserable, *Teniente*. Any reason for that?'

'Actually, sir, there is. I feel like no one cares about what I do in this job.'

'You're absolutely right, *Teniente*,' Guzmán said. 'No one gives a fuck. Now get out.'

He lit a cigarette and then reached for the green button, pleased at his growing facility with this new technology.

'Enrique Vilán?' Guzmán asked, staring at the young man who'd just come in. 'What the fuck are you, a mascot?'

'I prefer to be called Quique, sir,' the young man shouted, jumping to attention. He looked as if a gust of wind might blow him over, Guzmán thought. In fact, he probably wasn't even shaving yet.

'I saw a pram by the main gates this morning,' Guzmán said. 'If I was you, I'd go back and get in it before your Mamá realises you're missing.'

'Permission to speak, sir?' Quique bellowed. 'I've had three fights since I joined the *guardia* and I won them all. I'm good if things get rough and my shooting is slightly better than average.'

73

'All right, you're in. But if you bring your teddy bear to work, I'll shoot you both.' He glared at Quique for a moment. 'And stop shouting at me.'

'*A sus órdenes*,' Vilán shouted. He stamped to the door before turning and saluting with a last booming '*sus órdenes*.'

Guzmán rested his head in his hands, thanking God he hadn't got a hangover. He would need to impress on the kid that a secret operation required minimal noise.

He pressed the green button and the next man entered. Fair-haired, with a round, honest face. His uniform was neat, just as regulations required, though not annoyingly so.

'Luis Fuentes, *Comandante*.' A sharp salute.

Guzmán glanced down at the general's notes. 'General Ortiz says you're intelligent. In fact, he thinks you'll probably make *comandante* before you're thirty.'

'I'll do my best to live up to that assessment, sir.'

'The general's a good judge of men, so I'm inclined to trust his opinion,' Guzmán said. 'Don't give me any reason to change my mind. You're in.'

'Thanks, *Comandante*,' Fuentes stared straight ahead, eyes on the flag. 'I'll try not to let you down.'

'You're all fucking trying,' Guzmán muttered as the door closed. He looked at his watch and groaned: it was nowhere near lunchtime. With an exaggerated sigh he reached for the green button, wanting to get this next encounter over with as soon as possible.

He looked up as the newcomer came in. They shook hands hurriedly, like strangers. 'I bet you never thought you'd work with me again, did you, Ochoa?'

'That's what I was hoping, sir,' Corporal Ochoa said. The thick lenses of his glasses made his eyes seem vast. Provocatively so, Guzmán thought.

'Still taking photos of admirals fucking their secretaries?'

'That sort of thing, sir. Intelligence work.'

'*Hombre*, if you were intelligent, you wouldn't be so fucking miserable. You'd just get down on your knees every evening and thank God for having such a good job.'

'As the *comandante* says,' Ochoa said, stiff and formal.

'For fuck's sake, Corporal, I have to deal with officers I can't stand sometimes, but I make a better job of it than you.'

'I've only a month to go before I retire, sir. I didn't expect to be called back into the field at this stage, especially by you.'

'Then you should be grateful to see a bit of action before you retire,' said Guzmán. 'Incidentally, did you ever find your wife?'

Ochoa shook his head. 'But once I'm retired, I'll have the money to pay for a private detective, now I qualify for the pensioners' delivery.'

'What's that?'

'It's a *guardia* thing. If you've been involved with dirty jobs during your career they give you extra monthly payments to keep quiet about them.'

'I should get those.' Guzmán made a quick pencilled note on his pad.

'You haven't retired, *Comandante*.'

'Then I should get them when I retire.' Guzmán underlined the note. Twice.

'You aren't in the *guardia*, sir.'

'Fucking hell.' Guzmán scowled as he underlined the note yet again. 'I serve my country and get fuck all while someone like you takes a few photos and then retires with a small fortune.'

Ochoa shrugged. 'I'm a member of the *guardia*, sir. The fact that I've been seconded to you in the past is incidental as far as pensions go.'

'And you're an expert on finances as well?' Guzmán tossed the pencil across the room. 'Enough of the small talk. Do you understand what this operation entails?'

'Yes, sir, and it sounds like we might run into trouble, I reckon.'

'Not at all: as long as we keep a low profile, no one's going to notice we're spiriting away a few boxes of records. And then, after that, no one will ever know what we did for Franco over the years.'

'That should suit you nicely, I imagine, sir, now the Socialists are about to win the election? First thing they'll do is come looking for people like you once they're in power.'

'What would suit me is for someone to shoot you, Ochoa,' Guzmán snapped. 'And by the way, you mean "People like us". I don't seem to remember you ever refusing to shoot Reds, or anyone else, for that matter.'

'Perhaps the *comandante* would prefer it if I didn't take part in the operation?'

Guzmán's fist slammed down on the desk. 'I never had you down for a coward. Annoying, argumentative, obstinate and fucking stubborn to the point that a mule would look obliging in comparison, maybe. But scared of a mission? Christ, I asked for you because I thought you'd be reliable.'

'You know I am. I was just saying, that's all.'

'Then it would be better if you didn't say anything, Corporal. I was about to mention that I need a sergeant. How would a temporary promotion suit you?'

'No thanks. I saw how you treated the old sarge.'

'That was different. I had to beat him from time to time or he'd have turned feral on me.'

Ochoa shrugged. 'If you really want a sarge, there's always his son.'

'The sarge had a son?' Guzmán's eyes widened. 'I never knew that.'

'Oh yes.' Ochoa nodded. 'He's called Julio, same as the sarge.'

'Fuck me, I didn't even know the sarge had a name.'

'Julio was in the Legion for fifteen years,' Ochoa said.

'Really?' Guzmán asked. 'An ex-legionnaire is just what we need.'

Ochoa shuffled uncomfortably. 'I should have said he was in the Legion before he went to prison.'

'What did he do?'

'Murder.'

'Is that all? I'd never have had a squad if I'd refused to take murderers. When did he come out?'

'A few days ago. I came across him begging outside the Metro.'

Guzmán thought about it for a moment. 'Go and get him. A good sarge is exactly what this bunch of vestal virgins need to keep them in order.'

The corporal saluted as he left. At least his salute wasn't annoying.

Ochoa was back within the hour. It was not often Guzmán showed surprise at anything these days but his eyes widened as he saw the figure standing in the doorway.

The sarge's son was tall and muscular, though any further evidence of physical health was very well hidden. On the other hand, the ravaged face seemed very familiar.

'Christ, did you dig up his papa from the cemetery?' Guzmán pushed back his chair and went towards him. 'I'm Guzmán, I worked with your father in Calle Robles. He was a good man.'

'You reckon?' Julio scoffed. 'He put my mother on the street, whoring.'

'Well, at least it was regular work. Do you want the job or not?'

'A job?' Julio had a slightly breathless voice, like a panting dog. Another of his father's traits. 'Do I get a gun?' His smile revealed a few widely spaced rotten stumps protruding from his gums.

'Fuck, you've got the same teeth as your father.' Guzmán waited for Julio to take his hand. 'Are we going to shake hands or not?'

'Dunno,' Julio said, furrowing his brow. 'Why?'

'Because I'm offering you a job,' Guzmán said, impatiently.

Julio tilted his head to one side and gave another disconcerting grin. 'Is it dangerous?'

'Does that bother you?'

Julio's laugh sounded even more like a dog than before. 'Don't bother me, boss.'

Guzmán sniffed the air and frowned. 'There's one condition: you have to take a bath.'

'Shit, it's always the same,' Julio grunted. 'Join the Legion, they make you wash, in prison it's the same. Can't seem to get away from it.'

'Make sure you get cleaned up,' Guzmán said, 'because I'm not getting in a vehicle of any description with you until you have. Where are you living?'

'I've got a room somewhere.' Julio gestured vaguely at one of the walls.

'Is it a *pensión*?' Guzmán asked, hoping it was worse than his.

'Sort of. It's next to a stable.' He paused. 'Tell the truth, it is a stable.'

'Just make sure Corporal Ochoa can get in touch with you when you're needed. And there's one more question I need to ask.'

'I've already answered it,' Julio said. 'I never killed him. In any case, the witness fell under a truck so his word don't count either.'

'That's not the question. I want to know if I can trust you.'

'Me?'

'Who do you think I'm talking to?'

'What was the question?'

'Can I trust you?' Guzmán said, running out of patience.

'Hard one that, boss.'

'For Christ's sake, it isn't hard at all. Just answer the fucking question.'

The sarge's son grinned, exposing his devastated teeth. 'You can't catch me out with trick questions like that.'

Guzmán took a deep breath. 'I need a drink.'

Julio took out a bottle from his jacket pocket. 'Have some of this, boss.'

Guzmán examined the label on the bottle and handed it back. 'This is surgical alcohol.'

'It's got alcohol in it, boss, what more do you want?'

'A new liver if I drink that,' Guzmán said. 'We start tomorrow. Be here early.'

Julio lumbered to the door. 'You know, my dad liked you, *Comandante*.'

Guzmán raised an eyebrow. 'I wish I could say the same.'

'Yeah, me too,' Julio said as he opened the door. 'Thanks for the job.'

Ochoa showed him out.

Guzmán was lighting a cigarette when he returned. 'Can we trust him, Corporal?'

'As much as you could trust his father,' Ochoa said, after a moment's thought.

Guzmán took a long drag of his cigarette. 'That's what I was afraid you'd say.'

CHAPTER 6

MADRID 2010, GUARDIACIVIL HEADQUARTERS

'*L*et me get this straight: you don't want to transfer to Profiling?' Ramiro's voice was getting louder. On the other side of the general's office door, the adjutant was savouring every explosive phrase as Ramiro gave Galíndez the benefit of his extensive lexicon of profanities.

'Don't shout, Uncle Ramiro, you'll deafen me.'

'Deafen you? I should call my adjutant in here and have him horsewhip you.'

'Go ahead, I'll break both his arms.'

He sighed. 'I can never stay angry at you for long, Ana.'

'That's not the impression I'm getting, General.' That was a dirty trick, she knew. The moment she addressed him by rank, Ramiro started to melt.

'So what was wrong with Profiling anyway?'

'It would be boring.'

Ramiro stared at her. 'No offence, Ana, but you've always been a serious girl.'

'Serious?' Galíndez looked at him with horror. 'You think I'm boring, don't you?'

'Let's say I thought you'd enjoy the rarefied atmosphere of Profiling.'

'Two years ago, I would have. But I prefer the challenge of an investigation now.'

'You know, I'd always hoped you'd join an operational unit. What kind of investigative work are you interested in?'

'The research centre still has four years of funding left. Since we know Guzmán's alive, why don't I focus on tracking him down? After all, kidnapping's a serious offence.'

'There's only you and Señorita Morente at the centre. What makes you think you could track down someone like him?'

'I want to start by going after that skinhead, Sancho, first,' Galíndez said. 'If I can find him, he'll lead us to Guzmán, I'm certain. And I promise the moment I get a lead, I'll call in backup and do things by the book.'

'As long as you do. I mean it, Ana. Do it right or I'll send you back to Profiling and have Coronel Mascarell chain you to the desk.'

'I'll keep you informed throughout the investigation, General.' She started to get up.

'Have you bought a camera?' Ramiro asked, as he saw the case she was carrying.

'I borrowed it from Forensics. I'm going to take photos of the documents we've collected at the research centre.' She opened the case and took out the camera. 'Digital: zoom lens, the works. It's really powerful. Have a look for yourself.'

'Who'd believe it?' Ramiro said after he'd inspected the camera. 'Those Japanese, eh? It's so small and light yet I bet it cost a fortune?'

A sudden idea struck her. 'Shall I take your picture? I'll get it printed out and have it framed for you.'

He smiled indulgently. 'Why not take one of me signing your authorisation to investigate Guzmán? I've got a pen here, some-where.' He rummaged in his desk drawer, piling handfuls of pencils, rubber bands and other office detritus into a heap on his blotter. It looked like the contents of a schoolboy's desk, Galíndez thought, though, sensibly, she refrained from saying so.

Finally, Ramiro shoved the jumbled items from his drawer to one side. 'Here it is.' He held up a green fountain pen. 'My great-grandfather carried this throughout the war in Cuba in 1898, Grandfather took it with him to the Rif mountains in the twenties and my father used it in the Civil War. Now it's mine. Fantastic workmanship, never leaks. It has the name of Grandfather's house at military school engraved on it. It's a piece of family history.' He looked up at her, his blue eyes twinkling. 'One day, of course, it will be yours.'

'Let's hope that's a very long time away,' she smiled. 'OK, sign the authorisation then, Uncle.' She lifted the camera and squinted through the viewfinder at him.

'Wait,' Ramiro said. 'Move to the left so you get my father's portrait in the shot.'

Galíndez's heart sank. She'd hoped to avoid including the gaudy life-size oil painting of the late General 'Iron Hand' Ortiz in the picture. It was bad enough having the old boy staring down from the wall at her every time she visited Ramiro's office.

'Make sure you get as much of Papa in as you can,' Ramiro barked, arranging himself into a stiff, self-conscious posture.

Galíndez took the first picture: Ramiro posing with the pen, looking down at the sheet of paper as he signed his name. Behind him, his father glowered down from his ghastly portrait. Beneath the general's feet lay a trampled red flag bearing a hammer and sickle. In the background, smoke rose from a distant village surrounded by piles of bodies. They hadn't called him Iron Hand for nothing. As she pressed the shutter, Galíndez sincerely hoped she wouldn't inherit that painting.

She took a couple more shots and lowered the camera. 'Very handsome, General.'

'Right.' Ramiro screwed the cap back on his pen and put it in his top pocket. 'Back to work then.' He looked up, sensing her reluctance to leave. 'Unless there's anything else?'

'There is one thing,' Galíndez said. 'Do you know anything about the *Centinelas*?'

Ramiro shrugged. 'How long have you got? I could spend hours talking about them.'

'That shouldn't be necessary.' Galíndez started to sit and froze as she realised her mistake. 'Sorry, is it all right to...'

Ramiro laughed. 'Sit down, you don't need to ask. Not after

what happened to you.' His expression became serious. 'Speaking of which, when they had you in that cellar, did they...' He paused, embarrassed.

'I wasn't raped, if that's what you're wondering.'

'Thank God. Your Aunt Teresa will be so relieved.'

'I know I was,' Galíndez muttered.

'Why do you ask about the *Centinelas*?' Ramiro asked.

'Because Guzmán and Sancho are working for them,' Galíndez said.

'That's not surprising,' he growled. 'The *Centinelas* always used thugs like them.'

'When I was being tortured, Guzmán questioned me about what I knew of them.'

Ramiro's eyes narrowed. 'The bastard. What did you say?'

'I told him the little I knew: that they were a secretive bunch of Franco's most faithful officers who were involved in carrying out assassinations.'

'That was how they started out after the Civil War.' Ramiro nodded. 'Over the years they grew stronger and more secretive. Later on, they established links with organised crime. They tried to infiltrate the police, the *guardia* and the military. In fact, they practically ran the police force in the early nineteen eighties, but they always drew a blank with the *guardia*, largely due to my father's efforts – and mine, I might add. We had to fight damn hard to keep them out. It wasn't easy, I can tell you, they were bloody secretive. Rather like the Freemasons, though better armed. They used to swear oaths to defend Spain and Franco and they wore gold rings as a sign of membership, engraved with a two-headed serpent. They claimed the gold came from Peru. The conquistadores discovered it, apparently.'

'The conquistadores looted it from Peru, you mean,' Galíndez said, sternly. 'And they gave the Aztecs smallpox and syphilis in return.'

'I sometimes forget your generation feels it has to rewrite history, Ana.'

'The *Centinelas* had a leader, didn't they – apart from Franco?' Galíndez asked, gently steering him back onto the subject.

'They had several, though each leader always used the same code name: Xerxes. We never got near to the man at the top, unfortunately.'

She nodded, deep in thought. 'I wonder if maybe Guzmán's their leader now?'

'He could be.' Ramiro nodded. 'I'll step up our surveillance activities, see if we can find out what they're up to and then put a stop to it.'

Galíndez glanced at her watch. 'I'd better not keep you any longer, Uncle.'

'Always a pleasure, Ana,' Ramiro said as he showed her out. The adjutant didn't look up as she went down the corridor to the lift.

As the lift doors opened, she heard her uncle's booming voice as he extolled her virtues to his sour-faced adjutant as he always did. 'Young women like her hardly eat these days, that's why they're all flat-chested.'

Mercifully, the lift doors glided shut before she could hear any more.

It was the hour of siesta as Ramon Villanueva made his way down the main street, slowed by the ponderous weight of the sun. In the distance, the line of new hotels along the coast shimmered in the violent heat. Villanueva took off his panama hat and mopped his face with one of the handkerchiefs his wife had given him two Christmases ago. He then removed his jacket, deciding to carry it, exposing the .38 resting in the holster on his hip. Not that it mattered: all thirty-seven villagers knew their chief of police had never fired his pistol in twenty-five years of service.

As Villanueva went into the cool of the comisaría, *his* sargento *looked up from his desk, bleary-eyed. For some, the siesta started early.*

'All quiet, Alberto?'

He already knew the answer. There was no crime here apart from the odd problem with tourists or city people. One day soon, they would close this comisaría. *When that happened, he planned to use his pension to buy a share in his brother's hotel, just up the coast road. There had been a time when he thought he would miss being a policeman. That time was long gone.*

'Nothing new to report, Inspector,' Alberto said, squinting at his day book. 'Señora Manzanares came in half an hour ago, she said the school bus hasn't arrived at the school yet.'

'The engine's had it,' Villanueva said. 'They really need a new bus.'

He sank into a chair in his tiny office and stared at the black-and-white photo of Franco on the wall. The heat was fierce now and the wet patch on the back of his shirt was getting bigger. He needed some new shirts. At times like these, confronted by minor domestic needs, he missed his wife all the more.

'They ought to replace that bus,' Alberto agreed. 'It must be thirty years old.'

'I wish I was.' Villanueva took a bottle from his drawer and poured himself a glass of tepid red wine. He found his cigarettes, lit one and sat back. His lunch would be arriving soon. After that he would doze for an hour, more if he finished the bottle. And then home to an empty house and his memories. Another quiet day in Llanto del Moro.

CHAPTER 7

MADRID, OCTOBER 1982, TORRE DE MADRID,
PLAZA DE ESPAÑA

Guzmán strolled across the plaza towards the gleaming skyscraper that had once been the tallest building in Europe. Now, that accolade was held by some Belgian construction. He found that depressing.

As he walked, he watched the changing reflections in the pool below the monument to Cervantes. The still water mirrored the statues of Don Quixote and Sancho Panza and Guzmán paused, wondering why he found the statues so annoying. Only as he went into the lobby of the tower did he realise: the statues resembled Corporal Ochoa and him.

General Ortiz was waiting for him by the entrance.

'We'd better hurry,' Ortiz said. 'We need to get ourselves in position before those bastards get here.' He led Guzmán to a service elevator at the side of the lobby. On the fifth floor, they got out and followed a long corridor. At the end of the corridor, a young woman was sitting at a desk. She got up as they approached.

'You're in the yellow room, gentlemen. I'll show you in.'

They followed her into a small dimly lit office that resembled a stationery cupboard. On one wall was a dark square of curtain. Covering a painting, perhaps, Guzmán thought.

'I'll leave you to it, General,' the young woman said. 'There's a bottle in the drawer of that desk if you need it.'

'Thank you, *Sargento*.' Ortiz watched the movement of her hips as she went to the door. When the door closed, he went over and turned the key.

'*Sargento*?' Guzmán asked, raising an eyebrow. 'You're using women now?'

'Don't look so surprised, Leo.' Ortiz went to the desk and took a bottle of bourbon from a drawer. 'We can hardly have men posing as secretaries, can we? As soon as we found out the *Centinelas* were renting a meeting room here, we moved some of our ladies in, next door. They pretend to be typing all day, but really, they're keeping an eye on the opposition. Take the *sargento* you just saw. Out of uniform, she looks like any other office worker. Who'd suspect her?'

'I would,' Guzmán said.

Ortiz laughed as he poured bourbon into two plastic cups. 'You suspect everyone.'

'It's kept me alive this far.' Guzmán took a swig of bourbon. 'So what happens now? Is the meeting room wired, or do we press our ears to the wall?'

'Neither,' Ortiz said. 'When they arrive, the *sargento* will press a button and that light on the wall over there will flash. That's the signal to lower our voices.'

'And how long have you had the *Centinelas* under surveillance?'

'Not long enough. I never realised how fast they were working. One minute they weren't a threat, next minute they were. Things change quickly these days.'

'I'd noticed,' Guzmán muttered.

The light on the wall flashed. Ortiz put a finger to his lips and went over to the curtain. Carefully, he pulled it to one side, exposing a square of glass that gave a direct view into the meeting room next door. 'Two-way mirror,' he whispered. 'I'll point out some of their people to you as they come in.'

Guzmán peered through the glass. The conference room was dominated by a big oval table set with the usual corporate paraphernalia: pads of notepaper and complimentary pens were arranged alongside plates of mints and bottles of water in the centre of the table. Guzmán found the sight of so much water dispiriting. In the old days, meetings were always awash with drink. Unless they were with Franco, of course. Franco didn't drink much and he didn't smoke. No wonder he never looked happy.

General Ortiz took a packet of cigarettes from his pocket. 'Want one? Black tobacco, rough as a gypsy's sister.'

'I don't mind if I do.'

More people were arriving now and General Ortiz kept up a commentary for Guzmán's benefit. 'That's the deputy head of the *policía nacional* and there's the commander of the Brunete armoured division.' He continued, pointing out various civic dignitaries, a couple of captains of industry and several members of parliament. The *Centinelas* were very well connected indeed, Guzmán realised. No wonder Gutiérrez was so worried about them.

Behind the group of politicians coming through the door, Guzmán saw a burly man in a general's uniform, glancing round disdainfully as he took a seat at the head of the table.

'Isn't that General Alvaro?'

'It is,' Ortiz nodded. 'The King's personal advisor, though he's not advising His Majesty today. He's number two in the *Centinelas* hierarchy.'

Guzmán raised his eyebrows. 'Does the King know?'

'I don't know, Guzmán, why don't you ask him?'

The door opened again and a woman entered, weighed down by armfuls of cardboard files and bundles of papers.

'Who's the blonde?' Guzmán asked, approvingly.

'Her?' Ortiz sneered. 'Paloma Ibañez, one of their top lawyers. See the guy behind her, the tall one with the long hair? That's Javier Benavides, the other half of their legal team. He and Paloma are the human face of the *Centinelas'* central council. Not that either of them is remotely human. Ibañez is so cold you could chill a bottle of wine in her pants.'

Guzmán was not inclined to agree with the general about Señorita Ibañez though he was more than willing to take an immediate dislike to Javier Benavides. From his suntan to the exquisitely cut suit and his manicured nails, Benavides' appearance spoke of money. That was reason enough to hate him.

Ibañez and Benavides sat on either side of General Alvaro though he barely acknowledged them and continued writing on his pad.

General Ortiz pressed a button and the tinny sound of voices from the conference room filtered in through a small speaker in the wall.

'I'd like to begin this meeting by extending a welcome to you all,' said Paloma Ibañez. 'I thought Brigadier General Gutiérrez might attend today, God knows we've invited him enough times.'

'Sometimes I think the *Brigada Especial* don't like us,' Benavides said.

A ripple of laughter ran round the table. On the other side of the glass panel, Guzmán clenched his fists.

'Actually, his absence is understandable,' Ibañez said. 'He has a session of radiotherapy booked for this afternoon.'

'Let's hope it's not successful,' General Alvaro grunted, still writing.

Guzmán stared through the two-way mirror at the King's advisor, imagining throwing him through the window that ran the length of the conference room. Maybe Gutiérrez was a cold bastard, but that was for Guzmán to decide, not some overfed sycophant like Alvaro.

'I didn't know about Gutiérrez,' Ortiz whispered. 'Sorry, Leo.'

The door of the conference room opened as a big, thickset man entered.

'Late again, Señor Ricci?' General Alvaro asked.

'Traffic's bad,' Ricci said, slumping into a chair. 'Did I miss anything?'

'Nothing at all. Let's get down to the business of the day.'

General Ortiz leaned over to whisper to Guzmán. 'That big bruiser is Eduardo Ricci, Eduardo *el Bastardo* they call him. His mob act as the *Centinelas*' enforcers.'

'The central council have instructed us to inform you they're unhappy with the recent operations by the police against foreign narcotics importers,' Paloma Ibañez said, looking at the Deputy

Director of the National Police. 'From now on, such operations must be carried out in a less efficient manner.'

The deputy director flushed with anger. 'You want the police to turn a blind eye to large-scale drug pushing, señorita?'

Ibañez shrugged. 'It's nothing you haven't done before.'

'Even so, there's a limit as to how far we can go along with these things.'

Paloma Ibañez's eyes narrowed. 'You know, I believe in the old days, the *Centinelas* had a phrase: "You pay with your dead." It refers to the fact that when they first were formed, they pledged to repay any affront by killing not only the person who'd offended them but also three generations of his or her family.'

The deputy director seemed to be on the verge of a seizure. 'This is intolerable. First, you demand the police tone down their anti-narcotics operations, and then you threaten me?'

'I'm only the messenger, though the answer to both those questions is yes.'

'You took the money,' General Alvaro said, emerging from his brooding silence.

'And you knew it was a binding agreement,' Benavides added. 'End of story.'

The deputy director ground out his cigarette in an ashtray. 'As you wish.'

'Back to business,' General Alvaro sighed. 'And try to keep any further moral outrage to a minimum. I hate hypocrisy before lunch.'

Most of the business that followed consisted of further instructions for non-intervention by the forces of law and order in various areas of the *Centinelas'* extensive business interests.

Finally, Ibañez reached the end of her imperatives. 'Before we end this meeting, does anyone have anything else for discussion?'

'No takers?' General Alvaro asked, impatient for his lunch. 'Are we done?'

'There is one other piece of business, General,' Benavides said, shuffling through his papers. 'The arrival of Comandante Guzmán in Madrid.' He took off his reading glasses as he looked round the table. 'Anyone know why Guzmán's here?'

Paloma Ibañez turned to him, suddenly curious. 'I'm not familiar with this Guzmán, Javier.'

'I'll soon fill you in.' Benavides looked down at a typewritten sheet of paper. 'Leopoldo Guzmán, Civil War hero, awarded the Laureada de San Fernando for almost single-handedly wiping out a Republican unit following the battle of Badajoz, at the age of eighteen, no less. Following the war, he's been employed by the *Brigada Especial*, specialising in undercover operations and, more lately, counter-espionage and anti-terrorist activities. He was a firm favourite of Franco, though that doesn't count for much now, of course.' He turned the page. 'Utterly ruthless, violent and with a tendency towards insubordination, he's only stayed in his post so long because he gets results.'

'You won't get your fucking head through the door now, Leo,' Ortiz chuckled.

Guzmán frowned. He didn't care what the *Centinelas'* legal team thought about him. It was the fact that they knew he was back in Madrid that bothered him.

'Is he here to do a job for the *Brigada Especial*?' General Alvaro asked. 'You're supposed to know these things, Señor Benavides.'

'There was an incident in the Retiro, I believe. Isn't that right, Señor Ricci?'

Ricci looked at Benavides with contempt. 'Just a local problem. This Guzmán was collecting cash from old Franco supporters and he got into a dispute with some of my boys.'

'Two dead seems quite a dispute,' Benavides said, pursing his lips.

Ricci grinned. 'I doubt you know much about that kind of thing, son.' He reached for a glass of water. 'The casualties don't matter. The guys who were killed were Bulgarians, we've already replaced them. And just so we're clear, it wasn't me told them to go after Guzmán. Guillermo Masias called them in after Guzmán roughed him up.'

'Then perhaps you shouldn't let your friend give orders to your employees?'

Ricci stared at Benavides without blinking. 'Don't tell me how to do my job, son.'

Benavides looked away, suddenly nervous. 'It would be best if such scenes weren't repeated, especially with the election coming up.'

'Like I said, it was no big deal.' Ricci took a sip of water and banged the glass down on the table.

'Any other business?' Paloma Ibañez asked. When there was no response, she gave the men around the table a last cold smile. 'The meeting is over. Thank you all for your cooperation.'

Behind the two-way mirror, Guzmán and Ortiz watched the *Centinelas'* lawyers and associates file out of the conference room.

'What do you think?' Ortiz said. 'Nice bit of surveillance, wouldn't you say? Every time they meet, we have one of our people here to tape their conversations.' He looked at his watch. 'Fancy getting some lunch?'

Guzmán ground out his cigarette in the ashtray. 'What do you think, General?'

MADRID, OCTOBER 1982, TABERNA DE ANTONIO SÁNCHEZ, CALLE MESÓN DE PAREDES

A pale sun was emerging from the clouds as General Ortiz's Jaguar XJ6 pulled up at the end of the street. The general's bodyguard got out and opened the door. 'Does the general want us to come into the restaurant?'

'No, piss off and get a bite to eat. Pick me up at three.'

The bodyguard nodded. '*A sus órdenes, mí General.*'

The dark wooden frontage of the taberna was almost unchanged since its opening in 1884. Through the door, they saw the long narrow room, the tables and diners in deep shadow. Long arrays of bottles on gleaming shelves. The air of a bygone era.

Guzmán pointed to a building across the road. 'I used to live there.' Idly, he wondered if the weapons he'd left under the floorboards were still there. Not that it mattered, most would be obsolete by now.

'Are we going in or not?' Ortiz asked, impatient as he smelled the aroma coming from inside the bar. 'It's years since I was last here and I plan on eating myself stupid.'

Guzmán led the way into the crowded tavern. A group of business people were pressed together in noisy conversation at the bar. As Guzmán and Ortiz went to the dining room, one of the men at the bar turned and Ortiz found himself face to face with Javier Benavides. 'General, what a pleasure,' Benavides beamed, offering his hand.

'You can put that away,' Ortiz scowled, glaring at the man's outstretched hand. 'I don't know where it's been.'

Ignoring that, Benavides turned his attention to Guzmán. 'I don't believe I've had the pleasure, señor?'

'Leo Guzmán.'

Benavides' eyes widened as he heard the name. They widened much more as Guzmán gave him a particularly brutal handshake.

'It's funny, *Comandante*,' Benavides said, rubbing his hand. 'Your name cropped up in conversation only today.'

'They say the only thing worse than being talked about is not being talked about,' Guzmán said, turning to follow Ortiz into the dining room. He sat with his back to the wall. 'How did that orange-faced clown know we were coming here?'

'Coincidence, I hope.' Ortiz raised a hand to attract one of the waitresses and she came over, smart in her stiffly starched uniform. A gypsy, Guzmán noticed.

'Good afternoon, gentlemen.' Her eyes suddenly fixed on Guzmán. 'You owe me a thousand pesetas.'

'Like fuck I do,' Ortiz snapped.

'Not you, him.' She indicated Guzmán with a nod of her head.

Guzmán reached into his wallet, took out a banknote and handed it to her.

'About time,' she grunted. 'Will the gentlemen be drinking?'

'What do you think?' Guzmán said.

Her smile revealed a missing front tooth. 'Rioja, same as before?'

Guzmán nodded.

'But you have to pay this time,' she said. 'No waving your ID and then walking out.'

Guzmán sighed. 'Maybe you could bring us the wine before we die of old age?'

'You must have pulled that number a few times for her to recognise you.' Ortiz laughed as the waitress bustled away to get their wine.

'Maybe,' Guzmán said. 'I don't remember her at all.'

'So why give her the money? She might have been lying.'

'A gypsy wouldn't lie like that,' Guzmán said, looking down the menu. 'I'm going to have the tripe stew, how about you?'

'Bull's tail,' Ortiz said. 'Just the thing for a hangover.'

'I didn't know you'd got one.'

'I haven't, I was thinking about later.'

A sudden bellowing laugh a few tables away made them look up.

'Fucking hell,' Ortiz said. 'It's Eduardo Ricci.'

At a table near the bar, Guzmán saw Benavides and Ricci together with two heavyset thugs. One glanced over and saw Guzmán looking at him. He tried to hold Guzmán's gaze for a moment, then quickly looked away.

'What do they want, I wonder?' Ortiz muttered.

'You'll soon find out,' Guzmán said. 'Here comes one of their goons.'

Ortiz glared at the dull-faced bruiser as he came to the table. 'We've already ordered.'

The man treated him to a yellow-toothed grin. 'Señor Ricci sent you this.' He put a bottle of wine on the table. 'Thought you'd like it.'

Guzmán looked up from the menu and stared at him. 'You can go.'

'Most people would have the manners to say thank you,' the man said, scowling.

'I'm not most people. So fuck off while you can still remember your name.'

The man's face hardened. 'You need to be careful, *amigo*.'

'And you're going to need a wheelchair.' Guzmán started to get to his feet.

'OK, I'm going.' The man grinned. 'I'll see you next time you decide to leave some more money in the Retiro Park, eh?' He chuckled as he went to join Ricci and the others.

'He's one of the bastards who stole my money.' Guzmán reached into his jacket for the Browning.

Ortiz put a hand on his arm to restrain him. 'Leave it, Leo, it was only money.'

Guzmán stared at him, incredulous. 'It's not the money I'm angry about, it's this.' He lifted the bottle so Ortiz could see the label. 'Fucking cava, the cheapest you can get.' He stared at the wine with unbridled hatred. 'I wouldn't give this to a dying priest.'

'Even so,' Ortiz said. 'This isn't the time.'

Unconvinced, Guzmán put the bottle down on the table and glared at the waitress as she returned with their wine.

'Here we are.' She put two bottles of Marqués de Cáceres in front of them. 'What's this?' she asked, pointing to the bottle of cava. 'Did you bring your own?'

'It's a gift for a friend,' Guzmán said, reaching for the Rioja.

'He can't be much of a friend.'

'And you're not much of a gypsy if you can't tell how much you're annoying me.'

'I'll get your food.' She went away, cursing the bitch who'd borne him, though she did it under her breath, grateful that he didn't remember her.

The restaurant was getting crowded and Ricci and his companions were soon obscured by a line of people waiting to be seated. With Ricci and his crew out of sight, Guzmán calmed down a little. Then he tasted the tripe and calmed down a lot more.

A second helping was called for, he decided. When they had finished, Guzmán ordered brandy and cigars. It seemed churlish not to, since the general would be paying.

'That was excellent,' Ortiz said. 'I had lunch with the prime minister yesterday and the food wasn't half as good. I just hope the Socialists get better caterers if they get elected.'

'Did the prime minister say if he was expecting to win the election?' Guzmán asked.

'He said he was hopeful, which means he's lost it already.' Ortiz looked at his watch. 'This is on me. Well, the taxpayer anyway.' He gestured to the waitress to bring the bill.

'Thanks,' Guzmán said, as if Ortiz's generosity came as a surprise. 'I'm off for a piss.'

'They say you only ever rent your drink, Leo.'

As he looked across the crowded bar, Guzmán saw Ricci's dough-faced lackey go through the wooden swing doors into the toilet. Casually, he turned and took the untouched bottle of cava from the table.

The men's toilets were sharp with the familiar smell of alcohol and urine. At the door, Guzmán stepped back to let an elderly gentleman make his exit. Inside, he saw Ricci's lackey taking a long splattering piss. Guzmán walked softly towards him, the bottle in his hand. 'I'm returning your gift.'

The man turned, still holding his dick in his hand. As he did, Guzmán swung the bottle into the side of his head. The bottle didn't shatter, which surprised him, though the man went down as if he'd been shot, which came as no surprise at all. Guzmán stood over the unconscious man, unzipped his fly and took an extravagant piss over his face and clothes. Before he left, he laid the bottle on his chest. When he came to, he might need a drink.

'Though you'd got lost,' Ortiz said as Guzmán came out of the restaurant into the autumn sun. Across the road, the general's bodyguards were waiting listlessly by the Jaguar. 'You want a lift?'

Guzmán shook his head. 'I'm going to take a walk, see how things have changed.'

'It's hard to know what hasn't changed, these days,' Ortiz said as they shook hands.

Guzmán looked him in the eye. 'I haven't.'

'I know, Leo, but let me give you a bit of advice, for what it's worth. You know I told you the *Centinelas* keep trying to infiltrate the *guardia*? Well, that's the way they operate all the time. Keep an eye on the men in your squad. It only takes one traitor to ruin everything.'

'I'll do that, General.'

Guzmán watched Ortiz's car drive away before he set off down the road towards Puerta del Sol. The afternoon sun lit up the tall buildings around him. As he walked, Guzmán noticed a young man wearing a leather jacket and jeans standing in a doorway. Selling drugs, most likely. That was a matter for the police and he kept walking.

Behind him, the young man casually left the doorway and started following him.

Being followed was not a new experience for Guzmán. Sometimes it could be annoying, though it was always an interesting contest, particularly when the pursuer had no idea their target was aware of them. Most died without realising they had been marked for death from the moment Guzmán sensed their presence. But the man following him now was an amateur and within a few minutes, Guzmán had shaken him off. He could have dawdled, maybe even retraced his steps so the young man would pick up the trail again. But there was no sport to be had with someone so inept and he decided to make his way back to the *pensión*, taking a nostalgic route of shadowy streets and alleys he recalled from other times, when bars and cafés were dark with smoke and packed with dubious customers.

Selecting a particularly insalubrious establishment, he sat on a scuffed leather stool, nursing a brandy as he watched the clientele in the cracked mirror behind the bar. The noisy conversations around him were soothing, reminding him of Madrid after the war. Fond memories: the subtle unfolding of dawn, the sun stealing over the irregular horizon of roofs and spires. That first hour of soft light. And the noise: the rattle of horse-drawn carts on cobbles, voices echoing in narrow streets, overlayed by the murmur of traffic.

There were other, less aesthetic memories too, a recollected haze of winter mornings, faces pressed against barred windows watching vehicles pull up in the prison yard. Groups of men carrying rifles, smoking as they waited for orders. The thin line of light on the horizon marking the hour when the firing squads started their work. And Guzmán remembered much about that work. The pleading and weeping, the sudden blows of rifle butts urging the prisoners towards a wall pockmarked by bullets. Those things he remembered in detail, even the songs the condemned men used to sing. Only their faces escaped his memory, though the city was always present in his recollections, probably because it was so much like him, violent and capricious, cruel and yet unexpectedly generous on occasion.

There was a hidden rhythm to this city, a kind of violent inheritance etched into history by fire and steel. The tides of history ran red over these cobbles. And that tide was changing: his instinct told him so, as did the newspaper headlines. People wanted change. Change and happiness. To his mind, those things did not sit easily together.

As he turned up Calle de Preciados, a car pulled to a halt fifty metres ahead. Three men got out, adjusting their jackets, or rather, adjusting the pistols beneath their jackets. Hard-faced men, one sporting a large white dressing on the side of his head.

Guzmán's first thought was to draw the Browning, dive behind a parked car and open up. But though the men looked aggressive, no one made a move towards him. Someone was getting out of the car and one of the goons rushed to get the door. As the man got out, Guzmán recognised the tobacco-coloured features of Javier Benavides.

'*Comandante*,' Benavides said, giving him a friendly smile, though this time, he didn't offer his hand.

Guzmán stayed where he was, happy to let Benavides block the line of fire between him and the three armed men. 'I see you brought your friends.'

'They're not here to harm you.' Benavides smiled. 'They're here to protect me.'

'Clearly you're an optimist.'

'It's always best to take precautions, *Comandante*. As my mother keeps telling me, it's not been safe on the streets since Franco died.'

Guzmán shrugged. 'It wasn't all that safe when he was alive.'

Benavides looked past Guzmán to the dingy bar he'd just left. 'Do you have time for another, Señor Guzmán?'

'If you're paying,' Guzmán said, leading the way.

Once inside, Guzmán took a seat near the door where he could keep an eye on the heavies waiting by the car. He called to the barman for brandy. Benavides ordered beer.

As the barman got the drinks, Benavides leaned closer. 'You're probably wondering why I'm approaching you like this.'

'I'm sure you're going to tell me.'

'You've been away from Madrid, I understand?'

'I've been busy.' There was no need to go into detail about his work, Guzmán decided. It would only frighten Benavides and he didn't want to do that until he'd heard his offer. And he would make an offer, Guzmán was sure. They wouldn't be sitting here otherwise.

'I know what that's like,' Benavides said. 'I also know the *Brigada Especial* recalled you to Madrid. Might I ask why?'

'They owe me money,' Guzmán said, trying to keep the bitterness from his voice. He took his drink from the barman and then glared at him until he retreated back behind the bar.

Benavides sipped his beer. From his expression, he didn't like it much. 'I heard the *Brigada* had some financial irregularities. Accounting seems to be a common problem for those old departments of the Franco era. Money so often was misplaced.'

'My money certainly was.' This time Guzmán didn't even try to hide his bitterness.

'I understand Brigadier General Gutiérrez hasn't been well?'

'He's not so ill he can't sign a cheque.' Guzmán finished his brandy and shouted to the barman to bring another. 'I think his problem is that he can't count.'

'Can't count,' Benavides repeated, deadpan. 'Very droll.' He lifted the beer to his mouth and then put the glass down again without drinking. 'It's well known that he's not in the best of health. Word is that it's serious. If that's the case, he'll have to be replaced by someone of exceptional calibre.' He sat back, waiting for Guzmán to agree.

Guzmán glanced out at the men by the car. He said nothing. When the barman caught his eye, he lifted a finger and pointed to his glass.

'I'm authorised to offer you his post should it become available,' Benavides said, unable to bear the silence.

'Ten, fifteen years ago, I'd have said yes,' Guzmán replied, taking his brandy from the barman. 'But I want out now. That's why I'm back: to sort out the pay-off.'

Benavides' face twitched. The man wouldn't make a poker player, Guzmán thought, guessing what would come next.

'The thing is, we wanted to offer you Gutiérrez's post in return for something of yours. I wonder if perhaps a cash offer would be acceptable?'

Guzmán raised an eyebrow. 'Who's "we"?'

'You know very well who I work for. You were having lunch with General Ortiz, I'm sure he apprised you of the situation in Madrid.'

Guzmán took another sip of brandy. 'What is it you want?'

'I understand from a colleague that you devised a powerful code some years ago?'

This was something Guzmán hadn't anticipated, though his expression didn't change. 'Your colleague worked for Admiral Carrero Blanco, did he? I let his department use the code years ago.'

'And very useful it was too, I understand. Several of our people looked at it and they think it's exactly what we need.' Reluctantly, Benavides drank some of his beer. 'How did you come to write a code like that?'

'I didn't write it,' Guzmán said. 'I was given the prototype of a Nazi code machine in return for getting a ticket to Paraguay for a German fleeing the Allies. The machine was the only model that survived the war.' There was more to it than that, even if he left out the fatalities, though Benavides didn't need to know. 'Naturally, I used it from time to time.'

Benavides gave him a sly look. 'I imagine it helped protect your secrets?'

'If I'd had any.' Benavides didn't like eye contact, Guzmán noticed. He leaned forward and met his gaze. A few moments of that was usually enough to prompt most people into speaking and Benavides was no exception.

'I understand there's a key that makes the code impossible to break?'

'That's right,' Guzmán said. 'The key is a piece of poetry in a foreign language. It has to be translated into Spanish and then applied to the coded text.'

'And could this machine and the key be made available to an interested party?'

'They could, though naturally, they wouldn't be free.'

'Everything has its price, *Comandante*.' Benavides smiled. 'What would you say to eight million pesetas and regular payments into your bank account for the next ten years in return for sole use of the code machine?'

'Then the interested party could have the code in a heartbeat,' Guzmán said. 'The original key to the code was engraved on a sword, though I had it transcribed into a notebook for convenience. You'll be the only person in the world with a copy of that key. As long as you keep the key safe, no one's going to be able to crack your communications.'

That was not quite true, though there was no way Benavides could know he was lying. The sword was buried somewhere beneath a ruined house in the wilds of the Basque country. He doubted anyone would ever find it.

'So do we have a deal, *Comandante*?'

'If you can come up with the money this week.' Guzmán glanced round the bar. 'I'm staying at the Pensión Paraíso on Calle del Carmen.'

'We know where you're staying, *Comandante*.' This time, Benavides didn't smile.

'Then I'll get it ready for you. Once I get the money I'll hand over the code machine, the key and the paperwork that goes with it.'

'Excellent.' Benavides picked up his briefcase and tucked it under his arm. 'You know, with that sort of money, you'll be able to travel. In fact you'd be advised to, if you get my meaning?'

It was the nearest Benavides had come to threatening him and Guzmán's first thought was to punch him to the floor. His second was more pragmatic. 'Nice doing business with you.'

'Everyone does in the end,' Benavides said, holding the door for Guzmán. 'Because everyone has their price.'

CHAPTER 8

MADRID 2010, UNIVERSIDAD COMPLUTENSE,
GUARDIA CIVIL RESEARCH CENTRE

'You've been here half an hour now and hardly said a word,' Isabel said. 'Just tell me if you're in a foul mood.'

Galíndez glanced up from her computer screen. 'I'm in a foul mood.' With a sigh, she closed down the laptop and gave Isabel a detailed account of how she handled the attempt at reconciliation with the Fuentes family.

'What happened to all that stuff they taught you in the academy about conflict resolution?'

'I was angry,' Galíndez said. 'I just went into meltdown.'

Isabel put a hand on her arm, surprised at the tone of Galíndez's voice. 'Surely you could forgive Inés? You really liked those girls.'

'All that's over now. I'm through being Auntie Ana.'

'Come on, that's a little harsh, even for you.'

Galíndez narrowed her eyes. 'What do you mean, "even for me"?'

'Nothing.' Isabel held out a piece of paper. 'Before I forget, this guy from HQ called you earlier. Someone called Torrecilla. He works in cryptographics.'

Galíndez's eyes widened. 'He's the guy who's trying to decode Guzmán's diary. What did he say?'

'He said he was starting to understand it.'

'Really?' Galíndez grabbed her leather jacket as she went to the door. 'I'm off to HQ.' She paused in the doorway. 'By the way, do I look pale?'

Isabel took a long look. 'A bit, yes. Why, are you feeling ill?'

'Never felt better,' Galíndez said as she went out the door.

MADRID 2010, HEADQUARTERS OF THE GUARDIA CIVIL,
CRYPTOGRAPHY DEPARTMENT

Capitán Torrecilla looked up as Galíndez came into his office. 'Sounds like you're out of breath, Ana. Training for another marathon?'

She shook her head. 'The lift wasn't working so I used the stairs.'

'God, that's nine floors,' he said. 'The thought of it makes me breathless.'

'The exercise will do me good,' Galíndez panted as she took a seat facing his desk. 'My colleague said you've made progress in your work on the Guzmán file?'

Torrecilla shook his head. 'Not quite. I suspected it was encrypted with a Nazi algorithm but I've carried out a statistical analysis of Guzmán's cipher text and compared it to known World War Two ciphers and it doesn't resemble any of them. It's much more sophisticated.'

'So what now?' Galíndez tried to keep the disappointment from her voice.

Torrecilla shrugged. 'Are you familiar with Kerckhoff's principle that the security of a system should only be based on the secrecy of the key?'

'And we don't have the key?' Galíndez frowned. 'Can't you work out what it is?'

'That's not how things work, Ana,' said Torrecilla. 'Without a key, we'll have to use brute force and even then, there's no guarantee of success.'

Galíndez shrugged. 'Do it, then. Anything's worth trying.'

Torrecilla mopped his face with his handkerchief. 'When I say brute force I don't mean we're going to kick someone's door down. We'd need to use computer time, lots of it.'

'Then use it, what's the problem?'

'Money. My boss won't sanction it and neither will General Ortiz. Austerity and all that. Everyone's having to make cuts. No one thinks it's worth spending a fortune to crack a seventy-year-old code.' He smiled. 'No one but you, that is.'

Galíndez went quiet. 'I think I might know how the code could be deciphered.'

'That's great, as long as it doesn't involve overspending my department's budget. What makes you think you've got the answer all of a sudden?'

'There's a scimitar in the evidence room that belonged to Guzmán. I found it in the Basque country earlier this year. It has a poem by Omar Khayyam engraved on the blade in Farsi. You think that could be the key?'

'It's worth a try,' Torrecilla said. 'If you can let me have a look at it, I'll see what I can come up with.'

Galíndez jumped to her feet. 'I'll go get it.'

Torrecilla grinned. 'There's no need to run. I'm not going anywhere.'

'You'd better not,' Galíndez said, starting to run.

As she heard the door of the Forensics office open, Mendez looked up and saw Galíndez coming towards her. 'Come to apologise?'

Galíndez ignored her. 'I want that scimitar I found in the Basque country. You put it in to the evidence room for safekeeping, remember?'

'I remember.' Mendez's fingers rattled on her keyboard. 'Here we go.' She wrote the reference number on a slip of paper. 'Give that to Enrique, the clerk. He'll dig it out for you.'

'I know how the system works.' Galíndez turned and headed for the door.

'Really? I thought you might have forgotten since you don't work here any more.'

Ignoring her, Galíndez went out into the corridor without closing the door.

'Use the stairs,' Mendez called after her. 'The lift isn't working.'

Galíndez had already reached the stairwell and her answer was muffled, though the tone of her reply was clear enough. Mendez sighed and went back to work.

Ten minutes later, Galíndez was back, her cheeks flushed from running.

Mendez hit *save* on her document. 'Are you in training for something, Ana?'

'It's not me who needs any training.' Galíndez's voice was tight with anger. 'I asked you to put that sword somewhere safe.'

'It is safe: it's in the store, tagged and bagged, as always. Didn't you ask Enrique to have a look?'

Galíndez ran a hand through her hair, exasperated. 'Of course I asked him. And he went away like an old mole into the evidence store and found a space with the right label, but no fucking sword. So where is it?'

Mendez leaned back in her seat. 'Don't talk to me like that. I outrank you.'

'Not now I'm on secondment, you don't. So let me ask you again, what are you going to do about that sword?'

'Given your tone of voice, I'm going to do fuck all. How's that?'

'In that case, I'll fill in a complaint and send it to Professional Standards.'

Mendez gave her a hard look. 'Don't be ridiculous. I'll be filling in forms for weeks if you do that.'

Galíndez gave her a malicious smile. 'Oh dear.'

'Look, Ana. There are some things you don't do, and setting Professional Standards on a colleague is one of them.'

'Find that sword by tonight or I swear to God I'll complain. Then you'll spend the next week buried in paperwork while Professional Standards go over every last procedure in the department. That should keep you and Capitán Fuentes busy, since he'll have to explain to them why the procedures don't work.'

Mendez banged her fist on the desk. 'Know what? You're a real pain in the arse.'

'Five o'clock tonight or I file that complaint,' Galíndez said as she left. 'Your call.'

'Bitch,' Mendez called after her.

————

Galíndez found Torrecilla slumped over his desk, surrounded by pages of what looked like algebra. 'Bad news: they've misplaced the sword.'

'How did that happen? They got someone new in the evidence store?'

'Same people,' said Galíndez, 'but they're getting sloppy.' She slumped into a chair. 'My dad would never have stood for that when he worked here.'

Torrecilla shoved his pile of papers to one side. 'Looks like you're sunk, Ana. Without that sword, we've got nothing.'

'Can I make a suggestion?' Galíndez didn't wait for an answer. 'If I could find a copy of the poem that was on Guzmán's sword, we could get it translated from Farsi into Spanish. Then you could try using that as a key to decipher the diary.'

'You speak Farsi, do you?' Torrecilla laughed. 'Because I don't.'

'No, but Teniente Bouchareb on the third floor does. He's the one who identified it.'

Torrecilla shrugged. 'It's worth a go, though I'm not promising anything.'

'I'm off back to the university. Give me a call if you find anything, will you?'

As she went into the corridor, Torrecilla called after her. 'The lift's working again, by the way.'

'Since when?'

'About half an hour.' Torrecilla heard a muted curse as she left.

Outside, banks of dark clouds hung over the city and the air was humid. Galíndez got into her car and opened the windows. In the mirror, she saw beads of sweat on her forehead and wiped them away. She slumped in the seat, replaying the standoff with Mendez in her head, though each time it always ended the same way.

She sighed. Some days, it felt like everything and everybody was against her. With the exception of Isabel, of course. Increasingly, Galíndez found herself relying on her. One of these days, Isabel would get another job working in radio. The thought of being without her was troubling and Galíndez had been thinking about that a lot recently.

She saw her face in the mirror, her dark eyes stared back at her, daring her. Slowly, she took the plastic tube of painkillers from her shirt pocket and shook a couple of tablets into the palm of her hand. After a furtive glance around the car park, she raised them to her mouth and swallowed them.

Her phone suddenly blared into life. A text from Isabel. Galíndez felt her skin prickle as she read it: Positive finding on Guzmán. Call me. She snatched up her phone and called.

Isabel answered at once. 'Ana, you won't believe this. I've got the address of a place Guzmán stayed at years ago. It's a *pensión* on Calle del Carmen, at the top end of the street, between House of Cod and Lush. It's called the Pensión Paraíso. Want to meet me there?'

'Do I?' Galíndez started the engine. 'I'll see you in a few minutes.'

MADRID 2010, PENSIÓN PARAÍSO, CALLE DEL CARMEN

It had begun to rain and Isabel was standing under the awning of a grocery store when Galíndez arrived. She hurried across the street and gave Isabel an unexpected hug.

'Are you OK, Ana?'

'Of course,' Galíndez said. 'So, how do you know Guzmán stayed at this place?'

'You know how people used to have to show their identity card when they checked in to a hotel so the proprietor could forward their details to the police? Well, I've been searching a new database that holds thousands of those old hotel entries.'

Isabel took a sheet of paper from her pocket and unfolded it. Galíndez saw a scanned image of a form with details taken from an old DNI, the national identity document. 'Look, it's in the name of a Leopoldo Ramirez. That was Guzmán's alias, wasn't it?'

'It was,' said Galíndez. 'But look at the date he checked in: October 1982.'

'A few days before the elections.' Isabel took another paper from her pocket. 'Now take a look at this headline from the same week: "Bombing at Bar Navarra Was Attempt to Disrupt Election, Say Police." Maybe it's a coincidence, maybe not. What do you think?'

'I think he checked in at the *pensión* under an alias so he could plant a bomb.' Galíndez linked arms with her. 'Good job, Izzy. Let's take a look at this place.'

Isabel gave her a curious look. 'You don't have to keep holding on to me. I'm not going to run away.'

'Sorry,' Galíndez said, embarrassed, 'I'm excited, that's all.'

They went up the stairs of the *pensión* into a spartan reception area with a long desk by one wall. A window on the far side of the room overlooked an alley. Beside the window was a cane chair piled with old magazines.

Galíndez went over to the desk and hit the tarnished brass bell. As they waited, she noticed a doorway behind the desk, covered by a curtain of coloured glass beads. Behind the curtain, she heard the blare of a television. Probably the receptionist was watching TV instead of working. Wearily, she brought her fist down on the bell, and then again, harder. The noise of the TV continued, competing with the drone of traffic from outside. Then it stopped as the TV was turned off. Irritated, she looked round, seeing a staircase with a sign: HABITACIONES 1–4, COMEDOR. The cheaper rooms, she guessed, exposed to the noise of the street and the smell from the dining room.

The glass beads suddenly rattled as someone walked through them. Galíndez stared at the swinging rows of beads in surprise. There was no one there. Even so, she heard footsteps on the other side of the desk and then a stool seemed to drag itself to the counter. As she watched, a head appeared, followed by the rest of the body, as an elderly well-dressed dwarf clambered up onto the stool. He gave them a courteous bow. 'I rarely have the pleasure of one beautiful woman in my humble *pensión*,' he said in a deep voice, 'much less two.' He beamed at Isabel. 'I do hope you'll enjoy your stay here, Señorita Morente. You don't mind being recognised, I trust? I was a huge fan of your show. It was a disgrace when they got rid of you, an absolute disgrace.'

'I'm glad you liked it.' Isabel smiled.

He bowed once more. 'If it isn't too much trouble, might I beg an autograph?'

Isabel took a small notepad from her pocket and signed a sheet of paper.

The dwarf took the paper from her and put it into the pocket of his waistcoat. Then he gave Isabel such a low bow he almost toppled from his stool. 'Perhaps your servant here could bring your luggage in, while I show you to a room?'

'We're not staying.' Galíndez pushed her ID across the desk. 'Agent Galíndez, *guardia civil*. I'd like to ask you some questions.'

'Ah.' A note of resignation. 'The long arm of the law at last.'

'We're interested in someone who stayed here a long time ago. I wondered if you might remember him.'

A deep sonorous laugh. 'I'd prefer to forget most of the guests I've had here, to tell you the truth.'

'This is the man I'm talking about,' Galíndez said. 'Comandante Leopoldo Guzmán, also known as Leopoldo Ramirez.' She put the scanned details of Guzmán's fake DNI on the counter. 'According to this, he stayed in room number three.'

The dwarf's face set with concentration as he studied the document. 'I don't remember him, officer. This document is dated 1982 and I didn't take over here until 1983.'

Galíndez leaned against the counter. 'You know, a moment ago, it sounded as if you were expecting a visit from us.'

'Not at all. I was expecting other people. Tourists, definitely not the police.'

'That's odd, because the sign on the door says full.'

The dwarf took out a handkerchief and mopped his face. 'It does, though not in the literal sense. It means we'll be full once the tourists arrive. I expect they'll be here this afternoon.' He leaned forward, careful not to lose his balance. 'Is there something wrong with your eyes, señorita?'

Galíndez looked away, quickly. 'No there isn't. Why?'

'No reason. Will that be all, Agent Galíndez? I don't want to keep you.'

'I'm not finished yet,' Galíndez said, curtly. 'Can we take a look round?'

'Certainly, but at another more convenient time perhaps? You could call and make an appointment in a week or two when I'm less busy.'

'I could always get a search warrant,' Galíndez said, 'Señor...?'

'Leonidas Espartero, at your service, señorita. There's no need for a warrant, none whatsoever. Room three, you said? That's upstairs.'

She pointed to the sign over the stairs. 'I notice there are only four rooms up there. Where are the others?'

'There are no more, apart from the bathroom and dining room and neither have been overused by our recent clientele. Come, I'll show you round, ladies.'

Espartero slid across the counter and jumped down onto the shabby carpet. They followed him up the flight of stairs along a narrow corridor. At the end was a small room with several tables, each with a single place setting. On the wall a faded poster of some long-dead matador looked down on them.

'This is the dining room,' Señor Espartero said, proudly. 'If a guest is staying for a while, I set a table just for them. They have their own napkin, little bottles of oil and vinegar and everything. Almost a home from home, assuming their home is somewhat dilapidated.'

'Can we see the room Guzmán stayed in please?' Galíndez said, suddenly impatient.

They watched as Espartero opened the door to room number three. 'The room overlooks the street, so there's a bit of noise.'

'It hardly matters,' Galíndez said. 'We're not going to be stopping.'

'I might,' Isabel said, noticing Espartero's hurt expression. She took a step towards the window and gave Galíndez a dig in the ribs. 'If I get a new radio show, I might stay here from time to time. It's very central.'

Señor Espartero executed a deep bow. 'Naturally, I'd offer celebrity discount.'

Galíndez looked around the dingy room with its scuffed wooden floor, a wardrobe that must have come from a funeral sale and a nightstand with a smeared glass. The window was open and the thin curtain wavered in the humid air. 'Not very big, is it?'

'Perhaps the señorita thought the sign outside said "The Ritz"?' Espartero murmured.

'Can we have a minute to look round?' Isabel said.

'With pleasure, señorita. Perhaps I could prepare you both a coffee or something?'

From his voice, she guessed there was no *or something*. 'Coffee would be nice.'

Once Espartero had gone, Isabel rounded on Galíndez. 'What's up with you? You don't have to be so sharp with him. He's doing his best.'

'He's hiding something,' Galíndez muttered. She sat on the edge of the bed, taking in the lacklustre surroundings. The bed trembled as she got up and went to the window. Through the streaked glass, she saw a narrow alley scattered with bulging refuse sacks. From the walls came the murmur of water pipes and soft indistinct voices. She went back to the bed and sat down.

Isabel joined her. 'What makes you think he's keeping something from us?'

'For a start, when I asked him about Guzmán, his eyes almost crossed. I think he knows more than he's letting on.'

'He's wary of you, Ana. People of his generation are nervous about the police.'

'Maybe.' Galíndez went across the room to examine a pale mark on the wooden tiles. 'Look at this.' She ran her hand over the wood. 'The lacquer's been scrubbed away.'

'So? People make the most revolting messes in hotel rooms.'

'You could hardly call this a hotel.' Galíndez turned to the wall near the window and started scraping pieces of plaster from a small indentation.

'What's that?' Isabel asked, noticing her sudden concentration.

Galíndez shrugged. 'Probably nothing.'

Out of habit, she searched the room. In the wardrobe a few antiquated hangers dangled from a sagging wire. 'Not a trace of Guzmán,' she said, dejected.

The door opened as Señor Espartero returned. He gave them a languid bow. 'What do you think of the room?'

'How long did you say you'd been running this place?' Galíndez asked.

'It was 1983 when I took over from the previous owners,' Espartero said. 'If you're interested, I have the paperwork in the office. It would be no trouble to unpack it from the boxes. Just a few hours' work.'

Her face fell. 'You're sure you never had a guest called Guzmán or Ramirez?'

'Not to the best of my knowledge. May I be put to work in a circus if I lie.'

'Well, thanks anyway.' Isabel smiled. 'We'll leave you in peace.'

'He's lying,' Galíndez muttered as they went into the street. 'I could sense Guzmán's presence in there.'

'You're not clairvoyant, Ana.'

'Someone had scrubbed blood off those wooden tiles,' Galíndez said. 'And that hole in the wall looked like it was made by a bullet, I'd swear.'

'I think you're trying to make two and two equal five,' Isabel said as she unlocked the car door. She took Galíndez by the arm and peered into her eyes. 'You know what? Señor Espartero was right about your eyes.'

Galíndez pulled away. 'What's wrong with them?'

'They're dilated. You're still taking those painkillers, aren't you?' She pulled a sheet of paper from her pocket. 'I looked up your tablets on the net. These are some of the possible side effects: aggression, paranoia, sudden mood swings and overly emotional behaviour.' She gave Galíndez a stern look. 'You were aggressive with Señor Espartero and you frequently blow hot and cold with me when we're at work.' Angrily, she opened the car door and got behind the wheel. 'If you don't want my help, that's fine, but you'd better sort yourself out before it becomes a real problem.'

Galíndez leaned in through the window. 'Christ, Izzy, I was kidnapped only a few days ago, cut me some slack, will you?'

'You need to face up to this,' Isabel said. 'I know you're not comfortable talking about yourself, but sometimes you have to do these things.'

Galíndez ran a hand through her hair. 'I told you before, I can't do that.'

'If you can't even talk to me, then I'm not much of a friend, am I?' Isabel started the engine and the car pulled away from the kerb. Fifteen metres down the road, she braked and reversed. Galíndez hurried over and opened the passenger door.

Isabel held out her hand. 'Give me the tablets.'

Galíndez hesitated for a moment before handing over the plastic tube. 'What now?'

'You tell me.' Isabel kept her hands on the wheel, staring ahead.

'We talk?' Galíndez said, uncertainly. 'I could try, anyway.'

'Get in.' Isabel sighed. 'We'll go to my place.'

MADRID 2010, CALLE DE LAGASCA

Isabel stood at the window, looking out into the night. On the dining table a large pizza lay untouched. She picked up a bottle of wine from the table and poured two glasses. 'How do you feel now you've got all that off your chest?'

'You must have been a brilliant agony aunt on the radio.'

Galíndez was lying on the sofa, surrounded by crumpled tissues. 'I've never talked about myself like that before.'

Isabel shrugged. 'I like to think I helped a few people.'

'You've helped me,' Galíndez said. 'My life's been a mess the last couple of years.'

'That wasn't all your fault, Ana. There are lots of positives as well.'

'I know you're right. I just don't know where to start making changes.'

'You could start with the tablets.'

Galíndez dabbed her eyes with a tissue. 'Throw them away, I'm done with them.'

Isabel shook her head. 'No, you should be the one who does that.' She handed Galíndez a glass of wine. 'Can I ask you something?'

'One more question can't hurt. Go ahead.'

'Why are you so angry? Some days, you seem to be angry at yourself, at your colleagues and even me. Why is that?'

Galíndez lowered her eyes. 'Sometimes I need to blank it all out. Being angry helps.'

'Blank all what out?'

A long sigh. 'That's the trouble, Izzy. I don't know.'

'Is it Guzmán? You're angry because of what he did in the past?'

'It's not what he did in the past that makes me angry,' Galíndez said, quietly. 'It's because of what he did to me.'

'You mean mentally?'

'I mean physically.' Galíndez's dark eyes shone with anger. 'Want to see what he did?' Without waiting for an answer, she got to her feet and started unbuttoning her shirt.

Isabel watched her, confused. 'What are you doing?'

Galíndez unfastened the last button on her shirt and held it open, exposing her left side. She pointed to a pale line of scar tissue that began under her arm, disappeared beneath the side of her bra and ran down her ribs, ending just above her hip. When she spoke, her voice trembled with emotion. 'I survived the explosion at his *comisaría*, but I still see his mark on me every day of my life. Jesus, Izzy, I can't get away from him.'

Isabel put her arms around her. 'We'll find him, Ana. I promise.' Softly, she stroked Galíndez's hair. 'We'll find him and Sancho and they'll spend the rest of their lives in prison.' She pulled Galíndez closer, tracing the scar with her finger.

Galíndez took a deep breath, about to tell her that she already had a plan. A plan that didn't involve Guzmán or Sancho seeing the inside of a prison cell: when she found them, she was going to kill them.

But then Isabel's lips pressed against hers and for now, the time for talking was over.

CHAPTER 9

MADRID, OCTOBER 1982, PENSIÓN PARAÍSO,
CALLE DEL CARMEN

Guzmán pushed his empty plate away and watched as Daniela poured his coffee. 'That was good, did your Mamá teach you to cook?'

'No, Papa was a cook in the army.'

'I bet he didn't cook very often then: the Republicans only had chickpeas.'

'You said you weren't going to talk about the war, Señor Ramirez.'

'That was when I didn't know I'd be living cheek by jowl with a Red chef.' Guzmán slurped down his coffee and pushed the cup and saucer across the table towards her.

'A young man called at the desk half an hour ago, asking for you,' Daniela said as she stacked his crockery onto a tray. 'Remember my cousin Luisa asked you to take part in her research project? I didn't want to interrupt your breakfast, so I told him to come back later.'

'Of course,' Guzmán said, though he had forgotten completely. 'I can spare a few minutes, I suppose.'

'He's very nice,' Daniela said, blushing. 'He's Irish.'

'It's a good Catholic country,' Guzmán said, exhausting his knowledge of it. 'I'll be down in a couple of minutes, tell him to wait in reception for me.'

Ten minutes later, Guzmán came downstairs. A stocky red-haired young man was sitting by the window, leafing through a magazine. He leaped up as Guzmán approached.

'Señor Guzmán, thanks for seeing me, I'm Michael Riley.'

He held out his hand and Guzmán crushed it routinely, causing the lad's ruddy features to become even more florid.

'So you're the kid who wants to talk about the war?'

'I am. We could do the interview here if you like – since there's no one around?'

Guzmán would have preferred to talk about the war in a bar, preferably at the student's expense, but time was getting on. He shrugged and took a seat.

Riley placed several bulky files on top of the magazines scattered over the table. 'Mind if I take notes?'

'Go ahead,' Guzmán said, making himself comfortable.

Daniela brought them coffee. 'Here we are, gentlemen.' She was still a little flushed, Guzmán noticed. 'Would you like anything else, Señor Riley?'

'We don't need anything, thank you,' Guzmán said firmly.

Riley looked down at his notebook. 'There's a number of questions I'd like to ask.'

'I've got one for you first,' Guzmán said quietly. 'How do you know my name?'

Riley's face turned pale. 'I won't lie to you, señor.'

'No, you won't,' Guzmán leaned forward until his face was disturbingly close to Riley's. 'You speak Spanish well enough, so answer my fucking question.'

'It was Luisa,' Riley stammered. 'She recognised you.'

Guzmán smiled. *Always the same: threaten them and the first thing they do is betray someone else.* Some things never changed. 'How did she know who I was?'

As Riley reached into his jacket, there was a sudden flurry of movement, though not from Riley, who stayed very still, staring into the muzzle of the Browning.

'You reach into your coat like that and my first thought is that you've got a weapon,' Guzmán said, thumbing back the hammer.

'I haven't,' Riley mumbled, 'I swear.'

'Maybe so, but I'd have only found out when I searched your body. What were you reaching for?'

'A newspaper cutting.' Beads of sweat trickled down his face. 'May I show it you?'

'By all means,' Guzmán said, returning the Browning to its holster.

Riley retrieved a piece of yellowing newsprint from his pocket, an old clipping from the conservative daily, *ABC*. The page was badly faded, the contrast between light and shade so sharp the photograph seemed almost a sketch. In the picture, a tall, heavyset young man in combat gear was having a medal pinned on his chest by a short man in a uniform with big epaulettes, his spindly legs clad in gleaming riding boots. Behind them, neat ranks of troops were drawn up at attention. And beyond the lines of soldiers, the wooden *barrera* of a bullring. It had been a long time since he'd seen this headline:

HERO OF BADAJOZ DECORATED
BY GENERALISIMO FRANCO

'I can keep this, can I?' Guzmán asked.

Riley seemed to have lost the power of speech. He nodded.

'If Luisa realised who I was, how come she didn't want to do the interview?'

'She thought it would be good experience for me, *Comandante*.'

'And much safer for her.' Guzmán put the paper in his wallet. 'Any more questions?'

'I recently talked to a lady whose husband worked with you in the *Brigada Especial*.'

Guzmán frowned, unhappy with the idea of people discussing him. He took out a cigarette from his packet of Ducados and lit it. 'Give me their names.'

'That information is confidential, I'd never forgive myself if I betrayed a source.'

Guzmán exhaled smoke into Riley's face. 'And you'll never walk again if you don't.'

'Señora María Peralta,' Riley said quickly. 'Her husband was Teniente Francisco Peralta. He was your assistant.'

'I know who he fucking was.' Guzmán blew more smoke in Riley's face by way of encouragement. 'What did she have to say?'

'Her husband told her things about you,' Riley stammered. 'There was an incident at Las Peñas, that's a place in the Sierra de Gredos.'

Guzmán inclined his head, suddenly attentive. 'What's that noise?'

Riley darted a nervous glance at the papers on the table. 'Traffic, I think.'

Guzmán leaned forward and lifted the pile of cardboard files from the table in front of him, exposing a small cassette recorder, its spindles gently whirring as it captured their conversation. Riley opened his mouth, trying to say something.

Guzmán punched him in the face. Not a hard blow by his standards, but hard enough to send the young man tumbling from his chair. As Riley got to his feet, Guzmán seized his arm and marched him to the door.

'Señor Guzmán—' Riley's words were cut short as Guzmán hurled him down the steps into the street. A few passers-by paused to watch, amused by the sight of the young man crawling in the gutter. Their amusement was abruptly replaced by a need to be somewhere else as Guzmán came raging down the steps. He tore the cassette from the recorder, pocketed it and then proceeded to stamp the recorder underfoot until all that remained were small pieces of plastic and metal strewn across the road.

He pointed a meaty finger at Riley as the young man struggled to his feet. 'If I see you again, I'll do the same to you.'

'I only want the truth,' Riley called as Guzmán went back into the *pensión*. 'You can't hide it for ever.'

'I've managed this far, kid.' Guzmán slammed the door behind him. Then he set to work, gathering up Riley's notebooks and papers from the table. He would burn them later.

Behind him, he heard a faint tinkle of glass as Daniela came out through the bead curtain. 'Señor Riley hasn't gone, has he?'

'He's going back to Ireland,' Guzmán said, irritated by her crestfallen expression. 'He's been missing his girlfriend.'

'Oh.' Dejected, she fetched a sweeping brush from behind the desk and started work.

As Guzmán went upstairs, he heard a long sigh. She could sigh all she wanted, he thought, it would never have worked out. Not from what he knew about the Irish.

VALDEPEÑAS DE LA SIERRA, OCTOBER 1982

The truck rattled along the country road, leaving a cloud of tan dust hanging in its wake. On either side, the road was flanked by barren slopes strewn with stunted bushes and shrubs. As the vehicle accelerated over an old stone bridge, the men in the cab saw a meagre trickle of dark water sidling through the dry stones of the river bed.

'I can't move,' Quique wailed, not for the first time. He was trapped between Ochoa who was driving, and Guzmán, who was trying to ignore him. 'The gear stick keeps hitting my leg.'

'That's why we put you there,' Guzmán said, lighting a cigarette. 'Stop bellyaching.'

'I'm hungry as well, boss.'

'You should have asked Mamá to make some sandwiches. I said it was a long drive.'

'Here, kid, have one of mine.' Fuentes handed Quique a length of bread stuffed with ham. 'My wife always makes more than I can eat. I think she's trying to fatten me up.'

'I'd better test that.' Guzmán plucked the sandwich from Quique's hand and took a large bite before handing it back.

'How long till we get there, boss?' Quique asked through a mouthful of sandwich.

'Half an hour, maybe less if Corporal Ochoa remembers where the accelerator is.'

'You said we were going to an archive, sir,' Galíndez called from the back of the truck. 'This is the middle of nowhere.'

'Christ, stop complaining,' Guzmán snapped. 'We're going to an archive, all right, though I bet you've never seen one like this.' The truck shuddered violently as it went over a rock and Guzmán glared malevolently at Ochoa. 'Try and avoid the ruts in this road, Corporal.'

'There's more ruts than road, sir. I'm trying my best.'

'You're trying my patience.' Guzmán sighed. 'Look, there's the village coming up. The turn-off is a couple of kilometres further up the road.'

'How come the truck's full of shovels and pickaxes if we're going to an archive?' Galíndez asked.

'We've brought more than shovels,' Guzmán said. 'Open that box with the red label.'

He heard a rustle as Galíndez tore open the box. A long whistle. 'Fuck me.'

'Jesús.' Fuentes saw the dark shapes, gleaming with oil. 'There's an arsenal in there.'

'Uzis.' Guzmán nodded. 'Just in case.'

'Are you expecting trouble, sir?' Fuentes didn't sound entirely happy at the prospect.

'You never know,' Guzmán said. 'Any of you ever fired your weapon in the line of duty?' He listened to the embarrassed silence for a moment and then twisted round to peer at the men in the back. 'You're very quiet, Ramiro. Travel sickness, is it?'

'I'm fine, sir. Just looking forward to some action.'

Guzmán glanced at him in the driver's mirror. Ramiro's expression was not the face of a man anxious for combat.

'Wish I could have worn my uniform,' Quique said, to no one in particular.

Guzmán sighed. 'You haven't grasped the idea of a secret operation, have you, kid?'

'There's the sign.' Ochoa turned onto a track winding up the steep hillside past a large sign that read: BONAVENTURA MINE. PRIVATE PROPERTY, DANGER! KEEP OUT.

'Why is it dangerous?' Ramiro asked.

Guzmán gave him a hard look. 'It doesn't matter, we're going there anyway.'

At the top of the track, the ground flattened out. A few hundred metres away, set in the sheer hillside, was the bricked-up entrance to a railway tunnel. Running towards the tunnel, they saw a line of rotting sleepers and time-worn rails, overgrown with shrubs.

'That track connected the mine with the rest of Spain once,' Guzmán said. 'The tunnel runs right through that hillside to the mine.'

Ramiro frowned. 'How do we get inside if it's bricked up?'

From his tone, Guzmán gathered he was hoping they might have to turn round and head back to Madrid. The lad was certainly nothing like his father.

'What's that look like?' Guzmán snorted, pointing to a small wooden door set in the bricks at the side of the arch.

'A door, sir.' Quique's bellowed reply sent a chorus of overlapping echoes rolling over the arid hillside.

'I told you before, I'm not deaf, kid.'

The truck ground to a halt in a cloud of ochre dust and the men climbed out. Miguel Galíndez was last and Guzmán rounded on him. 'Move it, Galíndez. Grab one of those picks and get that door smashed down.'

Galíndez peered uncertainly at the thick wooden door. 'Couldn't we just unlock it?'

'We could,' Guzmán agreed. 'But the people who bricked up that tunnel didn't leave a fucking key, which is why you're going to hit it with that pickaxe until it opens.' Muttering obscenities, he moved away to give Galíndez room to work, shouting for Ochoa to accompany him.

'For fuck's sake, hit it properly.' Guzmán stood, hands on hips, watching Ramiro and Galíndez take turns to swing their pickaxes into the thick wooden door. Though each blow sent flurries of woodchips into the air, the door displayed only minimal signs of damage. At this rate, they'd be here long after dark.

'Give me that.' Guzmán snatched the pickaxe from Ramiro and

hefted it in his big hands before driving the point of the blade into the wood just below the lock. Furiously, he brought his weight to bear as he twisted the blade in the wood and then tore it free, ready to strike another blow. Before he swung, he paused as he saw the others watching.

'Fucking hell.' Guzmán shoved the pickaxe back into Ramiro's hands. 'You think you're going to lie back like a lazy whore while I do all the work? Take this and hit the fucker, anywhere near the lock will do.'

He stepped back, not trusting Ramiro's aim. 'Come on, swing it, you flabby bastard.'

'I'll have a go, *Comandante*,' Quique shouted, rushing forward with his pick. Sensibly, Guzmán stepped back as young Quique smashed the blade into the lock from above, sending a cascade of small metal parts tinkling onto the dusty soil.

'That's more like it.' Guzmán nodded, approvingly.

Quique grinned. 'I've always had a strong right arm, *Comandante*.'

'And I can guess why, Private Vilán. Just be careful you don't go blind.'

A loud crack interrupted them as a blow from Ochoa finally tore the lock away from the door. Ochoa gave the door a violent kick and it swung open, unsteady on its rusty hinges. The men peered into the darkness, coughing as clouds of dust floated out into the brilliant sunshine.

'Don't stand there gawping,' Guzmán said. 'There's a box of flashlights in the truck, go and get them, Private Vilán.'

'*Sus órdenes*,' Quique yelled before he scampered off to the vehicle.

'I'm going to be stone fucking deaf before we've finished this operation,' Guzmán growled. He took one of the torches and led the way into the tunnel. The others followed, the lights playing over the drifting clouds of dust. Some ten metres ahead, the tunnel curved to the right, making it impossible to see any further. That didn't matter: on the track ahead were stacks of boxes and crates, each with a number chalked on its side.

'This is what we came for,' Guzmán said. He took the list Gutiérrez had given him and gave one page to Ramiro and another to Quique. 'Find the boxes with these numbers and take them out to the truck. Corporal Ochoa will load them once he's double checked the numbers.'

'What about me and Fuentes, *Comandante*?' Galíndez asked.

Guzmán pointed towards the bend in the tunnel. 'Scout out the track around that bend and see if there are any more files stored there.'

As Fuentes and Galíndez moved away down the tunnel, Guzmán saw Quique staggering to the entrance, carrying three heavy boxes piled one on top of the other. He was about to tell him to take things slowly, but decided against it. If the young trooper collapsed with heatstroke it would not only teach him a valuable lesson, it would keep him quiet for a while.

Half an hour later, Ochoa stood by the rear of the truck, surrounded by piles of boxes. As he ticked off the last one on his list, Guzmán emerged from the shattered entrance to the tunnel, carrying a dusty crate stuffed with files.

'No sign of the other two, sir?'

Guzmán shook his head. 'I don't know where they've got to. Get those last few boxes loaded while I go and look for them.' As he reached the mouth of the tunnel, he saw Fuentes hurrying towards him, his face smudged with dust. 'Where the fuck have you been?'

'You need to see this, sir,' Fuentes said, lowering his voice. 'You won't believe it.'

'What have you found?' Guzmán asked, hoping it was money.

'A train,' Fuentes said as they went back into the tunnel.

'You mean one of those little things the miners dump the rubble in?'

'No, sir.' Fuentes led the way. 'Bigger than that.'

As they turned the bend, Guzmán played the flashlight over the brick-lined walls. 'There's nothing special about a—' He stopped dead. 'What the fuck is that?'

Ahead of them was a large steam engine, its powerful curves and muscular angles vague under thick layers of cobwebs and dust, but a train nonetheless.

Guzmán looked at it, bemused. 'That's a passenger train,' he muttered. 'How did it get here? This tunnel only leads to the mine.'

'You haven't seen what's inside, sir.' Fuentes stopped by the first carriage and shone his flashlight into one of the compartments. The light glowed dully in a mirror above the seats and then, as the light moved higher, Guzmán saw the sagging luggage rack, full of heavy bags.

'Let's have a look at this.' He hauled himself up into the carriage. As he did, he saw a reservation number on a pale ceramic disc by the window seat. Then the flashlight moved lower, illuminating the passenger slumped by the door, staring at him.

'For the love of Christ,' Guzmán said, playing the light over the interior of the carriage. Sprawled on the seats were more passengers, black holes where their eyes had once been, grinning with the slack-jawed smile of the dead.

'What killed them, sir?' Fuentes had stayed outside the carriage, Guzmán noticed.

'Let's see.' Guzmán slipped a hand under the lapel of the dead man's jacket, feeling the material crumble under his touch. He found a wallet in one pocket. Inside was a thick wad of banknotes. Suddenly interested, Guzmán lifted the flashlight to examine the money more closely. 'Fucking hell,' he snorted, 'it's Republican money, totally worthless.' He threw the wallet back onto the seat. 'This beats everything,' he said, lifting the dead man's skull. 'See that hole? He's been shot in the back of the head.' He handed the skull to Fuentes.

'How come it didn't blow his face off, sir?'

Guzmán shrugged. 'The bullet must have exited through his eye, I suppose.'

Fuentes put the skull back on the seat, next to the remains of its owner.

Guzmán climbed down from the carriage, still wondering about the possibility of finding valuables on the train. His thoughts were suddenly interrupted as he heard Galíndez screaming for help.

Two carriages down, he saw an open door and ran to it, shining the flashlight across the crumbling seats. Galíndez was sitting on the far side of the compartment, by the door to the corridor. He seemed on the verge of tears. 'Holy Mother of God, please help me.'

'What the fuck's up with you?' Guzmán barked. 'There's no reason to be terrified by a few mummified passengers.'

'I tried to open the door, to see what was in the corridor,' Galíndez whined.

'And what did you find?' Guzmán snorted. 'A big spider?'

'Dynamite, kilos and kilos of it. And then I put my hand on the door and got hold of this wire.' His voice trailed away.

In the white beam of his flashlight, Guzmán saw Galíndez's hand, still gripping the handle of the sliding door. And, from under his hand, he saw a wire, snaking down under the door into the corridor, where it connected to a pile of canvas bags.

'Don't let go,' Guzmán said. 'That's an order. Do not let go of that fucking wire.'

'Do something, *Comandante*.'

Guzmán turned towards the door. 'Stay calm,' he told Galíndez. 'Whatever you do, don't move.'

'Please don't leave me, *Comandante*, I don't want to die.'

'If I had a hundred pesetas for every time someone said that—' Guzmán cut himself short. 'Just keep calm. I'm coming back.'

He climbed down from the carriage and called Fuentes over. Fuentes' face was a study as Guzmán explained the situation. 'Tell Corporal Ochoa he's in command if it goes up,' he whispered, careful not to let Galíndez hear.

Fuentes swallowed hard. 'Can I help, *Comandante*? Cut the wire or something?'

'Just go back to the corporal,' Guzmán said. 'He'll know what to do.'

As Fuentes set off up the tunnel, Guzmán hauled himself back into the carriage. 'Tickets, please.'

'Don't joke, *Comandante*,' Galíndez pleaded. 'I feel sick.'

Guzmán examined the wire again. 'Clever bastards,' he said, kneeling to get a better look. 'They wedged the wire into the door frame so the moment it opens, the wire slackens and detonates a charge in the middle of the dynamite. You're lucky it didn't go off.'

'I don't feel lucky.'

'Well you are,' Guzmán snapped. 'This dynamite's been here years and it's highly unstable. Even your footsteps could have set it off.' He examined the wire again. 'Got any chewing gum?'

'My mouth's too dry, sir.'

'I don't want you to chew it, you moron. Just give it to me.'

Galíndez fumbled awkwardly in his pocket and extracted a wrapper of gum. Guzmán took it from him, ignoring the violent shaking of his hand.

'Keep a tight grip on that wire,' he said, mashing the gum between his teeth.

'I'm worried it will explode, sir.'

'So am I, *Teniente*,' Guzmán murmured as he pressed the gum onto the wire, pushing it firmly into the groove of the door. 'This should hold it in place for a while, I reckon.'

'Long enough to let us get out?'

'Let's see, shall we?' Guzmán got to his feet. 'Don't make any sudden moves.'

He swung down from the carriage and then shone the torch into the compartment to light Galíndez's path. 'Take it slowly, *Teniente*, and don't look at those bodies.'

On reflection, he realised it might have been better not to draw attention to the bodies.

As Galíndez brushed against one of the mummified corpses, he stumbled and fell full length on the carriage floor. His scream sent brittle echoes fluttering along the tunnel. When he opened his eyes, Guzmán was staring at him. 'Are you coming or not?'

'Yes, sir.' Galíndez climbed down from the carriage and followed him back along the tunnel. 'Shouldn't we run, *Comandante*?'

'Just keep walking, we're nearly there.'

MARK OLDFIELD

The afternoon light was dazzling as they came out of the tunnel. 'Wipe your face, *Teniente*,' Guzmán said, quietly. 'Otherwise the men will think you've been crying.'

A hundred metres away, Ochoa and the others were waiting by the truck. As the two men came out of the tunnel, Fuentes and Ramiro ran forward to help Galíndez.

'No problems then, sir?' Ochoa asked.

Guzmán shrugged. 'Clearly not, Corporal.' He walked over to the truck where young Quique was already in the cab, wedged against the gear stick. 'See him?' Guzmán said. 'He's the only one of this lot who looks happy.'

'Must be a mental case then,' Ochoa grumbled.

'You're too cynical by half, Corporal. I think if he plays his cards right, that young man could have a good career ahead of him.' He took a look up at the arid hillside. 'Let's get going, I could do with a drink.' As he climbed into the cab, he saw Galíndez huddled in the back of the truck, pale-faced and trembling.

By the driver's door, Ochoa was grinding his cigarette into the dirt with his boot, taking what seemed like an inordinate length of time to do it.

'Get a fucking move on, Corporal, will you?' Guzmán barked.

Ochoa climbed into the cab and started the engine. The truck rolled forward down the track, heading for the road that led back to Madrid.

Guzmán had just begun to calculate the amount of alcohol that would be needed to quench his thirst when the hillside above the tunnel entrance disintegrated as a vast explosion tore through the tunnel, sending a rain of debris rattling down around the shuddering vehicle. The sound of the blast was still echoing around the hillside as Ochoa accelerated on to the main road.

Guzmán turned to look at the others sitting unhappily in the back. 'That, gentlemen, is a day's work,' he said. 'So now, I reckon it's time we had a look at this Café León General Ortiz told me about.'

130

MADRID, OCTOBER 1982, CAFÉ LEÓN, CALLE SOTOMAYOR

'This is the kind of place I like,' Guzmán said as he led the squad into the bar. At one side of the room was a long zinc-topped bar with an enormous selection of bottles on the shelves behind. Across the hallway, large double doors led to the dining room. Work had already begun in the kitchen, given the strong aroma of roasting meat drifting into the bar.

Guzmán saw the barman skulking at the far end of the counter and called him over. 'Give me six beers.'

The barman nodded. 'Six beers for the gentlemen.'

'You'll have to ask the others what they want, these six are for me.'

It took a moment for the barman to realise Guzmán wasn't joking.

'I feel like I'm drunk already, boss,' Galíndez said, as the barman poured the drinks. 'I'm high as a kite.'

'Sitting in a train full of dynamite can upset the system, I've heard.'

'You weren't bothered though, boss,' Galíndez said. 'You saved my life back there.'

'I saved mine as well.' Guzmán looked at the glasses of beer on the bar and waved to the barman. 'Keep them coming.'

'But, sir, you haven't drunk those yet.'

'I will have by the time you've poured six more.' Guzmán reached for the first glass and downed it in one long swallow. He let out a loud appreciative belch and reached for another.

'I mean it, sir,' Galíndez said. 'I'm really grateful for what you did.'

Guzmán frowned. 'For fuck's sake, the last person who said that to me was a whore and she was lying. It's over now, stop going on about it.'

'But if you hadn't known how to fix that wire, the whole train would have gone up.'

Guzmán picked up his beer. The glass was sweating with

condensation as he held it to the light, admiring it before he took a long swig. 'I didn't have a fucking clue what to do with that wire,' he said, wiping his mouth with the back of his hand. Galíndez had turned rather pale, he noticed.

Tiring of Galíndez, Guzmán cast his eye over the bar. At the far side of the room, near the doors to the restaurant, young Quique was leaning round a corner, watching something in the hall. Quietly, Guzmán sneaked up behind him to see the object of his attention.

Further along the hall, a young woman was trying to retrieve a packet of cigarettes from the vending machine, though it was not her inability to manoeuvre them through the small flap that was the focus of Quique's attention. 'Look at that,' he muttered, unaware Guzmán was bearing down on him, 'a perfect arse.'

Guzmán grabbed Quique by the collar and pushed him towards the bar. 'Go and join the others, Private, you're out of your league here.' He turned the corner and strolled down to the cigarette machine. 'Can I be of assistance, señorita?' he asked, noticing that Quique had been correct in his evaluation.

She pointed angrily to the cigarette machine. 'Do you know how these things work?'

'In theory or in practice?'

'Just my luck, a comedian. Just get the packet out for me, would you, it's stuck.'

'At your service.' It only took Guzmán a moment to break the flap from its hinges and extract the cigarettes. He scoffed as he saw the brand. 'American cigarettes? You might as well not smoke.'

'Actually, I'm not smoking,' she said. 'That's because you've got my cigarettes.'

Guzmán handed her the packet, noticing the way her long dark hair matched the colour of her eyes. It certainly matched her mood.

'The least I can do is give you a light,' he said, producing his Zippo. 'Leo Guzmán, by the way, at your service.'

'That James Bond approach doesn't work with me, so drop it.'

She put the cigarette in her mouth. 'Christ, will you stop staring and just give me a light?'

Guzmán lit her cigarette and snapped the lighter shut. 'I was just thinking that you're the most beautiful woman I've ever seen.'

She exhaled smoke. 'Really? And I'm thinking that's the worst line I've ever heard.'

'Should I keep you company until your husband arrives? This place can get quite rowdy, I've heard.'

'So can I. But I'm sure I'll manage on my own.'

'It's no trouble.'

'You're with the *guardia*, aren't you?' Her tone suggested she was not impressed.

'What makes you say that?'

'I saw you drinking with my brother, earlier.'

'Your brother?' He stared, trying to find a resemblance between her and a member of the squad.

'Yes, the son of my parents.' She sighed. 'I'm Carmen, Miguel Galíndez's sister.' She cast a glance towards the door. 'And here's my date, so you'd better get lost, he doesn't like me fraternising with the ranks.'

Guzmán's eyes narrowed. 'I'm not in the ranks. I'm a *comandante*.'

'You might be a sergeant soon if you don't push off. *Hasta luego.*'

'Guzmán?' A loud voice behind him.

He spun round and saw a familiar face. 'General Ortiz?'

'I told you this was a good bar, didn't I?' Ortiz laughed. 'I didn't expect you'd be chatting to my girlfriend though.'

Guzmán gave Carmen a knowing look. 'No one should drink alone.'

Ortiz slapped him on the arm. 'Then you'd better take your own advice and have a few drinks with your boys over there, Leo. The lady and I are off to dinner.'

'*Adios*, sergeant.' Carmen smiled as she followed the general into the dining room.

Guzmán returned to the bar where Ochoa was nursing a large

glass of anis. 'The rate you're drinking, Corporal, you'll finish that drink some time in 1992.'

When Ochoa didn't rise to the bait, Guzmán shouted to the barman for a brandy. As he raised the glass to his lips, he noticed Ochoa's expression. 'What's the matter with you?'

Ochoa lowered his voice. 'It's Galíndez, he's up to something. I just saw him take a parcel of magazines from one of the drivers a while ago and he went away looking like he'd robbed a bank.'

'What magazines?' Guzmán asked.

'I don't know, but it looked suspicious to me.'

'It would.' Guzmán gulped down his brandy. 'But then the baby Jesús would look suspicious to you, Corporal.' He threw some coins onto the bar. 'I'll see you in the morning.'

'If it's any consolation, sir, she was far too good for you.'

'No consolation whatsoever, Corporal.'

Guzmán pushed open the swing door and went out into the night, thinking Ochoa would have been better off employed in a funeral parlour, where his congenital air of misery would have fitted in nicely.

CHAPTER 10

MADRID 2010, CALLE LARGASCA

Galíndez opened her eyes slowly, blinking as she saw the figure highlighted against the light streaming in through the blinds. A momentary sense of dislocation: the nightmare memory of lying bound to the wooden pallet with Guzmán and Sancho standing over her. But the figure coming towards her was no nightmare, she realised. Quite the opposite.

'Good morning.' Isabel put a steaming cup of coffee on the bedside table.

'What time is it?' Galíndez asked. 'I feel like I've slept for a week.'

Isabel slipped back under the sheets and nestled alongside her. 'Nine fifteen, we're late for work.'

'I'll have a word with the boss.' Galíndez smiled. 'She'll understand.'

'You know, this feels a bit weird,' said Isabel. 'Normally I'd be coming into the office around now and we'd be making small talk – with our clothes on.'

'I wasn't expecting this, either.'

'So is this where you tell me it's been a mistake but we can still be friends?'

'There's no mistake. We're more than friends.' Galíndez leaned closer to kiss her.

A sudden burst of Shakira blasted out from the pile of clothes scattered on the floor. Galíndez groaned as she scrambled out of bed and rummaged for her phone. She frowned as she saw the name on the screen: *Mendez*. There was no attempt at pleasantry as she answered. 'Did you find the sword?'

'And good morning to you too,' Mendez said. 'I spent half the night going through the evidence store looking for that sword of yours and it's vanished. No one signed it out so I think we can assume it's been stolen.'

'I could have worked that out for myself,' Galíndez muttered.

'So, shall I expect a visit from Professional Standards?'

Galíndez sighed. 'No, they won't get it back.'

'Thanks, I owe you.'

Galíndez cut the call, suddenly aware of Isabel watching from the bed. 'That was Mendez. Someone's stolen Guzmán's sword.' Angrily, she snatched up her clothes. 'OK if I take a shower?'

'Help yourself.'

Ten minutes later Galíndez returned, towelling her hair. 'Is that toast I smell?'

'It is.' Isabel took a couple of slices from the toaster and put them on a plate. She watched Galíndez as she ate. 'You've got a good appetite all of a sudden.'

'Must be the pep talk you gave me last night. No more pain-killers for me.'

'You still need to throw them away, Ana. Prove to yourself that you can.'

Galíndez nodded. 'I'll do it before I leave, OK?'

'Fine. So what are your plans for today?'

'I'm going to see if I can locate Sancho. Remember I told you he kept going on about Legions of Death just before I was tortured? He said one track could have been written just for me: "Death is for Losers". He said it as if he was quoting from the Bible.'

Isabel's face grew serious. 'I used to come across crazies like that on my radio show. I'd play a track and then next minute there was some jerk on the phone offering to shoot the King because he'd heard voices in the music.'

'I think Sancho might be like that.' Galíndez nodded. 'That's why I'm going to check out the Legions' old record company to see if they had anyone of his description hanging round the band. It's worth a try.'

Isabel put a hand on her arm. 'Be careful, Ana, he's dangerous.'

'Don't worry, if I find out where he is, I'll call in backup.' Galíndez slipped an arm round Isabel's shoulders as they kissed. After a few moments, she groaned and pulled away. 'I'd better get going.'

'Haven't you forgotten something?' Isabel saw Galíndez's blank expression. 'The tablets?'

Galíndez took the tube of painkillers from her top pocket and emptied the pills into the palm of her hand. 'Want to watch?'

'No, just flush them away. I trust you.'

Galíndez went into the bathroom and a moment later, Isabel heard the sound of the flush. Galíndez came out and put the empty tube on the table. 'All gone.'

'But that doesn't mean it's over,' Isabel said. 'You're bound to get cravings.'

'If I do, I'll call you.' She reached out and touched Isabel's cheek for a moment, about to say something, but stopped, flustered, and hurried off down the stairs.

Galíndez sat in her car, browsing the names of record companies on her phone. She soon found what she was looking for: *Hispano-Americano Records.* The label that published all the Legions of Death albums. The phone rang for a while before someone answered and she was put through to one of the company's senior staff. He was less than helpful. 'Señorita Galíndez? Is this a paternity suit? We get at least one a month connected with the Legions. I never realised how many groupies they'd had until we started getting these calls. Don't you girls ever use contraception?'

'Sorry, I forgot to mention I'm from the *guardia civil*,' Galíndez cut in. 'So you can either tell me how to get in touch with the Legions of Death or I'll be round with a search warrant to turn your office over.'

'Whoa, just a minute. We're always happy to cooperate with the forces of law and order. It's just that we parted with Legions on bad terms. They owed us a considerable sum of money which, it turned out, they'd invested in heavy-duty drugs to sell at their gigs.'

'Just tell me who I contact, would you?'

'Nacho Rosell is the guy you want, he was their manager. A good one too. It's a shame the band were a set of morons.'

'Give me his phone number.' Galíndez listened carefully, writing down the number on the back of her hand. 'Thanks for your cooperation.' She ended the call and dialled Rosell's number. A husky, smoke-wracked voice answered.

'Is that Nacho Rosell?'

'It is if you're Penelope Cruz.'

'I work for the *guardia civil*, Señor Rosell, so let's not play games, OK?'

'I deny it all. She said she was eighteen and in any case, it was a long time ago.'

'Look,' Galíndez said, exasperated, 'I want to talk to you about Legions of Death, so give me your address, or a whole lot of my colleagues are going to be knocking on your door. And when I say knocking, I'm talking about taking the door off its hinges and dragging you out in handcuffs.'

'No need for all that negative karma, babe. I'm in Lavapiés on Calle Tribulete. It's the penthouse apartment over the bakery.'

'Thank you so much. I'll see you soon.'

Galíndez found the apartment situated above an old renovated building that now housed an organic cooperative, with one wall replaced by glass, displaying the complexities of the bread-making process to passers-by. At the side of the building was a flight of steps leading up to a balcony. A small gilded sign: ROSELL INTERNATIONAL ENTERTAINMENT, MADRID, LONDON, PARIS, ROME, NEW YORK, MILAN. She paused for a moment and reached into her shoulder bag to turn on the digital recorder hidden in one of the pockets.

As she reached the balcony, Galíndez saw another sign by the door: VISITORS TO THE PENTHOUSE PLEASE KNOCK LOUDLY. Happy to oblige, she hammered on the door and waited for someone to answer. After a couple of minutes, she pressed her face to the glass door, her eyes widening as she saw the apartment. The place was more greenhouse than penthouse, filled with huge plants in large earthenware pots and clumps of small trees and shrubs arranged in apparently random patterns. Señor Rosell appeared to live in a small jungle. And, from his tardy response to her knocking, he also appeared to be deaf.

She pressed her ear to the glass. Inside, she thought she heard signs of life, though the vast collection of plants made it hard to see anything. Angry now, she tried the handle and the door opened. After a look round to make sure no one was watching from the street, she slipped into the apartment and closed the door behind her.

Inside, the air was warm, a damp tropical heat, cloying and uncomfortable. She walked slowly through the trees, surrounded by the sounds of a rainforest: shrill bird calls, the occasional shriek of a monkey and other, more disturbing, sounds that she didn't recognise.

As she went further into the apartment, following an aisle between thickets of tall bamboo, she saw the source of the sounds: several speakers, arranged discreetly behind the plants. But though the sounds of the jungle were fake, the smell was not: a dank, earthy fragrance, oddly familiar, an odour she remembered from her days at university. Sure enough, as she left the bamboo grove, she saw lines of potted cannabis plants, hidden between other, more legal shrubs.

Close by, she heard the sound of water and started to move towards it. Nearby, someone groaned, 'Oh fuck.' A few metres ahead, a waterfall tumbled down over a bed of artificial rocks into a pool. And another sound now, someone having trouble breathing. Moving quickly, she drew her pistol, keeping it raised as she crept forward. '*Guardia civil*, don't move.'

A man was sprawled on a lounger by the side of the pool. Dressed entirely in leather, he appeared to be dead. Then, as she approached, she heard a sudden, noisy intake of breath. He was fast asleep, she realised, she'd been listening to the sound of his snoring.

One of his arms hung over the side of the lounger, fumbling for a huge joint smouldering in an ashtray on the floor nearby. Slowly, his eyes opened and he stared at Galíndez, puzzled for a moment. Then he grinned. 'Are you the chick from the agency?' He raised himself on his elbows and ran a jaundiced eye over her. 'You're a bit skinny, but you'll do, sweetheart.' He gave her another addled look. 'I hope you take Visa?'

'Before you say anything else,' Galíndez said, 'I'm with the *guardia civil*. We spoke on the phone about half an hour ago.'

'If you say so.' He shook his head, groggily. As he staggered to his feet, Galíndez heard a strange creaking sound. The tight leather clothes might have fitted once but they were now taking a terrible revenge, given his restricted range of movement.

'So you're the chick who phoned earlier?' Rosell asked, suddenly remembering.

'I'm also the chick who might bust you for running a cannabis farm.' Galíndez shoved him into a chair beneath a clump of palm trees. 'I've got some questions for you.'

'You're not supposed to lay your hands on me,' Rosell grunted. 'Police brutality.'

'And you're not supposed to fill your apartment with industrial quantities of cannabis plants,' Galíndez said. 'You're already looking at jail time and I've only been here five minutes.'

Rosell raised his hands in surrender. 'How can I help you, officer?'

'Tell me about the Legions.'

'Of Death?'

'No, of Julius Caesar. What do you think?'

'I was their manager,' Rosell said. 'Is that why you're here? You want a free album?'

Galíndez laughed. 'I wouldn't touch one of their albums if you paid me.'

'A lot of people would. They're highly collectable. I've got the set. Want to see?'

'Why not?' Galíndez kept an eye on him as he went over to a

cabinet hidden among some ferns and returned with a pile of vinyl albums still in their shrink-wrapped covers.

'Here we go.' Rosell spread the albums on the table, like a huge hand of cards.

She looked at the first album. *Louder than Sound, Brighter than Light*. 'How does the title connect with these two girls in bikinis?'

Rosell looked at her in surprise. 'Everyone likes a girl in a bikini, right?'

'Can't argue with that.' She started leafing through the albums. Most of the covers were variations on the first. 'So how come the band broke up?'

'For a cop, you don't know much, do you, babe?'

'I know I could break your arm if you call me babe one more time.'

'No need to be like that,' Rosell said. 'Anyway, the band didn't so much break up as become extinct.' He saw her puzzled look. 'They're all dead, lady. One after another over a five-year period. Too fast to live, too... fill in the blanks, you know what I mean?'

She picked up another album. The cover showed a woman in a tiny silver bikini astride a Harley Davidson. The title picked out in glittering letters: *Too Fast to Die, Too Young to Live*. 'How did they die?'

Rosell counted the deaths on his fingers. 'Overdose, car crash, cardiac arrest.' He shook his head sadly. 'If you live the rock'n'roll lifestyle, it comes with the territory, I guess. You only have to read some of their lyrics to see where they were heading. When you play hardball, you have to have...' He frowned, trying to remember what came next.

'A hardball?' Galíndez suggested.

'Lyrics,' Rosell said. 'You know how some bands have songs that are life-affirming? They were the opposite.'

'Did people ever read things into the lyrics? Hidden messages, that sort of thing?'

'Yeah, a few. Most of the fans were bigger junkies than the band.'

'Did they ever have a stalker?' Galíndez asked, casually. 'Someone who hung round them a lot, idolised them maybe?'

'No, though if they'd had more money, the guys would happily have paid for a stalker. They always wanted a better class of fan.'

Galíndez picked up the last album cover and froze.

'Trouble was, success came too late for the Legions,' Rosell sighed. 'They were too old for that kind of lifestyle. Hello? Am I talking to myself here, babe?'

Slowly, she looked at him and then back at the album. Black Gothic lettering: *DEATH IS FOR LOSERS*. No bikini-clad girl here, just a black-and-white photograph of the band in a recording studio lined up alongside the drum kit, one behind the other, peering through manes of matted hair at the camera.

All but one. Standing at the back of the line, illuminated by the faint light from the studio door, his shaved head gleaming in the dimly lit studio.

She held out the cover towards Rosell. 'Who's this?'

As if she needed to ask.

MADRID, OCTOBER 2010, UNIVERSIDAD COMPLUTENSE, FACULTAD DE HISTORIA CONTEMPORÁNEA

Isabel parked behind the Faculty of Contemporary History and made her way down into the basement where the small room housing the *guardia civil*'s research unit was located. As she unlocked the door, she saw several polythene-wrapped chairs piled against the far wall. The office furniture had finally arrived.

Isabel heard singing in the corridor and went back to the door as a large black woman emerged from an office further along the corridor. Middle-aged, her hair tied in a brilliant multicoloured scarf, a broom in one hand, and a large plastic sack in the other.

'*Bonjour*, Mademoiselle Isabel. I already cleaned your office. All ready for you and Mademoiselle Ana.'

'*Buenos días*, Madame D'Nour. I like that song you were singing.'

'It's a song we sing in Senegal for girls who can't find a man. Girls like you and Mademoiselle Ana, no?' She gave Isabel a wide smile. 'Don't worry, *chérie*, there's time yet. The right man will come along just when you least expect it. It'll be such a surprise, no?'

'A very big surprise,' Isabel agreed.

'There's always hope, *mademoiselle*. Love finds you when it's least expected.'

'Doesn't it just.' Isabel smiled as she went into the office.

She sat at her desk, though work was the last thing on her mind this morning. Ending up in bed with Ana was something she hadn't been expecting. Perhaps Madame D'Nour was right.

A sudden knock at the door interrupted her daydreaming. Before she could say anything, the door opened and a woman came into the room. A tall, black woman, wearing the uniform of the *guardia civil*. The usual clutter of equipment hanging from her belt. Isabel heard the creak of her leather gunbelt as she came forward.

'*Buenos dias*. You must be Isabel.'

'Can I help you?'

'I'm Sargento Mendez, I brought some stuff over for Ana María.' Mendez held up a thick folder, crammed with papers. 'These are details of some new databases that have just been made available. She might find them useful.' She put the folder on Isabel's desk.

Isabel looked at the papers and saw a series of coloured photos. 'What are these?'

'The latest wanted notices from Interpol,' Mendez said. 'I doubt you need them but Ana's still *guardia* so she needs to be kept in the loop.'

'She never said anything about it.'

'I'm sure she has other things on her mind,' Mendez said, sarcastically.

'Like a lost sword?' Isabel regretted that at once as she saw Mendez's angry look.

'That sword was stolen. I'm pissed off about it as well, not that Ana cares what I think.'

'I don't really care to discuss a colleague when she's not here.'

Mendez looked at her, amused. 'Good for you. Don't bother about returning those papers, we've got copies at HQ. Maybe there's something in them to help with Ana's obsession.'

As Mendez went to the door, Isabel's voice stopped her. 'What obsession?'

'Guzmán, who else? She's spent the last two years chasing a dead man, causing havoc as she goes. But you can do that when your uncle's the boss, I guess.'

'Ana was kidnapped and tortured by Guzmán. That's hardly indulging an obsession.'

A mocking laugh. 'How do you know she was tortured?'

'She told me, of course.'

Mendez opened the door. 'She tells people lots of things. It doesn't mean any of them are true.' A cold smile. 'I'm sure she said she wants you around for your investigative skills?'

Isabel stared at her, angrily. 'What are you implying?'

There was no reply. Mendez had already closed the door.

MADRID, OCTOBER 2010, CALLE DE LA TRIBULETE

Rosell looked at Galíndez, blank-faced. 'That's Sancho, one of our roadies. Actually, he was our only roadie, we couldn't afford any more. Good at his job, mind. Strong, as well.'

'How long was he with the band?'

'Let's see.' Rosell leaned back in his chair. 'I think he joined us in 1990, maybe '91. Yeah, '91. The first album came out that year, remember?'

Galíndez shook her head. 'I was seven.'

'We never really appealed to that demographic.' Rosell sighed. 'It was hard to tap into for a band like us.'

Galíndez brushed aside his nostalgia for lost marketing opportunities. 'What was Sancho's surname?'

'Your type, is he? Always was one for the ladies.'

'Not this one. What's his surname?'

'Hernández. Is he in some sort of trouble?'

She nodded. 'It's important I find him as soon as possible.'

'That guy always sailed close to the wind. He's good company, though, don't you think?'

Galíndez had a sudden image of herself, straining against the leather straps as the electricity surged through her. 'How come he left the band?'

'He lost heart when the drummer died. Said the band was jinxed. Turned out he was right. After Sancho left, things just fell apart. Worst of all, no one cared.'

Galíndez picked up the bag and slung it over her shoulder. 'You did.'

'Yeah, we were like brothers. When you find him, tell him I said hello, will you?'

Galíndez had a sudden image of Sancho, her Glock 17 aimed at his chest. Her finger squeezing the trigger. The sharp echo of the shot. 'Sure, I'll tell him.'

Rosell accompanied her to the door. As Galíndez said goodbye, he held his arms wide as he approached her. 'Big hug, yeah?'

She planted her hand against his chest to keep him at bay. 'Let's just shake hands.'

Rosell frowned as he held out his hand. 'Hey, did you ask Ramona about Sancho?'

'Who are you talking about?'

'His wife, babe. Big Ramona?'

'Have you got an address for her?'

'Kind of, she works in an S&M bar called Cuero y Acero.'

'The one on Calle Espino?'

'That's the one. How come you know that?'

'A lucky guess,' Galíndez said. 'Thanks for your time.'

For a moment, as the door closed, Galíndez glimpsed her reflection in the glass, watching as Señor Rosell turned and ambled back into his jungle of cannabis plants.

CHAPTER 11

The barman looked up from his newspaper. In the doorway, he saw the owner of the bar, brushing rain from his coat as he came in.

'*Buenos días*, Alberto.'

'*Muy buenos.*' The barman quickly started polishing the counter. 'Quiet today.'

'At least we've got one customer, I see.' The bar owner indicated the young red-haired man sitting in the window, staring across the street at the Pensión Paraíso.

'Him?' The barman scoffed. 'He's been nursing that coffee since seven. Two hours, he's been watching that place.' He stopped polishing. 'Want me to throw him out? At least it would give me something to do.'

'I'll do it,' the owner said. He walked over to where the young man was sitting. 'Can I get you something, señor?'

Michael Riley turned away from the window. He seemed distracted. 'Sorry?'

'Can I get you something? We're not a charity, you know.'

'No, thanks.'

As Riley started to turn back to the window, the owner put a hand on his shoulder. 'Thanks for your custom.' He steered the student to the door and pushed him out into the rain. 'Call again.'

The barman laughed. 'That showed him.'

'Maybe he'll have more luck somewhere else,' the owner grunted.

Outside, Riley took shelter beneath the awning of the grocery next door. Luisa's idea of keeping a watch on Guzmán hadn't gone according to plan. Still, he wasn't too unhappy at abandoning his vigil, not after the way Guzmán treated him the previous day. The last thing he wanted was to have the *comandante* manhandle him again. Luisa hadn't told him Guzmán might become violent. Worse, when Riley told her what happened, she seemed excited rather than concerned for his welfare. And she owed him for the tape recorder.

'*Scusi.*'

A green car was idling at the kerb. Riley had been so engrossed in thinking about Guzmán he hadn't even noticed. He walked over to the car and bent to look in. The driver was a middle-aged man with short, cropped grey hair. Though his Spanish was good, he had a slight accent that Riley couldn't quite place.

'Can I help you?'

'The question is whether I can help you,' the man said. 'I've driven past this bar several times this morning and it looks to me like you're keeping a watch on that *pensión*.'

'No, not at all,' Riley said quickly.

The man grinned. 'I think you're interested in Comandante Guzmán.'

'Are you a friend of his?' Riley asked, hoping he wasn't.

'Not at all, though I know a lot about him,' the man said, 'and about his crimes.' He slapped a hand to his forehead, 'Sorry, I haven't introduced myself. Professor Luca, from the Institute of Social History.' He held out his hand through the window and Riley shook it.

'I'm doing a PhD at the Complutense on the Civil War,' Riley said.

'Really? That's a coincidence, because I've been researching Guzmán's activities for years. Maybe you'd like to take a look at my findings? You might like to use some of them in your thesis.'

The young Irishman's head spun at the prospect of getting fresh material for his dissertation. 'That would be great, thanks.'

'Hop in,' Luca said. 'I'll take you for lunch and we can discuss this some more.'

Riley slid into the passenger seat, glad to be out of the rain. 'Nice car.'

'An Alfa Romeo Spider,' Luca said. 'My little extravagance.' As the car surged forward over the cobbles, he switched on the radio. A sudden static-laced burst of Italian came from the speakers. 'Hope you don't mind?' he asked Riley. 'They're previewing tonight's game. My team's playing Palermo.'

'Who are your team?' Riley didn't like football but it seemed best not to say so.

'Napoli,' Luca said. 'Our star striker just returned to the squad after an injury. At one point it seemed he'd miss the entire season.'

Riley looked out of the rain-spattered window. He had no idea where he was. 'Must've been a bad one,' he said, trying to show interest. 'At least he's back now.'

'True,' Luca agreed. 'He makes a big difference to the team's performance.' He turned into a street lined with dilapidated tenements and crumbling warehouses. The car came to a halt at the side of a derelict factory. The rain was falling heavily now.

'Where are we?' asked Riley.

'This is where I work,' Luca said. 'Come on, I'll show you.'

MADRID, OCTOBER 1982, GUARDIA CIVIL HEADQUARTERS

As Guzmán went into the squad room, Quique came rushing up to give him the news about the bombing in central Madrid.

'I know, it's probably ETA,' Guzmán said. 'I heard it on the radio at my *pensión*.' He pushed the kid out of the door before he could do any more damage to his hearing. As he took a seat, there was a tap at the door as the orderly came in.

'Phone call, *Comandante*, it's Brigadier General Gutiérrez.'

'In that case, you'd better bring me a pot of coffee to keep me awake.'

Guzmán went into his office. Once he'd settled himself in his chair, he picked up the phone. 'What?'

'You've heard about the bomb, I expect?'

'It's the only thing I've heard since I got up,' Guzmán muttered, wondering where his coffee was. 'Who's responsible, ETA or one of the right-wing groups?'

'ETA, without doubt,' Gutiérrez said. 'We've been expecting them to make a move in the run-up to the election. But I wanted you to know the press are also speculating that the bomb might be an attempt to disrupt the elections by certain pro-Franco elements.'

'Do they mean us?' Guzmán scoffed. 'We couldn't afford the explosives.'

'Even so, they're asking whether the *Brigada Especial* might be involved. They want to know why the government still employs a unit that was once a death squad.'

Guzmán saw the orderly in the doorway and gestured for him to put the coffee tray on his desk. 'So what did you tell them?'

'I played it down, naturally,' Gutiérrez said. 'But you and your squad have to be careful, it's vital you don't get involved in any acts of violence while you're collecting the files. The press will crucify us if that happens.'

'For once, I agree with you.' Guzmán lifted his cup and inhaled the aroma of coffee.

'What's that noise?' Gutiérrez asked.

'Fault on the line,' Guzmán said, sipping his coffee. 'Anything else?'

He was answered by a flurry of coughing as Gutiérrez wheezed a hasty goodbye.

Guzmán finished his coffee and then pressed the button on his desk. A moment later, Fuentes and Galíndez came in.

'Morning, sir,' Fuentes said, snapping off a sharp salute. His appearance was a stark contrast to the other man, Guzmán noted. Fuentes was clean-shaven and his uniform looked as if he'd been up all night ironing out the creases. Or, more likely, his wife had. 'Look at the state of you, Galíndez.' Guzmán scowled. 'You look like you've been to a gypsy's funeral.' He gestured for them to sit. 'I hope you're sober enough for this job?'

'I'm up for anything, boss,' Galíndez said, stifling a yawn.

'Well, even you should be able to manage this.' Guzmán slid two typewritten sheets across the table. 'The target is a municipal archive. There are two guards on duty during the day.'

'And you want us to take them out?' Galíndez asked, suddenly interested.

Guzmán gave him a dark look. 'Of course not. Do this right and they won't even know you've been in the building.' He pointed to the sheets of paper. 'Take a look at those. You'll see the guards have a coffee break each morning at eleven, regular as clockwork. Park across the road and wait till they go to the café. Then you go in and get the files.'

'How do we gain access, sir?' Fuentes asked, making notes.

'There's an alley at the side of the building. It's big enough to take the truck.'

Galíndez nodded eagerly. 'And then we smash the door down?'

'And then you open the fucking thing with this.' Guzmán slapped a key down onto the table. 'Don't interrupt me again.'

'Sorry, sir.'

'Anything else we should know, *Comandante*?' Fuentes asked. 'Alarms or dogs?'

Guzmán decided he approved of Fuentes. 'Nothing like that. Any more questions?'

'Sounds easy, boss.' Galíndez grinned.

'The time to say a job's easy is when you've finished it.' Guzmán waved at the door. 'Dismissed.'

He waited until they were gone and then got up and poured more coffee before hitting the green button. The door opened at once and Ochoa came clattering in at the double, followed by Quique.

'Christ, were you two leaning on the door?'

'Come in when you see the green light. That was what you said, sir.'

'I didn't tell you to come in so quickly.' Once they were seated Guzmán gave them their instructions. 'This job's at the technical institute in Vallecas. Here's the list of files. It's the same procedure as before: the files we want are hidden among other, less important documents. This list has the reference numbers of the files we want. Nothing there to complain about, I hope, Corporal?'

Ochoa shook his head. 'Looks all right to me, sir.'

'Thank the Blessed Virgin for that.' Guzmán started gathering up his papers.

'And where will you be if I need you, sir?' Ochoa said, as he got up.

'The same place I'll be if you don't need me. Minding my own fucking business.'

'I meant if there's any trouble, sir.'

'There shouldn't be any trouble, Corporal,' Guzmán snorted. 'But if there is, you're armed, I seem to remember. How about you, kid? Did Mamá take your service pistol away in case you hurt yourself?'

'No, sir. It's right here.' Quique began fumbling with the catch on his holster.

Guzmán stopped him before he shot someone. 'I know what a gun looks like, thanks. Get on with it, Corporal,' he sighed. 'And take Billy the Kid here with you.'

After they had gone, Guzmán waited a few minutes and then went out into the squadroom. Ramiro was sitting in a corner reading the paper. He leaped to attention as he saw Guzmán approaching.

'I want you to go over to the warehouse to give Brigadier General Gutiérrez a hand,' Guzmán said. 'Here's the address.'

'Begging the *comandante*'s pardon, but I'd prefer a role with the chance of some action,' Ramiro said. His face told another story.

'I know,' Guzmán nodded, 'but the work at the warehouse is complicated. The brigadier general needs someone who's used to working with a high-ranking officer. You're the man for this.' He paused. 'You and the sarge's son, that is.' He saw Ramiro's troubled look. 'He'll do all the manual work, obviously.'

'Thanks, *Comandante*, I won't let you down.'

'Good man. Now get going and don't keep Gutiérrez waiting.'

As Ramiro marched off down the corridor, Guzmán breathed a sigh of relief. Command was so much easier in the old days. None of this man-management stuff. Just physical violence and a lot of shouting. Still, while his men were out collecting the files, that gave him time for a bit of old-fashioned police work. And he knew just the bar to do it in.

MADRID, OCTOBER 1982, LA CEPA, CALLE DE VALVERDE

Guzmán strolled through the crowds on the Gran Via heading towards the towering Telefónica Building. He noticed the passers-by as he walked: well dressed, laden with shopping, a certain air of confidence about them. It was unsettling.

More and more, he saw the city like a stranger. Not because the extent of change had swept away its former appearance, but because the little details by which he recognised the streets and their buildings were not as they were. He recalled Madrid as a city of closed shutters and darkened shops with empty windows. Old women peering from neglected doorways with sallow looks of reproach. Large empty squares, rustling newspapers blown across them by the cold wind from the sierra. Now, shop windows were full of all manner of consumer goods. Even the beggars looked well dressed.

At the corner he took a right into a narrow street hemmed in by tall buildings. Outside a bar, workmen in blue overalls were unloading crates of wine. Their jovial voices echoed off the walls, sending pigeons flapping for shelter on the tiled roofs.

After a few minutes' walk, he came to a small grimy bar. The name was picked out in tarnished paint over the door: LA CEPA. The place looked much as it had years ago, apart from the flashing lights of a pinball machine in a corner. As he entered, Guzmán was transported back to a simpler world where everything was routinely forbidden and people obeyed authority without question. Or at least pretended to.

He stood at the bar, careful to avoid resting his arms on the sopping zinc counter. Behind the bar, the shelves were packed with an esoteric collection of bottles bearing names Guzmán hadn't seen in years. On the wall behind the bar, he saw a ragged tangle of wires hanging from an ancient socket, just as it had twenty years earlier.

'Just admiring the place or are you going to have a drink?'

A fat balding man peered at him across the bar. His sagging features twitched, betraying the mental struggle going on in his domelike head. 'Fuck's sake, it's you,' he said, almost pleasantly. 'Come to arrest me for not washing the glasses, have you?'

'You still don't wash them?'

'It was my father's idea, to save money. He's gone now, but I remember you.'

Guzmán leaned forward, conspiratorial. 'Keep it to yourself, will you?'

'It'll cost you.'

'That's blackmail, I could arrest you for that. Still, you look like you need a kicking.'

The man's attitude softened. 'How about a drink? On the house, of course.'

'Now you're talking,' Guzmán said. 'Give me a brandy and none of that cheap rubbish either.' He waited as the man filled a large glass. He saw the label and scowled, though there was no point complaining: this dive wouldn't stock Carlos Primero and even if it did, none of the customers could afford it. Besides, drinking it here would smack of ostentation. This was not a place where a man wanted to stand out.

He heard a noise behind him as several rowdy women bustled in from the street, reeking of cheap perfume, all talking at once in loud voices. The place was still a meeting place for tarts, then. That piece of historical continuity pleased him.

To avoid the incessant babble of the whores, he found a table in the corner. At the next table a sad-faced elderly gentleman was nursing a glass of beer. It was clear he'd been nursing it for a while since it was now flat. Guzmán kept his voice low as he leaned towards the old man. 'You're not ignoring me, are you, Ignacio?'

MADRID, OCTOBER 1982, LIBRERÍA TÉCNICO, CALLE DE FERNANDO EL CATÓLICO

Ochoa pulled the battered Ford Transit to a halt by the side of the library. 'Here we are, kid.' He reached into the back and grabbed a couple of brown warehouse coats. 'Put this on,' he told Quique, 'you'll look like you've got a proper job.'

As they stood by the van, Ochoa decided to do what any working man would do in a situation like this. He lit a cigarette and leaned on the van for a few minutes while he smoked. When he'd finished the cigarette, he opened the back doors and pulled out a heavy wheeled trolley. That done, he sat on the trolley and lit another cigarette.

'Bit early to start taking things easy isn't it, Corporal?' Quique asked.

Ochoa shrugged. 'Who's taking it easy, kid? I'm blending in. Anyone who sees us will just see a couple of workmen in brown coats. If someone asks about us later, all they'll remember are the brown coats.' He took a long drag on his cigarette. 'You ready?'

Quique tore his gaze away from a shop window where a young woman was struggling to dress a mannequin in a pair of hot pants. 'Yes, Corporal.'

Ochoa sighed. 'Don't call me corporal again. I'll be Juan, you can be Pedro. Right?'

'Fine by me, Juan.'

'Our first stop is the assistant librarian in the maritime section,' Ochoa said. 'She's a *guardia* sergeant, working undercover.'

'A woman?' Quique raised his eyebrows. 'Is that legal?'

'She's one of General Ortiz's undercover team. She'll direct us to the files we want.'

'Maybe we could borrow a couple of books as well, Corp? I like Westerns.'

Ochoa shook his head. 'This is a technical library, kid. It's where they store all the old material that no one wants.'

'Why do they store it if nobody wants it?'

Ochoa gave a patient sigh. 'Someone might want it one day. And if they do, they can come here and read it even though the rest of the world's forgotten all about it.'

'A library of forgotten books?' Quique looked across the road at the dull, grey-stone building, its weathered Doric columns spattered with dirt and pigeon shit. 'Imagine that.'

'Just imagine doing your job, kid. That's what keeps the pay cheque coming, or hasn't anyone explained that to you?'

'They never say anything else some days, Corporal.'

'Address me by rank again and you'll get a slap.' Ochoa saw the traffic come to a stop as the lights changed. 'Come on, let's get this over with.'

The old trolley rattled as they dragged it across the road between the stalled lines of traffic, hearing exasperated cat-calls from the stationary vehicles as they went.

Once on the pavement, Ochoa pointed to the door at the side of the building: STAFF. 'That's us, kid.' They manhandled the trolley through the door and found themselves at the end of a long tiled corridor with drab brown walls. On either side, open doors gave views of shadowy rooms where badly dressed people clustered around the shelves, examining the dusty tomes with reverential care.

At the door of one cavernous room, Quique stopped and pointed to several bearded men at a table piled high with books. Most wore jackets with leather patches on the elbows. All were furiously taking notes. 'Are they scholars, Corporal?'

Ochoa glared at the men through his thick spectacles. 'They're Reds, kid, I'd bet your life on it.' He gave the trolley a violent shove. 'Come on, let's find this lady.'

The office of the maritime section's assistant librarian was located near the end of the corridor. When no one answered his knock, Ochoa pushed the door open. A dusty-looking office, a desk littered with books and papers around a large Bakelite phone. On the walls, several cabinets stuffed with books. No sign of the librarian.

'Shit.' Ochoa went over to the desk and took a look behind it. Suspicious, he reached down into the waste basket. 'Look at this, kid.' He held up a crumpled piece of paper.

'What's that on it?' Quique asked. 'Lipstick?'

'Looks like blood,' Ochoa said. 'And look, her handbag's still here.'

'Can't have gone far then, Corp. Women take their handbags everywhere.'

Ochoa looked up from examining the scattered papers on the desk. 'I'd forgotten you were an expert on women.' He shuffled though the papers and selected a large brown envelope. 'This is what I'm after.'

'How can you tell just by looking?' Quique asked, impressed.

'Because it's got my name on it. Now stop asking questions.'

'Funny the lady isn't here.'

'Come on, kid, we need to find another librarian.'

Leaving the trolley outside the office, Ochoa led the way down the corridor until they came to another office. The door was open. Inside, a rotund lady was sitting behind a desk. When Ochoa tapped on the door, she looked up, staring at him through thick reading glasses. Her eyesight seemed to be even worse than his.

'Can I help you?' Her tone suggested she would rather not.

'We've come to collect some documents from the maritime archive,' Ochoa said, politely. 'We were supposed to see Señora Davila but she's not at her desk.'

The woman sighed as she struggled to her feet. 'I'll show you where to go.'

They followed her along the corridor into a small lobby, and waited as she opened a door with a key from the copious collection hanging from her belt. A sudden odour of damp paper drifted out.

'This is the archive you're looking for, gentlemen.' She paused. 'Will you need to visit any of the upper floors?'

'I can't say, señorita,' Ochoa said. 'If we do, which way do we go?'

'You go up those stairs over there, cross the first floor and then go up the spiral staircase to the next floor and then do the same again if you need to go up another floor.'

Ochoa looked at Quique. 'Got all that, did you?'

'I think so,' Quique said, frowning.

The trolley rattled on the tiles as Ochoa and the kid went into the maritime archive. The lights were out and Ochoa fumbled for a moment, trying to find the switch. When the light came on, they were confronted by a large room, filled with row after row of cobwebbed shelves, packed with cardboard boxes of files.

Ochoa took the paper from the librarian's envelope. 'I'll call out the reference numbers and you fetch the boxes.'

The job was easier than Ochoa had expected. The files were located exactly where the list indicated. Apart from Quique looking a little sweatier than when he started, things were going to plan. At this rate, they'd be done by two at the latest.

'You know what this is all about, Corp?' Quique panted as he put another armful of boxes onto the trolley.

Ochoa shrugged. 'What all what's about – life?'

'No, collecting these old files.'

'It's about collecting them like the *comandante* ordered. That's all you need to know.'

'I'd hate to work in a place like this all day. You can't even see out the window.'

Ochoa struggled as he carried one of the heavier boxes to the trolley. 'Stand on that chair over there, kid. You'll get a good view of the street.'

Quique took his advice and peered out at the passing traffic. 'Busy out there, Corp.'

Ochoa sighed heavily. 'Tell you what, why don't you go outside and get a smoke? I can work better if I don't have to listen to you.'

He breathed a sigh of relief as Quique wandered off down the corridor. It was worth having to lift a few dusty boxes just to be rid of the kid for a while.

Outside, Quique watched the traffic, picking out cars he'd like to own one day when he was a *capitán*. There were some nice sets of wheels, he thought, watching the slow-moving vehicles intently. Best of all were the cars that had been polished until the bodywork gleamed, unlike the dirty Opel Ascona that had just pulled up across the road. That would never do for him. A nice saloon like that, the least the owner could do was wash it from time to time. He imagined himself as a traffic cop on a motorbike, pulling the car over, pointing out the danger of having such a dirty rear window. And then he'd give the driver a ticket, he decided, since the car's rear number plate was missing. He put his hand into the pocket of his warehouse coat, resting it on the butt of his Star 400, imagining the stern lecture he'd give the driver before writing the ticket.

As he watched, still daydreaming, four men got out of the car, glancing round furtively as someone inside the vehicle handed something to each of them. The passing traffic partly obscured what was going on but not so much that Quique couldn't see the pistols the men were now pushing into their belts. He swallowed, hard. Then he turned and ran back to the side door of the library. Desperately, Quique twisted the handle. The door was locked. Quickly, he dashed round to the back of the building, looking for an entrance. He found a door halfway along the building with a large sign that said No ADMITTANCE. This time, when he turned the handle, the door opened. As he went inside, he found his way was blocked.

'How's it going, young man?' It was the large librarian with glasses like Ochoa's. Quique stared at her as if she were talking a foreign language. 'Perhaps you and your colleague would like a coffee?' she asked. 'I can show you to the kitchen if you like?'

'No, thanks, señora,' Quique stammered, edging past her into the building. 'I've got to get back to work.' He hurried off up the corridor.

Ochoa had just put the last box of files on the trolley when Quique burst in, gasping for breath. 'What it is it, kid?'

'A bunch of men just got out of a car across the road, Corp. They've all got guns and they're coming this way.'

'Fuck.' Ochoa ran to the chair by the window and stood on it. He saw the Opel and further along the road, the four men, patiently waiting for the lights to change so they could cross. He jumped down and went to the trolley. 'Move it, kid.' Quickly, he pushed the trolley against the wall and shoved a couple of waste-paper baskets on top of the boxes to cover the labels. That done, he grabbed Quique by the arm, and hurried down the corridor looking for somewhere to hide.

A couple of metres along, they came to a narrow room filled with wooden file drawers. Just inside the door, someone had left a mop and bucket. Ochoa pointed to the mop. 'Pick that up, kid, and start cleaning the floor.'

As Quique obeyed, Ochoa flattened himself against the wall, hidden from the doorway by a filing cabinet. 'When they come past the door, pretend you're the cleaner,' he told Quique, drawing his pistol. 'If they start anything, hit the floor. I'll take care of the rest.'

For once, Quique had nothing to say and began running the mop over the floor with studied concentration. Somewhere up the corridor, they heard a door bang, footsteps echoing on the tiles, coming nearer. Just before the men reached the door to the filing room, they paused and held a brief, muted discussion. The footsteps started again.

Ochoa cocked his pistol and held it at arm's length, aimed at the door. The men outside wouldn't see him unless they came into the room. In which case, Ochoa was the last thing they'd see.

Quique lowered his head, swabbing the floor industriously as the men approached.

A voice from outside. 'Hey, kid.'

Quique looked up. 'Can I help you, señor?'

'Seen anyone new around here this morning? Not the library staff, workmen maybe?'

Quique thought quickly. 'Is it the builders you're looking for?'

A humourless laugh. 'Yeah, that'll be them. How many are there?'

'Two.' Quique rested his hands on the mop handle. 'They're up on the fourth floor.'

'So how do we get there?'

'Follow this corridor and you come to a flight of stairs. Go up those to the next floor and then follow the signs.'

'We've got them,' someone muttered.

'Thanks for your time, kid,' the man said, turning away.

Ochoa wiped sweat from his brow with his free hand. He started to lower the pistol.

Outside, the footsteps stopped and then came back. 'Hey, you know what, kid?' The same voice as before.

Quique stopped mopping the tiles. 'Yes, señor?'

'Why don't you show me where they are?'

Ochoa weighed up the odds. If Quique went with them, he was dead the moment they realised he was bluffing. If Ochoa tried to open fire, he would have to move out into the room and show himself. Sweat dribbled into his collar. Decisions weren't his strong point.

'I can't, señor,' Quique said. 'I'm the only cleaner on this floor. If I leave my post, that head librarian will fire me. She already hates my guts.'

At some point, the men were going to guess Quique was playing them, Ochoa realised. Better to start things now than wait for them to do it. He started to count. *One.*

Outside the door, the men were laughing. 'How long have you worked here, kid?'

'Four days,' said Quique. 'I was out of work for two years before I got this job. My mamá will kill me if I get fired.'

Two. Ochoa tensed. Hopefully, the kid would throw himself out of the way when the men went for their guns. Hopefully.

'That staircase at the end, you said?'

'That's it, señor,' Quique said. 'Straight ahead.'

'OK, kid, we'll find it. Here, take this and forget you ever saw me, right?'

Ochoa flattened himself against the wall as he saw the man standing in the doorway.

'Thanks very much, señor,' Quique said, putting something in his pocket.

The footsteps faded as the men went down the corridor.

Quique went to the door. 'They've gone, Corp.' As Ochoa came out from hiding, Quique gave him a broad grin as he held up the thousand-peseta note the man had given him. 'Split this with you?'

'You keep it, kid.' Ochoa led the way back to the trolley. Heavily laden now, the trolley creaked and rattled as they pushed it along the corridor. As they passed the assistant librarian's room, the door was still closed. 'Let's see if she's back,' Ochoa said. He knocked on the door softly. When there was no reply, he went in.

Nothing had changed. The woman's handbag was still on the desk, the scattered papers still on the floor. As he turned to leave, Ochoa stopped abruptly, staring at the metal cabinet he'd tried to open earlier.

Quique saw his expression change. 'What is it, Corporal?'

Ochoa pointed to the floor where a small pool of blood was steadily growing along the base of the filing cabinet. He reached for the handle and tried it. The cabinet was no longer locked. As he opened the door, the body inside rolled onto the carpet, looking up at them with blank staring eyes. A bloody, ragged cut across the woman's throat.

Quique crossed himself, suddenly pale.

'I think we've found our librarian,' Ochoa said.

MADRID, OCTOBER 1982, LA CEPA, CALLE DE VALVERDE

The old man rigorously avoided eye contact. 'You know how it is, Señor Guzmán. It's not wise to know policemen in here.' Slowly, he hauled himself out of his chair and came over to sit at Guzmán's table. 'You haven't changed,' he said, taking a mouthful of beer. As he put down his glass, he saw a thousand-peseta note on the table. Expressionless, he placed a hand over the note. Guzmán looked away. When he looked again, the note was gone. Ignacio looked at him uncertainly. 'Buy you a drink?'

'Why don't I get you one?' Guzmán said. 'Like old times.'

'Old times are gone, *Comandante*. It's all foreigners in slick suits now, pushing drugs and selling women. Killing them too, if they don't behave. What are you drinking?'

Guzmán asked for brandy. He watched the old man totter to the bar, picking his way through the throng of gaudy-faced hookers who were smoking so much it seemed they were standing round a camp fire.

A blast of cold air as the door opened. A man came in, a sallow face beneath a helmet of brilliantined hair. He ordered a drink and then removed his coat with a practised flourish. The whores broke out in a brittle chorus of false laughter as the newcomer began telling anecdotes. 'Pimps never change,' Guzmán said when Ignacio came back from the bar.

'They do, *Comandante*, they get worse.' Ignacio put the drinks on the table and sat down. On the table in front of him was a piece of notepaper, folded in half. The way it had always been done.

'You were the best informer I ever had,' Guzmán said.

'Mother of God, keep it down, will you? You never know who's listening.' Ignacio picked up the paper though he kept it folded. 'What is it you want to know?'

Guzmán pointed to the paper in the old man's hand. 'The addresses of those two.'

Ignacio took a pair of reading glasses from his pocket and then unfolded the paper. He peered at Guzmán's broad, angry script. 'Is this a joke?'

'Do I look like I'm laughing?'

'You do know who these people are, I suppose?'

'I wouldn't want their addresses, otherwise, would I?'

Ignacio's red-rimmed eyes grew wider as he carried out the

calculation every informer made before committing themselves: *How much and what's the risk?*

His reticence was annoying: in the old days, Guzmán wouldn't have given him time to calculate. A beating usually provided sufficient incentive.

'I'll want a lot for this,' Ignacio said.

'Don't worry, I'll make it worth your while. You can take the wife somewhere nice.'

'She's already somewhere nice, *Comandante*,' Ignacio laughed. 'Two metres down in the Almudena cemetery.' He blinked as Guzmán's smoke curled around his face. 'I hoped it'd be a while before I joined her, but maybe not. What you're asking for is dangerous.'

'When did you ever care about danger? Or are you getting past it?'

Ignacio sighed as he reached for his drink. 'All right, I'll do it.'

Guzmán put a card on the table. 'Call me on this number.'

When Guzmán offered him another drink, Ignacio shook his head. 'I'll be pissing all night as it is. I'll give you a call as soon as I've got something.'

Guzmán got up and made his way past the whores propping up the bar. Outside, the air felt thin and cold, though as he strolled up Calle de Valverde, he was in good spirits. For a few moments back in La Cepa, it felt like he was back in the old days. The days when things were done properly. His way.

Cheered by his memories, he took his time making his way back to *guardia* HQ. When he arrived, he discovered that things had not been done his way at all.

'Thank you, señora.' As Alberto put down the phone, he saw Villanueva, asleep in his chair, his mouth open. On the desk in front of him was the tray with his lunch plate and an empty wine bottle. Alberto didn't blame the inspector for drinking. Anyone who lost his wife like that deserved some cheer, even if it did come from a bottle.

'Who was that on the phone?' Villanueva asked, without opening his eyes.

'Señora Manzanares. The bus still hasn't arrived. By the time it turns up it'll be time to bring the kids back again. It was much better when the village had its own school.'

Villanueva yawned. 'That bus is always breaking down.' He got up, groggy from the heat and the thick bull's tail stew. 'I'll take the car and go and look for it,' he said, fumbling for his keys. 'They could be stuck in a ditch or something.'

Villanueva went out into the bleached afternoon glare. Across the road, his car was parked in a patch of brilliant sunshine. He opened the doors and, as he waited for the seats to cool, he looked up towards the spot where the coast road came over the brow of the hill. As traffic breasted the hill, their windows caught the sun, creating brilliant flashes of light before they were lost from sight again. Usually, traffic was sparse. It had never been a busy road.

It was now.

Villanueva stared at the long procession of vehicles coming over the brow of the hill. Big dark cars, driving slowly. As the convoy snaked down onto the road to the village, he called Alberto to come and take a look.

164

'What's happening, Inspector?'

Villanueva noticed Alberto wasn't carrying his service pistol and ordered him to fetch it. While Alberto rummaged through his desk drawers for the pistol, Villanueva drew his .38 and checked it was loaded. As he slid it back into its holster, he realised that, for the first time in his career, something was happening in Llanto del Moro.

CHAPTER 12

MADRID 2010, CALLE LAGASCA

The curtains trembled in the cool morning air. Outside, the early-morning sounds of a city coming to life: the drone of traffic, mothers and children, on their way to school.

'Third time you've stayed here this week: it's getting to be a habit,' Isabel said, watching as Galíndez laid their breakfast on the table by the window. 'Not that I'm complaining.'

'Make the most of it,' Galíndez laughed, 'this is as domestic as I get.' She sipped her coffee, deep in thought. 'Are you going in to the research centre today?'

Isabel frowned. 'From the tone of your voice, I'm not going to like this, am I?'

'I know you don't think it's a good idea, but I'm going to get the DNA samples from Ramiro's family tomb.'

'You mean you're going to break in, don't you?'

'Yes, but I won't do any damage. I'll just take the samples and then, once they're analysed, I'll know if Ramiro's daughter was his natural child or not.' She poured herself another coffee. 'And whatever the result, I won't mention it again, I promise.'

'I still don't think you should do it.'

'Then don't come.' Galíndez shrugged. 'I'll hide until the cemetery closes and take the samples once it's dark.'

'I don't like the idea of you being in there on your own,' Isabel said. 'Do you want me to come with you or not?'

'It would make things easier.'

'OK. When do you want me to get there?'

'About six? It closes at seven thirty. We'll wait for it to go dark and then...'

'Go grave robbing?'

'Do a little scientific investigation.' Galíndez suddenly noticed the pile of papers on the sofa. 'What are those?'

Isabel slid the papers across the table. 'Mendez brought them to the office yesterday. They're wanted notices from Interpol.'

Galíndez pointed to a photo near the top of the first page beneath a large heading in bold capitalised letters: **WANTED**. 'God, look at this ugly bastard.'

The photo showed a man with a dark, sun-leathered face. Greasy black hair tied back in a ponytail, a long, vivid scar snaking down his cheek. Cruel, pitiless eyes.

Isabel leaned over to take a look. 'You're right, he looks evil. Who is he?'

Galíndez read from the text beneath the photo. 'Joaquín Rodríguez, aka "The Hammer of Reynosa". Wanted by the FBI, DEA and the Mexican government for murder and narcotics offences. Highly dangerous and should be approached with caution.'

'Do they call him the Hammer because he's tough?'

Galíndez read the text under the photo. 'No, it's to do with the way he kills people.'

'Christ, I'd run a mile if I saw him.'

'That would be a good idea,' Galíndez said. 'Because he's thought to be in Madrid.' She saw Isabel's worried look. 'Don't worry, he'll be hiding out with some drug gang or other. Birds of a feather and all that.' She glanced at her watch. 'I'd better go. See you at the cemetery?'

'Unfortunately yes.'

As she got into her car, Galíndez glanced across the street to see if Isabel was watching from the window of her apartment. There was no one at the window. Quickly, she opened the glove compartment and rummaged around until she found a balled-up tissue, wedged at the back. She unwrapped the tissue and looked at the five painkillers for a moment, wondering whether to break into her emergency reserve. She resisted the temptation briefly and then swallowed two of them dry. Slumped in her seat, waiting for the tablets to kick in, she began to think about what she needed to do to track down Sancho. It was not going to be easy, though as long as she worked to a plan, as she usually did, she was sure she could do it. Still, one thing at a time. Right now, she needed to focus on planning how she was going to break into Ramiro's family tomb.

MADRID 2010, CEMENTERIO DE NUESTRA SEÑORA
DE LA ALMUDENA

It was late afternoon as Galíndez drove up the narrow road leading to the cemetery. The sun was low and slanting shafts of light danced through the trees as she parked the car. Ahead was the main entrance, a beige and cream mix of *fin-de-siècle* modernism blended with neo-Moorish columns and arches. By day, the building's appearance was slightly eccentric. What it would look like in the dark, she could only guess. Not that she feared the cemetery. Dead people couldn't hurt her. The living were far more problematic.

She went through the gate into the cemetery. In front of her, seemingly endless ranks of tombstones, plaques and statues stretched away into the distance. She followed the path, standing aside at one point to let a group of elderly nuns go by. Clearly a tour group: she heard their guide explaining that the cemetery contained the remains of five million people, two million more than the living population of Madrid. The nuns responded with appropriate gasps of surprise. Galíndez had heard it all before and pressed on.

After a few minutes' walk, she reached a wide, curved section of the cemetery. The graves here were modest, a stark contrast to the areas where the wealthy of Madrid lay beneath ostentatious memorials that served as a testament to their loved ones' lack of taste.

She stepped off the path and picked her way through the lines of gravestones. Some of these memorials were weathered, others were in better order, clearly still maintained by their families. Many were adorned with flowers, often accompanied by a rosary or a small laminated photograph of the deceased. Here and there were simple crosses, the names bleached away by the sun, the graves and their occupants long forgotten.

As she walked, Galíndez remembered her first view of this cemetery, clinging to Aunt Carmen's hand as they followed the line of mourners, the men in their green uniforms and shiny black tricornes, the women's faces pale behind dark veils. Carmen had lifted her in her arms to see the firing party as they stood by the open grave. It was the first time Galíndez had seen grown men cry.

She remembered the stern faces of the men at her father's funeral. Her mother's loud, inconsolable grief as the honour guard bore the casket to the grave. And she remembered Aunt Carmen's harsh words later to her mother, though what was said that day, or why, Galíndez had no idea.

She counted the rows as she walked, the late-afternoon sun on her back. Despite walking slowly, she came to row ten much too soon. She stared at the large white stone, a mute reminder of the tragedies that had blighted her life. Not that she needed reminding. Never a week went by without someone sharing a reminiscence with her about her father, bemoaning the tragic waste of life, cursing the cruelty of terrorists who would assassinate a man in front of his daughter. *We'll never forget him, Ana María.* Usually the phrase was accompanied by a tearful hug or a firm pat on her arm. Perhaps their outpouring of sorrow made them feel better. It did nothing for her.

Not one of the people who expressed their admiration and respect for her father knew Galíndez's secret. She had never visited the grave since Aunt Carmen died. God, she'd only just managed to attend her funeral. That had been the bad time, the time when she had been tested. And now, here she was, facing another test, though this time she would meet it head on, without falling back on the things she'd done to dull the pain after Carmen's death.

She took a deep breath and forced herself to look at the memorial, seeing the tragic sequence of her family history, carved in stone. Her father's name first: *Made the Ultimate Sacrifice for his country*, then her mother, though there were no comments, neatly avoiding any reference to her suicide. And finally Aunt Carmen, only two years ago. *Dearly beloved aunt of Ana María.* As if words could ever sum up her love for Aunt Carmen.

She breathed slowly, confronting her feelings, trying to face them down. Sometimes that worked, though not often, and she waited, fists clenched, biting her lip until the pain began to pass and she felt aware of life around her once more. The rumble of traffic on the M-23. Distant voices. And, somewhere among the headstones, the sound of someone approaching. Instinctively, she reached into her jacket and drew the Glock from its holster.

As the footsteps came closer, she got to her feet, staying hidden behind the big headstone, holding the pistol with both hands as the footsteps came nearer.

'Jesus Christ,' Isabel gasped, staring at the pistol aimed at her chest.

Galíndez lowered the Glock and slipped it back into its holster. ' I thought you were going to call me?'

'I did.' Isabel frowned. 'But your phone's off.' She gestured towards the path. 'A party of nuns said they'd seen a woman coming up here who fitted your description.'

'I'm glad you came.' As Isabel turned to read the inscriptions on the headstone, Galíndez took the opportunity to slip on her sunglasses. The last thing she needed was for Isabel to notice her eyes.

Isabel left the headstone and came to sit with her. 'Are you OK, Ana?'

'I'm fine.'

'Do you visit the grave often?'

'Why would I? It wouldn't change anything.'

'I only meant—'

'Drop it, will you? We're not here to visit, we're here to get those DNA samples.'

Isabel gave her a curious look. 'Did you bring the tools?'

'They're in my car. I put them in a couple of bags, so it'll look like we're going to clean up a headstone.' She took Isabel's hand. 'Sorry I snapped at you. I'm a bit stressed.'

'No wonder, is there, Ana? We're sitting in a cemetery, waiting for them to lock us in so we can break into a tomb.'

'Well, at least there's only a couple of hours to go.'

Isabel glanced at the sun, now sinking into the horizon. 'Quite.'

The sun was setting as they made their way to Uncle Ramiro's family vault. The tombs and memorials here were considerably more imposing than the simple headstone on the Galíndez family plot. Isabel shook her head at the life-size statues, growing sinister in the fading light. 'Your Uncle Ramiro's father must really have been someone to be buried in here.'

'He was a famous general. Iron Hand Ortiz, they called him.'

Isabel pointed at a white marble memorial. 'I don't believe that.'

Galíndez came up behind her and peered over her shoulder. 'Do you speak German?'

Isabel shook her head. 'Doesn't matter, does it? Look, there's a Spanish translation: "German Aviators, died for God and a Free Spain. Still Present".'

'Let's hope they're not,' Galíndez said, lowering her voice.

The sun finally slipped below the dark line of the horizon and around them, the statues and headstones melted into the shadows. Galíndez took two flashlights from her bag and handed one to Isabel. She played the light over the graves ahead. 'This is it, Izzy,' she said, her voice tight with excitement.

Isabel joined her beneath the statue of General Ramiro Ortiz Senior standing guard over the marble vault of the Ortiz family.

Worn by Madrid's fierce sun and winter rains and spattered by birds who cared nothing for rank, the statue was still recognisable as the man in the oil painting hanging in Uncle Ramiro's office at *guardia* HQ.

Isabel turned as she heard the chink of metal. Galíndez was kneeling, arranging her tools on the grass. She selected one, feeling the weight as she swung it to and fro.

'What's that?' Isabel whispered.

'An ice pick. The blade should be useful for levering the side of the vault open.'

Galíndez inserted the pick into the thin gap between the lengths of marble. Tensing, she began moving the pick from side to side, loosening the slab. Finally, with a sudden grinding of stone, the piece of marble came loose. Carefully, she pulled it away and laid it on the grass. As her flashlight shone into the opening in the side of the vault, small flurries of dust rose from below, accompanied by a cloying odour, like damp earth, though more unpleasant.

Galíndez opened one of her bags, pulled out a white forensic overall and shook it.

Isabel watched as Galíndez started to pull on the overall. 'What's that?'

'My bunny suit,' Galíndez said, as she wriggled into the overall. 'You wouldn't want me coming back to your place covered in bits of dead people, would you?'

Isabel preferred not to think about that. Instead, she took the torch and shone it down on Galíndez as she eased herself into the vault and dropped down to the floor below.

'Keep that light on me,' Galíndez called as she went towards the far wall of the vault. As Isabel tracked her with the light, the coffins suddenly emerged from the darkness. Four of them in a row, furred with cobwebs, the glazed wood mildewed and cracked. Carefully, she scraped dust from the rusty plaque on the nearest coffin and read the words on the plaque: *Señora Angustia Ortiz y Flor 1923–1966.*

'Whose coffin is that?' Isabel called.

'Ramiro Senior's wife. She died in her forties.'

Galíndez moved to the next coffin, once more brushing accumulated grime from the name plate. *General Ramiro Ortiz Senior, 1922–1982.* 'Here's Ramiro's father.'

She took a screwdriver from her case and began loosening one of the rusty screws in the coffin lid. It was hard work and sweat trickled down her forehead from under the band of the head torch, stinging her eyes. Finally, the screw began to loosen and within a few minutes the remaining screws were neatly lined up on one of the adjoining coffins. She wiped her face with the back of her hand. 'I'm going to open the lid now, Izzy. You might not want to look.' She took a face mask from the case and pulled it on.

'I've seen skeletons before, Ana.'

Galíndez inserted the blade of the ice pick under the coffin lid and pushed, hard. The lid creaked as it opened and fell to the floor.

Galíndez backed away from the stench from the coffin. Above her, she heard Isabel retching. Using the head torch, she peered at the remains of General Ortiz Senior. There was little left of his face, she noted, as she tugged a tuft of hair from his scalp and put it into a plastic evidence bag.

'What are you doing, Ana?' Isabel called.

'I'm pulling his hair out by the roots,' Galíndez said. 'That's where the DNA is.'

Isabel stayed quiet.

As Isabel shone the flashlight over the coffin, Galíndez noticed something she'd overlooked. Gently, she touched the top of the skull and turned it to one side. 'Oh shit.'

A worried voice from above. 'Christ, what is it?'

'I just decapitated the general.'

'That's not funny.'

'I'm serious. His head came off.' Galíndez bent forward, examining the corpse with new-found interest. 'Well, well.'

'Have you found something?'

'Nothing important,' Galíndez said, distracted as she examined the bulge in the breast pocket of General Ortiz's uniform. The material disintegrated under her touch, revealing what appeared to be a plastic tobacco pouch stuffed with papers. She labelled and bagged it and then took her camera from its case. Two brief flashes of dazzling light. The rustle of plastic as she put the object into her case with the other items.

'Jesus, are you nearly done? My nerves are in shreds.'

'A few minutes more, then we're through.'

Galíndez went over to the last two coffins. One was tiny, forcing her to kneel to read the plaque: *Ramiro Jnr. 1980–1981*. The other was larger. *Lucia Estrella Ortiz 1969–1981.*

For the first time since she'd climbed into the tomb, Galíndez felt emotion. So far, her actions had been cold and detached, informed by her training. But here she was, about to open the coffin of a child she never knew existed until recently: a child who killed herself and her infant brother, wiping out a whole chapter of family history. It was hard not to think *what if?* If Estrella had lived, she'd be forty-two now and baby Ramiro almost thirty. They'd have families of their own, Uncle Ramiro and Aunt Teresa would be proud grandparents and maybe Galíndez would be a godmother. An alternative family history, though one now lost for ever.

'What's happening?' Isabel asked, suddenly aware of the silence.

'I won't be long.' The screwdriver turned again. The same routine: the faint tinkle as the screws hit the ground, the creak of the coffin lid. She reached into the coffin, her movements slow and considered. Stupid, she knew: she wasn't going to wake the girl. There would be no surprises here.

Galíndez looked down at the girl's shrivelled corpse, seeing the slack-jawed grimace of death, the dark empty sockets of her eyes. Gently, she took a sample of hair. Deep in thought, she replaced the coffin lid and went to Baby Ramiro's coffin to get the final sample.

Then it was over. A brief struggle as Isabel hauled her through the opening in the vault. She sat for a few moments breathing in the cool night air, clean and fresh after the dust and decay of the tomb.

'What did you find?' Isabel asked as Galíndez struggled out of her overall.

'Dead people.' Galíndez went over to the length of marble by the opening in the wall of the vault and levered it back into place.

As they gathered the tools together, she wondered whether to mention to Isabel what she'd found down there. Later, she decided. Once she knew herself.

CHAPTER 13

MADRID, OCTOBER 1982, GUARDIA CIVIL HEADQUARTERS

L ate afternoon was merging into dusk, turning the window into a dark rectangle that reflected the glow from the lamp on the desk. Outside, vehicles came and went, troopers' boots crunched on gravel. Guzmán's office was quiet, though anyone listening at the door would have heard the sound of nervous voices within.

Guzmán stared across the desk at Fuentes and Galíndez as he listened to their explanation. For a while, he listened patiently, though his eyebrows rose from time to time when he doubted he was being told the truth. For the most part, he stayed quiet, letting the two men give him the details. When they had finished, both were sweating profusely.

'It went wrong,' Guzmán said, finally.

Neither of the men replied.

'How could it go wrong?' Guzmán's voice dropped into a lower, more threatening register. 'I thought you were capable of carrying out a simple job like this with your eyes closed.' He picked up a pencil and twisted it between his fingers until it broke. 'You incompetent bastards.' 'The security men came back earlier than we expected,' Fuentes said.

'That's right.' Galíndez nodded. 'Nothing we could do about it.'

'You shut the fuck up.' Guzmán leaned forward, belligerently. 'I'll come to your part in this in a minute.' He glared at Fuentes. 'You had the boxes by the door and the van was waiting outside. All you had to do was load it up and drive away.'

'We did load it, sir,' Galíndez said.

'But then, like the fucking goat's prick that you are, you went back inside. Why?'

'To take a last look, sir,' Galíndez muttered. 'Check there was no one there.'

'Why? There was no need,' Guzmán said, verging on apoplexy. 'Why go back?'

Out of the corner of his eye, Guzmán saw Fuentes give Galíndez a dark look. 'I know why, Galíndez. Because you thought you'd have a chance to wave your fucking pistol about and scare two old men shitless, didn't you?'

'You can't blame me for wanting some action, sir.'

'Blame you? I'm wondering whether to court martial you.' Guzmán struggled for words. 'You went back looking for trouble and because of that, some old guy gets his skull fractured.'

'I don't know why you're so upset, boss,' Galíndez said. 'Golden boy here loaded the truck and when I hit that old guy, he pulled me off before I did any real damage.'

'Fuentes did well,' Guzmán said, 'but he made one mistake and that was not shooting you in the back for being a prick.'

'That's unfair,' Galíndez said.

'Unfair?' Guzmán jumped up, sending his chair clattering backwards to the floor. He looked at Fuentes and pointed to the door. 'Get out.'

Fuentes didn't need telling twice. The door slammed shut behind him.

Guzmán went over to the emergency door at the side of the office and kicked it open. 'Outside.' He stormed out into the darkened car park. Reluctantly, Galíndez followed.

'Look, boss, I had to do something. We couldn't stand around arguing with them.'

Guzmán's punch hit him in the face, sending him staggering into the wall.

'Know what? I reckon I should have shot that guard,' Galíndez muttered, wiping blood from his lip. 'I used my initiative.'

Guzmán hit him again, in the chest, this time. 'I didn't tell you to use your fucking initiative. I told you how to handle it and you blew it.' He stormed forward, seizing Galíndez by his lapels and slamming him against the wall. 'You obey orders, understood?'

'You can't treat me like this, it's not like the old days. The war's over. You've had your day. People like me are what the *guardia* needs these days.'

'People like you, you moron?' Guzmán swung his fist and Galíndez went sprawling to the ground once more. 'I'll tell you this, disobey orders again and your career is over.'

'You can't do that.' Galíndez unleashed a half-hearted punch that Guzmán blocked easily before jabbing his fist into the man's belly. He heard the sudden rush of air from Galíndez's mouth as he crumpled to the ground. Terrified, Galíndez cried out for help as Guzmán seized his lapels, intent on dragging him to his feet.

In a blind panic, Galíndez lashed out with his foot as he tried to escape. His boot caught Guzmán in the crotch and the world burned in a sudden moment of dazzling, vertiginous pain. Guzmán sank to his knees, clutching his groin. He spat a string of bile onto the tarmac, fighting the urge to vomit.

'I didn't mean to do that, *Comandante*,' Galíndez whined. 'It was an accident.'

'Fuck off,' Guzmán grunted, still hunched on the ground. 'Go on, get out of here.'

'I won't mention this to anyone,' Galíndez said, backing away. 'Not a soul, I swear.'

Guzmán waited until Galíndez had slunk back into the building before he threw up. The pain was considerable and he wiped sweat from his face as he waited for the immobilising spasms to pass.

On the far side of the car park, Corporal Ochoa was sitting on a low wall, hidden in shadow. He had been having a quiet smoke when the fight started. Quickly, he stubbed out his cigarette and sat watching, invisible to both combatants. It came as a surprise when Guzmán lost the fight. Galíndez was a big brute who deserved a good beating, in Ochoa's opinion. Still, one lucky kick wouldn't save him from Guzmán's wrath later, he knew.

Ochoa stayed quiet, waiting until Guzmán finally got to his feet and staggered away. Ochoa expected him to go back into the main building but instead, he took the path to the main gate, clearly not wanting to be seen. Once he was out of sight, Ochoa got up and headed off in the opposite direction, to Café León. It was probably best to give the *comandante* some time to himself after such a humiliation, he decided. Not that he knew for sure: Guzmán had never lost a fight before.

MADRID, OCTOBER 1982, CALLE SOTOMAYOR

It was a night like any other in Madrid, the pavements echoing as laughing groups of people headed for bars and restaurants. Guzmán walked slowly, waiting for the pain to subside. Around him, he heard the rumble of traffic, felt the air charged with a sense of things happening, people enjoying themselves. He paid no attention, unable to endure the thought of other people's pleasure while he was still fighting an urge to spew. Even smoking didn't help. There was nothing that would relieve this pain, he knew, because though the physical pain would inevitably diminish, the memory of losing the fight would not.

As the pain in his groin eased a little, he tried to remember how long it had been since he'd lost a fight. A long time, for sure. So long he couldn't remember. No matter how badly an opponent injured him, he had always come out on top. All but once of course, though Alicante had been very different.

The traffic and the passers-by blurred as he walked, deep in thought. There was more to it than just a kick in the balls. This was another sign of things that once seemed permanent becoming transient and vulnerable. The message was clear. Men like him inevitably reached a point where their powers declined. It was the way of the world.

Ahead, sparkling light spilled from a string of coloured bulbs around the terrace of a café. He strolled onto the terrace and took a seat. As he called the waiter, he heard a slurred voice behind him.

'Buy a girl a drink, señor?'

MADRID, OCTOBER 1982, CAFÉ LEÓN, CALLE DEL
GENERAL IBAÑEZ DE IBERO

General Ortiz was propping up the bar, his arm round Carmen's waist. 'There you are, Corporal,' he bellowed as Ochoa came through the door. 'Where's Guzmán? It's his round.'

'I think he's busy, sir. He might be along later, I'm not sure.'

'Have a drink then, Corporal.' Ortiz grabbed a bottle of wine from the bar and filled three glasses to the brim. 'Here's to beautiful women,' he bellowed. 'Well, one actually.' He grinned mischievously as he raised his glass in a toast to Carmen and drank it in one swallow. 'Keep Ochoa company for a minute, will you, Carmencita? I just saw someone I need to talk to.'

'So, Corporal, what shall we talk about?' Carmen smiled.

Ochoa stared into his glass. Being in the presence of a beautiful woman always put him on edge. 'I was looking for your brother actually, señorita.'

'Well, you're in a bar, so there's every chance he's here.' Carmen brushed a lock of hair from her eyes. 'Or you could try a few whorehouses. The ones that give credit, that is.'

'I'll take a look in a minute.' She was exceptionally beautiful, he thought, unhappily.

'Has Miguel done something wrong?' Carmen asked. 'Or does he owe you money?'

Ochoa shrugged. 'It's personal.'

'If it's so important, go and find him. I'm used to standing at this bar on my own.'

'I wouldn't want the general to think I'd gone off and left you alone.'

'For God's sake,' Carmen sighed, exasperated, 'it's 1982. Women are liberated now, haven't you heard?'

That came as news to Ochoa, though since he didn't know what it meant, he said nothing. Over Carmen's shoulder, he saw Miguel Galíndez hanging about in the car park. 'I'll be off.'

'Nice talking to you, too.' Carmen turned and called to the barman to bring her a vodka Martini.

As Galíndez parked his car, he saw Ramiro waiting in the shadows.

'Your man got back from Sweden then?' Ramiro said.

Galíndez glanced around nervously. 'Have you seen the sarge from the motor pool? He's down for three of these. That's twelve thousand pesetas I've made without doing anything.' He sniggered. 'Which is more than I can say about the kids in these magazines.'

'That's a tidy profit,' Ramiro said. 'I'd say the first round is on you.'

Galíndez took two thin packages from his bag. 'You want a couple? You can owe me till payday.'

'Not me,' Ramiro said, shaking his head. 'I think my father knows what you're up to, so you better be careful.'

'What's the harm?' Miguel snorted. He pushed the packages inside his uniform jacket. 'I'm off to the crapper. Why don't you get the drinks in?'

Miguel watched Ramiro go into the bar. Behind him, he heard a sudden rustle as something moved in the darkness. He turned and gasped as a fist hit him in the chest, sending him staggering back, gasping. The bag fell from his hands, spilling the brown paper packages onto the ground. When he looked up, Ochoa was standing over him, his eyes magnified by the thick lenses of his glasses.

'What the fuck?' Miguel bellowed. 'Didn't you see me?'

'I saw you all right,' Ochoa said. 'Just like I saw you a few days ago.' He bent down and picked up one of the parcels.

'That's private property,' Miguel shouted. 'Put it down.'

Ochoa stared him in the eye. 'Make me.' Miguel stayed where he was, shifting uncomfortably as Ochoa ripped open the package and slid out a magazine.

'Christ, Corporal, put that away,' Miguel hissed. 'It's nothing to do with you.'

Ochoa opened the magazine and stared at the contents. 'What the fuck is this?'

Miguel lowered his voice. 'You can see what it is: porn. I buy it from the long-distance lorry drivers who've been to Sweden.'

'These are pictures of children.' Ochoa took off his spectacles and put them in his top pocket.

Nervously, Miguel ran a hand over his hair. 'Now look here—'

Ochoa's headbutt knocked him to the ground. Before Miguel could get up, Ochoa was astride him, raining blows into his face, ignoring his cries for help.

'What's going on over there?' General Ortiz came strutting across the car park. 'Ochoa, is that you? You can't go brawling in the gutter when you're in uniform, man. What the hell's come over you? Get up at once.'

Ochoa got to his feet, though he took the opportunity to take a last vicious kick at Galíndez's ribs as he did.

Miguel got up slowly, wiping blood from his nose.

'What's the meaning of this?' General Ortiz bellowed.

Ochoa gave a cursory nod at Miguel Galíndez. 'Ask him, sir.'

'It's nothing,' Miguel stammered, 'just a difference of opinion.'

'You can't go round punching my officers, if you don't agree with them, Corporal,' Ortiz said. 'Explain yourself.'

Ochoa picked up the magazine from the ground and handed it to the general.

'That belongs to Ochoa,' Miguel spluttered. 'I told him not to—'

His words were sheared off as General Ortiz punched him. As Miguel rolled on the tarmac, dazed, the general tore up the magazine and threw the pieces over Galíndez's prostrate body. 'I warned you about this before, you piece of shit, and you've disobeyed me.' He shook his head. 'You're a disgrace.'

Seeing General Ortiz about to launch another attack on Miguel, Ochoa stepped between them. 'Perhaps you shouldn't be brawling in public, General?'

'You're right, Corporal,' Ortiz said, panting with anger. He glared at Miguel. 'If I catch you with any more of that filth, I'll court martial you.'

He turned on his heel and stamped off back into the bar.

'He won't court martial you,' Ochoa muttered, 'because I'll kill you first.'

MADRID, OCTOBER 1982, BAR LA PERLA,
CALLE SOTOMAYOR

Guzmán twisted round in his seat to get a better look at the woman. She was clearly a better class of whore. Reasonably well dressed, her hair tied back tight, exaggerating her pale face. A silver chain around her neck accentuated her tan.

'Have a seat.' He would have got up to hold the chair for her but such details never counted for much with whores. Behave like a gentleman and they put the price up.

When the waiter arrived, she asked for gin and tonic. He ordered a double brandy.

While the waiter was getting the drinks, he leaned closer. 'You look tired,' he said. 'Maybe you should spend less time on your back?'

'Excuse me?' She stared at him, puzzled.

'It doesn't matter to me.' Guzmán shrugged. 'But it's bound to put the punters off if you look like you're about to doze off at any minute.'

She looked away as the waiter brought the drinks. Guzmán noticed her flushed cheeks. 'You are on the game, aren't you?'

'For heaven's sake, stop saying that. Of course I'm not.'

'I'm sorry, I didn't realise. It was your line about buying a girl a drink.'

'I lost my purse on the bus, if you must know, señor.'

'Leo Guzmán.' He shook her hand, careful not to crush it. Her hands were chapped, he noticed. A different kind of working girl, obviously. 'You lost your purse?'

'Yes. I phoned my friend and asked her to meet me here. She's going to lend me a few pesetas so don't worry, I'll pay you for the drink.'

'No need,' said Guzmán. 'I hope I haven't offended you?'

'Not at all, I'm sure you said it because you found me attractive?' Her attitude was skittish: nervous one moment, confident the next. An interesting mix. She was pretty too: dark brown eyes, deep and intense as if trying to work him out. If that was true, it would be a long time before her observations paid off.

He saw her face turn pale. 'What's the matter?'

'Santa María.' She raised a hand to hide her face as she turned towards him. 'That's one of my neighbours over there. If he sees me with you, the whole neighbourhood will know and so will my husband.' She leaned closer, draping an arm round Guzmán's shoulder, pulling him closer. 'Kiss me.'

Guzmán obliged.

After a couple of minutes, the neighbour went off down the steps of the terrace into the street. Relieved, she rested her head on Guzmán's shoulder. A faint air of soap and citrus.

He took a sip of brandy. 'What are you laughing at?'

She took a tissue from her handbag and dabbed his mouth. 'Lipstick. You don't want to go home to your wife looking like that.'

'I don't have a wife.' He was tempted to add 'thankfully', but decided against it. She might think he was a cynic.

'What do you do for a living, señor?'

'I'm a police officer,' Guzmán said, omitting the detail.

'A detective?'

'Sometimes.'

She looked at him, suddenly curious. 'So, what do you deduce about me?'

Guzmán looked her over. The intensity of his gaze made her blush. 'Don't keep me waiting,' she said, suddenly uncomfortable.

He took a swig of his brandy and set the glass down slowly. 'You work in a laundry, you're unhappily married and you drink too much, though you probably manage to stop before anyone can tell you're drunk.'

Her eyes widened. 'Why do you say that?'

'Your hands gave away the laundry work. Too much bleach, perhaps? It's clear you're unhappily married though since you wouldn't be tapping strange men for a drink unless you were sick of your husband. And the story about losing your purse is bullshit. Your purse is sticking out of your handbag. That suggests your husband checks how much you've spent when you go out. To avoid that, you cadge drinks off mugs like me.'

She flushed deeply. 'Maybe I'm not married at all? I'm not wearing a ring.'

'Not now, you aren't, but there's a white mark on the third finger of your left hand, even though the rest of your hand is tanned.'

'My husband doesn't love me,' she said abruptly.

Guzmán called the waiter over and ordered another gin and tonic for her. He let the waiter move out of earshot before speaking. 'What did you expect when you got married? Love and affection for the rest of your life?'

A sudden petulant look. 'It would have been nice,' she sighed. 'I hate him.'

'That's normal,' Guzmán said, as if he knew anything about the subject. 'They ought to mention it in the marriage vows, it would save time later.'

'I suppose you think I'm a terrible person now?'

'Not at all, I like a woman who drinks. As long as she can hold it anyway.'

'I mean, being married.' Her voice trailed away.

'That's none of my business, señora.' He noticed the thin silver chain round her neck. 'Are those your initials on the chain?' Not that he had any interest in her jewellery but women appreciated men who paid attention to such detail, he had noticed.

A shy nod. The gesture of someone he'd known years ago. Another woman with chapped red hands. A woman who blushed. A woman long dead.

'How about dinner?' he suggested, thinking the evening was picking up nicely, especially now the pain in his groin had died down.

'Another night perhaps? I have to get home.'

Guzmán handed her his card. 'Call me at my *pensión* and leave a message.'

She frowned as she read the card. 'It says Ramirez on here.'

'You're not the only one with secrets.' He got to his feet. 'I'll see you to the Metro.'

'I'd like that.' A complicit smile.

'I can't keep calling you señora, what's your name?'

'Lourdes.'

'That's a pretty name,' Guzman said, though he wondered whose initials those were on the necklace since none of them was an 'L'. Not that it mattered: he was on to a good thing here. It would be a shame to spoil it.

They walked arm in arm along Calle Sotomayor past the geographic institute. Spots of rain were starting to fall and when Guzmán offered to pay for a taxi, she accepted the money without protest.

He watched as the taxi drove away. He had never understood women so it was unlikely he was about to start now. She seemed rather old-fashioned, a woman who expected a man to open doors or to hail a taxi when necessary. A woman who made him feel like a gentleman. Even so, he was relieved she was gone. They had been followed since leaving the bar and the last thing he needed in such a situation was a woman on his arm. Some things were best done alone.

The sun was setting, softening the familiar contours of the city with gentle light. As he walked, listening to the footsteps behind him, the sun slipped below the horizon and the city was reborn as a place of shadows, feral and threatening. He walked on, his senses straining to detect the sounds men make when trying to conceal their presence.

And those sounds were all around him now. Soft, subtle echoes, the faint scrape of a shoe, a muffled cough. Sounds that followed him along the darkened cobbles as he took a convoluted route down narrow streets ripe with possibilities for ambush and escape. By no means a direct route, more an examination of the ability of the man dogging his footsteps.

He continued his circuitous journey, irked by the persistence of his pursuer. It was an annoyance, though an unavoidable one. Dealing with people like the *Centinelas* inevitably meant becoming the object of their attention at some point.

At the corner of an alley, he paused, listening to the sullen silence as he he lit a cigarette and then stooped as if to tie his shoelace. Carefully, he eased the big trench knife from the scabbard on his calf and tucked it into his belt. Then he started walking. As he went down the street, he heard the man start following again. It was not a problem. Over the years, the men changed, but the night did not. And the night was Guzmán's territory.

MADRID, OCTOBER 1982, CALLE DEL CARMEN

It was just after midnight as Guzmán pushed his way through the crowds on the Plaza del Callao. He had lost his tail half an hour ago, though it had taken some doing. Whoever followed him had been good, though not so good that Guzmán couldn't shake him off in the end. He had planned to lure the man into a quiet spot and kill him. But when he initiated that tactic, his pursuer backed off, though without giving up. That was impressive in one way, annoying in another. But if it happened again, it would have to end in death and fuck what Gutiérrez said about keeping a low profile. Some things were a matter of professional honour.

The square was awash with coloured light. High above, he saw the blue Schweppes advert on the modernistic Carrión building. The bars and clubs were teeming as he continued on to Calle del Carmen. Across the road, he heard the heavy thump of music coming from a club. A neon sign over the door illuminated several life-sized cardboard images of young women wearing strategically placed red tassels. He looked up at it:

RICCI'S EL TOPLESS – GO GIRLS-MUSIC-DANCING

In need of a drink, he decided to take a look, out of curiosity. The entrance fee was a hundred pesetas. He paid and followed the line of people ahead of him through a black-curtained entrance into the club.

The music hit him at once, thick and physical. From the dance floor, waves of heat rose from the swaying crowd, packed so tightly that Guzmán could only make out the men from the women when the flashing lights of the mirror balls played over them. He smelled perfume, cigarettes and sweat, a carnal odour that clung to him as he pushed his way through to the bar.

As he leaned against the bar, he found himself suddenly diverted by the three women dancing in a gilded cage at the far end of the dance floor. To Guzmán, they appeared to be doing gymnastic exercises, though since they were so scantily dressed, he felt obliged to watch. After a few minutes, he was thirsty and raised a hand to attract one of the bar staff.

She came at once. 'What can I get you?' Her voice died away.

Guzmán stared at the girl behind the bar. 'What the hell are you doing here?'

'What does it look like? I work here.' Daniela was wearing a halter top with the club's logo emblazoned on it: *El Topless, Numero Uno*. And, as far as Guzmán could see, a pair of silver hot pants.

'How long have you worked here?'

'About two years now.'

'You can't,' Guzmán said. 'What would your father say?'

'My father hasn't earned a *céntimo* since the sixties. Mamá used to go out to work to keep the *pensión* going. Then she died. So now it's down to me.'

'Everything all right, Dani?' A deep voice close to Guzmán's ear.

Eduardo Ricci was standing half a metre away. He recognised Guzmán at once. 'Come to piss on my staff again, have you?'

'It's not like anyone's going to stop me.' Even as Guzmán spoke, he saw three men emerge from the pulsing shadows of the dance floor. One was stocky and heavily muscled, his pallor suggested he'd been released from Carabanchel after a particularly long sentence. Another was an Arab, thin and wiry, with a scar across his forehead. Guzmán couldn't see him taking a punch and staying on his feet. The third man was a joke. Guzmán already knew what he was capable of and it wasn't much.

'You're on our turf now,' the fat man said, unhappy as he recognised Guzmán.

Guzmán gave him a malicious smile. 'How's your gypsy pal?'

The fat man didn't answer.

'Is he with you, Dani?' Ricci asked.

Daniela nodded. 'He's a friend.'

Ricci frowned. 'Better pick your friends carefully if you want to keep your job.'

'I didn't know she worked here,' Guzmán said. 'Leave her out of it.'

'Please don't make any trouble,' Daniela whispered.

'Yeah, don't make any trouble,' Ricci echoed, 'or she's fired.' He nodded to the three men. 'Show him the door.'

The fat man reached for Guzmán's arm. Guzmán gave him a dark look that made him step back. 'I'm going,' Guzmán muttered.

The three goons escorted him through the swaying bodies on the dance floor. At the front door, the big bruiser with the prison tan pushed him towards the stairs. 'Better not come back, *amigo*, looks like the boss took a dislike to you.'

Guzmán wiped sweat from his forehead. He heard a voice in his head calling for blood. The knife was still in his belt, easily available. The only difficult part of slaughtering these three sons of whores would be deciding who was to die first. As he planted himself in front of them, he had a vision of Daniela in her gaudy top and silver hot pants. Her father in his wheelchair. She was right: how would she pay the bills? He turned and went down the stairs, burning with humiliation.

'Next time you come here, you might find that little girl dancing in the cage. They all do in the end,' the Arab called.

Their mocking laughter followed him down the street. When he reached the *pensión*, the lights were still on in Garcia's grocery and he went in to buy a bottle of Carlos Primero.

Guzmán let himself into the *pensión*. As he passed the reception desk, a cracked voice came from behind the glass bead curtain. 'Is that you, Señor Ramirez? Can you give me a hand?'

Guzmán pushed though the strings of glass beads into the windowless room. Señor Argüello was slumped in his wheelchair near the table.

'Dani left me some sandwiches,' Argüello whined, 'but I dropped them. See over there, under the table? I can't reach them.'

Guzmán bent to retrieve the package from under the table and gave it to Argüello.

'Thanks, I haven't eaten all day,' Argüello said, unwrapping the sandwiches with shaking hands. 'Want one?'

'You need them more than me,' Guzmán said. 'Although, there's a lot there for just one man. What are they?'

'Chorizo and peppers,' Señor Argüello mumbled, his mouth full. 'Have one, you'd be doing me a favour, I'll never eat all these.'

'As a favour then.' Guzmán picked a sandwich from the pile and took a large bite, suddenly hungry. 'This is really good.' He held out the bottle. 'You want a brandy to wash down your supper? It's good stuff.'

Argüello nodded. 'Just a drop, I can't handle it like I used to.'

Guzmán poured him a generous glassful. 'This will help you sleep.'

'So you fought for Franco?'

'What about it?'

'Nothing. What does it matter now?' The old man shrugged. 'If I ever mention the war, Daniela tells me it's over and to forget about it.'

'Hard to forget something like that, no matter which side you were on.'

'Exactly.' Argüello nodded. 'I always say the war won't be over until people like you and me are dead and buried.'

Guzmán thought about that for a moment. 'You're right. They say you fight a war twice: once on the battlefield and once in memory. One day, there'll be no one left to remember. Then it will be over.'

'Sad though, isn't it?'

Guzmán finished his brandy in one long swallow. 'Everything's sad if you think about it for long enough.'

Argüello looked up as the outside door opened and slammed. 'That'll be Daniela,' he said. 'She often works late at that college.'

'I want a word with her.' Guzmán got to his feet. 'Thanks for the sandwich.' He pushed his way through the curtain of glass beads. Daniela was standing by the reception desk, wearing a coat to cover her glittering outfit. 'Don't start.' A tired voice.

'Come up to my room,' Guzmán said. It was not a request.

In his room, he switched on the cadaverous light and then took a seat by the window. Daniela sat on the edge of the bed. She looked exhausted.

'I didn't tell your father about the club,' Guzmán said. 'He doesn't need shocks like that in his condition.'

She glared. 'Why did you have to annoy Señor Ricci? I could have been fired.'

'You're not doing a college course, are you?'

She shook her head. 'Someone has to pay the bills. After Mamá died, I had to make a choice: find work or put my father in a home.'

'You know how Ricci makes a living, do you?'

'I know. But he's never suggested anything improper to me.'

'He will,' Guzmán said. 'He's just waiting for the right moment.'

'I'll deal with that when it happens.' She got up and went to the door.

Guzmán poured a finger of brandy into the glass on the night-stand. 'You can't handle someone like Ricci. You're out of your depth.'

'That's my business. You don't have to worry about me.' The door closed behind her.

He listened to the sharp clack of her heels as she went down the hall, the sound abruptly silenced as she went into her room. He lay back on the bed, staring up at the ceiling, noticing the dark stains and cracks in the plaster. Suddenly, a small patch of light appeared. At first, it seemed to be a reflection from the street outside. But as he watched, the light began to expand, forming a series of concentric circles, turning slowly above him, shimmering and imprecise.

It was the view of a drowning man, the circles turning faster as they rose through the darkness towards the surface and the light. But it was not the circles that were rising, he realised. He was sinking into the darkness.

He sat up with a jolt. His mouth was dry. Too much brandy or perhaps not enough. He reached over for the bottle on the nightstand and poured another drink. It had been a long time since those lights had appeared to him. Perhaps it was an omen.

If it was, it was not a good one.

CHAPTER 14

MADRID 2010, CALLE ESPINO

avapiés was buzzing. Galíndez left her car at the end of Calle Tribulete and made her way through the bustling crowds of tourists, declining offers of dope from the dealers lounging outside the bars and cafés. After a few minutes, she turned into a familiar cul-de-sac of residential buildings punctuated by a few commercial premises. At the far end was a nondescript bar, the door flanked by heavily barred windows.

It had been a while, but the sign over the door was still the same:

CUERO Y ACERO
CLUB SADOMASOQUISTA SOLO PARA MUJERES

LEATHER AND STEEL, LADIES' S&M CLUB
HERE ONE SPEAK ENGLISH
DRINKS AND FOOD AVAILABLE
WE'LL TAKE YOUR CREDIT CARDS

As she went downstairs into the cool shadows of the bar, Galíndez felt the same edgy vibe she'd experienced when she came here as a student. The bar was pretty much the same: a sprawl of leather sofas and chairs, low tables, the lingering smell of last night's cigarettes. On the far wall was a zinc-topped bar and behind it, towering shelves filled with exotic-looking bottles. Afternoon was always a quiet time and the place was empty. She slid onto one of the high stools at the bar. The barwoman came out from the kitchen at the back, drying her hands on her jeans.

'What can I get you?'

Galíndez shrugged. 'Mineral water.'

'We don't serve soft drinks on their own. It's a house rule.'

'Since when?'

'Since we introduced it. You want a drink or not?'

'Give me a vodka and tonic.'

'Any particular kind?'

'Oh, I don't know. Schweppes. Whatever.'

'I meant what kind of vodka, *chiquita*.'

'A big one.'

The barwoman picked up a large glass and rattled ice into it. 'Great,' she muttered, half filling the glass with vodka and splashing in a few drops of tonic, 'amateur hour.' She put the glass on the bar and pushed it towards Galíndez. 'Knock yourself out.'

Galíndez waited for her to go before taking a drink. The vodka was cold and refreshing. And very strong. She put the glass down. Tempting though it was, she wasn't here to enjoy herself.

'Excuse me?' Galíndez called.

The barwoman turned, annoyed at having to interact with a customer.

'Is Ramona working today?'

A sudden, knowing grin. 'I thought I'd seen you before.'

'I don't think so.'

'If you say so, doll. So what do you want with Ramona?'

'I just want to talk to her.'

'She'll talk to you all right. Cost you fifty euros though – and that's just for starters.'

'Is she here?'

The barwoman leaned her elbows on the bar and looked at Galíndez, hard. 'You're not our usual type of customer. Not on a dare, are you? Seeing how the other half live?'

'I just want a quiet drink and a quick word with Ramona.'

'You want to be careful, darling.'

'Why's that?'

'Because people who come here don't usually just want a

quiet drink. You saw the sign over the door. We have dungeons downstairs.'

'I know.'

'Oh yeah? How?'

Galíndez took a long drink before answering. 'That's my business.'

A shadow fell over her shoulder. She sensed someone standing behind her. A deep, threatening voice. 'Was that you I heard asking for me, sweetheart?'

Galíndez twisted round on the stool. Ramona was big and tall. Spiked hair flecked with day-glo streaks, broad shoulders under her studded leather jacket. No wonder she'd married Sancho: she had a similar build.

'Are you Ramona?'

'I can be who you like, darling. It all costs, though.'

'That's not a problem.' Galíndez shrugged.

Ramona put a finger under Galíndez's chin and lifted her face roughly. 'You look like a stroppy little thing to me, kid.'

Galíndez stared back. 'I have my moments.'

'Yeah? You sound like a bad girl.' Ramona smiled. 'Come on.' She took Galíndez by the arm and led her downstairs into a small passage. On either side were fake medieval doors set with metal studs. Ramona shoved open the nearest door and pushed Galíndez inside. She flicked a not-so-medieval light switch, filling the cell with a dull red glow.

Galíndez glanced at her surroundings. One wall was taken up by a collection of whips and scourges. On the far wall, she saw wrist and ankle irons attached to the wall by chains.

Ramona pointed to a large wooden stake fitted with a cross-piece, handcuffs dangling from each end. 'Sixteenth-century whipping post,' she said proudly. 'At least that's what it said in the catalogue. Very popular.'

'I just want to talk to you,' Galíndez said.

'You'll talk all right, babe,' Ramona said, pushing her towards the wooden post. 'You can tell me what a naughty girl you've been.'

She yanked one of Galíndez's hands up to the nearest cuff and tried to close it around her wrist. 'Do you want to get undressed first?'

'No, I want you to stop,' Galíndez said, struggling to keep her from fastening the cuff.

'You've done this before,' Ramona chuckled as the cuff snapped shut. 'Don't be coy, sweetie. Those marks on your wrists are a dead giveaway. I knew you were the type.'

She forced Galíndez's free hand into the cuff on the far side of the crosspiece and closed it. She reached round Galíndez's waist and tugged at her belt buckle. 'Want me to gag you as well?'

'No, you don't understand,' Galíndez spluttered, finding it hard to talk with her face pressed against the wooden post. 'I was tortured a few days ago.'

'And now you want more? I bet I'll do it better, babe.'

'You're not listening,' Galíndez said, struggling against the handcuffs. 'I was tortured by your husband.'

The atmosphere changed. And not for the better.

Ramona let go of her belt and stepped back. 'What are you talking about?'

'Your husband and another man kidnapped me. They took me to a cellar and gave me electric shocks. For real, I mean.'

Ramona's eyes narrowed. 'So why come here and pretend to be a punter?'

'Because I'm looking for Sancho.' Galíndez twisted her head to try and make eye contact. 'I didn't want anyone to overhear us.'

Ramona grabbed Galíndez's hair and jerked her head back. 'You've got a nerve.' She kept a tight grip on her hair. 'Why are you looking for him?'

'Look, could you fasten my belt?' Galíndez said. 'My jeans are falling down.'

'Tough,' Ramona said. 'Tell me why you want Sancho or I'll flay you. These rooms are soundproofed, by the way, so don't expect any help.'

'I'm *guardia civil*,' Galíndez said hurriedly. 'Your husband's involved with a wanted criminal.'

Ramona scoffed. 'Know what? I don't believe you.'

'Sancho could be in danger as well,' Galíndez said, improvising. 'If I can nail the man he's been helping, he'll be a whole lot safer. It isn't Sancho I'm after.'

Ramona went quiet for a moment. 'Let me see some ID.'

'Look in the pocket of my jeans.'

Ramona took a few moments before she found her ID card in the pocket of her jeans. Galíndez could almost hear her thinking things through.

'OK.' Ramona unlocked the cuffs and Galíndez quickly pulled up her jeans.

'Look, I'm sorry I didn't say who I was at the start,' Galíndez said, 'but I didn't think you'd trust me.'

'I don't.'

'I can tell you're worried about Sancho.'

Ramona was suddenly wary. 'Like I said, I don't trust you.'

'All I want is to talk to him for a few minutes. Ask a few questions.'

'It's not that easy.'

'Do you keep in touch?'

Ramon gave her a knowing look. 'You try quoting anything I say, and I'll deny it. And I'll tell the *guardia* why you were here.'

'I'm making an inquiry, that's all.'

Ramona shrugged. 'You'll be on the CCTV in the bar. Talk your way out of that.' She laughed as she saw Galíndez anxiously scan the room for cameras. 'Don't worry, babe, you're not on film down here.'

'So how can I contact Sancho?'

'It's complicated.'

'It doesn't seem complicated. A phone number, an address, that's all I need.'

'It's not that easy, sweetheart. I know nothing. Put that in your fucking notebook.'

'Would he talk to me off the record?'

'You'd have to ask him.'

'Look, Sancho could be in danger. If something happens to him, it's on your head.'

Ramona's attitude seemed to soften. 'Thing is, doll, I'm supposed to report it if anyone tries to contact Sancho.'

'Report to who?'

Ramona sighed as she took a card from her pocket and handed it to Galíndez. 'You'd better talk to him yourself.'

Galíndez stared at the card. 'Really?'

'Yeah, he's the one you have to talk to.'

'Then that's what I'll do. Thanks for your help.' Galíndez went to the door.

'Hey.'

Galíndez turned. 'Yes?'

'You help Sancho and I'll let you have a session in here on the house.'

Galíndez hurried up the stairs and headed for the door. Behind her, she heard the barwoman laughing.

Once she was back in the car, she took a couple of painkillers from her jacket pocket and swallowed them. Then she took another look at the crumpled card Ramona gave her:

INSPECTOR JEFE ENRIQUE VILLENA
JEFATURA SUPERIOR DE LA POLICÍA NACIONAL,
AVENIDA DR FEDERICO RUBIO Y GALI

What interest Chief Inspector Villena had in Sancho, she couldn't imagine. But she intended to find out. She picked up her phone and dialled National Police Headquarters to ask if Villena was on duty.

MADRID 2010, JEFATURA SUPERIOR DE LA POLICÍA NACIONAL, AVENIDA DR FEDERICO RUBIO Y GALI

Galíndez saw the radio mast towering above the complex of red-brick buildings at the top of the hill. She pulled up at the barrier and gave the duty officer her details. Then she waited, drumming her fingers on the wheel while he made a call to reception. Patience was not her strong suit, she was starting to realise.

'Go straight to the car park, señorita. You'll see the door to reception over there,' the man said, gesturing towards another featureless part of the building, the dull monotony of its red-brick walls broken by dark glass windows that gave it the appearance of a particularly inhospitable airport hotel.

She parked and made her way to reception. The receptionist gave her a visitor's badge and then called to Inspector Villena. 'He'll be with you in a few minutes, Dr Galíndez.'

Villena kept her waiting twenty minutes. By that time Galíndez was pacing up and down the lobby, seething. Finally, Villena arrived, a sharp-faced man with serious acne scars. When Galíndez introduced herself and offered her hand, he ignored it. 'I don't have much time,' he said. 'Come this way.'

Glowering, she followed him down a flight of stairs and along a dark narrow corridor. Villena took out a key and opened a door. 'In here.'

'This is an interview room.' Galíndez frowned, looking at the spartan furnishings.

'It's all we've got available.' He slapped a file down on the table and took a seat, facing her. 'Sit down.'

'Are you this rude to all your visitors?'

He gave her a cold look. 'Why don't you let me ask the questions?'

'What the fuck is wrong with you? I want to make a routine request for information and you're treating me like a suspect. I'll be making a formal complaint about this.'

'Not for some time you won't,' Villena growled. 'Under anti-terrorist legislation I could detain you here for several days.'

'Detain me for what? I'm here to get information.'

'Exactly. Very sensitive information about Sancho Hernández.'

'Our agencies exchange information all the time,' Galíndez said, struggling to control her temper, 'so how come you're threatening me with illegal imprisonment?'

Villena's eyes narrowed. 'Why don't you start by telling me about your interest in Inspector Hernández?'

A long silence. '*Inspector* Hernandez?' Galíndez said, finally.

'That's right,' Villena said. 'He's one of my best undercover operatives, or I should say he *was* one of the best, since he's been missing for four years. Perhaps you could explain your sudden interest in him?'

'I'd be happy to. Sancho Hernández is implicated in several crimes including murder and an attack on the home of a civil guard *capitán*. He's also linked to the killings of the CEO of a group of private hospitals and the assassination of the Minister of the Interior and her husband, two weeks ago.'

'You have evidence of all that, do you?'

'I saw him at the scenes of some of those crimes,' Galíndez said. 'He was also jointly responsible for kidnapping me last week, assisted by a former member of Franco's secret police.' She sat back, breathing hard, angry at the memory of it.

Villena's eyes narrowed. 'You saw Sancho?'

'On several occasions, including the attack on Capitán Fuentes' house.' She leaned forward. 'It's clear to me your inspector's gone over to the other side.'

'What other side?' Villena snapped.

'I have no idea.'

'And you're sure it was him?'

Galíndez shrugged. 'Do you have any photos? I can identify him.'

'I won't be a minute.' Villena jumped to his feet and hurried out of the door.

Still angry, Galíndez listened to his footsteps fading down the corridor, leaving her alone. Alone, with only Sancho's file for company.

She pulled the file across the desk and flicked open the cardboard cover. Inside was a black-and-white photograph of Sancho, probably the one used for his police ID card. A few details: age, rank, blood group and his wife's address. She flipped the page and saw a handwritten address above a scrawled map: *Monasterio de*

Santa Eulalia, near Las Rozas. In the corridor, she heard the sound of footsteps. Villena was coming back.

She reached into her pocket for her phone, took a photo of the page and pushed the file back across the desk.

A moment later, Villena came into the room, clutching a handful of photographs. 'Have a look at these.' He spread the photos on the desk, careful to mix them up.

Galíndez looked at the photos in front of her. Two were of Sancho, one with his piercings and tattoos, one without, clearly taken earlier in his career. The other pictures were of men of a similar appearance. She examined the photos slowly, making Villena wait. Languidly, she tapped the pictures of Sancho with her finger. 'These two are Sancho,' she said. 'Now are you going to tell me what this is about or are you going to threaten me again?'

Villena slumped forward on the desk. 'I was out of order, I know. But you'd do the same in my position.'

'I wouldn't, but that doesn't matter. What can you tell me about him?'

'He was one of our best undercover operatives. The man was a natural. Four years ago, we set up an operation to infiltrate a group of ex-military officers and politicians who were affiliated with organised crime syndicates in Madrid.'

Galíndez felt her pulse quicken. He was talking about the *Centinelas.* 'Go on.'

'They were already powerful when we started planning to take them down. Once we sent Sancho in, we found out they were even more powerful than we thought. They had influence in various branches of the police, the armed forces and the *guardia.*'

'The *guardia*?' Galíndez cut in. 'Were we notified?'

He shook his head. 'We couldn't alert agencies that had been infiltrated by these people, it would have blown our operation. We wanted them to think no one was aware of their activities. That way, we could take them by surprise when we made our move.'

'And did you?'

'We never got the chance. Sancho sent a last message saying

there was a problem. Something had been lost and they were desperate to get it back.'

Galíndez's mind was racing now. 'Did he say what it was?'

'He never contacted us again,' Villena said quietly. 'We kept trying to make contact so we could get him out, even though we suspected he was dead. At the same time, communications between members of the group stopped. We couldn't get a lead, we had no informers, nothing. I swore to his wife we'd find him but it never happened.'

'Did the group he was investigating have a name?'

His eyes flickered with sudden interest. 'Not as far as I know. Why?'

'I just wondered.'

'Could you send us the material you've got on him?' Villena asked, conciliatory now. 'We've been assuming he's dead but from what you say, it sounds like there's still a chance of finding him.'

'Of course, I'll send you copies of my reports,' said Galíndez. 'But I have to tell you that everything I've found suggests that he's switched sides.'

'We'll deal with that once we find him,' Villena said. 'Any information you can give me will be helpful.'

'Don't worry, I'll send it over. Not that you deserve it after your behaviour earlier.'

He gave her a sheepish look. 'I really am sorry about that. I was Sancho's unit commander when he went undercover and it was my call to send him in. That also meant it was up to me to get him out. But I failed, which is why I'm desperate for information. I thought I could bully it out of you.'

'"Please" would have worked a lot better.'

'I'm really sorry. If I get any more info on Sancho, I'll copy you in on it at once.'

'Who said the age of diplomacy's dead?' Galíndez smiled.

Back in her car, she took out her phone and checked the picture she'd taken of Sancho's file. Then she set the satnav for Las Rozas.

MADRID 2010, MONASTERIO DE SANTA EULALIA,
LAS ROZAS

'Follow the A-6 to Pozuelo and then bear left at Majadahonda.'
Galíndez looked angrily at the crumpled map on the passenger
seat next to her. *Shit, why can't they make these things clear?* She
glared at the satnav, the wires hanging loose from its cracked
screen. That hadn't been much use either.

She was deep in the suburbs now. Commuter land: neat
gardens, swimming pools shaded by large palm trees. Expensive
cars parked on long drives.

And then a sign, no, two signs, one for Majadahonda and the
other a tourist sign, *Monasterio de Santa Eulalia, 12km.*

She sighed with relief as she turned onto a dusty country road
rising gently around the side of a hill. At the top, she passed a
grove of olive trees and then, as the car turned a bend, she saw
the outline of the monastery on the skyline, a big arched gate, a
steep grey slate roof, rows of ancient leaded windows. She slowed,
thinking of the centuries of austere habits and bleak comforts that
had passed here on this desolate hilltop, broken only by midnight
prayers in the dead of winter.

A couple of hundred metres up the road, she saw a long wooden
bar with a veranda overlooking the countryside beyond. A perfect
spot to sit and watch the sun go down with a cool drink. She
slowed to a halt alongside the only other vehicle in the parking lot.
As she climbed from the car, she looked up again at the hermitage.
By the gate, she saw activity: several small vans, people hurrying
in and out of the gate. Sancho was somewhere in there, she was
certain, though she doubted Inspector Villena would get his wish
to get him back. Villena was being naive: it was clear to her that
Sancho had changed sides. Yet another reason to put a bullet in him.

The barman was leaning on the counter, engrossed in the
sports pages of *El País.* He looked up as he heard her approach.
'*Buenas tardes.*'

Galíndez ordered a Coke.

'Just finished work?'

'Not yet, I haven't.' Galíndez gestured towards the monastery. 'Interesting old place. Is it open to the public?'

He pushed her drink across the counter. A tinkle of ice cubes. 'No, it's some kind of private members' club.'

'Really? What kind of club?' She tried not to sound interested.

'You tell me. We all have our own theories as to what goes off when they have their special nights up there.'

'Why, what happens?'

'Sometimes there's two dozen cars parked round that gate. People go into the monastery and then they leave in the early hours. That's all I know.'

'Maybe they have dinner dances or something?'

'Maybe.' His expression suggested he wasn't convinced. 'They have all the lights on, but I've never heard music. In fact, there's never any noise at all. Whatever they do, they do it quietly.'

'Maybe they're swingers?'

'Don't think we haven't thought of that. But if they are, they keep it to themselves.'

Casually, she slid Sancho's photo across the counter. 'Ever seen him round here?'

The barman gave her a long look. 'You a cop or something?'

She grinned. 'Me? Are you kidding?'

He joined in her laughter. 'Yeah, you're too pretty to be a cop.'

'Flatterer.' She took another sip of Coke. 'Actually, I'm a lawyer. That guy in the photo was married to a client of mine. He ran out on her and the kids. I'm trying to get some maintenance for her. It's no joke, looking after four kids. You can imagine, can't you?'

'I can. What a shit.' The barman picked up the photo and examined it. 'Yeah, I know him. He's the caretaker up there. Once in a while he drops by for a beer. Keeps himself to himself though.'

'You think he's up there now?'

'Who knows? You could try for nothing.'

'Know what?' Galíndez said. 'I'll do that.'

———

The road became a narrow track as she approached the monastery. At least she didn't have to climb the hillside, she thought, seeing the steep slopes littered with stunted trees and broken rocks.

Ahead of her, a line of vans was parked by the gate. The logos on the sides showed they were from a catering firm. Quite a big order, given the number of vehicles. She kept walking, deciding to wander in. If anyone asked, she'd bluff it out with a story about being a lost tourist.

As she went past one of the catering trucks, a man was standing at the back of the vehicle, talking into his mobile. He gave Galíndez an evil look. 'Hang on, I think she's here now.' He glared at her. 'You're Carla, I take it?'

Galíndez nodded.

'Well you're late. Do it again and I'll dock your wages. I know you said you weren't experienced but I didn't think you'd be forty minutes late.'

'Sorry, my car broke down.'

'I don't care. I expect you to be on time, OK?' He pointed to a woman standing by a van a few metres away. 'That's Elena, your supervisor. She'll tell you what to do.'

'Thanks.' Galíndez wandered over and introduced herself.

Elena gave her another warning about punctuality and then slid a big tray of canapés covered in cling film from the back of the truck. She pushed the tray into Galíndez's arms and went back for another. 'Follow me.'

Two men were standing by the gate. Both in black suits, earpieces and mikes. As she got nearer, Galíndez saw the bulge of sidearms under their jackets. Probably not a swingers' evening then, she guessed.

'Just got to check you two ladies out.' The bigger of the two smiled as he came towards them. Galíndez's stomach tightened. Even the most cursory search would find the Glock tucked in her waistband.

The man went up to Elena and lifted the cover on the tray she was carrying. 'Looks tasty.' He came over to Galíndez and checked her tray. 'OK, girls, go straight in, the refectory is down the corridor and on the right, you can't miss it.'

They continued walking.

'Hey, brown eyes.'

Galíndez stopped and turned.

'You married?'

'Yes.'

He looked over at his partner. 'Told you. The best ones always are.'

Galíndez stayed where she was, staring at them, stony-faced.

The man waved his hand dismissively. 'Carry on, señora.'

Slowly, Galíndez turned and followed Elena into the monastery.

The motorcade came to a halt, almost filling the main street with long black limousines. Men jumped out from both sides of the lead vehicle. Hard-faced men, wearing dark suits despite the heat.

One of them ran to the rear door of the car and opened it.

For the first time in a long time, Villanueva felt vague excitement, realising it was probably some foreign film star, making another spaghetti western in the arid countryside.

As the man got out of the car, Villanueva realised at once he was not an actor, though his face was familiar. He'd seen it often enough in newspapers and newsreels at the cinema. Alberto also had recognised him, and was now rigidly standing to attention, saluting with uncharacteristic formality as the prime minister came towards them.

'Almirante.' Villanueva raised his hat. 'Inspector Villanueva at your service.'

Admiral Carrero Blanco looked at him, expressionless. 'Who the devil are you?'

'I'm Chief of Police.'

Carrero Blanco gave him a cold look. 'Not any more.' He turned to one of the dark-suited men. 'Get the church hall opened up. I want all the villagers in there within the hour.'

CHAPTER 15

MADRID, OCTOBER 1982, CALLE DE MENORCA

Guzmán took a coffee at a café on Avenida de Calle Menéndez Pelayo before going in search of the Sepúlveda Garage. As always, Gutiérrez's instructions were annoyingly accurate. He turned into Calle Menorca and a hundred metres further on, he saw the sign.

Whoever Sepúlveda had been, he had not looked after this garage. The battered metal shutters were daubed in painted slogans from both left- and right-wing groups. Various slogans, most beginning with *Death to*. Others called for an amnesty for political prisoners; one hopeful soul had even painted *Viva Franco* across the door. Yet another sign of the times. In the old days his men would have hospitalised someone for this wanton vandalism.

Inside the garage, bolts rattled and a small metal door slid open. 'That you, Guzmán?' The words were lost in a sudden fit of coughing.

'No, it's the *Centinelas*, we heard you'd opened a library.'

'Don't make jokes like that,' Gutiérrez grumbled. 'It might be bad luck.'

Guzmán slammed the door behind him. 'When did you start caring about luck? You said you always placed your faith in science.'

'And which of us spends his time consulting fortune-tellers or asking dwarfs for their opinions?'

'I've lost faith in dwarfs,' Guzmán sighed, reaching for his cigarettes. 'This new generation don't want to work in fairs or circuses and even if they get a job in a hotel, they complain about being stuck in the lift all day.'

'Why would they turn their noses up at regular work like that?'

'Same reason people are wearing clothes that look they were made by a blind gypsy.' Guzmán fumbled in his jacket for his lighter. 'Got a light?'

'I'd rather you didn't smoke in here.'

'I'm in need of a cigarette. I promise not to exhale.'

Gutiérrez went to the wall and hit the light switch. 'This is why you can't smoke.'

The overhead lights fluttered on, revealing the interior of the old garage. By the far wall, Guzmán saw a small glass-sided office. Along the other wall were piles of rusty tools and worn tyres. But it was the huge shelves that caught his eye. At least two metres tall, they dominated the place, long metal racks loaded with boxes and files, arranged in rows that extended to the back of the garage.

'This is what I've been doing, Guzmán. While you and your squad have been collecting the files, I've started sorting and cataloguing some of the most damning material.'

'Including the stuff on us?'

'Some of it, though it's early days yet, I'm going to need more help.' Gutiérrez picked up a folder lying on a workbench. 'Remember this? You arrested twenty men from a village near Toledo in 1959. They were never seen again.'

Guzmán frowned. 'Can you be more specific?'

'They were all members of the PCE,' Gutiérrez said. 'If that helps?'

'Ah, the communists.' Guzmán nodded. 'It was a meeting in an abandoned church.'

'How convenient.'

'I'll say. We threw the bodies into one of the tombs and blew it up with grenades.'

'We?' Gutiérrez chuckled. 'It says here you did all the killing.'

'If you want a job doing properly...' Guzmán waved away the memory. 'So those documents really do have all the shit on us?'

'Indeed they do, which is why we ought to think about moving this material to a more secure location. I've had a feeling the place has been under surveillance these last few days.'

'I've been followed on a couple of occasions as well,' Guzmán said. 'He's good too. Tailed me for forty-five minutes and then, just when I'd decided to kill him, he melted away. A pro, definitely.'

'Then the sooner we move these files the better,' Gutiérrez said. 'I'll make some calls this afternoon.' He looked at his watch. 'How about lunch? It's on me.'

Guzmán was cheered by the thought of food and even more cheered by the prospect of Gutiérrez paying. 'There must be at least one five-star restaurant round here.'

'There's a bar just down the street,' Gutiérrez said. 'It's very reasonable.' He pressed a button on the wall and two men came out from the back of the garage, dressed in overalls though no one would take them for workmen since both were wearing shoulder holsters. 'We're going out,' Gutiérrez told them. 'No one comes in until I get back.'

'Got it, *jefe*,' one of the men grunted as he dragged open the metal door for them.

They went out into the street and the door grated to behind them. 'Those guys look like they can handle themselves,' Guzmán said.

Gutiérrez nodded. 'Ex-Foreign Legionaries. They've been working for me since they left the Legion.' He pointed to a small bar further down the road. 'You'll like it here, it's cheap and they have very good sandwiches.'

Guzmán's expression hardened. 'Sandwiches aren't lunch.'

The bar was small and homely. Guzmán was still studying the menu when a large woman in a grease-stained apron came to serve them. Gutiérrez ordered a cheese sandwich, annoying Guzmán no end. 'Got anything hot?' he asked.

'I've just made some *albóndigas*, señor.'

'Meatballs? That sounds good,' Guzmán said. 'Any tortilla?'

'We have potato tortilla.'

'Then I'll have both. And a bottle of Rioja.'

'Not for me,' Gutiérrez muttered. 'It's bad for my stomach.'

Guzmán gave him a disparaging look. 'I wasn't offering you any.'

The woman brought the wine and Guzmán poured himself a large one. He glared at Gutiérrez's empty glass and splashed a little Rioja into it. 'Here, it's unlucky to drink alone.'

Guzmán's head turned as a green Ford Fiesta drove slowly past the window. Cheap cars were of no interest to him and he looked away.

The food arrived and Guzmán attacked his meatballs with gusto. 'Ortiz was telling about how he's kept the *Centinelas* from infiltrating the *guardia*,' he said.

Gutiérrez nodded. 'It was brave of him: if he'd just given in, he could have been rich.'

Guzmán glanced out of the window. The green Ford had now pulled to a halt outside the garage. 'Looks like someone wants to get his car fixed. I hope your lads are qualified mechanics?'

'Not at all,' Gutiérrez said. 'Their orders are to tell prospective customers to get lost.'

Idly, Guzmán watched a man get out of the car and go towards the door of the garage. 'Looks like they'll have to do just that.' He frowned as the man turned and dashed off up the street. 'See that?'

Gutiérrez leaned across the table to get a better look. As he did, his elbow caught Guzmán's glass, sending a stream of red wine over the tablecloth.

'You clumsy bastard,' Guzmán said, 'that's a waste of good—'

The Ford exploded in a lurid fireball, shattering the windows of the café and showering the interior with broken glass and rubble. Guzmán hurled himself sideways, knocking Gutiérrez from his chair and pinning him to the floor as debris rained down around them. As the dust settled, Guzmán cautiously struggled to his feet, wiping dirt from his face.

The café was wrecked, the air thick with dust and the stench of burning gasoline.

Gutiérrez was still lying on the floor. 'Are you all right?' Guzmán asked.

'The archive,' Gutiérrez croaked, pointing to the door.

Guzmán ran out through the shattered doorway into the street.

In a shop across the way, several hairdressers were peering out through the broken windows of their salon. Behind him, a car alarm blared incessantly as he sprinted to the burning garage.

The door to the garage had been blown off its hinges. Inside, one of Gutiérrez's men was lying on his back in a pool of blood. The man had taken the full force of the metal door and his head was lying halfway down one of the aisles between the shelves, connected to the body only by a long trail of blood. The other guard lay face down near the office. Guzmán had no time to determine what had killed him as he heard the crackle of flames from the shelves near the door. He turned, aware of someone behind him. It was Gutiérrez, gasping as he staggered through the acrid smoke.

'Where's the fire extinguisher?' Guzmán yelled.

'In there.' Gutiérrez pointed to the small office by the far wall.

Guzmán ran in, seized one of the fire extinguishers and smashed it head down onto the concrete floor. The spray hissed as he aimed it into the flames.

'That's going to ruin the files,' Gutiérrez said, between bouts of coughing.

Guzmán kept the spray aimed at the fire. 'Go and wait outside, before you choke to death.' In the distance, the sound of approaching sirens.

By the time the fire engines had negotiated their way down the narrow street, the fire in the archive was out. Guzmán stood outside the wrecked garage, hawking and spitting, trying to clear the smoke from his lungs. Near the burned-out Ford, Gutiérrez was unsuccessfully arguing with two firemen who insisted that regulations required them to hose down the inside of the garage. Guzmán went over and convinced the firemen that it would be unnecessary, first, by showing them his ID and then, when that was unsuccessful, by showing them the Browning. The discussion over, the fire engine drove away, its commander muttering darkly about the Francoists still controlling the Forces of Public Order.

'You realise this was deliberate?' Gutiérrez said, between bouts of coughing.

'There was me thinking that car blew up by accident.'

'I went to great lengths to keep this place secret.'

'Clearly not great enough, since someone found out.' Guzmán went over to the blackened car and bent to examine the debris. Gutiérrez heard him curse as he took a blackened piece of metal from the smoking ashes, juggling it from hand to hand until it was cool enough to examine.

'What's that you've got, *Comandante*?'

'Part of a detonator, I'd say.' Guzmán handed him the lump of twisted metal. 'Get on the phone and have a forensic team sent over. Let's see what they can find in all this shit.'

'We should move the files. They're vulnerable now.'

Guzmán looked into the darkened garage. 'There's a lot of them.'

'We can separate out the most important and move those.'

'That'll still take all night,' Guzmán said. 'I'll call Ochoa and tell him to bring the squad down here. They can do it.'

'You've got something more important to do, I take it?'

Guzmán nodded. 'I'm seeing an informer.' It was a curious description for Lourdes but he saw no reason to discuss that with Gutiérrez.

MADRID, OCTOBER 1982

Only an hour had passed, though to Michael Riley it seemed very much longer. The day had started well, though everything had changed now, even his appearance. He saw that only too clearly from his reflection in the rust-spotted mirror set up in front of him. When he moved his head, he saw the small table at his side filled with the instruments of his suffering. Pliers, pincers and several knives. All had been used.

'Stop snivelling,' Professor Luca said. 'At least I know you're telling the truth now. It was foolish to try to lie to me.' He grabbed Riley by the hair and pulled back his head. 'I learned from the best in the business, Signor Riley. I could make you remember things you forgot years ago, if I wanted.'

'Pleesh lemee go. It hurth.' It was difficult to speak without his front teeth. An hour earlier, they had been in his mouth. Now, they lay on the table, next to the instruments.

'Don't speak,' Luca sneered. 'You sound ridiculous.' He reached over and took a small knife with an adjustable blade from the table. Riley gurgled and pleaded, struggling desperately as the knife came towards him.

The blade slid down his chest, scoring the flesh in a deep line that stopped just above the sternum. Luca put down the knife and dipped his index finger in the slick of blood on Riley's chest. Then he turned to the wall and began writing. From time to time he dabbed his finger into Riley's blood before continuing.

Riley looked away, sensing that whatever Luca was writing, it was better not to know. That thought rapidly blossomed into an obsessional belief and he turned his head, staring at a pile of dusty equipment in a corner of the room, half covered by a filthy tarpaulin. Pots of paint, a rusty hatchet. Plastic garden sacks.

Luca seized the student's hair and twisted his face to the wall. Riley closed his eyes. As long as he couldn't see what was written there, he was safe.

'Open your eyes,' Luca said, in the same flat voice he used when he began the interrogation. The same voice that had continued asking questions despite the screaming.

Riley opened his eyes and stared at the word scrawled in large bloody letters on the peeling paintwork. A name.

Luca looked at him with contempt. 'I know what you're thinking.'

Not that it was hard, Luca knew. The Irishman's reaction was commonplace. Commonplace but deluded. This was not some child's game where things went away if you shut your eyes: no matter what Riley did, the outcome would be the same.

'You've told me all I need to know, Signor Riley,' Luca said.

Riley's head slumped and a string of snot slid from his nose. 'I neeth a dotter.'

Luca pulled on a pair of gardener's gloves. Serviceable but cheap, 350 pesetas from the SEPU bargain store. Tomorrow he intended to buy several more. He would need them.

'That cut's not fatal by the way,' he said, gesturing at Riley's chest. Riley's eyes widened as he saw the thin bright wire pulled taut between Luca's gloved hands. 'But this,' Lucas stepped behind the chair, ignoring the student's gurgled pleas as he drew the wire round his throat, '*this* is fatal.'

MADRID, OCTOBER 1982, RETIRO PARK

'I can't,' Lourdes whispered, pulling away from him. 'I'm a married woman.'

When she had finished rearranging her clothes, she leaned against him, looking at the line of trees by the lake. He held her in his arms as she recalled a poem, something about love and trees. It was a reminder to Guzmán of how much easier it was just to pay for it.

'What's your favourite meal, Leo?'

Guzmán didn't have to think hard. 'Beef stew, fried fish, tripe, shellfish, pork.' He felt her shoulder moving against him. 'What's so funny?'

'It sounds like you'd eat anything.'

'As long as the cook's pretty.'

That made her laugh. A woman unaccustomed to compliments, he guessed. Probably that was why she kept fishing for them.

'Getting cool, isn't it?' she said.

'You're right. Shall we get a drink?'

'I thought you'd never ask. Look, there's a bar with music and dancing over there.'

They crossed the road and went into the bar. The chairs on the terrace were arranged in a circle to make space for the dancing. A few musicians stood under the trees, setting up their instruments. Guzmán led her to a table outside the ring of light, so they could watch from the shadows.

'This is my favourite tune,' Lourdes said, squeezing his hand as the music began.

'What's it called?' It sounded like any other bolero to him.

She gave a long sigh. '"*Historia de un Amor*". It's about a man who's thinking about his dead wife. He asks why God made him love her only to make him suffer so much by taking her away.' She sighed again. 'I can't imagine a man loving me that much.'

'Sounds morbid to me,' Guzmán grunted.

'I think about you all the time,' she said, watching the dancers. Her voice was so quiet, he thought at first he was mistaken. 'You're a good man.'

'No, you're a bad judge of character.'

The waiter brought their drinks. She waited until he had gone. 'Adultery's a sin, you know. I'll be so embarrassed in my next confession. Just think what the priest will say.'

'Why does he need to know? We haven't done anything yet.'

She gave him a reproachful look. 'It's what I believe, Leo. If you don't repent, you lose your place in heaven.'

'I doubt they've saved a place for me.'

'Don't be silly, there's always redemption for those who want it.'

The dance ended to a ripple of applause from the terrace. 'We could go to my *pensión*,' he suggested, not for the first time.

'No, I have to get home by eleven. My husband's been called out on a job. He'll want his supper when he gets back.'

'It's only eight thirty. I can call a taxi later to take you home.'

She was quiet for a moment. 'All right.'

'What was that?'

'I said let's go back to your *pensión*. The owner won't mind, will he?'

'No, he's an ex-Republican but he's all right, considering. I'll give him a bottle of brandy, that'll keep him happy.'

'Is that how you still think of people, Leo? As an ex-this or that? The war's over.'

That very much depended on your point of view, he thought,

leaving a handful of coins on the table. Across the street, he saw a taxi waiting by the kerb. 'Let's go.'

MADRID, PENSIÓN PARAÍSO, CALLE DEL CARMEN

The church bells were striking midnight as Guzmán watched her taxi drive off across the Plaza del Callao. He gave a last wave and went back up the steps into the *pensión*.

Daniela's father called to him through the glass bead curtains. 'That you, Leo?'

'You know it is.'

'I didn't want to bother you while your lady friend was here.'

'I should think not. What is it?'

'You had a couple of calls earlier. They're on the pad by the phone. Do you want your bottle of brandy back?'

'No, you finish it.' Guzmán reached over the reception desk to retrieve the notepad. The first caller was Ignacio. Guzmán dialled the number he'd left and heard the sounds of a bar in the background as someone answered. 'Is Ignacio there?'

A gruff voice: 'Who wants to know?'

'I do.'

'I'll get him.'

He waited while the barman called Ignacio's name. A scuffling noise as the old man picked up the phone. 'Guzmán?'

'You must be psychic. What have you got for me?'

'Exactly what you asked for.'

'Good man. And where are you?'

'Lavapiés. Remember the Bar Almeja?'

Guzmán frowned. 'Of course I do. It was always full of queers in the old days.'

'Still is. But no one knows us here, do they?'

'I'm on my way.' As Guzmán put down the phone, he glanced at the other number on the paper. A Capitán Serrano of the *policía nacional*. He dialled the number and waited with growing impatience for the dunderhead at the other end of the line to find out if Serrano was still in the building. Finally, the *capitán* came to the phone.

'Comandante Guzmán? I called you earlier about the explosion in Calle de Menorca. Brigadier General Gutiérrez asked me to pass on our findings about the bomb.'

'And?'

'We've come up with a few details. You know the detonator was made in Italy?'

'I do now. Keep going.'

'Not just the detonator, all the components we could identify were Italian.'

Guzmán gripped the phone tightly. 'Anything about the way it was put together?'

'Funny you should ask,' Serrano said, taking a deep breath.

Guzmán cut in before he could speak. 'Meticulous attention to detail, reinforced connections and top-quality wiring, almost as if he'd been entering it for a show?'

The *capitán* sounded surprised. 'That's right. You have to wonder who'd put that amount of effort into it, don't you?'

Guzmán hung up. There was no point wasting time speculating about the bomber's identity. He already knew.

MADRID 1982, BAR ALMEJA,
CALLE DE LA RIBERA DE CURTIDORES

As the taxi came down the steep cobbled hill, Guzmán noticed a flashing sign over the door, the bar's only concession to changing times, by the look of it. He got out of the taxi, taking care not to tip the driver since the man had made it clear from the start he was not happy conveying a passenger heading to a notorious gay bar. Naturally, it was not his prejudice Guzmán objected to so much as the fact the driver thought he was a *marica*.

As the taxi roared away, Guzmán pushed open the door to the

bar and stepped into a warm fug of cigarette smoke and cheap cologne. The bar was crowded and heads turned as he came in. His menacing build and hostile stare suggested he was not seeking company and most of those looking at him quickly lowered their eyes. It was not like the old days, he thought. They might be wary of him, but they were no longer afraid now the law against homosexuality had been repealed. He went to the bar and ordered two brandies before looking for Ignacio.

The old man was sitting in a corner and Guzmán went to join him. He sat with his back to the wall.

'Suspicious, aren't you?' Ignacio asked, taking the brandy Guzmán offered.

'I like to see who comes in and who goes out.' Guzmán lowered his voice. 'So what have you got for me?'

'It wasn't easy, *Comandante*.'

'I wouldn't need you if it was easy. Who gave you the information?'

Ignacio smiled. 'Professional secret.'

'Suit yourself,' Guzmán said, thinking he would have punched Ignacio to the ground for that comment a few years ago. 'How much did I say?'

'You didn't. But I said it might be risky and it was. I phoned a guy I thought could help me. He made a couple of calls and blow me, half an hour later he was chased by two heavies when he was bringing me the details over.'

'Did he know who they were?'

'He knew they were trouble, put it that way.' Ignacio took another sip of brandy.

'I hope you made sure you weren't followed here?'

'*Tranquilo, Comandante*. How long have I been doing this?'

'Long enough not to have a couple of heavies chase your contact, I'd say.'

'Coincidence, that's all it was.' Ignacio's cheeks were flushed by the brandy.

'Let's hope so. I like to keep my business to myself.'

'You always have, *Comandante*. I remember how organised you were at Calle Robles. You had everything on file back then. A man couldn't take a shit without you cataloguing it.'

'Not me personally.' Guzmán scowled. The drink was making the old man talkative so he decided to cut his reminiscing short. 'Where's the information I asked for?'

Ignacio nodded at the newspaper lying on the table between them. 'It's in the paper, if you see what I mean.'

'I do.' Guzmán reached into his jacket. 'How much?'

'Not here, *Comandante*. You never know with these nancies whether they'll shoot their mouths off if they see money changing hands. Do it like we used to.'

Guzmán narrowed his eyes. 'The toilet?'

'That's it,' Ignacio agreed. 'Tuck it behind the cistern. I'll pop in and collect it when you come back.' He smiled. 'Just like the old days.'

'Suit yourself.' Guzmán got up and casually took the newspaper from the table before making his way across the crowded bar to the toilets. They were cleaner than he remembered, though the graffiti were just as obscene and inventive – or optimistic – as they ever had been.

He went into the second of the two cubicles and locked the door before opening the folded newspaper. Inside was a sheet of white paper with the information he wanted written in Ignacio's old-fashioned script. Guzmán put the paper into his jacket pocket and, in an unusual act of generosity towards his fellow man, left the newspaper on the empty toilet roll holder. Finally, he pulled Ignacio's reward from his pocket and wedged the roll of pesetas behind the cistern. This was how he paid his informers during the dictatorship and it amused him to be doing it now, so much so that he was almost in a good mood as he returned to the bar.

The place was getting crowded and it took a moment to spot Ignacio slumped at the table, still clutching his glass. He was getting old: at one time, that old lag could drink anyone under the table, even the sarge.

Guzmán sat down and nudged Ignacio's arm. 'It's ready for collection.' When Ignacio said nothing, he nudged him again, harder. 'Wake up, you dozy old bastard.'

There was something wrong, he realised, and it was easy to see what it was: a thin metal stiletto protruded from the old man's chest. An assassin's weapon, thrust in from short range. He glanced round the room, seeing nothing to arouse his suspicions. That was to be expected: this was a professional job. One subtle thrust and then the killer was gone without anyone being aware of his presence. Ignacio probably hadn't even noticed.

Guzmán got up slowly, making a point of bidding Ignacio a good evening before he went back into the toilets to retrieve the roll of money.

Outside, he took a circuitous route around the Rastro, making sure he was not being followed. Once certain he was not, he relaxed a little, thinking about Ignacio. Another one of the old crowd gone, though it was the old man's fault. He should have taken the money when Guzmán offered it. Instead, he'd wanted to play cloak-and-dagger stuff like in the old days. And look where that got him.

There was a lesson to be learned there.

CHAPTER 16

MADRID 2010, MONASTERIO DE SANTA EULALIA,
LAS ROZAS

Galíndez saw the room at the end of the corridor, just as the hired muscle at the gate had said. A large ancient room with pillars, arches and leaded windows. A wide semicircle of chairs had been arranged facing a platform. A few chairs on the platform, a lectern facing the audience.

Elena's voice interrupted her thoughts. 'Carla, stop daydreaming, will you?'

By the sixth trip, she had to wipe sweat from her brow once she'd put down the tray.

'That's the lot for now,' Elena said. 'Make sure you're here at nine thirty tomorrow, won't you? I'll pay you then.' She narrowed her eyes. 'Assuming you turn up.' She pointed to Galíndez's overall. 'I'll have that back as well.'

Galíndez took off the overall and handed it over. 'See you tomorrow.'

'OK.' Elena softened a little. 'You need a lift or anything?'

Galíndez shook her head. 'I'm fine, thanks, you go. I need to find the toilet.'

Once Elena had gone, Galíndez went down the corridor. At the far end, she saw a pair of double doors, the dark carved wood reinforced by broad metal bands. Opening the door, she found herself in a spacious hallway, facing a spiral staircase that wound up to a landing bordered with elaborate balustrades.

She heard voices, from the refectory by the sound of it. Feet echoing on the stone tiles. A sign on a small door: CLOAKROOM.

Maybe there was somewhere in there she could hide. As she stepped into the room, she realised her mistake.

'Good evening, señorita.'

Galíndez looked at the attendant behind the desk, thinking that he must be a hundred at least. But what caught her attention was the long rail behind him, laden with what looked like monks' cowls. Dozens of them.

The attendant came out from behind the desk, holding one of the robes. 'Your first time at the convocation, señorita?'

Galíndez nodded.

'There's nothing to be afraid of.' The old man held out the robe and she threaded her arms into the sleeves and put it on. 'Don't speak unless you're spoken to, that's the golden rule for new initiates.' He smiled. 'At least you've got your initiation out of the way.'

'Yes, that's a great relief,' Galíndez said. The attendant pulled up the hood of the robe over her head, forcing her to rearrange it in order to see.

'It's not the best fit,' the old man said. 'But then, the idea is to invoke humility.' He tilted his head, hearing the sound of footsteps in the corridor. 'Now, remember, sit on the far right of the semicircle, look down at the ground at all times and never look anyone in the face, particularly the people on the platform. Got that?'

'Of course,' Galíndez said, wondering what the hell was going on.

'Head down then, and off you go.'

She went back down the echoing passage to the refectory. Through the open door, she saw several men standing on the platform, locked in discussion. Most were wearing dark business suits that emphasised their pale corporate faces.

One man stood out from the rest. There was nothing corporate about him. A lightweight suit, his greasy hair tied back in a ponytail. He seemed vaguely familiar, though whoever he was, he looked like trouble, given the long scar down his cheek. As she entered the room, he gave her a cursory glance and she lowered her head, letting the cowl fall over her face.

She walked past the platform to the rows of chairs and took a seat on the right near the front. On the platform, the discussion continued, though the men in the dark suits were talking in hushed voices, making it impossible to hear what was said. The man in the linen suit was not so discreet. His voice was loud and angry, punctuated by obscenities. A thick accent, possibly South American. His face seemed familiar.

The room was filling with people, all wearing cowls like hers. It was like no other meeting she had ever attended. The entire audience sat in silence, looking down at the worn carpet. No greetings to fellow initiates, no glances round to see who had arrived. Cautiously, she lifted her head and darted a glance at the platform.

One of the men on the platform was coming to the lectern. Silence fell over the cowled audience. Not just silence. The atmosphere was charged with fear.

'*Buenas noches*,' the man said, looking round at his audience. 'Greetings to all you initiates. You haven't been on the journey for long, but I know from your tutors and sponsors that you're making progress. Keep it up and soon you'll start reaping the rewards.'

Galíndez stared out of the corner of her eye at the man's hand, resting on the lectern, noticing the light playing on the gold ring on his finger. Furtively, she glanced at the person sitting on her left and saw a woman's hands, clasped on her lap. Once more, the glimmer of gold on her finger. Galíndez lowered her head and peered at the ring. Plain gold, engraved with a two-headed serpent. Carefully, she slid her hands under the broad folds of her gown, hiding them from view.

'I have a disappointment for you,' the man on the platform continued. 'Xerxes can't be with us tonight, though he asks me to express his satisfaction at your progress.'

Galíndez waited for the applause to start, ready to join in. She heard only silence.

'And now to business.' The speaker waved to someone at the back of the room. A moment later, she heard footsteps as the armed men from the main gate filed in and took up position by the doors. A sudden thought: she was trapped.

The speaker gestured to the men guarding the exits. 'No one leaves until we've dealt with the next item.' He raised his voice. 'You all know loyalty is paramount to the *Centinelas*. In your initiation, you pledged to uphold the things most dear to us: respect for hierarchy and order, submission to the will of the central council. But above all, loyalty.'

He paused and slowly looked over the rows of initiates arranged in front of the platform, their heads lowered. 'You all swore to uphold that oath knowing that the price of disloyalty is death.'

No one spoke. From the silence, it seemed no one was breathing either.

'The disloyalty of one dishonours all,' the speaker said, threateningly. 'Any attempt to betray the *Centinelas* is an attack on the very foundations of our organisation. Because of the binding nature of the oath, betrayal is rare, but when it happens, it must be dealt with quickly and decisively as an example to others.' He leaned on the lectern for emphasis. 'Ladies and gentlemen, it gives me no pleasure to tell you that there is a traitor among you this evening.'

Sudden muted gasps. Galíndez was suddenly aware of her heart beating faster.

'This is a distasteful business,' the speaker said, 'but we must face up to it as we always face the problems which beset us. Sitting among you is a woman who has sullied our fellowship, contaminating it with her lies and deceit. A policewoman.' Fiercely, he gripped the sides of the lectern. 'With us on the platform tonight is an honoured guest, Señor Rodríguez. I must apologise to him for this unfortunate incident.'

The man in the linen suit got to his feet. 'Don't bother me, señor. In my country, we have the same thing happen from time to time.' He grinned, revealing several gold teeth. 'Let me take care of this person for you, as a gesture of goodwill.'

A sudden image of breakfast in Isabel's flat. Gentle flirting, laughing about the strength of her coffee. The pile of wanted notices lying on the table.

Her stomach churned as she remembered where she'd seen the man's face.

The speaker looked out grimly at the audience. 'I now ask the traitor to stand up, disrobe and come forward. We have a saying in the *Centinelas*: "You pay with your dead". By that, we mean that we deal with our enemies to the third generation. If the traitor doesn't come forward now, not only will she die, so too will three generations of her family.'

Galíndez felt her heart pounding against her shirt. *They know I'm here.* A trickle of sweat ran down her back.

'Ladies and gentlemen, the traitor is skulking among you. I have her name here.' He waved a sheet of paper. 'She can either come to the platform now, or we'll drag her there.'

Galíndez's head felt ready to explode. *They knew all along.*

At least she had the Glock. Maybe she could take a couple down with her. Anything was better than sitting here, bathed in sweat, waiting for them to come for her. Slowly, she slipped her hand inside the heavy robe, feeling the frantic beating of her heart as she closed her fingers on the Glock. Seventeen bullets would do some damage, though not enough to get her out of here. Still, it was better to go for them before they came for her. She tensed.

'I'm here.' A clear, tremulous voice.

Startled, Galíndez turned in the direction of the voice. She was not the only one. Dozens of faces peered out from the black cowls, watching a woman in the back row throw off her cloak. Hesitantly, she began walking towards the platform.

The woman was late twenties, early thirties maybe. Blonde, her hair tied back tight. As she stepped onto the platform, each step reverberated in Galíndez's gut as she approached the speaker.

The speaker gave her a venomous stare. 'You would be Teniente Luz Reverte?'

'Yes.' A faint tremor in her voice.

'One of your colleagues told us you were coming here.' The speaker imparted the information with malicious pleasure. 'You were doomed the moment you got in your car.'

Teniente Reverte gasped. More from disappointment than surprise, Galíndez guessed. The sudden realisation she was alone, without any chance of help.

'You have children, *Teniente*?' The speaker smiled, enjoying the moment.

'Yes.' The terror in her voice was unmistakable now.

'How many?'

Galíndez wanted to scream. The bastard was prolonging things deliberately.

Her voice cracked. 'A girl and a boy.' She looked down, trying to compose herself.

Galíndez took deep slow breaths, wondering what she was going to do. There could be no fighting her way out of this. The moment she decided to act, she was dead.

Or she could do nothing.

At the rear of the platform, she saw the man in the lightweight suit get to his feet. His name suddenly came to her: Joaquín Rodríguez aka 'The Hammer of Reynosa'. Wanted by the FBI, DEA and the Mexican government. She remembered what she'd said to Isabel: *They call him the Hammer for a reason.*

The speaker stepped away from Teniente Reverte. 'You might like to pray, *Teniente*.'

The lieutenant let her head fall forward. Galíndez could see her shaking as she tried to contain her emotions. She was trying to die with dignity.

The Mexican came slowly across the platform. One arm hung at his side. As he turned, Galíndez saw what he held in his hand and something sour rose in her throat.

Teniente Reverte was fighting back tears. In the ominous silence, Galíndez heard the stammered words of her prayer. 'Hail, Mary, full of grace...'

Behind her, the Hammer of Reynosa's arm rose, drawing

muffled gasps from the audience as the claw hammer swung through the air. The blow knocked the lieutenant to the floor, though she was still conscious when the second blow struck.

For what seemed for ever, Galíndez listened to her screams as the Mexican rained blows down on her. She kept her head lowered, grateful now for the cowl as she tried to shut out the sounds from the platform. Finally, they stopped.

'Initiates, look up, please.' The speaker's voice.

Galíndez raised her eyes and saw the *teniente*'s body lying by the lectern. There was more blood in the human body than she had imagined.

The Mexican was chatting with two of the men sitting at the rear of the platform.

'Remember this night,' the speaker said. 'Be instructed by this woman's death. Now go. You'll be informed of our next meeting in due course.'

The initiates began to file out, heading back down the passage to return their cowls. Galíndez hurried after them, not wanting to be the last to leave.

There was a queue at the cloakroom. Further down the passage, she saw a sign: WC. Once inside the small cubicle, she pulled off the heavy cowl and splashed her face with water. Outside, the initiates were starting to leave the building. She glanced at her watch. The sun would be setting soon. If she could find a door or window open, maybe she could slip away into the night. Finding Sancho would have to wait till another day.

Quietly, she went down the passage, away from the refectory and its gory secret. A few metres along, she saw an arched entrance and her hopes lifted. As she got nearer, she saw the great double doors with their heavy latches and double locks. There was no getting out this way. To her right was a simple wooden door with a sign above the lintel: CHAPEL. It was worth a try. She pushed open the door and slipped inside.

The chapel was huge. Dominating one wall was a large medieval fireplace with ornate andirons supporting a pyramid of great logs.

On the far wall, a huge stained-glass window depicted the martyr-
dom of a young woman lying on the ground next to a cross, her
naked body draped with a cloak across her waist, a vast swirl of red
hair around her head.

The evening sun flooded through the multicoloured glass in a
torrent of vibrant light, leaving the rest of the hall in shadow. As
Galíndez glanced at the rear of the chapel, she saw doors. Some
sort of exit, by the look of it.

Something behind her moved and she spun round, raising a
hand to shield her eyes from the kaleidoscopic light shining
through the window.

'*Buenas tardes, señorita.*' A deep, sonorous voice.

Galíndez looked up, still shielding her eyes with her hand.

'That's Santa Eulalia you're admiring, young lady. Her window
is one of the greatest jewels in this monastery. I often contemplate
it at this hour.'

Squinting, she could just make out the priest, silhouetted
against the stained glass. 'It's a little difficult to talk like this,
Monseñor. I can hardly see you.'

'There's a chair just in front of you if you'd care to sit down.'

She moved forward, one arm outstretched, feeling for the chair.
Once seated, she looked up again. The priest was a tall shadow
figure against the radiant light.

'I was looking for the exit, *Monseñor*. I seem to be lost.'

'So many people are these days, señorita. That's because they
have no faith. You could do worse than emulate Santa Eulalia. She
refused to deny her faith and was put to death by fire, hooks and
the scourge. The flesh was ripped from her body with pincers yet
she stayed true to her faith. Which of us can truly say we'd stay true
to our beliefs in those circumstances?'

She felt a dull throb in her temples. The feeling she got just
before one of her seizures.

'You're young enough to repent, Señorita Galíndez, though I
doubt you will. It's in the nature of those with your perverse nature
to reject spiritual advice.'

A sudden silence. 'How do you know my name, *Monseñor*?'

'God knows everything, my child. All those who go against the laws of nature are known to him, though whether they're forgiven is another matter. Repentance is what you should be thinking about now. How to atone for your sinful ways.'

'I asked how you know my name.'

A deep chuckle. 'Our paths have crossed before.'

'Not in church, they haven't. In any case, what do you know about my sinful ways?'

The sun was setting now and the angle of the light began to shift.

'The last time we met, you weren't quite so haughty.'

Galíndez squinted into the poly-coloured light. 'What are you talking about?'

'You pleaded,' the priest went on. 'When you weren't screaming, that is. Splayed on that wooden pallet like Santa Eulalia there.'

The dying rays of the sun rose higher, lifting the blinding patterns of light from her eyes. She saw the detail of the stained-glass window, the small panes of leaded glass, the great grey stones of the wall, the worn tiles on the floor below. And the priest standing by the window, the final rays of the sun around his head, like the halo of a dark angel, the pistol glinting in his hand. 'We should have killed you there and then, without relying on that Bulgarian inbred.'

Her eyes widened. 'Guzmán?'

The sound of the shot was magnified by the walls of the chapel.

Galíndez hit the floor, rolling as she tugged the Glock from her belt. Panting with anger, she raised herself into a crouch, the pistol held two-handed.

Footsteps in the darkness, a sudden oblong of pale light as a door opened at the side of the stained-glass window. Even as Galíndez tried to aim, the door slammed and she heard the key turn in the lock. Outside, shouts echoed along the passageway. Sounds of people running, coming closer. She had a sudden image of the Hammer of Reynosa, the bloody weapon in his hand as he chatted to the men on the platform, laughing.

She turned and ran to the doors at the back of the chapel. At the centre of them, she saw the large key in an ancient lock. She seized the key with both hands, the rusty metal sharp and painful as she twisted it furiously. Behind her, fists banged on the chapel door. Desperately, she twisted the key again and this time the door opened.

As she stepped out into the deepening shadows, Galíndez paused to lock the door and then hurled the key into a patch of dry scrub. Then she ran, trying to orient herself in the dusk. Ahead of her, the hillside was lined with trees, sharp silhouettes against the night sky. Further away, she saw the lights of the bar where her car was parked. There was only one thing to do now. Bail out: get back to the car and put some distance between her and the *Centinelas*.

She set off across the hillside, stumbling as she tried to keep the lights of the bar in sight. Behind her, she heard faint shouts. Somewhere to her right something moved and she spun towards it, aiming the Glock. And then a furious rustling of branches as a startled owl flapped upwards into the night sky.

Galíndez kept moving. Five minutes, ten at most, and she could be driving back to Madrid. She just had to stay calm, though that was difficult on this darkened hillside as she tripped and stumbled over the rocky ground, sharp branches clawing at her face and clothes. She slowed and moved more cautiously. No point rushing and breaking an ankle.

The blow hit her in the stomach, driving the air from her lungs. She fell, clutching her belly as she hit the ground, her lungs burning as if she would never breathe again. A hand closed on her wrist and twisted her arm behind her back. The pain was excruciating and she fought to keep herself from crying out.

'Gotcha,' Sancho whispered.

CHAPTER 17

MADRID 1982, PENSIÓN PARAÍSO, CALLE DEL CARMEN

Guzmán was just finishing his breakfast when Daniela came into the dining room.

'Can't you wear something quieter?' he grumbled. 'Those shoes make you sound like a mule.'

'There's a gentleman to see you in reception, Señor Ramirez,' Daniela said, tidying her hair with her hand. 'He's very good-looking, I must say.'

'Tell him I'll be right down.' Daniela took off her apron before she went, he noticed. Clearly, the girl was awash with hormones. He decided to have a word with her father later.

Back in his room, he put on his shoulder holster and cocked the Browning before going downstairs.

Javier Benavides was sitting by the window, leafing through one of the faded magazines. As he saw Guzmán coming down the stairs, he jumped to his feet, greeting him like an old friend.

Guzmán was more restrained. 'To what do I owe this pleasure, Señor Benavides?'

The lawyer lifted a large brown paper package from the floor and laid it on top of the ancient magazines on the table. 'The payment for your code, *Comandante*. Eight million pesetas, just as we agreed. The rest of the payments will be made to your bank account on the first of every month. Perhaps you'd like to count it?'

Guzmán wanted to count it very much but decided it would be bad form. 'I'll fetch the code,' he said, reaching for the parcel.

'Can I get the gentleman a coffee?' Daniela called from behind the desk.

Guzmán stared at her in surprise. She had changed into a dress, combed her hair and put on make-up. This thing with her hormones was getting out of control. The old man would need to think about marrying her off before she took matters into her own hands.

Benavides gave her a dazzling smile. 'That's very kind, señorita.'

Guzmán went up to his room and locked the door. Then he ripped open the package and stared at the wads of bills in their cashier's wrappers. Quickly, he knelt by the nightstand and lifted the floorboards before transferring the money to the dusty space below. Once that was done, he pressed the floorboards back in place and went downstairs with the leather case containing the code machine.

Benavides looked at the sleek metal encryption device, entranced for a moment, before Guzmán closed the case. 'This is exactly what we need,' he said, as they shook hands. 'You've done a marvellous job, *Comandante*. I believe this will make our communications untouchable.' He got up, ready to leave, and then paused, his artificially tanned face suddenly serious. 'Now we've concluded our business, it would be better for all concerned if you were to leave Madrid. Within the next four days, say?'

'I don't like people setting deadlines for me, Señor Benavides.'

A nonchalant shrug. 'That instruction comes from above, *Comandante*. Now you've got the money, there's no reason to hang around. Four days: after that, things could become unhealthy for you.'

'Don't worry about my health,' Guzmán growled.

'Believe me, I won't.' Benavides picked up the leather case and left.

He watched the lawyer go out into the street. Four days then. That was enough time to complete the job for Gutiérrez, collect his money and take off before Benavides discovered the code machine he'd bought was not quite complete. Certainly it was genuine, and it was definitely unique, though it was missing a couple of key features that would soon become apparent with use. Still, those features might form the basis of a subsequent trans-action, though one Guzmán would conduct at a distance.

There was no use worrying about that now and he set off to the Plaza del Callao in search of a taxi.

MADRID, OCTOBER 1982, BRIGADA ESPECIAL HEADQUARTERS, CALLE DEL DOCE DE OCTUBRE

One of Gutiérrez's men showed Guzmán down a flight of stairs to the meeting room. The room was impeccably –and expensively – decorated. No wonder the accountants had been set loose on Gutiérrez's finances. Even a casual glance revealed new heights of ostentation. Gutiérrez had clearly been spending like a gypsy on payday.

Gutiérrez was sitting at the far end of the table. His black pinstripe suit gave him the appearance of an undertaker. That was appropriate for a number of reasons, Guzmán thought. There was something wrong, he realised, though he did not ask what. Instead, he waited in silence, knowing it would annoy Gutiérrez.

'Have you gone mad?' Gutiérrez said, finally. He saw Guzmán's blank expression. 'I'm talking about the student.'

Guzmán frowned. 'What student?'

'The Irish student, Michael Riley.'

'Has he complained? I only broke his fucking tape recorder. Twenty years ago I'd have broken his legs.'

'He hasn't complained to anyone,' Gutiérrez muttered. 'Not in this life anyway.'

Guzmán raised an eyebrow. 'He's dead?'

'He was tortured first.' Gutiérrez's shoulders heaved with the effort of breathing.

'He was a devious little bastard,' Guzmán said. 'He said he was working on a university project about the Civil War and tried to get me talking so he could tape it.'

'And you killed him for that? After all I said about keeping a low profile?'

'I smashed his tape recorder and threw him into the street.

He walked away in one piece.' Guzmán narrowed his eyes. 'When did this happen anyway?'

'Yesterday.' Gutiérrez pushed a black-and-white photograph across the table.

Guzmán stared at the photograph. The picture showed Riley bound to a chair, his mouth wide open, straining for a breath that never came. It had not been an easy death, that was clear. There was a large cut down his chest and his face was dark and congested, no doubt due to the wire garrotte embedded in his throat. Most unpleasant, Guzmán thought. Even less pleasant was that his name was scrawled on the wall behind the dead student in large letters.

'I take it my name was written in his blood?' Guzmán said.

'The police think he managed to write it just before he died.'

'That means the fucking police are cretins, just as you are if you believe it,' Guzmán snapped. 'His hands are tied so how could he write anything?' He glowered at Gutiérrez. 'Frankly, I'm surprised you didn't notice that.'

'But if you didn't kill him, who did?'

'Given the melodramatic touch of writing my name in his blood, I'd say someone's trying to damage my reputation. The *Centinelas*, probably.'

'We can do without incidents like this,' Gutiérrez muttered. 'The situation's explosive enough as it is.'

'Speaking of explosions,' Guzmán said, 'that brings me to the bomb in your warehouse yesterday. I spoke to the *policía nacional* last night. They gave the remains of the car a good going-over. Every part of the bomb that they could identify was Italian. Extremely well made, like a craftsman, they said.'

Gutiérrez fell silent.

'It's him, isn't it?' Guzmán said, angrily. 'All that shit about him being in retirement or consumed by grief in a monastery. That was all lies: it was the Italian. And since the bastard only works for money, you have to wonder who's funding him.' Furiously, he drove his fist into the palm of his other hand. 'I'd say it's the *Centinelas*.'

Gutiérrez kneaded his forehead, deep in thought. 'I think you're right. There've been several bombings this week that I thought were the work of ETA, trying to disrupt the election. But they could just as easily have been his handiwork.'

'But how did he find the archive? We're the only ones who knew about it.'

'I don't know,' Gutiérrez sighed. 'But I do know he has to die, *Comandante*.'

'That's easy for you to say,' Guzmán sneered. 'Since it won't be you who has to do it. I want my pay-off first. You arrange that and I'll take care of the Italian.'

'You're sure you can do it?'

Guzmán clenched his fists. 'Of course, though I'll do it my way, this time.'

'Then perhaps this time you'll get it right,' Gutiérrez said. 'I'll arrange the payment.'

'And the files will need to be moved somewhere safe.'

'Leave that to me, I'll find somewhere even he can't get at them.'

Guzmán glanced at his watch. 'I've got to go. The lads are off to another archive today and I don't want them to fuck it up this time.'

'I told you my plan would work,' Gutiérrez wheezed. 'Our war records will disappear and the *Centinelas* will be destroyed by theirs.'

Guzmán got to his feet. 'Don't count your chickens. Not now there's an added complication.'

'The solution isn't complicated,' Gutiérrez said wearily. 'Just kill him.'

Guzmán's reply was masked by the sound of the door as it slammed behind him.

MADRID, OCTOBER 1982, PENSIÓN PARAÍSO, CALLE DEL CARMEN

As Guzmán came up the stairs of the *pensión*, the TV was still blaring out behind the bead curtain. Daniela was sitting at the desk, reading a magazine. She looked up as she heard him come in. 'Señor Ramírez, you're back early.'

'I need to talk to you,' Guzmán said.

'Is anything wrong?'

'Not at all.' Guzmán motioned for her to sit with him at the table. 'I know you and your father have tried hard to keep the *pensión* going,' he said, 'but look at it: the whole place needs renovating.'

Daniela laughed. 'You think I don't know? But we can't afford it, it's that simple. Lots of people have pointed out what's wrong with it, but there's never anyone who can help us put things right.' Her eyes flashed with tears.

'You can't keep going like this,' Guzmán said. 'One day, something will go wrong and you won't be able to afford the repairs. You'll have to close down.'

'We get by, Señor Ramirez,' said Daniela. 'Maybe if my father hadn't fought against Franco he'd have been able to get a job and do the place up. But things are what they are. He couldn't make money because of his injuries and his war record so it was down to Mamá to keep things going. Now it's my turn to run the place and that's what I'm going to do.'

'I admire a hard worker,' Guzmán said. 'That's why I'm going to help you.'

Daniela frowned. 'How?'

'I've come into some money so I'm going to give you the cash to do the place up. Two million pesetas, to be exact. I want you and your father to make the place a going concern like you always wanted.'

'Are you serious?' She wiped something from her eye. 'I don't know what to say.'

'Don't say anything. But in return, I want you to quit your job at El Topless.'

She raised a hand to her mouth, trying to stop the tears. 'Of course I will.'

'Then I'll sort out the money and get it into your bank account in the next day or so,' Guzmán said. 'You can decorate the rooms and make them more comfortable. If you want, you could even put a window in your father's room.'

Daniela gave him a dubious look. 'I can't do all that on my own.'

'You won't have to.' Guzmán smiled. 'I've found someone who can help. He's experienced in hotel work and he comes well recommended. I'll get him.' He went to the front door and called to someone waiting outside.

Daniela looked up as the dwarf came in. A smart dwarf, wearing a well-cut suit though it had clearly been owned by a couple of generations before him. '*Buenas tardes*, señorita. Leonidas Espartero at your service. Señor Ramirez has told me all about your establishment and suggested I might have the impudence to approach you regarding work.'

'I've known this gentleman a long time,' Guzmán said. 'He's a good worker and you can afford his wages, though whatever you do, don't play cards with him.'

Espartero gave Daniela a sheepish grin. 'We all have our little vices, señorita.'

She offered Espartero a seat. 'Would you like a coffee, señor?' His reply was interrupted as the phone rang. Daniela went to the desk and answered. 'Pensión Paraíso.' She looked puzzled. 'Guzmán? No, señor, there's no one of that name here.'

Guzmán snatched the phone from her hand. He motioned towards the curtain of glass beads. 'Go and introduce Señor Espartero to your father, will you?'

The beads rattled as Daniela ushered Espartero into the other room.

Guzmán lifted the phone to his ear. 'Who is this?'

At the other end of the line, he heard faint crackling. And then a voice, low and distant, speaking to him from across the years. A harsh voice, taut with threat. 'Who do you think, *Comandante*?'

It was true then: he was back. There might have been a moment when Guzmán wondered if he was mistaken, but that thought was dispelled now. 'What do you want?'

'Oh, many things, my friend. Justice, freedom for the oppressed.'

'Bullshit,' Guzmán said. 'You've always been out for yourself.'

The voice grew colder. 'There are accounts to settle. The innocent won't rest until that's done.'

'She wasn't innocent,' Guzmán said. 'She was made from the same stuff as you.'

'An eye for an eye, *Comandante*. That's how it works.'

'So what do you want? Pistols at dawn?'

'I have some information about Alicante.'

'What information?'

'There are things you ought to know.' A mocking tone in his voice now. 'Shall we say the Bar Navarra on Calle de San Bernardino at two tomorrow? I'm sure you know it.'

'I know you're a dead man.'

'Until tomorrow then. *Ciao.*' The line went dead.

Guzmán slammed down the phone. Without doubt, it was a trap. No one in their right mind would turn up for such an assignation, knowing what he knew about the man. But then, no one in their right mind would have done the things Guzmán had over the years. Which was why he would be there, at two o'clock in the Bar Navarra.

But the Italian would have known that, the moment Guzmán picked up the phone.

MADRID, OCTOBER 1982, GUARDIA CIVIL HEADQUARTERS

The squad were packing their kit into a truck as Guzmán arrived. Galíndez gave him an embarrassed look and quickly made himself scarce.

Ochoa left the men and came over to join Guzmán. 'What's the target today, boss?'

'Another archive, Corporal, what else did you expect?' Guzmán took out his cigarettes and offered the packet to Ochoa. He took one and leaned forward to get a light.

'I never expect anything, sir. That way I'm never disappointed.'

'That's ridiculous,' Guzmán snorted. 'I never met a man as disappointed as you.'

Ochoa shrugged. 'If you say so.'

Guzmán took a folded piece of paper from his pocket and handed it to Ochoa. 'This is today's target. It should be straight-forward.'

Ochoa studied the paper for a few moments. 'I agree with you, sir.'

'Try to smile when you say that, Corporal,' Guzmán sighed. 'Let's get started, before you become even more disappointed.'

The men lined up at the rear of the truck and Guzmán went to speak to them. Galíndez was sporting a few cuts and bruises, he noticed.

'I'll keep this short,' Guzmán said. 'We're off to an archive near Torrejón airbase. It's a little different from anything you've come across.'

'Why's that, sir?' Quique shouted.

'If you'd let me speak, I'd tell you, kid. Shut up.'

'Sorry, sir.'

'The archive's underground,' Guzmán said, noticing their expressions suddenly change. 'And it's huge,' he continued. 'So make sure you stick together. No one goes wandering off unless I tell them.' He noticed Galíndez gazing into the distance, bored. 'Got that, Galíndez?'

'Don't worry about me, boss.' A faint smirk on his lips. 'I can look after myself.'

Guzmán narrowed his eyes. Galíndez clearly thought that one lucky kick meant he could get away with such sneering innuendo with impunity. He wouldn't think it for much longer.

'There's another thing you need to bear in mind,' Guzmán went on. 'The archive is awash with armed guards.' That was a lie, though it had the intended effect as the men climbed into the truck, suddenly preoccupied. All but Ochoa, Guzmán noticed. He was probably looking forward to being shot at. It would give him something to complain about later.

MADRID, OCTOBER 1982, PENSIÓN PARAÍSO,
CALLE DEL CARMEN

Daniela hummed a tune to herself as she polished the reception desk. It was a stupid little song about dancing birds that had been played throughout the World Cup. Stupid or not, it was hard to get it out of her mind.

Behind the glass beads, her father was taking a nap, exhausted since Daniela had allowed him a glass of wine to celebrate Señor Ramirez's generous investment.

She still had no idea why Señor Ramirez was going to help them. For all she knew, he travelled through Spain handing out money to those he deemed worthy of help. She'd read of those things in *¡Hola!* though she'd never met anyone who'd received such assistance. For the hundredth time, she imagined the transformation of the *pensión*: light, airy colours, comfortable seats for people to sit and watch the street. New magazines to read, a modern bathroom and nice wallpaper in the dining room. She would even have Señor Espartero to assist her.

Lost in her daydream, Daniela was unaware of the man standing a metre away on the other side of the desk. Finally, he ran out of patience.

'*Scusi?*'

She looked up, startled. 'I'm so sorry, I was miles away.'

'It doesn't matter.' The tone of his voice implied that it did.

He was quite handsome, Daniela noticed. Close-cropped grey hair, an immaculately trimmed beard and a pristine suit. 'How can I help you, señor?'

'I'm looking for a friend who's staying here: Leo Guzmán.'

Daniela shook her head. 'There's no one of that name here.'

'You're sure?' A sudden edge to his voice.

'Definitely. We haven't had anyone called Guzmán staying here.'

'I see.' A last, cold look. 'Thanks for your trouble.'

'It was no trouble, señor.'

'No, it wasn't.' He turned away and hurried down the steps.

The man's sports car was parked outside the *pensión*. As he went towards it, he saw a blonde woman in the driver's seat. He tugged open the door and got in beside her. 'Do I know you?'

The woman's smile was almost as cold as his. 'Not yet. But I think you'd like to.'

'I'm not very good with women, I should warn you.'

'That's what I heard. Rather violent, in fact, to put it mildly.'

'So you realise the risk you've taken getting into my car without being invited?'

'I think you'll overlook my forwardness on this occasion.'

He lifted his hands in mock surrender. 'So what is it you want?'

The blonde woman started the engine. 'Was Guzmán in there?'

'He's been there all right, though they denied it. I wanted to leave him a message.' He shrugged. 'So now, I'll send him a different kind of message. Him and that little whore behind the desk. She lied about not knowing him and I don't like women lying to me.' He narrowed his eyes. 'So who are you? Not the police, I hope, for your sake.'

'Far from it,' Paloma Ibañez said. 'But you'll be interested in the people I work for.'

MADRID 1982, TORREJÓN AIRBASE

Guzmán peered through his binoculars, watching the comings and goings around the airbase. Further along the road, past the perimeter fence, was a side road leading into a concrete structure, the entrance blocked by a red-and-white barrier, manned by two military policemen. Beyond the barrier, the road sloped down into darkness.

'That's where we go in,' Guzmán said.

Quique squirmed uncomfortably, trapped as usual between Guzmán and the gear lever. 'Got you, boss.'

'I was talking to Corporal Ochoa.'

'Sorry, sir.'

'Are we going to force our way in?' Fuentes asked.

'Of course not. And we're not going to take out an advertisement in the local paper either.' Guzmán took a sheaf of papers from his pocket. 'These documents are signed by General Ortiz, they say we're here to collect personnel records needed by the admin department at HQ. Something about calculating pensions, I believe.'

'That'll be me in another month,' Ochoa said. For once, he didn't sound disappointed.

Guzmán banged the dash with his fist. 'Let's go.'

As they neared the barrier, a cluster of signs warned of the dangers of trespassing. The truck slowed to a halt in front of the red-and-white barrier and a military policeman emerged from one of the sentry boxes to check their papers.

'That's fine, *Comandante*.' The MP waved to a man inside the glass-fronted booth to lift the barrier. 'Drive down the ramp and leave the vehicle in the parking area. You'll find the lifts on the far wall.'

The barrier started to rise before Guzmán could thank him. Ochoa put the truck in gear and drove down the ramp. The daylight rapidly faded as they went into the subterranean parking area.

'It's like a huge cavern,' Quique muttered, twisting in his seat to look at the great stone walls around them.

'That's what it is, kid.' Guzmán nodded. 'Franco had it built so he and the government could hide down here if the Russians dropped an atomic bomb. Park over there, near the lifts,' he ordered, pointing to a pair of big metal doors set into the wall. For once, Ochoa obeyed without comment.

The squad climbed out and lined up by the lift doors. Guzmán gave each of them a document with the details of where the files were located. 'I'll give you thirty minutes,' he said. 'So set your watches when you get out the lift. Collect the files on your list and then make your way back to the lift and stay there until we're all ready to leave. Got that?'

As the squad mumbled their assent, Guzmán punched the button by the lift doors. Far off, they heard the slow metallic grumble of the winch mechanism as the lift started to rise. Finally, the doors opened and the squad filed in.

A few minutes later, they stepped out into another great, man-made cavern. The ceiling was much lower here, creating a claustrophobic atmosphere. Ahead of them, serried ranks of long metal shelves stretched away into the gloom. A few weak spotlights in the roof illuminated the archive with a baleful half light.

'Get started,' Guzmán ordered, setting his watch. 'Get back here in thirty minutes.'

He listened to the men's footsteps fading as they went down the darkened aisles. Once he could no longer hear them, he took a paper from his pocket and unfolded it. As he examined the paper, Guzmán shook his head, rebuking himself for not having thought of this before. In fact, the idea had occurred when he was talking to Ignacio in the Almeja, the night the old man was killed. His ancient informer's words came back to him: *I remember how organised you were at Calle Robles. You had everything on file back then.*

So very true, Guzmán recalled. They logged every operation, no matter how serious or trivial. Naturally it was not done to attribute blame, merely to comply with procedures and to demonstrate the job had been completed. You did the job, left the dead behind and then returned to the office to complete the paperwork. And then after, the drinking and the whores.

All those operations, all of them secret, carefully guarded from prying eyes. But the files were not hidden from everyone. Not, for example, someone who possessed a copy of Franco's list. The list Guzmán now held in his hand. He looked at the reference number again. The weak lights barely illuminated the faded typewritten heading:

Alicante 1965 GZ986443R53/S92

A faint sense of satisfaction: the hunter scenting his prey.

He made his way to row 53 and started down it, looking for section 92. From time to time, the narrow aisle between the shelves was crossed by horizontal walkways, giving the feeling of being on an enormous chessboard. At each intersection, a square of card was attached to a shelf, bearing the reference number. And there it was, *S92*. Guzmán knelt by the shelves, and ran his finger along the spines of the cardboard files. Of those, there were many, and it took several minutes to find the section beginning with 'G'. More time passed as he moved along the files, GA, GH, GL. Impatiently, he got to his feet and examined the top shelf of yet another section, poring over the titles, dogged by a sullen concern that the file probably didn't exist. After all, these documents recorded success, not failure. And no one had ever considered what happened at Alicante to be a success.

GZ. He stared at the file, checking its serial number. Slowly, he eased it from the shelf, dusting off the cover to reveal the title:

> Brigada Especial: Top Secret
> (Restricted Access)
> Report on the incident at Llanto del Moro,
>   Alicante
> September 25th 1965
> *Classification: Top Secret [Permanent]*

His eyes narrowed as he saw the file was still classified as secret. All files were, in the sense that access to them was restricted, but this one had permanent status. It was hard to understand why.

Somewhere in the archive, he heard the dull grating of the lift doors, the metallic grinding as the lift ascended. From another direction, he heard muffled footsteps. Possibly his squad. Possibly not. He pulled his shirt loose and put the file under it, tucking the file under his belt to hold it in place.

The footsteps were coming closer, soft and measured. A sudden thought that it might be Galíndez sent adrenalin surging through him. That was unfinished business, as far as he was concerned.

In the war, there had been men like Galíndez who challenged his authority, thought they could slight him with impunity. Those men were long dead. Instinctively, he dropped to a crouch and ambled forward, easing the Browning from its holster. After a few more steps he paused, realising the problems killing Galíndez would bring. General Ortiz wouldn't take kindly to losing one of his men, especially in these circumstances. And the sound of a shot might alert the military police. The last thing Guzmán needed was to draw attention to his squad's activities in the archive. There was nothing for it, he would have to deal with Galíndez later. But for now, the least he could do was give the bastard a surprise.

The footsteps were very close now, coming down one of the horizontal aisles. Guzmán positioned himself against a row of shelving, bracing himself as the man came past the end of the aisle. In one fluid movement, Guzmán moved forward and pressed the Browning to the man's head. He sensed the fear immediately: that was only to be expected, he'd always had Galíndez down as a coward. And then the weak light fell over the man's face and it was Guzmán's turn to be surprised as the fat bouncer from El Topless stared at him with horror.

'One word and you're dead,' Guzmán whispered. 'Got that?' He kept a grip on the man's collar as he marched him to the lift. As he walked, an idea came to him, something that would remind Galíndez and the rest of the squad who they were dealing with.

The men were standing by the lift, clutching their bundles of files. He saw their looks of surprise as he came out of the shadows, pushing the fat man in front of him.

'Who's this?' Ochoa asked.

'He works for Ricci.' Guzmán shoved the man with his pistol. 'That's right, isn't it?'

'Yes, señor,' the fat man stammered.

'So what are you doing here?' Another shove with the Browning, harder now. Guzmán saw the concerned looks on the men's faces. That was good. They would all learn from what was about to happen. Guzmán pushed the fat man to his knees. 'I asked what you're doing here.'

'I can't say.'

He cocked the Browning even though it was not technically necessary: all he had to do was squeeze the trigger. But the sound of a gun being cocked while pressed to a man's head was a powerful inducement to comply.

'I'm looking for something.' The words tumbled from the fat man's lips. 'Señor Ricci was asked to find it and he sent me.'

'And who asked Ricci for it?'

'I can't say,' the fat man said. 'I wasn't supposed to know.'

'But you do.' Guzmán smacked the man over the head with the pistol. 'Who?'

'Paloma Ibañez.'

Guzmán's eyes lit up. 'And what did she want?'

'A file, señor. On you.' The fat man took a paper from his shirt pocket. Guzmán snatched it from him and stared at the details. They seemed familiar, and no wonder: these were the same reference numbers on the file hidden under his shirt. Still, he would worry about Paloma Ibañez later. The squad still needed a lesson.

Guzmán screwed up the paper and put it in his pocket. 'You know why she wanted it?'

'No idea, señor,' the fat man spluttered. 'I'm only the errand boy.'

Guzmán slugged him again with the pistol, sending him sprawling. 'So what do I do with this joker?' he asked, glowering at the squad.

'Lock him up, boss,' Fuentes said. 'Bring charges against him.'

'Knock him about a bit,' Galíndez muttered. There was no smile on his face now. There wouldn't be for some time, Guzmán reckoned.

'Make him walk back to Madrid,' Quique suggested.

Guzmán kept an eye on the fat man as he struggled to his knees. 'Corporal Ochoa?'

'You already know what you're going to do, sir,' Ochoa said, turning away.

Guzmán took hold of his belt and slowly pulled the wire from its hiding place. A long wire, the ends wrapped with electrical tape.

The fat man was on his knees, his head hanging forward. Guzmán looped the wire over his head and dragged it around his throat, pushing his knee into the man's back as he pulled the wire taut.

The effect on the squad was electric. He saw their pale faces and gaping mouths as he pulled the garrotte tighter with all his strength. With a huge effort, he twisted the man round to face Galíndez. 'This is how it's done,' he snarled, giving the wire another violent twist as he pushed the man closer, so close that his flailing hands clutched at Galíndez's uniform. That was too much for Galíndez and he screamed as Guzmán shoved the dying man into him again and again, until his struggling stopped. Finally, he let go of the wire and stepped back, letting the dead man sag to the floor at Galíndez's feet.

Galíndez slumped back against the wall, covering his face with his hands as he sobbed. He was still weeping when Guzmán punched him, a hard jab in the belly that drove the air from his lungs, sending him falling onto the corpse at his feet.

Guzmán was panting from the exertion, rubbing his hands where the wire had cut them. 'That, gentlemen, is how you kill someone.' He turned to Ochoa. 'Get the men back up to the truck. Not you, Galíndez.' Guzmán waited until the rest of the squad were in the lift and then pressed the up button. The doors slid to and the lift started to ascend.

'Do we understand each other now?' Guzmán said.

'Absolutely, *Comandante*.'

'Then I reckon we've time for a few drinks in El León once we've delivered these files, what do you think?'

'Whatever you say, sir.'

Guzmán nodded. 'Keep saying that and you'll do all right.'

MADRID, OCTOBER 1982, CAFÉ LEÓN, CALLE SOTOMAYOR

Guzmán leaned closer to make himself heard about the noise of the bar. 'Nothing like a killing to bind men together,' he bellowed into Ochoa's ear.

'It did the trick, sir, that's for sure.' Ochoa tried to grab a bottle from the bar and sent it crashing onto the tiled floor. He blinked, surprised at his lack of coordination.

Things were getting raucous. But that was good, Guzmán knew. First the stick then the carrot. Discipline had to be enforced sometimes and the fat man – unluckily for him – had arrived just in time to provide the lesson.

'There's the one who got away,' Ochoa said, looking across the crowded bar at Carmen who was engaged in conversation with one of General Ortiz's staff officers.

'Tell me about it.' Guzmán poured more brandy into his glass and then attempted to do the same for Ochoa. Most of it went down Ochoa's uniform. Neither of them noticed.

'It's a tragedy to think I'll never fuck her,' Guzmán said, staring bitterly at Carmen.

'And they say romance is dead,' Ochoa laughed.

'Who says so?' Guzmán demanded, suddenly belligerent. 'Christ, I've had a few too many. I'm off home. No point hanging round watching her if it's never going to happen.'

'Unattainable. That's what she is, sir.' Ochoa's eyes were starting to close.

'Thanks for those words of encouragement,' Guzmán muttered as he pushed his way through the crowd around the bar. The air was warm, thick with the smell of cooking. Above the clamour, he heard someone shout his name.

'*Comandante*, over here.'

It was Miguel Galíndez, his face flushed and sweaty, sitting at a table strewn with empty bottles and dirty plates. 'Sit down, *Comandante*, and have a drink.'

'I'm going in a minute,' Guzmán said, raising his voice to make himself heard. He saw one of the bottles was almost full. 'I'll have a glass of that.'

'There you go, boss.' Galíndez sloshed red wine into a glass and handed it to him. 'I hope we're OK now, sir? I should've apologised for the other day, I realise that.'

'Forget it.' There was something Galíndez wouldn't forget, he thought.

A figure emerged from the crowd and sat down next to Galíndez. Guzmán peered unsteadily at her over the top of his glass as he drank. The wine tasted sour.

'Sorry, *Comandante*.' Galíndez made an attempt to fill his glass and splashed most of it over the tablecloth. 'Let me introduce you. This is the missus.'

Señora Galíndez smiled. 'Nice to meet you, *Comandante*.'

'Nice to meet you too, Señora,' Guzmán said with polite formality to the woman he usually referred to as Lourdes.

Suddenly, the street was alive with men in dark suits, shepherding the protesting villagers down the street towards the church hall.

'May I ask what's going on, sir?' Villanueva said.

Carrero Blanco gestured at a white Ford Cortina parked by the church. 'See the man by that car? Go and introduce yourself. Maybe you can help with his operation.'

Villanueva stumbled as a man in a dark suit pushed past him. 'What operation?'

'I don't answer questions, Inspector.' Carrero Blanco turned away and went into the comisaría *with several of his men. Quickly, Villanueva sent Alberto after them with instructions to provide refreshments.*

As Villanueva approached the white Ford, a man in his shirt-sleeves was unloading things from the boot. As he got closer, Villanueva saw they were rifles. Other weapons too, pistols and a sub-machine gun.

The man came round the car. Big and muscular, another hard-faced man, though not like the men with Carrero Blanco. This was a different hardness. Frighteningly different. He crushed Villanueva's hand in his powerful grip. 'Guzmán, Brigada Especial.'

'The school bus is late,' Villanueva said, after he had introduced himself. 'I need to go and see if the kids need a lift back to the village.'

Guzmán looked at him curiously. 'Haven't they told you yet?'

Villanueva shook his head. 'Told me what?'

All his life, Villanueva would remember that moment, standing in the shade of the church, listening as Guzmán told him, quickly and concisely, what had happened. As he took in the information, Villanueva had a sudden clear insight: things were never going to be the same again in Llanto del Moro.

CHAPTER 18

MADRID, OCTOBER 2010, MONASTERIO DE SANTA EULALIA

'Keep still or I'll break your arm.'

Sancho knelt astride her, pinning her face down on the dry soil, unable to move without provoking a firestorm of pain in her arm.

'I'm going to let go of you now,' he growled. 'Then we're going to have a little chat.'

He released his grip on her arm and moved away from her. Galíndez sat up slowly, grimacing at the pain.

'Keep rubbing it, the pain will soon go.' Sancho sat with his back resting against a tree trunk, keeping his pistol pointed at her. 'I suppose that was you who fired that shot in the chapel?' He sighed. 'That wasn't a smart move, I have to tell you.'

'It was Guzmán, he recognised me.' She started to push hair away from her eyes but froze as he raised the pistol, pointing it at her face.

'Best not to make sudden moves like that, Ana.'

She put her hands back in her lap, slowly. 'Are you going to hand me over to that Mexican psychopath in there?'

'Of course not,' Sancho snorted. 'But you know what? Whoever sent that woman here killed her just as if they'd put a bullet in her head. Though a bullet would have been quicker. How did that make you feel, by the way, seeing as it was your fault?'

'Why was it my fault?'

'It's not rocket science, babe. You've been to see Inspector Villena, haven't you? That made him curious, so he sent her here to spy on the *Centinelas'* meeting. Unfortunately for her, she walked straight into a trap.'

'How do you know I'd been to see Villena?'

'Ramona called me right after you ran away from her S&M bar. She said she'd given you Villena's card.' His lips creased into a lewd smile. 'I didn't know you liked that sort of thing, by the way.'

'I just wanted to ask her some questions, that was all.'

'Oh yeah? She said you'd been there before.'

'I'm not discussing it with you. You're a murderer and you work for the *Centinelas* so that's enough to think about without you trying to take the piss out of me as well.'

'It's not a problem, I'm prepared to spend any amount of time winding you up.'

She carried on kneading her injured arm. 'Why?'

Sancho shrugged. 'Because I can't stand you. You're sanctimonious, opinionated and you keep fucking up my investigation.'

'That investigation stopped the moment you joined the *Centinelas*.'

'Not at all,' Sancho said. 'That was when it started. Anyway, what did Villena tell you about me?'

'That you were a good undercover cop who'd infiltrated the *Centinelas* and then disappeared.'

'That was it?' He waved the pistol at her. 'Didn't he say he'd sworn to get me back no matter what it took?'

'More or less.'

'And you bought it, of course? What kind of detective are you?'

'I'm a forensic investigator, if you must know.'

'Well, pardon me for my fucking inaccuracy, Dr Frankenstein.' He put the pistol on the ground by his side. 'What did you make of Villena?'

'He's a little strange. At first, he threatened me, though he said that was because he was so keen to get you back.'

'You want to know about Villena? Four years ago, he asked me to work undercover, collecting information on the *Centinelas*. After a few months, I reached a point where we almost had a case against several members of their central council.' He paused, suddenly troubled by the memory.

'Go on,' Galíndez said, impatiently.

'They sussed me. They grabbed me off the street and brought me here. For some reason, they didn't kill me. Instead, they decided to turn me so I'd work for them.'

'And you agreed?'

'I refused. I thought, what was the worst they could do?'

'And what did they do?'

'The worst.' His face was blank. 'They threw the lot at me.' He reached down and tugged his shirt up. 'See?'

'Jesus Christ.' She turned away, her hand over her mouth. 'How did they do that?'

'Hot irons, electric shocks, things much worse than anything we did to you. Beatings, kickings, brainwashing-type stuff. There was only one problem.'

'I know. You haven't got a brain.'

'Don't steal my punchlines, babe. Anyway, after a few months, I reached a stage where they thought I could be trusted. And once they started trusting me, I began collecting information on them again.'

'So that's what you meant about your investigation starting when you disappeared?'

'See? You're not so stupid after all. Anyway, it's time for me to go back to being a cop now.' He started to get to his feet.

'Wait,' Galíndez said. 'How did you come to be working with Guzmán?'

Sancho shrugged. 'He was hired to help the *Centinelas* search for something. They ordered me to help him.'

'What were the *Centinelas* looking for?'

'Something to do with a code. I don't know all the details, but there was a sword involved. They thought it might be somewhere called the Western Vault. We couldn't locate the vault, but when we started looking for the sword, you know what? Everything led back to one person.'

Galíndez frowned. 'Who was that?'

'You. That's why Guzmán tortured you. You're lucky I was able to get you out.'

She stared at him, outraged. 'You handed me over to that Bulgarian madman so he could kill me.'

'Well, yeah, if you're going to be picky about it. But I knew you could take him. Why do you think I got him to take you to a room with two bolts on the door? I knew you'd work something out – particularly since I'd cuffed your hands in front of you.' He grinned. 'See? I had faith in you, sweetheart.'

She shook her head, trying to take it in. 'How do I know I can trust you?'

'Because the alternative is that I leave you here and the *Centinelas* get hold of you.'

'You tortured me. I thought I was going to die.' Her eyes glinted with anger.

'So cross me off your Christmas card list, but honestly, right now we're better sticking together.' He picked up his pistol and shoved it into his belt. 'Where's your car?'

'Parked near the bar at the bottom of the hill.'

'Then we'll have to work our way down the hillside. We can't risk using the road. Just be careful not to trip and break something.'

Galíndez took an elastic band from her pocket and tied back her hair. 'You don't need to worry about me.'

'I won't, babe, believe me.'

She followed him through the shadows onto the steep hillside, moving slowly, trying not to slip on the dry shifting soil. After a few hundred yards, Sancho stopped and signalled to her to take cover behind a clump of stunted bushes. Somewhere below, they heard the rumble of engines. As they watched, a row of vehicles slowly came up the road, coming to a halt near the bar. Doors swung open and men jumped down onto the dirt road. In the beam of the vehicles' headlights, Galíndez saw dark uniforms and ski masks.

'Special forces,' she whispered. 'Villena must have sent them after the *Centinelas*.' She heard his gruff laugh. 'What's so funny?'

'Villena's inside that monastery right now. Who did you think gave the woman cop away?' He reached out and gripped her arm, hard. 'Who do you think betrayed me to them? Those guys down there aren't looking for the *Centinelas*. They're looking for us. Or, more accurately, they're looking for you.'

'Are you saying Villena's one of them?'

He sighed. 'Give the woman a cigar.'

'But why send a policewoman to spy on the *Centinelas*, if Villena's a *Centinela* himself?'

'God you're dumb.' Sancho sighed. 'It's not the first time this has happened. They do it to show the initiates what happens if they don't toe the line.'

Hidden among the harsh dry shrubs, they watched the policemen hurrying up the dirt road towards the monastery.

'Now's our chance,' Sancho whispered as he started to get up.

'Wait.' She put a hand on his shoulder. 'Look over there.'

He turned his gaze away from the policemen and peered down at the darkened road near the bar. Lines of light moved through the darkness in careful, methodical movements. After a couple of minutes, the lights started to move up the road.

Sancho nudged her. 'Look, those cops down there are joining the others. If we can get to your car, we're out of here.'

He led the way, stooping low, trying to avoid making noise. It took a while to get to the bottom of the hill and as they reached the road, Galíndez paused to wipe sweat from her eyes before carrying on.

'You start the car,' Sancho whispered. 'I'll cover the road in case they come back.'

She did as he said, keeping low, holding the Glock two-handed as she scanned the darkness around her. She reached the car and slid the key into the lock, wincing at the sound. She opened the door and then froze, listening intently to the silence. Further up the road, she saw Sancho lumbering into a clump of bushes and swore, realising he was too far away for her to attract his attention without shouting. Angrily, she made for the bushes, wishing they'd stuck together.

She tensed as she heard someone running towards her, their boots crunching on the dry ground. As she raised her pistol,

Sancho burst from the bushes. 'Get back to the car and start the fucking engine.'

Before she could move, the brilliant beam of a flashlight silhouetted Sancho from behind. She saw Villena's acne-scarred face, the raised pistol in his hand.

Galíndez raised the Glock, unable to shoot with Sancho between her and Villena. She called a warning but her voice was lost in the sound of the shot as Villena fired. Sancho grunted and fell face down onto the parched ground.

For Galíndez, time seemed to slow. She heard Sancho shouting, his voice thick with pain, telling her to go to the fucking car and get out of there. A few metres away, she saw Villena lift the flashlight as he aimed his pistol at Sancho again.

She fired three times. The shots rolled over the hillside in dry staccato echoes as Villena staggered back, his flashlight clattering on the parched ground. Keeping the pistol aimed, she moved towards him, saw his dazed expression turn to a snarl as he recognised her.

As Villena raised his pistol again, Galíndez squeezed the trigger. Villena pirouetted back, collapsing like a broken doll into the undergrowth. Behind him, another black-clad figure came out of the shadows. Galíndez fired once more and the man sank to his knees and pitched forward onto the baked earth.

Ears ringing, she hurried over to Sancho. 'Get up, for Christ's sake.' She seized his collar, pulling with both hands. 'Stand up, damn you, you've got to get to the car.'

Sancho groaned. 'I'm hurt bad, doll, you'd better leave me.'

'Like fuck I will.' She shoved the pistol into her belt and struggled to get him to his feet. 'Jesus, you're built like a gorilla.'

He grunted as he leaned against her for support. 'I knew you liked me.'

It seemed an eternity before they reached the car and even longer as she struggled to manoeuvre Sancho into the passenger seat. As she got behind the wheel, she saw clusters of flashlights raking the undergrowth further up the road. She started the engine, suddenly aware her hands were wet.

'Where are we going?' Sancho muttered, fumbling with his seat belt.

Galíndez accelerated down the dirt road, sending a rain of stones and dry soil rattling against the bodywork. 'I'm getting you to a hospital.'

'No, you're not. The medics will report a gunshot wound to the police straight away.'

'Where then?' When she glanced at him, she saw the black glint of blood.

He clutched his side as a spasm of pain lanced through him. 'Do I have to do all the thinking?'

She saw the lights of the motorway ahead and floored the pedal. 'My sports kit's on the back seat. Use it to stop the blood.'

Painfully, he followed her instructions and pressed a rolled-up sweatshirt to his side. He grunted as a fresh dart of pain shot through him and spat blood. 'Sorry about that.'

Galíndez shrugged. 'That's OK. You can clean it up later.'

'Listen,' Sancho said, 'I could black out at any time, so listen. The information I collected on the *Centinelas* is on a USB stick. It's got the names of their central council, the civil servants and the police who're on their payroll. The whole fucking thing.'

Ahead, she saw the lights of Madrid approaching. 'You'd better hand it over to the *guardia* or security services.'

'You think? The way things are, the minute I give that memory stick to someone, it's going to be like a curse. They'd be dead in days. Talk about a poisoned chalice.'

'So who are you going to give it to?'

Sancho put his hand to his mouth as he coughed again. Blood ran though his fingers.

'You.'

MADRID 2010, PENSIÓN PARAÍSO, CALLE DEL CARMEN

Rain was falling as Galíndez pulled up outside the *pensión* and the wet cobbles gleamed with the light of the street lamps. Señor Espartero was waiting by the door and hurried down the steps as Sancho staggered from the car.

Sancho's eyes widened. 'What the fuck? You've brought me to a circus?'

Espartero gave Sancho a fierce stare as he drew himself up to his full height. 'Considering the condition you're in, señor, you'd be wise not to reject any offer of assistance on the grounds of stature.'

'Exactly my thoughts,' Galíndez muttered, struggling to keep Sancho on his feet. 'Let's get him inside.' She leaned against him, using her weight to keep him on his feet. 'Put your arm round my shoulders.' Sancho draped his arm around her as she helped him across the pavement to the steps of the *pensión*.

'Why have we stopped?' Sancho asked.

'Put your hand on my shoulder or I'll leave you in the gutter.'

'Sorry, babe, I was just trying to get a better grip.'

'I said my shoulder. Now.'

'You'd never make a nurse,' he groaned, moving his hand back onto her shoulder.

Ten minutes later, Sancho was propped up in the one comfortable chair in reception, resting his feet on the coffee table. He looked round at the dusty surroundings, the pile of ancient magazines by the window, the curtain of glass beads behind the desk.

'Nice place you've got here.'

Señor Espartero executed a neat bow. 'I like to think of it as home.'

'I'm not moving in.'

'As you wish,' Espartero said, 'though I offer good rates for the economy rooms.'

'I'll let you know,' Sancho said, looking at Galíndez. 'It depends on nurse here.'

'Your nurse is going to call the *guardia*,' she said. 'I'll see how fast they can get you into witness protection.'

Sancho frowned. 'Don't do it from here. They might trace the call.'

'For once, you're right. I'll call later on my mobile,' Galíndez said. 'Give me your number.'

'You heard her say I was right, little man, didn't you?' Sancho laughed when Galíndez finished putting his number into her phone. 'That's a first.' He pointed to the pile of magazines. 'Pass me one of those, would you, babe?'

Galíndez bent to take one of the old journals from the pile by the window.

'See that?' Sancho asked, nudging Espartero. 'It's her best feature. Shame she's sat on it most of the time.'

'You ungrateful bastard.' Galíndez threw the tattered magazine onto his lap. Brushing dust from her hands, she went to the door. 'I'll call you later from Isabel's once I know what's happening.' The door slammed behind her.

'Just you and me, then,' Sancho said.

'Apparently so,' Espartero agreed. 'Is there anything I can get for you?'

'There is,' Sancho said. 'Can you use your contacts to get me Isabel's address?'

Espartero shrugged. 'Of course. Is that all?'

'No, there's something else as well, once you've got the address.'

'Just tell me what to do, Señor Sancho. It's the least I can do.'

'Listen carefully, then,' Sancho said, 'because this is important.'

Sancho was dozing in the chair when Señor Espartero returned. 'You did it?'

'Just as you asked.' Espartero locked the front door and then went behind the reception desk to get a chair. He carried it over to where Sancho was sitting and sat facing him. 'Forgive me for mentioning this, but I recognise a bullet wound when I see one.'

Sancho winced at another stab of pain. 'Thanks for that incisive diagnosis.'

'The thing is,' Espartero said, 'I know a doctor.'

'If it's all the same to you,' Sancho grunted, 'I'd rather carry on talking about Galíndez's *culo* than worry about doctors. How do you know we can trust him?'

'For a start, he's less than legitimate, Señor Sancho. Much less. His father was a Nazi who fled here after the war. He provided a much-needed service to those whose situation made using conventional facilities difficult. I've had a number of guests who needed his services over the years.'

'Were they satisfied with him?'

'The ones who survived were effusive in their praise.'

Sancho turned to get a better look at Espartero. The effort made him wince. 'Do you always talk like you've swallowed a dictionary?'

'Probably. Shall I call the good doctor?'

Another shaft of pain burned in Sancho's side. 'Yeah, why not?'

Isabel gasped as Galíndez staggered through the door. 'I'm calling an ambulance,' she said, reaching for the phone. 'You've been shot.'

Galíndez looked down. Her clothes were soaked in blood, from her throat down to her knees. 'It's OK, it's not mine.'

'Whose is it?'

'Sancho.'

Isabel raised a hand to her mouth. 'Did you kill him?'

Galíndez shook her head. 'It's hard to believe but he's an undercover cop. He's been collecting evidence on the *Centinelas* for years. Enough to put them all in jail.' She reached into the pocket of her jeans and took out the memory stick. 'It's all on this.'

'Are you sure you can trust him?'

Galíndez nodded. 'He was wounded so I've left him at the Pensión Paraíso with Señor Espartero.' She raised her bloodied hands. 'OK if I take a shower?'

'You'd better.' Isabel nodded. 'I'll get you a drink.' She paused as Galíndez went over to her laptop and lifted the lid. 'I thought you were getting showered, Ana?'

'I'm having a look at Sancho's USB stick.' Galíndez stared at the screen for a few moments and then removed the memory stick from the computer and put it in her top pocket.

'What did you see?' Isabel asked.

Galíndez shrugged. 'Loads of names and addresses, just like he said.'

As soon as she had washed away the blood, Galíndez dressed and then called Mendez.

'Ana? It's just like old times.'

'No it's not. But I want you to do something for me.'

'As I said, like old times. The sword hasn't turned up yet if that's why you're calling.'

'It isn't: I need you to arrange witness protection for someone.'

'I can do that. Who's the lucky person?'

'I'll tell you later. He's got some major evidence so he needs a high level of security.'

'OK, I'll contact Witness Protection and arrange it. Is he with you at the moment?'

'I've got him tucked away at a little *pensión*, the Paraíso on Calle del Carmen. He's been injured but I think he'll be OK for now.'

'I'll call Witness Protection the moment we hang up, but realistically, it probably won't happen until tomorrow.'

'I'll let him know, thanks, Mendez.'

'No problem.'

'By the way...' Galíndez took a deep breath.

'Go on.'

'I've decided to drop the lawsuit against Capitán Fuentes. Life's too short to go through weeks of court proceedings.'

'That's nice, he'll appreciate it. I need to talk with him this evening, shall I tell him?'

'Please. I'm still mad, but I'll get over it.'

'OK. I'll get back to you once I've talked to Witness Protection.'

Galíndez put down the phone and sank onto the sofa alongside Isabel. 'God. What a day this turned out to be.'

'And it's not over yet,' Isabel said. 'You left something next to your toothbrush this morning.' She held out her hand, palm up. On it was the yellow tube of painkillers.

Mendez sat in the darkened office, staring into the shadows. From time to time the window glowed with the headlights of passing cars. She sighed as she reached for the phone and pressed speed dial.

'Fuentes speaking.'

'It's Mendez, *Capitán*.'

'Working late, *Sargento*?'

'When don't I, boss? Listen, I've been talking to Ana María.'

'How is she?'

'Fine, in fact, she's more reasonable now. She says she'll accept an apology from Inés as long as you're all present.'

'That's great. Inés really does want to make things right, you know how she idolises Ana. To tell the truth, we all miss her.'

'Then now's the chance to sort things out, boss. She wants to meet at eight thirty tomorrow night at a little place called the Pensión Paraíso. It's on Calle del Carmen.'

'Tell her that's fine by us. We'll be there at eight thirty.' Fuentes hung up. Mendez waited a few minutes and then dialled another number.

'So, what's happening with Witness Protection?' Galíndez said.

'It's all arranged. They're setting up a safe house somewhere outside Madrid.'

'Do we know where?'

'That's always a secret, you know that. But you can meet them when they come to pick your boy up. Do the introductions and so on.'

'Fine, when will that be?'

'Eight thirty tomorrow night at the *pensión*.'

'I'll be there. Thanks, Mendez.'

Mendez cut the call and called another number. It was answered at once. 'It's done,' she said and hung up.

The office was silent, the terminals on the other desks all logged out. The only light came from the glow from her computer screen, though her work was now done for the day. She logged out and closed down the computer.

Outside, a car went by, its headlights dancing along the wall and over her desk. For a fleeting moment, the object in front of her glittered with pale fire. She reached out and ran a finger over it, tracing the patterns engraved on the curved blade. Then, slowly, she picked up the sword and left the office.

CHAPTER 19

MADRID, OCTOBER 1982, PENSIÓN PARAÍSO, CALLE DEL CARMEN

G uzmán looked up as he heard a soft tapping on the window. It was raining again. One of those autumn mornings when old men sat in cafés, staring out at the rivulets of water running down the windows, oblivious to the world beyond.

He went to the window and opened the shutters of his tiny balcony. Below, the cobbles in the alley glistened black with rain. Sharp staccato footsteps as a woman came out of one of the ground-floor apartments. Dressed in black, her head covered with a shawl. Going to mass, no doubt. At least someone still had something they could believe in.

A knock at the door. Guzmán turned and picked up the Browning before opening the door. A gypsy woman stood outside with a mop in one hand and a bucket of filthy water in the other.

'Who are you?'

'Señora Chavez, I'm the new cleaner.'

'It's not convenient.'

'If I don't do it now, it won't get done.'

He grunted and returned to the bed, careful not to sit on the weapons hidden under the flimsy sheet. 'There's no money in here,' he growled, 'so don't waste your time looking.'

She shrugged. 'There's no money anywhere in this country, señor.' When he ignored her, she persisted anyway. 'Is the gentleman from Madrid?'

'No.'

'Perhaps the gentleman's here on business?'

'That's correct.'

'What kind of business?'

'My business.'

'Have you brought your family with you?'

'I don't have any family.' Guzmán's tone emphasised his growing annoyance.

'What, no children?'

Her persistence surprised him so much that he gave her a civil answer. 'A daughter.'

'Girls are a blessing, señor. How old is she?'

'She died a long time ago.'

The gypsy crossed herself. 'I'm sorry.'

Guzmán went back to the window and leaned against the balcony, looking out over the rooftops. Through an attic window, he saw a family around a table, eating. 'So am I.'

Señora Chavez decided against further conversation and dipped her mop into the bucket, moving it over the wooden tiles in listless sweeps that left dark wet tracks in the dust. Guzmán soon tired of her presence and told her to leave. Once she had gone, he spent a while lost in dark thoughts. But such introspection was not helpful and he abandoned it in order to prepare for his meeting with the Italian.

Like a matador preparing for the afternoon's *corrida*, he worked slowly and methodically, checking and rechecking his weapons. The Browning loaded with thirteen soft-nosed bullets that would punch a hole in a man the size of a fist, the big trench knife strapped to his leg, the garrotte hidden in his belt. Dealing with the Italian merited this attention to detail. Those who neglected such things usually discovered their error the hard way.

His preparations complete, he selected a grey suit from the wardrobe. A blue silk tie would complement it nicely, he decided. It was always best to dress well for a meeting.

MADRID, OCTOBER 1982, BAR NAVARRA, CALLE SAN BERNARDINO

It was lunchtime and the tables outside the bars and cafés were full.

Despite the earlier rain, the sun was out now and the air was unseasonably warm. In this relaxed atmosphere, life slowed. But despite the autumnal glow, there were some whose business was so pressing there was no time to enjoy the day.

Further down the street, a man crossed the road, not waiting for the lights to change as he dodged through the traffic surging towards Plaza Cristino Martos. Once across, he strolled along the pavement past the crowded terrace of the Bar Navarra, casually scanning it for signs of surveillance. Inside the bar, he saw the large dining room with its zinc-topped counter and antique beer pumps, absorbing the detail in a glance, careful to disguise his interest.

At the end of the street, he took a left and went along a narrow alley behind the shops and bars of the main road. Once in the alley, he was hidden from view by its high walls and he paused to put down the package he was carrying. Then he waited, scanning his surroundings with a hunter's instinct. This was how he always worked, following a plan that would be enhanced by improvisation depending on his surroundings and circumstances. And for a man with his skills, each set of circumstances always presented new possibilities.

He heard a noise and turned, smiling to himself at how quickly such possibilities opened up to those who sought them.

A woman was making her way down the alley, pushing a pram. It was not easy for her: garbage cans and discarded boxes slowed her progress, forcing her to manoeuvre around them. He wondered why she had taken this route: the road would have been far easier. No matter: he would not look this gift horse in the mouth.

The woman stopped as she saw him, realising one of them would have to give way. He waved her on with a calm, elegant gesture, standing back to allow her to pass. An attractive woman, he thought, subtly appraising her as she passed. She gave him a demure 'thank you', in response to his old-fashioned courtesy.

In a moment he was on her, his left hand clamped over her mouth, pulling her against him, his right hand driving the stiletto into her heart, letting the body fall, anxious to avoid the blood. Rows of garbage cans were lined up along by the wall and when he lifted the lid of the nearest, it was almost empty. Quickly, he bundled the woman head first into the metal container, folding her legs to make sure the lid would close. As a final touch, he threw several small boxes in on top of her to hide his handiwork.

From the pram, he heard the quiet gurgling of the child. Yet another gift of fate. But then, he had always been lucky. He looked down at the chuckling baby, quickly completing the final details of his plan. It did not take long. Improvisation was his trademark skill.

MADRID, OCTOBER 1982, CALLE DE GARCÍA DE PAREDES, ORTIZ RESIDENCE

Ramiro Ortiz Junior was polishing his father's boots. The general was not at home, Ramiro had made sure of that before he started the task. It was bad enough being treated like a servant, but if General Ortiz caught his son polishing his boots in the living room, the result would undoubtedly be violent. *You're younger than him: hit him back.* Teresa's words echoed in his head. But what did his wife know? She hadn't been on the receiving end of a beating from the general. Ramiro had, many times.

The doorbell rang and he froze. Quickly, he gathered up the brushes and shoved them behind the sofa before answering the door. As he opened it, he breathed a sigh of relief as he saw a well-dressed man holding a briefcase.

The man beamed at Ramiro, revealing a dazzling array of dental work that contrasted with his deep tan. 'Teniente Ortiz, I believe?'

Ramiro nodded. 'Can I help you?'

'I'd say it's more a question of how I can help you, *Teniente.*'

Ramiro shrugged and stepped back to let him in. They went through the hall to the lounge and Ramiro took a seat in one of his father's favourite armchairs.

'So what's this about, señor?' Ramiro asked, suddenly impatient as he watched the man take a wad of documents from his briefcase and arrange them on the sofa next to him.

'I'll be frank, *Teniente*. There are certain things you should know about your father,' Javier Benavides said.

MADRID, OCTOBER 1982, BAR NAVARRA,
CALLE SAN BERNARDINO

Guzmán crossed the terrace, picking his way through the crowded tables. At the door of the dining room he paused to cast an eye over the converging mass of fashions and styles at the tables within, secretaries, clerks and business people all intent on enjoying the three-course special lunch.

Across the road, obscured by the stop-start line of traffic, people were sitting outside a similar café, drinking coffee or beer, eating sandwiches or plates of calamari or jamón, concentrating on their food. The entire world was doing exactly what Guzmán would normally be doing at this time of day. If he had not come to kill someone, that was.

He went into the dining room and took a table facing the French windows, giving himself a good view of the terrace and the road beyond. A waiter came over and Guzmán ordered beer. Then he leaned back and lit a cigarette.

He glanced at his watch: ten past two. The Italian was late. He picked up his glass and raised it to his lips, his eyes fixed on the crowded terrace. As he put the glass down, he considered the possibility that the Italian might not show up. But that was ridiculous. How could he miss such an opportunity after waiting all these years? Though why he should seek revenge now, after all this time, was hard to guess. But motives didn't matter. Actions did.

A sudden flash of white among the throng of diners on the terrace. Someone in a white linen suit. Casually, Guzmán slipped his hand into his jacket and gripped the Browning. He watched the white suit move through the crowd towards the door, the man's face obscured by waiters and customers drifting across his line of vision. Carefully, he began to slide his chair away from the table, ready to raise the pistol the moment the Italian came through the door.

At the door of the dining room a waiter stepped back, blocking Guzmán's view as the man in the white suit entered. Guzmán started to get to his feet then stopped and slowly sat back down, his hand still inside his jacket as he saw the woman in the white suit at the bar, now ordering a couple of drinks.

He took a long swig of beer and watched her return to the terrace with the drinks. 'Looks good in that white suit, doesn't she?' the waiter said, noticing his attention. He grinned as he wiped Guzmán's table with his cloth. 'Just like in that *Yanqui* movie.'

'What movie?' Guzmán asked.

'*Saturday Night Fever*. Haven't you seen it?'

'Of course,' Guzmán said, though he had not. Ignoring the waiter's attempt at further conversation, he went back to his surveillance of the terrace. The tables were less crowded now, as people drifted back to work or to resume their shopping. Casually, he scrutinised the faces of the remaining customers, trying to imagine how the Italian might have changed over the years.

He reached for his beer, drank it and ordered another, still watching the people on the terrace, enjoying the sunshine. Beyond them, the slow lines of traffic crawled by, bathed in a haze of exhaust fumes. From time to time, daring pedestrians darted across the road through the vehicles, provoking sudden blasts from the horns of short-tempered drivers. And there were plenty of those, Guzmán smiled to himself, though his smile lasted only a moment.

Across the street, a man was watching him.

A familiar face, despite the years that had passed since he last saw it. The white linen suit, the close-trimmed grey beard and cropped hair. The savage insolence of his smile. A memory of circles of light, rising through dark water.

As the waiter brought his beer, the traffic thickened, obscuring Guzmán's view of the road. When the traffic started moving again, the man was gone. He glanced around the terrace, tense with violent anticipation.

The phone on the bar rang, loud and shrill.

The barman answered. 'Phone call for Señor Guzmán?'

Guzmán went to the bar and took the phone. Behind him, the steady grumble of traffic continued. Bright voices rattled around the terrace. He lifted the phone to his ear and heard the voice from his past. The voice of the dead.

'Sorry to keep you waiting, *Comandante*.'

'What kind of game is this? I thought you had something to tell me?'

'Look across the road.' A soft, mocking tone.

Guzmán stepped back from the bar, pulling the phone cord taut as he moved to a spot where he could look out over the terrace. He saw the café on the far side of the street, the crowd of people outside. And next to the café, a phone box. A man was standing inside it. A man in a white linen suit.

'I see you.'

'Now look at the terrace, *Comandante*.'

'I am.'

'See that red pushchair? The one near the large potted palm?'

Guzmán saw the pushchair. Saw the tiny hand rising and falling, trying to reach the plastic toys dangling from the hood. And he saw the wire running down the side of the pushchair, disappearing beneath the chassis.

The Italian breathed the words into the phone. 'His Mamá had an accident.'

The phone hit the wooden floor as Guzmán ran towards the bar, shouting a warning as he hurled himself across the counter. Behind him, sudden shouts and screams, the tap of high heels as someone started running.

Guzmán pressed his face to the floor as the explosion tore through the bar in a murderous storm of fire and smoke. Above him, the fake art deco mirror shattered in a hail of jagged glass and the floor ran with spilt liquor as bottles rained down from the collapsing shelves. Stunned, Guzmán lay, protecting his head with his hands until the cascade of broken glass was over. He pulled himself to his feet, blinking and coughing in the thick cloud of dust now settling over what had been the dining room.

The room was destroyed. The glass French windows had vanished, leaving only a few jagged shards in place. Not a table or chair remained intact. Most had been hurled against the far wall, shattered like firewood. Amid the wreckage, he saw the waiter who liked movies. What was left of him.

He staggered outside, his ears ringing from the blast.

Bodies were scattered across the terrace. A slick of blood marked the spot where the group of women had been chatting earlier. There was no sign of the pushchair or the baby.

He heard the wail of approaching sirens. People were shouting, though the ringing in his ears made it hard to tell what they were saying. At the roadside, a man was kneeling by the body of a woman. Her clothes were shredded and, as the man rolled her onto her back, Guzmán saw she had lost an arm. That would not bother her now, she was beyond help.

He crossed the road, wending his way through people running towards the Bar Navarra. The sirens were growing louder. Someone put a hand on his arm, asked if he was all right. Guzmán pushed them away and went to the pay phone. He yanked open the metal door, expecting some taunting message amid the graffiti and adverts for prostitutes. Sure enough, it was there, taped to the phone. A personal message consisting of a small cheap business card: *Pensión Paraíso, Calle del Carmen.*

Guzmán punched the side of the phone box. He had no idea how the Italian had located the *pensión*, though it was entirely consistent with the man's warped logic. *An eye for an eye.* Or in this case, a woman for a woman.

The Italian had gone after Daniela.

MADRID, OCTOBER 1982, PENSIÓN PARAÍSO,
CALLE DEL CARMEN

The roads around Bar Navarra were gridlocked as the emergency services tried to get through to the carnage. Guzmán raged as he passed lines of stationary traffic, in search of a taxi. He turned down Calle San Leonardo and ran towards the Gran Via before he finally managed to flag down a cab. He pushed a wad of notes into the driver's hand as he gave him the address. 'Drive like a lunatic and don't say a word.'

The cab driver was not inclined to argue and drove off at speed.

Guzmán took the Browning from its holster and put a round in the chamber. Things were going to happen quickly when he reached the *pensión* and he had to be ready.

A hundred metres from the *pensión*, he ordered the driver to stop and jumped out, not bothering to close the door as he ran up the street. The gun in his passenger's hand discouraged the driver from asking for a tip and he turned the car and headed away in the opposite direction.

Guzmán ran up the steps to the *pensión*, the pistol raised. The door was slightly ajar and he nudged it open, scanning the reception area with the Browning. No sign of a struggle. No sign of anyone. Unusually, there was no sound from Señor Argüello's TV. He stepped inside, calling Daniela's name.

A weak voice called for help from behind the glass bead curtain.

Guzmán pushed his way through the coloured beads. Daniela's father lay on the floor, alongside his upended wheelchair. 'Leo.' His voice was sharp with fear. No wonder, Guzmán thought, as he saw the pool of blood under the old man's body.

'What happened?' Guzmán asked.

'A man in a white suit came in,' Argüello wailed. 'He asked where your room was. Then he took Dani upstairs.' His voice cracked. 'I heard him say that he'd teach her not to lie to him. I told him he could have all our money, but he shot me.' Trembling, he lifted a bloody hand, palm upward, as if Guzmán needed further evidence.

'What about Dani?'

'There was a bang, I think it was the door slamming. He must have taken her.'

Guzmán pushed his way through the bead curtain into reception and went slowly up the stairs. The door to his room was open and he raised the Browning, ready to confront the Italian. But the Italian was long gone, he realised as he peered into the room.

Daniela lay on her side near the far wall, her dark hair spilled around her head like a halo. So dark, it was difficult to tell where her hair ended and the blood began. One arm was extended, as if she had tried to protect herself. As if there were any protection from that lunatic's bullet. He touched her cheek. It was soft and cool and very dead. Shot through the head as a punishment for knowing him. For what he'd done in Alicante. And then, as he checked the room, he saw the full extent of the disaster.

The floorboards by the nightstand had been torn up. The weapons were still in their oilskin bags where he'd left them. But the money, all eight million pesetas, was gone.

Downstairs, he holstered the pistol as he went back through the bead curtain. Señor Argüello had not waited to find out what had happened to Dani. He was dead. That was perhaps just as well, Guzmán thought. Argüello had suffered long enough. Slowly, he leaned over and switched on the TV. As in life, so in death. Then he went back upstairs.

Daniela seemed to weigh nothing as he scooped her up and laid her on the bed. Carefully, he closed her eyes and covered her with one of the threadbare sheets. Then he went downstairs. As he went into reception, he heard a soft noise by the door and spun towards it. Leonidas Espartero came out of the shadows, his hands raised.

'How long have you been here?' Guzmán asked.

'Five minutes,' Espartero said, blinking unhappily. 'I came to ask Señorita Daniela if I could start work tomorrow. But I can see this is a bad time. I'll come back.'

'How do you know it's a bad time?'

'An educated guess,' the dwarf said. 'There was no one in reception so I looked in there.' He pointed to the glass bead curtain that hid Señor Argüello's windowless room. Slowly, he started backing away to the door. 'I'll not trouble you any further.'

'Wait.' Guzmán gestured at one of the chairs by the table. 'Sit down.' He took a seat facing the dwarf. 'There's still a job for you here, despite what's happened, though it's somewhat different from the one you were interested in.'

'That's fine: I can cook,' Espartero said, 'and I don't mind dirty work, though preferably not at the same time as I'm cooking.' He waited in vain for Guzmán to acknowledge the joke. 'May I ask what you meant by "despite what's happened"?'

'You saw Daniela's father in there, didn't you?' Guzmán said. 'Her body's upstairs.'

'Perhaps it would be best if I withdrew?' Espartero said. 'I can be out of the city within the hour.'

'I didn't kill them, you fool,' Guzmán snorted. 'I'm going to make you an offer. How would being hotel manager suit you?'

Espartero's expression changed. 'I suspect you're making fun of me.'

'Not many dwarves get offered a position like this,' Guzmán said. 'You'll be in charge of everything. But you'll have to make the place pay, because there's no money.'

'I don't understand.'

'The *pensión* is yours. But you have to take it on this minute. And there are a couple of problems that need addressing. You need to dispose of the bodies and clean up the blood.'

Espartero drew himself up to his full height. 'I always relish a challenge, *Comandante*.'

'You may be sorry you said that.'

Espartero smiled. 'I'll take my chances.'

Once he'd put the dwarf to work, Guzmán called Gutiérrez. The brigadier general sounded less than happy. 'The media have been harassing me, Guzmán. They think the explosion at Bar Navarra was an attempt to delay the election.'

'They can think what they like, it was the Italian's handiwork.'

'Trouble is,' Gutiérrez said, 'they're referring to the *Brigada Especial* as "Franco's Old Guard". Before long, they'll be accusing us of trying to derail the election.'

Guzmán sighed, thinking that if he'd still had the money Benavides paid for the code, he could be miles away, leaving Gutiérrez and the Italian behind. He saw a fleeting image of a long strip of yellow sand covered in bikini-clad women with sing-song Nordic accents. 'So what do we do?'

'You have to complete the job, Guzmán. First, we need to get the files you've been collecting to a safe place.'

'And where would that be?'

'I'll find somewhere, don't worry. Call me in the morning.' The phone went dead.

Down the road from the *pensión*, the bell of the Church of el Carmen struck midnight. Guzmán sat in the cane chair in reception, watching the street. He was tired and his ears were still ringing from the explosion that afternoon. Upstairs, he heard the sound of the dwarf scrubbing Daniela's blood from the wooden tiles of his room. For a moment he wondered about helping him to move her body but decided against it. Years ago, he'd buried his daughter with his bare hands: enough was enough. Besides, Señor Espartero had agreed to handle the burials using the services of an acquaintance. A dwarf with contacts: he would do well, Guzmán had no doubt.

He lit another cigarette, raising his hand in front of him, staring at the glowing tip. So it had come to this: despite all his efforts, he was living in squalor and still short of money. Without money, a man was no better than a beggar cowering in a doorway. He had never thought this would happen to him, not after all he'd done for Franco. He'd placed his faith in that bandy-legged popinjay, thinking he would always reward a faithful servant like Guzmán generously. He had no idea now why he'd thought that. If history showed anything, it was that the *Caudillo* by the grace of God, Francisco Franco Bahamonde, could not be trusted as far as a man could throw him.

All that killing, the bullets he took in defence of the State, the traitors he liquidated, continuing the malevolent violence of the war long after the Republic surrendered. All of it to enable Franco to have his revenge on those who opposed him. Such service deserved a better reward than this.

In his long bloody career, Guzmán had rarely asked questions. But he was faced by one now: had it been worth it? Could he truly look himself in the mirror and say that his was a life well spent? But when he thought about it, that question was easily answered: of course he fucking could. Because whatever he had done, he had always stayed true to his values: let no insult go unanswered and no challenge go unpunished. That had been the bedrock of his self-respect for a long time. There was no reason to abandon it now.

He went to the door and threw the cigarette down the steps, a brief trail of sparks in the cool night air. It was beginning to rain. Further up the street, he heard the rumble of traffic in the Plaza del Callao. And above that, the deep visceral thump of music from El Topless. Eduardo Ricci's club.

Fucking Ricci. *Eduardo el Bastardo.* There were always winners and losers in this life and right now, Ricci was a winner and Guzmán a loser. The perverse logic of history. And just to add to Guzmán's woes, the Italian had returned. The deck was rapidly being stacked, and not in his favour.

He looked up the street again, towards Ricci's nightclub. Ricci, a man who epitomised everything that was wrong with Spain. A man who'd humiliated him. No, that was not true: Guzmán had let himself be humiliated by Ricci's lackeys for Daniela's sake.

It was time to respond to that insult.

He started walking, indifferent to the rain. The smart thing to do now would be to cut and run. Head for the sea, make a new life somewhere, as he had once before. But Guzmán had never run from anything, and the last time he was by the sea was in Alicante.

He continued up the road and slipped along the side of El Topless, towards the emergency doors at the rear. Inside the club, the music was thick and physical, the pumping bass notes steady and strong, like a dark beating heart.

By the fire doors, two bouncers were chatting. He recognised them at once: the men he had allowed to throw him out of the club to save Daniela getting into trouble. Dani was far beyond their reach now.

A familiar odour of kif hung in the damp night air. The bouncers were getting stoned, hiding away by the back door, neglecting their duty. These were the kind of men Ricci hired. In the war, Guzmán killed men for much less.

The Arab laughed as he saw him coming towards them. 'What do you want?'

'Señor Ricci told me to see him about a job,' Guzmán muttered.

A lopsided grin. 'What job's that, *amigo*?'

Guzmán paused, staying outside the faint halo of light from the door. 'Bar work.'

That amused them. 'You can't see him now, he's in the VIP lounge with Señor Masias,' the Arab said. 'Come back this afternoon about one. Losers' hour, we call it. Maybe you'll pick up a bit of work then if you ask nicely.' He turned, about to make a quip to the other man.

Guzmán grabbed the Arab's arm, spinning him to face him as he drove the trench knife into the man's chest, up to the hilt. A dull grunt of surprise, a muffled sound as the Arab fell to the ground, already dead. As Guzmán turned to the second man, the volume of the music in the club rose in a violent crescendo. Voices whooping and shouting. As the noise intensified, the other bouncer came at him, trying to take the initiative.

Guzmán kicked the man's legs from under him and he fell heavily. As he tried to get to his feet, Guzmán seized him by the hair and dragged his head back, exposing his throat to the knife.

Once he had wiped the blade clean on the dead man's jacket, Guzmán went through the emergency doors into the club. On the dance floor, the dark mass of dancers ebbed and flowed under the fluctuating light of the strobes. He pushed through them, enveloped in warm, moist heat, an odour like the sheets of a brothel.

A woman stumbled into him, drunk. For a moment he felt the warmth of her skin, smelled the musk of her perfume before she was swept away again by the tide. On the far side of the dance floor, he saw a sign for the VIP lounge and made for it. The sign pointed up a flight of stairs and Guzmán went straight up, noticing there were no bouncers on duty. Another mistake on Ricci's part.

The VIP area was a black chrome and steel platform overlooking the dance floor. At the far end of the platform was the bar, an oblong of black marble, the bottles on the shelves glowing under the eccentric, fluctuating lights.

And at the bar, Eduardo Ricci, his back turned, taking a bottle of champagne from an ice bucket, leaning across to top up Guillermo Masias's glass. Both laughing with contagious drunken humour, unaware of Guzmán bearing down on them, silhouetted against the light storm raging over the dance floor.

He watched their reactions as they saw him. Ricci making some sneering comment, both of them laughing. All they saw was a man who had been pushed out of the club by Ricci's bouncers. Such a man posed no threat to them, they were certain.

So many over the years had shared that certainty. Guzmán had killed every last one.

Ricci's face changed, his laughter turning to a snarl, caught between amusement at Guzmán's audacity and fury at his intrusion.

On the dance floor, the music reached a thunderous climax, the dancers oblivious now to anything outside this world of pulsing light and swaying bodies. Above them, a sudden flash of light in the VIP lounge, the sound of the shot lost in 'Eye of the Tiger'.

Ricci stumbled in broken motion along the bar, feebly clutching at the gleaming black marble, trying to stay on his feet. Masias watched, open-mouthed, as Guzmán turned to him. Another flash in the darkness; a staccato image of Masias clutching his chest, his legs buckling beneath him as he fell.

Ricci clung to the bar like a man on a sinking ship, his mouth opening and closing as he called for help, his words swept away by the music. Guzmán shot him in the back of the head. There would be no open casket at that funeral.

On the floor to Guzmán's right, Masias lay on his back, his dead eyes staring up at the whirling lights. Guzmán leaned on the rail at the top of the stairs, peering through the kaleidoscopic patterns of light at the dancers below, moving like the sea at night, striped by roving strobes and spotlights. He holstered the Browning and went down into the ripe, sensuous warmth, taking his time as he worked his way across the dance floor to the entrance.

By the door, the staff were dealing with a woman who had just thrown up onto the red nylon carpet. Guzmán stepped round her, smiling indulgently. The harassed doormen ignored him, though Guzmán heard one asking where the fucking Arab was. That was a theological question now and he left them to it.

The rain had stopped and the air was soft and cool. Autumn air, a subtle promise of winter. Outside El Topless, a line of taxis stretched along the kerb. In the square, the lights glowed bright around the Cine Callao, advertising a film, *Laberinto de Pasiones* by someone called Almodóvar. Guzmán turned away and went down the street to the small bar next to Garcia's grocery. The heat of the club had given him a thirst.

He sat at the counter and ordered a beer. In the dark-flecked mirror behind the bar, he saw his reflection: a hard-faced man wearing a well-cut suit. The beer was cold and refreshing and he ordered another, reflecting on the image looking back at him from the speckled glass. A model of respectability to the casual observer, though whatever his appearance might convey, it was just that, an appearance. He was but one thing now and it had nothing to do with respectability. He was Guzmán. A man forged in the fires of war and its murderous aftermath. That war was long past. It was the war to come that concerned him now. The war he had just started.

In the sudden draughts of damp air that floated in when the street door opened, he smelled wood smoke. He looked into the mirror and smiled, lifting his glass in a toast to himself. As he put down the glass, he inhaled the aroma of burning wood again.

It was the smell of bridges burning.

CHAPTER 20

MADRID 2010, PENSIÓN PARAÍSO, CALLE DE CARMEN

'Good morning, Señor Sancho.' Espartero placed the tray on the table next to Sancho's chair. 'Are you sure you wouldn't be more comfortable in bed?'

Sancho shook his head. 'I'm fine right here, *amigo*. This way I can see anyone who comes in that front door.' He gave Espartero a complicit wink. 'And if I can see them, I can shoot them.'

'A practical philosophy no doubt,' Espartero said solemnly.

'That's me,' Sancho chuckled, 'a philosopher.'

'How's the wound?'

'Not too bad. Your Kraut doctor did a good job. You got any more contacts like him?'

'Of course.' Espartero nodded. 'How else would I make a living?'

'I don't know, take in paying guests maybe?'

'You've seen the *pensión*. Would you stay here?'

'No, but then I'm choosy.'

Espartero poured them coffee. 'I thought Señorita Galíndez and Señorita Morente were potential guests when they came here but they were less than impressed, I could tell. Particularly Señorita Galíndez.'

'No doubt. What was her problem this time?'

'There were a couple of things she disliked about the room I showed them. It was her own fault: she said she wanted to see the room Señor Guzmán used.'

'And what was wrong with it?'

Espartero took a deep breath. 'There was a bullet hole in one wall and the cleaner had made a mess of cleaning up some blood on the floor.' He shrugged. 'The cleaner was a gypsy, unskilled, but trustworthy. You can't have everything.'

Sancho's face set with concentration. 'So Guzmán stayed here? Was that recently?'

'Not really. It was 1982.'

'But you met him?'

'Indeed so. In fact, he was the one who gave me the *pensión*. There'd been an accident, necessitating a sudden change of owner.'

'I wonder if it was the same Guzmán I know.' Sancho took a noisy swig of coffee. 'Big guy, bald and violent?'

'More or less, though the man I knew had rather a good head of hair.'

'A lot can change in thirty years.' Sancho tore off a piece of croissant and crammed it into his mouth.

'This place hasn't,' Espartero said. 'It's almost the same as the day I took over. Apart from the bodies, of course. Disposing of them was the price I had to pay.'

'You're a dark horse, *amigo*,' Sancho laughed. 'This Guzmán, did he drink whisky?'

'No, brandy was the *Comandante*'s favourite libation, as I recall.'

Sancho shrugged. 'I guess we're not talking about the same person.'

'Speaking of strong liquor,' Espartero's eyes lit up, 'do you think Señorita Galíndez would mind if I were to offer you a small glass of the hard stuff before you go to your safe house?'

'Oh, she'd disapprove all right,' Sancho grinned. 'So I'll have a large one, my little friend, though only if you join me.'

'They do say it's bad luck to drink alone.' Espartero got down from his chair and went in search of the bottle.

MADRID 2010, DIRECCIÓN GENERAL DE LA GUARDIA CIVIL, SECCIÓN DE CRIPTOGRAFÍA

Capitán Torrecilla looked up as he heard the sharp knock on his door.

'I came as soon as I got your message,' Galíndez said, excited. 'Does this mean you've cracked Guzmán's code?'

'I wouldn't say we've cracked it, Ana. But we have identified a phrase in it.'

Her face fell. 'Just one?'

'Don't knock it. It means we're making progress.' He gestured to a stack of papers on his desk. 'All that paper is my work on extracting this one phrase.'

'Shit.' Galíndez slumped into the chair by his desk. 'I'd really hoped that—'

'Patience. It's a virtue, remember? Slow and steady wins the race, all that?'

She shook her head. 'Every race I've ever been in was won by the fastest runner. And I never put much store in virtue.'

Torrecilla smiled. 'Here's what we've found. Three words: "The Western Vault".'

Galíndez stared at him. 'Do you know where that is?'

'No, do you?'

'I've heard it mentioned, but I don't know what it is. A bank vault maybe?'

'That was what I thought. Want me to make a few calls, see if we can find anything?'

'That would be great,' Galíndez said. 'I'll call you if I get any ideas.'

'You know where I'll be,' Torrecilla said and went back to his notes.

MADRID 2010, PENSIÓN PARAÍSO, CALLE DEL CARMEN

'And the bishop says...' Sancho cackled, spluttering wine down his shirt, 'I'll have what His Holiness just had, but I'd like it peeling first.' His laughter was cut short by a sudden spasm of pain and he clutched at the wad of bandages taped against his side. 'Fuck, sometimes I wish I didn't have such a well-developed sense of humour.' He raised his glass, hopefully. 'Any of the good stuff left?'

'I'm afraid not,' Espartero said, suppressing another wave of laughter. 'In any case, perhaps we ought to slow down our intake of alcohol?'

'I suppose,' Sancho said, though he sounded doubtful. 'I want to appear professional when Witness Protection collect me.'

'Will Señorita Galíndez be accompanying them?'

'I expect so. She won't believe I'm capable of getting into a car on my own.' He shot a look at the little man sitting opposite him. 'You don't have a thing about her, do you? Because you're barking way up the wrong tree if you have.'

Espartero shook his head. 'Nothing like that, though I do find her interesting.'

'If you like humourless, flat-chested women with attitude, she fits the bill, I suppose.'

'A rather harsh assessment. The young lady seems to be a trier, as far as I can tell.'

'She tries my patience,' Sancho snorted. 'For two years she's been popping up here, there and everywhere, disrupting my investigation. And every time, she'd get herself into a mess. It was infuriating. She's got guts, that one, but fuck me, she can be stupid as well.'

'Which of us can say we haven't been like that?' Espartero said.

'So you're really not interested in her?'

Espartero gave him a scornful look. 'Not in the coarse way you suggest. The truth is, I like to think that I have certain psychic inclinations. I sense things, from the other side.'

'What, like in a crystal ball?'

A noncommittal shrug. 'There are many ways: the tarot, the shape of the head, coffee grounds and so on.'

Sancho laughed. 'I knew you'd worked in a circus.'

'A travelling show. I had a number of roles, fortune-telling was just one of them.'

'I have to ask: what do you sense about Galíndez?'

Espartero's face grew serious. 'There's a shadow over her.'

'And that's bad, right?'

'Very bad, unfortunately for her.'

'And what about me?'

Espartero met Sancho's gaze and held it. He said nothing.

'That bad?'

Espartero raised his hands. 'These things vary but I'd say your aura very much resembles Señorita Galíndez's.'

With a groan, Sancho sank back into the chair. He gave Espartero a long despairing look. 'I really wish you hadn't told me that.'

MADRID 2010, CALLE DEL CARMEN

The sun was setting, filling the street with elongated shadows as Galíndez parked the car. 'Aren't you worried about getting a ticket?' Isabel asked, seeing a No Parking sign.

Galíndez shook her head. 'We're on *guardia* business.' She tapped her watch, impatiently. 'It's eight fifteen, we should get a move on.'

'We don't want to miss your new best friend going off to the safe house, do we?'

Galíndez gave her a wicked smile. 'Are you jealous?'

'Of course not, but you have to admit it's weird the way he's turned out to be on the side of the angels.'

'I wouldn't go that far,' Galíndez said as they turned the corner. 'Hey, what's going on here?' Fifty metres ahead, the road was blocked by a line of police, two deep.

One of the officers came towards them. 'That's as far as you go, ladies, this is a controlled area.'

Galíndez held up her *guardia* ID. 'GC. I've got business in that *pensión*.' She pointed to the dilapidated building, hemmed in by The House of Cod and Lush.

The cop lowered his voice. 'It's a counter-terrorism operation, Agent González.'

'Galíndez.'

'Whatever. We've got strict instructions to close the road. That's all I know.'

Galíndez wasn't about to back down. 'Look, I really have to—'

'You heard me. It's more than my job's worth to let you through.'

Frustrated, Galíndez went back to tell Isabel what was happening.

'That's a coincidence, isn't it?' Isabel said.

'Maybe it's a part of Witness Protection's strategy for moving him, I don't know.'

'Maybe.' Isabel pointed at the line of police further up the road. 'Look, they're closing off the other end of the street now.'

Seventy metres away, a couple of men were putting red bollards across the road. Galíndez frowned as she took her phone from her pocket. 'I'll call Sancho.'

MADRID 2010, PENSIÓN PARAÍSO, CALLE DEL CARMEN

'Two hundred fucking euros,' Sancho grumbled. 'You've got to be cheating.'

'Have you seen a card up my sleeve or noticed a sleight of hand?' Espartero asked.

'No, but I've noticed you're talking a lot. For all I know you're shifting the cards around while I'm still trying to work out what you said.'

Sancho was interrupted by a sudden buzz in his shirt pocket. 'I'd better answer that and save myself some money.'

As Sancho answered the phone, Espartero began counting banknotes onto the table.

'You don't say. How long?' Sancho sighed, irritated. 'How many?' A long pause. 'You never fail to disappoint me, Galíndez.' He hung up.

'Is there a problem?' Espartero pushed the small pile of notes across the table.

Sancho stared at the money. 'What's this?'

'A refund.'

'I thought you said you weren't cheating?'

'What I actually said was that you hadn't seen me cheating – that's an entirely different proposition altogether.'

Sancho snatched up the money and stuffed it in his pocket. 'That was Galíndez on the phone. Apparently there's a crowd of police just down the road. Some counter-terror operation. Galíndez thinks they could be the Witness Protection officers.'

'And what do you think, Señor Sancho?'

'I think it's best never to trust what she says. Let's wait and see.'

Espartero gave him a troubled look. 'What's the worst that could happen?'

'The guys outside are from the *policía nacional*. I don't trust them an inch.'

'I see.' Espartero quickly put the rest of his winnings into his pocket.

'Wait.' Sancho reached for his phone as it went again. 'Maybe this is Galíndez saying everything's OK.'

Espartero watched nervously as Sancho looked at his phone. 'From your expression, I take it that's not good news?'

'You take it right, little man.' Sancho lifted the phone for Espartero to read the text.

You pay with your dead

'That would be a threat, I assume?' Espartero asked, loosening his tie. 'Who from?'

'My ex-employers. And it's more than a threat, it's a promise.'

He winced as he struggled to sit up. 'You'd better get going. Just walk out the door, get away from here and come back when it's all over. Anyone asks you anything, play dumb. Galíndez can give you lessons in that.'

'I think, Señor Sancho, that at my age, the time for walking away is long past.'

'And what does that mean?'

'It means we're in this together.'

'Don't be stupid, little man. You haven't even got a weapon.'

'That's true.' Espartero turned on his heel and trotted towards the stairs.

MADRID 2010, CALLE DEL CARMEN

Galíndez glared at her phone. 'Sancho's not answering.'

'Ana? Look over there,' Isabel said, pointing up the street.' See that car? Isn't that Capitán Fuentes driving?'

Galíndez stood on tiptoe to peer past the line of police in front of her. 'I wonder what he's doing here?'

'Who knows? But the guys with the bollards are letting him through.'

As the car slowly rolled forward over the cobbles, Galíndez saw Mercedes Fuentes in the front passenger seat, immaculate as ever in an expensive blouse. As she watched, Mercedes twisted round awkwardly, struggling against her seat belt, no doubt giving her daughters in the back a telling-off for something.

Fuentes slowed the car, gesturing for the men to move the rest of the bollards so he could get past. Maybe he was late for some appointment, Galíndez guessed. The *capitán* was a stickler for punctuality and even a minor hold-up like this would be enough to annoy him.

She looked over to the *pensión*. Nothing was happening there. Perhaps Witness Protection were already inside.

A sudden movement in her peripheral vision made her look up. There were people on the balcony of the building next door to the Pensión Paraíso. Maybe someone wanting to get a look at what the cops were doing. She narrowed her eyes, squinting against the evening sun as she saw the automatic rifles the men were carrying.

'Look, Izzy, Witness Protection have got snipers on that balcony.'

'They really must think Sancho's worth looking after.'

'That's because he's got so much evidence against the *Centinelas*.' Galíndez decided not to mention that evidence was on the USB stick in her pocket.

The Fuentes car came to a halt and Fuentes began unfastening his safety belt, clearly tired of waiting. In the road, the man with the bollards suddenly turned and disappeared into the crowd. Suspicious now, Galíndez glanced up at the balcony.

Her warning shout was drowned out by gunfire.

As the shooting began, Galíndez hurled herself at Isabel, knocking her to the ground, shielding her with her body. Around them, the sour whine of bullets, impacting on metal, glass and stone. Harsh rattling bursts of automatic fire, the gruff splutter of single shots. As she lay, pressing Isabel to the ground, Galíndez realised what was happening: the men on the balcony were shooting at the Fuentes family.

Raising her head, she saw Capitán Fuentes' car start to disintegrate. Pieces of ragged metal flew into the air, pulverised glass spilled onto the cobbles, steam and oil poured from dozens of holes in the engine. Around the street, the howl of ricochets mimicked the screams of fleeing bystanders.

Galíndez rolled away from Isabel and aimed the Glock up at the balcony, gripping the pistol in both hands. Her first shot raised a cloud of powdered stone from the balustrade and one of the men reeled back, trying to wipe the dust from his eyes. She fired again and saw him clutch his shoulder as he fell, suddenly lost from sight. As the firing started to die down, she scrambled to her knees, seeking another target.

She never got the chance.

Galíndez grunted as the policeman landed heavily on top of her, knocking the Glock from her hand as she struggled beneath him, her enraged shouts telling him who she was and where the shooters were. As she lashed out, other hands grabbed her ankles and wrists, pinning her down as her desperate cries competed with the final cadences of gunfire.

MADRID 2010, PENSIÓN PARAÍSO, CALLE DEL CARMEN

Señor Espartero was coming down the stairs when the shooting started. He saw Sancho, on the edge of the chair, struggling to get to his feet. 'You shouldn't strain yourself.'

'If I don't, we're going to be dead very soon.' Sancho looked at the two oilcloth bags in Señor Espartero's hands. 'What have you got there?"

'Señor Guzmán left these here a long time ago. I don't know if they'll still work.'

'Just tell me what the fuck they are, will you?'

'I believe they call them Uzis,' Espartero said, tipping the contents of the bags onto the table.

Sancho grabbed one of the machine pistols and wielded it in his big fist. 'Here, give me the other one.' He readied the weapon and handed it back to Espartero. 'We'll stand a better chance on the stairs,' he said, resting a hand on Espartero's head as he got to his feet.

With a good deal of grunting and a significant loss of blood, Sancho managed to get halfway up the stairs before he was forced to sit. 'This will do,' he said, toying with the Uzi. 'You'd better get out the back way while you still can.'

Señor Espartero sat down next to him. 'There is no back way, alas.'

'What about a fire exit?'

'This place was built in another era. Health and safety concerns were thought effeminate back then.'

'Then you're stuck with me, *amigo*,' Sancho said. 'Sorry about that.'

'Actually, a similar event led to my ownership of this *pensión*. Perhaps someone else will take it over, Señorita Galíndez, maybe.'

'Yeah, she could haunt it,' Sancho muttered. 'Listen, here's the plan. As they come into reception, they won't see us up here, so start firing at once. We'll take them by surprise.'

'That's your plan?'

'Only one I've got, *amigo*, sorry.' Sancho pointed the Uzi's snub barrel at the entrance as he heard shouting. Boots clattered on the steps and something hard struck the outside door, tearing it from its hinges. Sancho took a deep breath and aimed the Uzi at the doorway. 'They don't stand a chance,' he said. He was laughing.

MADRID, OCTOBER 2010, PENSIÓN PARAÍSO, CALLE DEL CARMEN

Pressed to the cobbles beneath several burly policemen, Galíndez realised her struggles were hopeless and stopped resisting. Finally satisfied she was no threat, the police allowed her to get up. She went straight over to confront the police commander and demanded an explanation.

'So none of you are from Witness Protection?' she asked, when he'd finished.

'We don't know anything about witness protection, as I keep telling you, Galíndez. We're from Counter-Terrorism. We were told there were suspects in the *pensión*. We assumed it was them who opened fire on your colleague's car.'

'The shooters were on the balcony next door,' Galíndez shouted. 'My witness was in the *pensión* for his own protection. You never gave him a chance. You had no right to do that. No right.' She repeated the words, as if that could undo what had just happened.

'We lost three men in there,' the commander snapped. 'If they were so innocent, how come they had machine pistols?'

Galíndez realised she was going to get nowhere for the time being and turned away. 'Izzy? I want to go over to the car and see Capitán Fuentes. Say goodbye. I owe him that. Will you come with me?'

As they walked up the cobbled street, they stopped as white-suited forensics officers came out through the shattered door of the Pensión Paraíso, carrying the stretchers. Galíndez raised her fist to her mouth as the first stretcher went past, carried by four men: Sancho's bulk had proved too much for two. The second corpse was a child-sized outline beneath the sheet.

Isabel brushed a tear away as they watched the stretchers being loaded into the ambulance. 'That little man was so polite.'

The *guardia* forensics team had arrived and the Fuentes car was already covered in numbered markers, identifying where the bullets had struck. Most of the team knew Galíndez. All knew Capitán Fuentes. As she approached the bullet-riddled car, they stepped away, giving her space to say goodbye.

Galíndez had seen a lot of dead people in her short career. Each time, she'd always managed to detach herself from the person she was dealing with. She'd learned to close down, focusing on them only as a potential source of information. In this job, you had to maintain a sense of detachment, keep your distance. They'd told her that when she first started. And she had.

There was no chance of doing that now.

Capitán Fuentes was slumped over the steering wheel, his clipped steel-grey hair splashed with blood. His left hand was pushed deep into his jacket pocket, Galíndez noticed. Probably he'd been reaching for his personal sidearm when he was killed. Gently, she lifted his hand from the pocket. Something slipped from his fingers onto the leather seat and she saw a glint of gold. His wedding ring. She picked it up and put the ring in her pocket. She would give it to the undertaker in due course. It was the least she could do.

At his side, Mercedes had taken the full force of the automatic fire and Galíndez could only bear to look at her for a moment. She turned and went to the rear door, looked in, carefully avoiding touching the vehicle, guided by her training, though no training could have prepared her for this.

The two girls were lying on the back seat. The upholstery had been ripped apart by the furious gunfire and torn wadding and springs protruded through the shredded leather. Clari had been coming up to her fifth birthday. She'd been looking forward to starting a new school. And Inés, thirteen years old, her teen years just beginning.

Mendez had just arrived as Galíndez rejoined Isabel. For a

moment Mendez stood, pale-faced, staring at Capitán Fuentes' shattered car. A bewildered expression, as if looking for words that had been lost for ever. Galíndez went towards her and they embraced. After a moment, Mendez pulled away. 'What were the Fuentes family doing here, Ana?'

Galíndez shook her head in despair. 'I keep wishing I'd told Inés that I forgave her.'

'These things happen when they happen. None of us have a crystal ball.' Mendez squeezed her arm. 'You and Isabel should go home. I'll talk to our forensic guys and start the search for whoever did this.'

The forensics team had waited quietly for the women to pay their respects. But there was work to be done now, and slowly they returned to the car to resume their work.

Galíndez and Isabel walked in silence down Calle del Carmen.

'I've had an idea,' Galíndez said as they reached the car. 'I'm going to give Sancho's memory stick to Judge Delgado. He's someone we can trust.'

Isabel gave her a dubious look. 'He's famous for his anti-corruption work, that's for sure. But he was also the subject of malpractice hearings a few months back. Something about money laundering, I think.'

'But he could generate publicity about the Centinelas in ways we couldn't. It's worth a try, surely?'

'Do it then.' Isabel opened the car door. 'I'll drive, you look exhausted.'

Wearily, Galíndez slumped into the passenger seat, turning her head to watch the buildings of central Madrid pass by in a haze. She reached into her pocket and took out Capitan Fuentes' wedding ring. The light glittered off the gold band as she held it in the palm of her hand, her thoughts coalescing into questions. Trite questions at first, slowly becoming more defined, though much more puzzling.

And what puzzled her most was the memory of Capitán Fuentes slumped against the steering wheel of his car, killed as he reached into his pocket for the ring now on her palm. The daylight was almost gone, but each time the car passed a street light, for a fleeting moment she saw again the engraving of a two-headed serpent on the ring.

Within twenty minutes, the men in suits had rounded up the villagers and herded them into the church hall at gunpoint. They sat on hard wood chairs, the men mopping their faces with handkerchiefs, the women waving fans. At the doors, men stood guard with machine pistols. As the last villagers arrived, they brought troubling news: roadblocks were being set up at each end of the village. No one could enter or leave.

Carrero Blanco stood at the front of the hall, looking out over the captive audience. Imperiously, he raised his hand, signalling for quiet.

'Something terrible has happened to your children,' Carrero Blanco said, his voice devoid of sympathy or concern. 'This is Comandante Guzmán of the Brigada Especial. *He's going to explain to you exactly what's happened.'*

Guzmán had taken off his jacket. Since that revealed the Browning hanging under his left arm in its shoulder holster, the villagers watched him with some trepidation.

'At about eleven this morning, we got a phone call saying your school bus and the children in it had been taken hostage.' He waited until the noise died down a little. 'The man who has them hostage is a wanted terrorist, Umberto Santorini, though he's usually referred to as "the Italian". He was involved in the hijacking of an Italian plane recently. He has an accomplice with him, a Palestinian, Leila Ahmed. She was responsible for a number of murders in Israel and the killing of an American in Crete last year.'

'*But what does he want with our children, señor?*' a man called from the back.

'An exchange,' Guzmán said. '*Fifty million dollars and the release of four ETA terrorists.*'

The *pensión* was as silent and lifeless as its former owners as Guzmán packed his clothes into a suitcase. Señor Espartero had done a good job during the night, there were no signs of death now, and no sign of the former occupants. Guzmán had not asked where they would be buried. It made no difference to the dead where they lay.

He stopped at the reception desk and tore the page with the details of Señor Ramirez from the register. From behind the glass bead curtain, he heard Señor Espartero snoring. He let the dwarf sleep. Espartero had all the old man's documents and the *pensión* was his now. Until he lost it in a card game with other dwarfs, no doubt. But that was none of Guzmán's business. He put his keys on the desk and left without looking back.

On the way to the plaza, he stopped at a phone box and called *guardia civil* HQ. The receptionist put him through to General Ortiz at once.

'I need to see you, General,' Guzmán said, 'urgently.'

'That sounds serious, Leo. Come over in an hour or so, I'll be free then.'

Guzmán took a walk, brooding about what had to happen next before someone else decided that for him.

His first option was clear: leave town before the *Centinelas* discovered the code he'd sold them was missing its key components. But running had never appealed to him, probably because of all the people he'd tracked down over the years. People could run, but if someone wanted to find them badly enough, they would. Death respected no boundaries.

His other option was to carry on helping Gutiérrez with his plan to discredit the *Centinelas*. There were other, more complex, possibilities, but for now that would have to do. *It's a bad plan that cannot be changed*, some Roman once said. Guzmán had always borne that in mind, despite his opinion of Italian military competence. But despite Gutiérrez's plan, Guzmán still had an agenda of his own, a violent agenda, one that would slake his need for revenge. Even so, he had to be careful. Daniela would not have wanted the kind of retribution he was thinking of. On the other hand, Daniela was dead. But out of respect to her, he decided to refine the plan and, as he turned into Calle de las Navas de Tolosa, he suddenly realised exactly how that plan could be refined.

He paused and peered into the window of the old print shop on the corner. The grimy window was filled with reams of paper, faded by the afternoon sun. In front of the paper, a jumbled display of ancient fountain pens and bottles of ink, a vast collection of outdated printing accessories that were probably obsolete forty years ago.

As he opened the door, he heard a bell ring in the back of the shop, the same bell that had been there before the war. It had not worked properly then either.

He stood at the counter, peering past large rolls of paper and boxes containing printer's ink, towards the small workshop in the back. After a moment or two, he heard heavy footsteps as a man came out of the darkened workshop, a thickset old man with white hair, rubbing his ink-stained hands on his leather apron. His eyes widened as he saw Guzmán.

'*Comandante*? Jesus, I thought you were dead.'

'Likewise.' Guzmán smiled as they shook hands. 'How's business, Geronimo?'

The old man shrugged. 'Not like the old days, *Comandante*.'

'You've stopped printing fake banknotes, have you?'

'I wouldn't say stopped, exactly.' Geronimo shot him a suspicious look. 'Is this an official visit?'

Guzmán shook his head. 'Business. If you're still up for it, of course?'

'Business is business,' Geronimo said. 'What is it you want?'

Guzmán took a handwritten list from his pocket and put it on the counter. 'All of these documents. I want them to look authentic. No cutting corners.'

'You know me, *Comandante*. I never cut corners. Do you want them in your name?'

'Of course not,' Guzmán snorted. 'The name and details are on the back of that list.'

Geronimo turned the list over with a podgy finger and gave a low whistle as he read the name. 'I know who this is.'

'You also know how to keep your mouth shut, as I remember,' Guzmán said, counting several banknotes onto the counter. 'You'll get the rest on delivery. Can you get them done by eleven tonight?'

Geronimo raised an eyebrow. 'That's a tall order, *Comandante*. I'll need special paper and ink for this job.'

'Know what? I'm willing to bet you've got them all in the back.'

The old man held up his hands. 'I've always been up for a challenge.'

'That's why you never went to jail,' Guzmán said, heading for the door. 'I'll send someone round to collect the order this evening.'

The dissonant clank of the bell reverberated above his head as he went out into the street, suddenly optimistic. Not everything had changed in this city.

MADRID, OCTOBER 1982, GUARDIA CIVIL HEADQUARTERS

Guzmán took a seat in the general's office and waited as Ortiz opened his drinks cabinet and poured them brandy.

'First of the day's always the best, eh, Leo?' Ortiz beamed as he slumped into his leather chair and put his feet on the desk. 'So, how's the file collection going?'

Guzmán leaned forward to take a cigar from the box the general offered. 'Excellent,' he sighed, exhaling a mouthful of fragrant smoke. 'Gutiérrez is finding a safe place for the documents. Once we've moved them there, that's my job done.'

'That should be enough to fuck the *Centinelas* up.' Ortiz nodded. 'All we need then is for the Socialists to get elected. Once they get the files, they can do the rest.'

'Let's hope so.' Guzmán took another swallow of brandy. 'I've got a favour to ask.'

'Name it, Leo.'

Guzmán reached into his jacket and took out a plastic tobacco pouch filled with papers. 'I'd like you to keep this safe for me.'

Ortiz frowned. 'Sounds like you're expecting trouble.'

'I always expect trouble. It's best to be prepared.'

'True enough.' The general took the packet from him and put it into the breast pocket of his uniform jacket. 'I'll put it in my safe. Just let me know when you want it back.'

'Thanks.' Guzmán glanced at the time. 'I'd better go, I'm seeing Gutiérrez later.'

Before he could get up, General Ortiz raised a hand. 'I've been thinking. If this plan to use the files against the *Centinelas* comes off—'

'Which it will.'

'*If* it does, that will leave Gutiérrez as the most powerful man in the city.' He raised his glass to his lips and took a long swallow of brandy. 'Or you, of course.'

'Not me,' said Guzmán. 'I'm through with all of this.' He drained his glass with an appreciative grunt. 'I'm off.'

'You should get yourself a wife, Leo. Someone to take care of you.'

'I've always taken care of myself,' Guzmán said, pulling on his coat.

'Even so, cooking, cleaning, sewing – you need a woman to do those things. There must be someone who fits the bill?'

There were several, Guzmán recalled. Unfortunately, all were dead. All but one, of course, and she was taken. 'I'll bear it in mind.'

'Before you go,' Ortiz said, 'how's my son been doing on this operation?'

Guzmán stuffed his hands into his pockets, suddenly uncomfortable. 'None of those lads are very experienced. But most of them have made an effort.'

'But not Ramiro?'

'I don't think his heart's in it.'

'Not got the balls, you mean?'

'It's not a career he would have chosen if you weren't his father. Put it that way.'

General Ortiz's face was like thunder. 'He doesn't have a choice. Christ, when I joined the Legion as a young officer, my father told me not to come back without a bullet wound or he'd thrash me.'

'Things were different back then.'

'Don't start on about change again, or I'll think you've gone soft.' Ortiz gave Guzmán a hard look. 'Was it you who blacked Galíndez's eye?'

'My corporal. He had a fall-out with him about some magazines.'

'I've had several fall-outs with him about those magazines,' Ortiz growled. 'The ones with children in them, were they?'

'Ochoa's a family man. He gets upset about children being mistreated.'

'Good for him,' said Ortiz. 'I'll add an extra increment to his pension.'

Guzmán winced. Ochoa seemed to attract money like shit attracted flies. At this rate, he'd be the wealthiest pensioner in Spain. 'He'll like that,' he said, through clenched teeth.

'One other thing,' Ortiz said. 'Somebody killed Eduardo Ricci last night.'

'There's a tragedy.'

'It could be for someone: you know he was protected by the *Centinelas*?'

'Doesn't sound like they did a very good job.' Guzmán went to the door.

'Look after yourself, Leo. These are tough times, and they're going to get tougher – especially for you, I imagine.'

'Why me?' Guzmán asked, suddenly belligerent. There were others who'd served the regime besides him, many others, yet people talked as if he'd been the only one.

'Men who stand out at what they do are always remembered, and there are plenty of people who remember you and what you did.' He looked up and met Guzmán's eye. 'You have to know when it's time to go.'

Guzmán narrowed his eyes. 'Why? Franco didn't.'

'Franco had been gone a long time before he died on that life-support machine,' Ortiz said. 'And even then, they only kept him alive so he'd still be here for the fortieth anniversary of the war. It's different for your sort. Men like you don't die in their beds.'

Guzmán closed the door behind him. He went into the court-yard and walked past the sentries at the gate into the street. A surly grey sky. More rain to come, given the dark layers of cloud moving over the city. Winter was coming and in winter things converged: ice and snow, TB and the grave, hunter and prey. A time when the weak fell and the strong stayed standing. Winter had always been his time.

Somewhere along the street, a dog was barking.

He crossed the road and used a payphone to call Gutiérrez. 'You asked about my code the other day. I think I can get you a copy.'

'Excellent,' Gutiérrez wheezed. 'I'll be happier knowing the *Centinelas* can't read our communications. Can you bring it to HQ at once?'

'Not yet,' Guzmán said. 'I have to collect it from someone.'

'Who might that be?' A sudden note of suspicion in Gutiérrez's voice.

'I can't say. But when I've collected it, you can have it for a reasonable sum.'

He heard Gutiérrez sigh. Or perhaps he was gasping for breath. 'That would be most helpful, *Comandante*.'

Guzmán hung up.

MADRID, OCTOBER 1982, SECRETAS DE LA NOCHE, LENCERÍA, CALLE DE NÚÑEZ DE BALBOA

Guzmán entered the shop and waited, glowering at the arrays of underwear until an assistant emerged from behind a display of lacy basques and came to serve him.

'Can I help you, señor?'

'I'd like some underwear,' he muttered. 'Not for me, of course, they're for a lady.'

'Of course.' The assistant beamed. Men's shopping habits were inevitably lucrative. Their embarrassment made them willing to part with far more money than they intended. For most, the aim was to make the purchase and get out before anyone saw them. 'Does the gentleman have anything in mind?'

Guzmán had a great deal in mind, though he was hardly going to tell her.

'Underwear,' he said. 'Red underwear.' He pointed to various items. 'Bra, panties. Suspender belt and stockings. All in red.'

'And the size?'

'A little taller than you, a bit stockier as well.'

'One size bigger than me then?'

'Larger,' he said, appraising her with a critical eye. 'You're bigger than you seem.'

The shop assistant wrapped his purchases in tissue paper and put them in a brown paper carrier. 'Anything else?'

He glanced along the counter, thinking quickly. 'Lipstick.'

'To match the underwear?'

'Of course,' he snapped, wondering why sales people made things so difficult.

Once he had paid, he hurried from the shop, clutching the

carrier to keep it from spilling its contents in the street. Such things were the stuff of nightmares.

The assistant watched him go, certain his wife or girlfriend would be calling in during the next couple of days to change the items for different sizes or colours. They invariably did.

The afternoon light was starting to fade. That cheered him. Most aspects of his business were best conducted in the dark. He looked again at the piece of paper Ignacio gave him. If the old man's information was correct, Javier Benavides lived only a few hundred metres further up the road.

He found the address without difficulty. A sombre, though well-kept apartment building. Its appearance spoke of money, which was hardly surprising, given Benavides' position within the *Centinelas*.

Guzmán stood in a doorway across the road from the apartment building, watching people go in and out. He saw the small desk inside the door where the *portero* lurked, making sure that visitors were expected, taking parcels from the postman and keeping out any lowlifes who might drift in to tap up the residents. Or rob them, of course. Another sign of change. But those things were problems for the police, not for him. He had his own problems.

He crossed the road just as the *portero* was helping an elderly resident into a taxi. Guzmán slipped inside, crossed the entrance hall and, without pausing, went down an unlit corridor. From the smell of damp, he guessed this was the tradesmen's entrance, accessed from a passage at the side of the building.

At the end of the corridor, he found an emergency door to one side and to the other, a flight of steps that led to the cellar. Quietly, he went down the stairs into the murky basement. A couple of rusting old washing machines stood against the wall and he hid the lingerie behind them before going back upstairs. The concierge glared as he came across the marble tiles.

'Can I help, señor?' The man's tone suggested that would not be his preferred option.

'Probably,' Guzmán said. 'I'm a reporter. I'm looking for someone called Javier Benavides. I'd like to interview him.'

'You've no right to come wandering around in here, señor.' The man's outrage turned his already unhealthy complexion puce. At this rate he wouldn't survive the encounter, Guzmán decided.

'I can go if there's a problem.'

'You'd better, before I call the police.'

Guzmán held his hands up. 'You don't have to tell me twice.' Outside, he crossed the road and slowly looked in every shop window on that side of the street, concentrating on shops that could easily be seen from the *portero*'s desk. He walked up and down a few times, each time making sure the man had seen him. When he checked his watch, half an hour had gone by. Surely to God the *portero* had instructions to call for backup when Benavides had unexpected callers? No one in Benavides' position could be that lax.

He turned again, planning to survey the shop windows and restaurant windows once more to try and provoke a reaction. A few metres up the road, a car pulled to a halt and Guzmán stopped his bogus window shopping.

The backup had arrived.

MADRID, OCTOBER 1982, CALLE DE GARCÍA DE PAREDES

'Pour me a proper fucking drink, for Christ's sake,' General Ortiz barked. 'No son of mine is going to give his father half a fucking glass of whisky.'

'Sorry, Father.' Ramiro opened the bottle and topped up the general's glass. Ortiz took a long drink and sank back into his favourite leather armchair. 'To what do I owe the pleasure of this visit? Has your wife sent you to borrow money again?'

'It… it… it's not that, Father,' Ramiro stammered.

It was quite common for people to develop a slight stammer when dealing with General Ortiz. Normally, he would have ignored it. But not with his son.

'It… It… It's not… wh-wh-wh-what?' Ortiz took an angry gulp

of his Scotch. 'How the fuck are you ever going to command men if you can't speak to your own father?'

'It's only a problem with you,' Ramiro muttered.

'That's where you're wrong, son. It's you that's fucking wrong. You're a coward, lazy and, worst of fucking all, everyone knows about those foreign magazines your pal Galíndez keeps buying.'

'He doesn't mean any harm, they're just a bit of fun, Papa.'

'Don't call me papa,' General Ortiz shouted. 'A bit of fun? Carmen's a bit of fun. Good-looking, big tits and a sense of humour. But she's a woman, not a child.'

'You know what? You spend more time talking to her than you do to me.'

'I'd rather spend more time with Corporal Ochoa than you. At least he was man enough to give Galíndez a thrashing for buying that filth.'

'Times have changed, Father. Spain's liberated now. Music, books, even porn. People smoke dope in public.'

'You think I don't know?' The general got to his feet and went over to the drinks cabinet to get a refill. 'Do you think that gives an officer in the *guardia* the right to sell smut to his colleagues like some impoverished pimp?'

'Miguel only sells them to his friends.'

General Ortiz slumped back into his chair. 'You keep protecting him like this and your career is going to end up down the fucking toilet along with his.' He unfastened his holster and pulled out his Star semi-automatic. 'Here, make yourself useful. Strip this down and clean it. And make a good job of it.' He tossed the pistol over his shoulder, forcing Ramiro to catch the weapon before it landed amid a collection of the late Señora Ortiz's porcelain. 'And get a move on,' Ortiz growled. 'I'm meeting Carmen later.'

MADRID, OCTOBER 1982, CALLE DE NÚÑEZ DE BALBOA

Guzmán watched the men come down the road, shadow figures

against the pale street lights. He watched carefully, looking for the subtle movement of a hand towards a hidden weapon. Even though they seemed relaxed, that didn't mean they weren't armed.

The men stopped a couple of metres away. The tallest took a pace forward, making him Guzmán's first target.

'You're looking for Señor Benavides, I hear?'

'That's right, I'd like to interview him about his views on the election.'

'We can take you to meet him, if you like. He's out at the Casa de Campo.'

'A country park is an odd place to carry out an interview, isn't it?'

The man shrugged. 'He's willing to spare you an hour for the interview.' A cold smile. 'We'll give you a lift back later.'

'Let's go, then.' As Guzmán followed them to their car, he glanced up at the windows of Benavides' apartment. In one of the upper windows, he caught a glimpse of a man, highlighted against the electric light, watching. At this distance, there was no mistaking Benavides. Not with that fake tan.

The tall man got behind the wheel. The other two sat in the back, leaving Guzmán no choice but to take the front passenger seat. That was unfortunate, since it left him open to being garrotted or shot in the back of the head. That was a risk he would have to take. As the driver started the engine, Guzmán got in and slammed the door.

Once the car pulled away from the kerb, he took a look in the mirror at the two men behind him. Neither seemed nervous or fidgeted in the way that men about to kill someone often did. There were usually at least some signs to be detected but these men were relaxed. That suggested he wasn't going to be killed yet. Maybe they planned to torture him to satisfy their curiosity about his interest in Benavides.

'You eaten, *amigo*?' the driver asked, making conversation.

'An hour ago.' Guzmán nodded, improvising. 'Seafood. It didn't agree with me.'

'I've had that,' one of the men in the back said. 'Mussels. I was sick for a week.'

'I've got a story to write,' Guzmán said. 'I can't afford time off work.'

A sudden furtive complicity passed between them. He glanced out of the window, noticing shabby buildings to either side. A badly lit alley ahead. He clutched his stomach. 'Fuck, I'm going to spew.'

'Don't be sick in the car,' the driver said, slowing.

'Over there,' Guzmán groaned. 'That alley.'

The driver exchanged looks with the two in the back as he slowed.

Guzmán felt the two men behind him relax as the car turned into the alley. He knew what they were thinking. *No way out.* They were correct.

'Sorry about this, gentlemen,' Guzmán said, opening the door. He crouched by the side of the car, stuck a finger down his throat and began retching.

'Doesn't sound too bad, *amigo*,' one called. Guzmán heard a metallic click as someone cocked a pistol. By the car's front tyre, he saw a dog turd among the other refuse.

'We haven't got all night.' The driver's voice, tense now.

Guzmán stuck his finger into the turd and then popped it into his mouth.

'Señor Benavides doesn't like to be kept waiting.'

The man's voice was cut short by Guzmán's sudden, agonised retching. He banged the side of the car with his fist as a stream of vomit burst from the deepest recesses of his gut, splattering the cobbles.

A voice from inside the car. 'Fuck's sake, he's making me feel ill.'

With each spectacular wave of nausea, he felt their discomfort growing. Finally, he spat a wad of bile onto the pavement. 'Fuck, that's better out than in.'

'I hope you're done,' someone growled as Guzmán raised his face into the open window. He saw their disgusted expressions. And then he retched violently, spraying vomit onto the empty passenger seat. Automatically, the men turned away in disgust.

Guzmán pushed the Browning through the window and shot the driver in the side of the head. The other two reacted far too late. The car shook with two sharp reports from the Browning and they sagged back against the seat, their faces set in a look of eternal surprise.

Guzmán took out his handkerchief and wiped the inside of his mouth. He left the car and walked back along the street until he found a bar. Inside, he ordered brandy, filled his mouth with it and then left. Once outside, he gargled with the brandy and then spat it out, carelessly splattering the shoes of a dark-clad passer-by.

'Sorry about that,' he called. Irritatingly, the man ignored him. That was typical of priests, he thought, they never saw the funny side of anything. A taxi turned the corner and he flagged it down. 'Núñez de Balboa,' Guzmán told the driver.

MADRID, OCTOBER 1982, CALLE DE NÚÑEZ DE BALBOA

Javier Benavides slipped a cassette into his tape deck and pressed play. The room filled with a slow smoky voice as Dionne Warwick sang 'Heartbreaker'. He mimed a little dance, swirling across the carpet with an imaginary partner.

A knock at the door. 'Parcel for Señor Benavides.'

Benavides sighed. How many times had he asked the *portero* not to send tradespeople up? Laziness, that was what it was.

With a sigh, he opened the double lock on the door. 'You could have left it with the—' The sentence ended as he stared into the muzzle of Guzmán's Browning.

Benavides backed away, raising his hands. 'What is this, *Comandante*?'

'Shut up.' Guzmán was holding a brown paper package in his free hand. He stepped inside and tossed the package to one side before locking the door. 'Take a seat,' Guzmán said. An order, not a request. Benavides did as he was told.

'Where's my code?' Guzmán asked.

Benavides smiled. 'Don't you mean *my* code, *Comandante*?'

Guzmán clubbed him over the head with the Browning, knocking him from the chair. As Benavides lay on the floor, clutching his head, Guzmán picked up the upended chair, righted it and then shoved Benavides back into it.

'That was unnecessary,' Benavides groaned. 'The code isn't here.'

That was not what Guzmán wanted to hear and he cocked the Browning as an indication of his displeasure. 'If you don't have it, who does?'

'I'm no expert on these things, *Comandante*, so I decided to get one of Spain's best mathematicians to look over it. He's a little eccentric, but an absolute genius with figures.'

'I don't want a fucking reference, just give me his address.'

Benavides reached for a rolodex card index on his desk and flipped through the cards. 'This is him, Alberto Pedraza. It's Dr Pedraza, actually, though you wouldn't think so to look at him: he dresses like a tramp.'

Guzmán snatched the card from Benavides' hand and stuck it in his top pocket.

'You know, you really aren't playing by the rules, *Comandante*.'

Guzmán raised the pistol. 'See this?'

Benavides blinked nervously at the pistol a few centimetres from his face. 'Yes?'

'Now tell me whose fucking rules we're playing to.'

Benavides opted for silence.

Strangely, that annoyed Guzmán as much as when he was talking. 'Where do you keep the drinks?'

'In that globe.' Benavides pointed to a large wooden sphere by the wall.

'Looks like it's ready for the dump,' Guzmán said. 'The paint's faded.'

Benavides gave him a hurt look. 'It's antique.'

Guzmán pulled open the hinged lid. 'Is there any Carlos Primero?'

'But of course.' Benavides started to get to his feet.

Guzmán raised the pistol again. 'One more move like that and you're dead. Hands behind your head and put your face down on the desk.' Benavides obeyed.

'What's your poison?' Guzmán asked, searching for the brandy.

'Whisky.'

Guzmán selected two heavy Venetian glass tumblers and poured himself an extremely large brandy and a small whisky for Benavides. Satisfied Benavides was keeping his face pressed to the desktop, Guzmán took two small tablets from his top pocket and dropped them into the whisky. The tablets dissolved within moments.

'Get this down you.' He put the glass on the desk.

Benavides raised his head slowly, cautious now.

'I was attacked at my *pensión*,' Guzmán said. 'One of my friends was killed.'

'That had nothing to do with me, *Comandante*. I know nothing about it.'

'Pretty much everything seems to involve you in one way or another,' Guzmán said. 'Or maybe I should say you and Señorita Ibañez. So don't insult my intelligence or I'll beat your brains out all over this desk. What do you know about the attack on the *pensión*?'

Benavides shrugged. 'Paloma and I are strategy people, *Comandante*. We collect data, we make suggestions. Most of our efforts go into policy making. The unpleasant stuff remains the domain of the central council. They're the ones who authorised the attack on your *pensión*.'

'I find it hard to believe that a bunch of elderly generals would spend time planning the killing of an eighteen-year-old girl.'

Benavides' hand trembled as he raised the glass to his mouth and swallowed half the Scotch in one long gulp. 'They don't share information like that with me.'

'How about Paloma Ibañez?'

'Paloma handles strategic and tactical issues as the need arises. I can't say which ones for certain.'

'Of course not,' Guzmán sneered, 'it's not like you work with her, is it?'

'I merely meant that—'

Guzmán cut him short. 'Does she socialise with any of the central council?'

'Well, naturally Paloma appeals to them as men. One hears rumours.'

'You'll hear this pistol rumouring through your head if you don't give me a straight answer. Does she sleep with any of them?'

'If the rumours are to believed.'

'Including General Amadeo?'

'She likes to get her way, and she knows how to get it.' A dull look of surprise crossed Benavides' face. He frowned, as if trying to remember something. He put down his empty glass and stared at it. 'There was something in that drin—'

As Benavides slumped forward on the desk, Guzmán went over to the wooden globe and got himself another brandy. Reaching into his coat pocket, he took out a pair of gloves and put them on. Then he pulled the chair from under Señor Benavides and tipped him onto the floor. Benavides grunted though he did not wake.

On the desk, Guzmán saw an electric typewriter. He put a sheet of paper into the typewriter and clumsily tapped out a couple of sentences. Then he dedicated the next few minutes to clearing up the flat.

First, he took the Venetian glass tumbler he'd drunk from into the kitchen and washed and dried it carefully before returning it to the drinks cabinet. The other glass carried Benavides' fingerprints and Guzmán handled it using a cloth from the kitchen as he placed it back on the desk. Then he wiped the bottles he'd touched free of prints. The cloth went into his pocket, for disposal later. The housework over, he went over to the sleeping man on the floor and started to unbutton his shirt.

It only took a couple of minutes to strip Benavides and stuff his clothes into a bamboo washing basket in the kitchen. In the bedroom, the wardrobe was fitted with a double shelf for Benavides' large collection of shoes and Guzmán shoved the pair he had been wearing alongside the others.

It was an impressive wardrobe: no doubt an antique, Guzmán guessed as he closed the door. On the top was a heavy, intricate carving, sculpted from a single block of wood. Some kind of pastoral scene, the thick wood laced with delicately carved loops and whorls. A robust piece of craftsmanship, he thought, as he returned to the living room to retrieve the brown paper package.

Dressing Benavides in the red underwear required a lot more effort than undressing him. The man was a dead weight and Guzmán had to struggle to get him into the lace panties and bra. Attaching the stockings to the suspender belt provoked a stream of colourful obscenities, though in the end, the result was satisfactory. It wasn't as though Benavides was about to be entered into the Miss World competition. Finally, Guzmán took the lipstick he'd bought and used it to turn Benavides' mouth into something resembling the grin of a particularly deranged clown.

Guzmán dragged Benavides into the bedroom and propped him against the bed while he went back to get the clothes rope he'd bought in the SEPU department store that afternoon. One end of the rope he attached to the carving on the top of the wardrobe, wrapping the rope around several of the carved pieces to distribute the weight. When he tested it, both rope and carving took his weight without any problem.

The rest was simple. He fashioned a noose with practised familiarity before hauling the unconscious Benavides towards the wardrobe, holding him awkwardly with one arm while he worked the noose around his neck. Slowly, he released him, watching the rope tighten until it supported Benavides' entire weight. Rather than listen to the noise of him choking to death, Guzmán went back into the living room.

The scene was just as he wanted it. When the body was found, the conclusions were already there, waiting to be drawn. One glass for Benavides' last solitary drink. His clothes in the wash basket and his shoes put away neatly. The actions of a careful, methodical person, albeit one with a terrible guilty secret. The evidence of that secret was clear for all to see on the single sheet of paper sticking out of the typewriter roller.

I can't go on living a lie.

Whoever found Benavides would understand at once, Guzmán knew. It was just a matter of creating a convincing impression and the red underwear would certainly do that. Within a few days of the body being found, even Benavides' closest friends would begin to remember that they'd harboured suspicions about him.

A faint reek of shit from the bedroom signalled Benavides' change of status to the late Señor Benavides. After locking the apartment, Guzmán went downstairs and left the building by the tradesmen's door.

A block away, he went into a call box. The sarge's son answered and listened carefully to the instructions Guzmán gave him. Guzmán pushed another coin into the phone as he rummaged in his pocket with his free hand for the paper Ignacio had given him and dictated the second address, thinking that Ignacio probably deserved a lot more than the amount he'd paid him. 'Got all that?' Guzmán said, ready to hang up.

'I'll do it now, boss,' Julio said.

MADRID, OCTOBER 1982, PLAZA DEL CORDÓN

'Ricci *and* Javier?' A momentary silence. 'Thanks for letting me know.'

Paloma Ibañez's hand was shaking as she put down the phone. She hurried across the room and turned out the lights, leaving the room illuminated only by the vague glow of the street lamps outside.

In four years of working for the *Centinelas*, Paloma had never experienced a moment like this. People got hurt, of course: she knew how those things were done and why, but it was not part of her job to witness them or to have them happen to people she knew. Orders were given, action was taken. But for her, those assassinations were abstract affairs, designed to remove people who got in the way of progress. The *Centinelas'* progress, that was.

Which made what was happening now all the more troubling.

She picked up the phone again and dialled a number. As she listened to the ringing at the other end, she ran a hand through her hair in an unconscious gesture of deference to the man she was calling.

An icy voice answered. 'Señorita Ibañez. I was expecting your call. Such a pleasure.'

Pleasantries, even fake ones, were beyond her tonight. 'Someone killed Javier earlier this evening,' she spluttered. 'It's bad enough Ricci got himself shot at that tawdry club of his but Javier? He was—'

'Shut up.' The voice was even icier than before. 'I know what happened. You need to come over, we'll keep you safe. You know where to come?'

'Yes.' Paloma nodded, hoping her voice wasn't shaking as much as her hands.

'Then get your car keys and leave the flat at once. You'll be safe here.'

'I understand, but—' She stopped talking. The line had gone dead.

Paloma went over to an ornate desk by the window. As she rummaged for her keys, she felt the panic rising. *If they can kill Ricci and Javier, they can kill any of us.* And another, more bitter thought: *They said we were protected.* Her fingers closed around the keys and she snatched them up and made for the door, her heels tapping on the parquet tiles.

As the door closed behind her, she wished she'd picked up the small pistol Javier had given her last Christmas. But then, why would she carry a gun around with her? Hadn't her employers told her that their protection was more than enough to keep her safe? Unfortunately, recent events made her question that.

She crossed the small cobbled square, wincing at the brittle echoes of her footsteps as she listened for the sound of someone lurking in the shadows. She heard nothing. That encouraged her. Once she was in the car, she would be safe.

Her hands were shaking badly, and she struggled for a few moments to get the key into the lock. Finally, the door opened, the sound of the catch magnified by the still night air. Once inside, she gave a sigh of relief as she locked the doors and pushed the key into the ignition. Calmer now, she smoothed her skirt and turned on the interior light to make sure her hair was tidy. Where she was going, she could hardly arrive looking as though she'd just got out of bed. Satisfied with her appearance, she switched off the light and reached for the ignition.

A hand clamped over her nose and mouth, pulling her head back against the headrest. She struggled, clutching at the hand, fighting for breath. Then something cold pressed against her neck and she felt the sharp edge of a blade pressed against her carotid artery. The hand relaxed a little and she gulped in air, tasting the strong bitter tobacco on the man's skin. Other smells too, none of them pleasant. And then, as her attacker raised himself from behind the driver's seat, she saw a face from hell, reflected in the mirror. Her scream was cut short as his hand pressed over her mouth again, harder this time. A deep, rasping voice. Stinking breath.

'Keep quiet or I'll cut your throat.'

Paloma obeyed, offering no resistance as he bound her with coarse rope. She was less compliant as he took a piece of cloth from his pocket and gagged her, though her resistance was short-lived. Lying across the front seats, she heard him get out, the sound of his footsteps as he went to the rear of the car and opened the boot. Then the footsteps returned and she moaned as he dragged her from the car. She realised what was about to happen and started to struggle, though it was too late to stop him now as he bundled her into the boot and slammed the lid. Then the driver's door closed and a few moments later the engine throbbed into life as the car bounced forward over the cobbles.

CHAPTER 22

MADRID, OCTOBER 2010, CALLE VELÁZQUEZ

The elegant shops bustled with customers as Galíndez made her way up the street, checking out the goods in the windows of the most expensive stores, taking the opportunity to cast an eye over the passers-by around her. No one seemed to be following her, though she wasn't stupid enough to think that meant no one was.

Across the road, the reinforced glass windows of Judge Delgado's office glinted dull in the autumn light. She took a last look to see if she was being trailed and then hurried across the road. Reaching for the buzzer, she caught a glimpse of her image reflected in the bulletproof glass. Pale face, dark circles under her eyes. Definitely not at her best. Still, a couple of painkillers would perk her up later.

The receptionist answered through the speakerphone. When she heard Galíndez's name, she operated the door mechanism, opening it just long enough to for Galíndez to enter before it closed and locked behind her. The receptionist opened the door to the side and Galíndez stepped out into the office.

'Judge Delgado is upstairs in the conference room.'

She followed the woman down the hall, pausing while she tapped a security code into a pad at the side of a thick metal door. Once through the door, the receptionist led her up a wide flight of stairs and ushered her into the conference room.

Judge Delgado was standing by the window, looking out at the bustle of Calle Velázquez through floor-length muslin curtains, his bouffant of grey hair backlit by the light from the window. Dismissing the receptionist, he came forward and took Galíndez's outstretched hand in such a formal manner she thought he was about to kiss it. Instead, he gave her a light handshake.

'A pleasure, Dr Galíndez,' Delgado said, holding a chair for her. Once she was seated, he strolled languidly round the table and sat facing her. 'Can I offer you a drink? Sherry, perhaps, or coffee?'

Galíndez asked for water.

Delgado went over to a drinks cabinet by the wall and came back with a large glass of mineral water. 'You said on the telephone that you have evidence on the *Centinelas*? I'm surprised.'

Galíndez frowned. 'Why? It's my job.'

'I wasn't doubting your competence,' Delgado said. 'I meant I'm surprised you're alive. Most people who've tried to expose them have died in somewhat unusual circumstances.'

'So I believe,' Galíndez said. 'In fact, I infiltrated a meeting of the *Centinelas* only two days ago. During the meeting, they identified an undercover police officer. She was beaten to death in order to intimidate their new members.'

Bernardino looked up sharply. 'You should be careful, if they were able to identify her, it would be reckless to think they couldn't do the same thing to you.'

Galíndez swallowed, hard. She'd been thinking the same thing herself.

'There was another policeman there,' she said. 'He's been working undercover in the *Centinelas* for four years.'

'Sancho Hernández?' Delgado said, leafing through his papers. 'He's the only man to successfully infiltrate them so far.'

She narrowed her eyes. 'How do you know about him, Judge?'

Delgado shrugged. 'Naturally, I keep abreast of what's happening in law enforcement agencies. You can never have too much information.'

'Unfortunately, Sancho was killed during a police raid on the Pensión Paraíso yesterday,' she said. 'The *policía nacional* claim there were terrorists in the *pensión*, though that was a lie. It's clear to me that the *Centinelas* have infiltrated the police force.'

Delgado gave her a curious look. 'You seem to know a great

deal about them. Why haven't you reported your findings to your superiors?'

'Because I don't know who I can trust any more.' The ice cubes tinkled in her glass as she took another sip of water.

'A very sensible attitude.' Delgado nodded. 'You've already seen the precautions I take to protect myself and it's no fun, I can tell you, living behind bulletproof glass. But that's enough about my problems, what do you want from me?'

Galíndez reached into her top pocket and took out the memory stick. 'This is the information Sancho Hernández collected during the four years he worked for the *Centinelas*. It has details of their membership and their finances as well as information about their connections with organised crime, both in Spain and abroad.'

'Good Lord,' Delgado said. Carefully, he ran a hand over his hair. 'That material has the potential to destroy them, if used properly.'

'Exactly, and I was hoping you might be the one to do it.'

'I'd have to decide how it should be done,' Delgado said. 'Do you have any ideas?'

'I thought if the contents of the USB stick were sent to media and law enforcement agencies, it would be impossible to stop that information from becoming public. The authorities would have to act.'

'An excellent idea,' Delgado said. 'Do you have a time frame in mind?'

'The sooner the better. Midday tomorrow, maybe?' She held out the memory stick.

Delgado took the stick from her and placed it on the blotter in front of him. 'You don't know what this means to me, Dr Galíndez.'

Galíndez got up from her chair, ready to go. 'I have a feeling that I do, Judge.'

MADRID 2010, CALLE LARGASCA

'The judge agreed to release it tomorrow?' Isabel said. 'That's brilliant news.'

She looked happier than she had for a long time, Galíndez thought. 'Midday tomorrow. He said it could go global.'

'We should celebrate.'

'Let's see what happens tomorrow first,' Galíndez said, starting to unfasten her boots. 'We can celebrate once we're sure the plan's worked.'

Isabel went into the kitchen and came back with two bottles of Alhambra. 'Here, let's have a pre-celebration drink.'

Galíndez took a long drink from the bottle and sighed. 'You can't beat a cold beer.'

Isabel joined her on the sofa. 'You really think all this will be over soon?'

'It depends on Delgado,' Galíndez said. 'I stopped off in the library after I visited his office and read up on the malpractice suit he was involved in. He was accused of corruption *and* money laundering.'

'It wasn't proved, though, Ana.'

'It wasn't disproved either,' Galíndez said. 'The charges were dropped because key witnesses declined to give evidence.'

Isabel frowned. 'You surely don't suspect he's one of them?'

'I trust you and I trust me. Everyone else is a suspect. And before you say anything, that's not paranoia. I haven't had a painkiller for days.'

Isabel leaned closer, and smoothed Galíndez's hair with her hand. 'That's my girl.' Her face grew serious again. 'But if you don't trust Delgado, how are you going to find out if he's on their side or not?'

'We won't, not until tomorrow, anyway.'

'OK.' Isabel got up. 'Then we should get an early night.'

'I'm not tired yet.' Galíndez looked up and saw Isabel's expression. 'I'll be right there.'

'Have you finished your shower?' Isabel called. 'It's almost midday, I'm putting the TV on. Let's see if Judge Delgado's on the news.'

Towelling her hair, Galíndez joined her in front of the TV. The 24-hour news channel was recycling footage of a Chinese earth-quake it had used the previous day.

'Did you tell anyone you were staying here, Ana?' Isabel went over to the table and picked up a package from it.

Galíndez shook her head. 'No, why do you ask?'

Isabel handed her a padded envelope. 'Someone sent you this package.'

'That's odd,' Galíndez muttered, examining it. 'It's very light, much too light to be—'

'Important?' Isabel cut in.

'A bomb,' Galíndez said. She saw Isabel's expression and tried to change the subject. 'Judge Delgado must have released the contents of that memory stick to the press by now.'

'Let's see.' Isabel grabbed the remote and surfed the channels until she found CNN. 'Look, it's just more footage about that earthquake.'

Galíndez frowned. 'If Delgado sent out the information, they ought to be discussing it by now.'

'They could still be editing it, Ana.'

'I told you I had my doubts about him.'

'Look,' Isabel gasped, suddenly excited. 'It's him.' She pointed to the TV screen.

The screen was showing a still photograph that flattered the judge. The familiar grey coiffure, the wry smile and mischievous blue eyes.

Galíndez turned up the sound. An excited voice.

'A leading figure in the judiciary was shot dead in Madrid this morning. Police named the victim as Judge Bernadino Delgado. Over now to a special report from our political reporter Roberto Peralta at the scene of the assassination.'

A stunned silence. Finally, Galíndez switched off the TV.

'Fuck,' Isabel said, taking in the implications.

'Precisely my thoughts.' Galíndez nodded. 'They must have found out I gave him the memory stick.' She looked down at the padded envelope in her lap. 'Let's see what's in here.' She upended the envelope and a small object slid out. 'There's a note.' She took a folded piece of paper from the envelope. As she read the note, Isabel saw her eyes widen.

'What is it, Ana?'

'It's from Sancho,' Galíndez said, blinking as she read it. '"Sorry, babe, I gave you a fake USB. If you've managed to stay alive long enough to read this letter, here's the real one. If you passed on the fake stick to anyone, they're now the proud owners of a copy of the Madrid phone directory. Thanks for sorting out the Witness Protection thing for me.'"

Galíndez stopped reading to wipe her eyes.

'Does he say anything else?' Isabel asked.

Galíndez shook her head. 'I think we'd better keep a low profile now.'

'As in go into hiding?'

'Not yet, though maybe we should go somewhere they won't find us easily.'

'How about the university?' Isabel said. 'It's teeming with people.'

'That might work. Let's go in an hour, when the traffic's heavier. It'll make it harder to follow us.'

'Are you certain?' Isabel's voice sounded strained.

'I'm not certain of anything now, Izzy.' Galíndez got up and went to the window, looking out nervously into the street. Then she lowered the blind. As she came back to the sofa, she picked up the evidence bag containing the packet she'd found in General Ortiz's pocket when she took the DNA samples. 'I've been meaning to have a look at this.'

'I thought you said it was a tobacco pouch?'

'It is.' Galíndez pushed a finger under the flap and opened it. 'But there are some papers inside it.' She slid one of the papers from the plastic pouch and started unfolding the yellowing outer layer. 'Shit, it's disintegrating.'

More careful now, she teased the time-worn sheets apart with her fingernail. Despite her delicate touch, the outer layers crumbled into yellow flakes. She put the crumbling paper to one side and reached into the pouch again, lifting out a folded square of what seemed to be thick card. 'This is some sort of parchment.'

Isabel leaned closer, watching her unfold the parchment. 'Is that a map?'

'A building plan, I think,' Galíndez said, examining it. The lines were faded, though there was no mistaking the linear precision of an architect's pen. She pointed to a long corridor with regularly spaced rooms on either side. Her eyes narrowed as she felt a strange sense of familiarity.

'Look at that,' Isabel said, watching over her shoulder. 'It's laid out like a hotel.'

Galíndez shook her head. 'It's not a hotel, those are cells.' Her voice was taut. 'I know exactly what this is: it's the layout of Guzmán's old *comisaría* on Calle Robles.'

'Are you OK?' Isabel asked. 'You're white as a sheet.'

'It's where I was injured in the explosion.' Galíndez rubbed her hands together as she remembered the chill air of the ancient building. 'There are rooms on this plan I didn't know existed.' She pointed to the plan, indicating a doorway at the far end of the corridor. Beyond that was the sweep of a spiral staircase leading to other chambers below. Each chamber bore a label, though the lettering was smudged and faded.

'What does that say, Ana?' Isabel asked, pointing to one of the labels.

'Eastern Vault,' Galíndez said. Slowly, she traced her finger over the plan to a second chamber. 'And this one is the Central Vault.' In one corner of the chamber was the entrance to a passageway leading to another vault. This time, the layout of the vault was slightly different: a strange sloping line ran upwards, like a staircase without stairs, reaching up to the street, three storeys above. Galíndez pointed to the label: *Western Vault.*

'That's it,' she said, quietly. 'Whatever the *Centinelas* are looking for is in there.'

'Shouldn't you call the *guardia* and have them send someone to investigate?'

Galíndez shook her head. 'We've no idea who we can trust now.'

'Oh, come on,' Isabel said, sharply. 'Not everyone's working for the *Centinelas*.'

'No? Capitán Fuentes was wearing a *Centinela* ring on the day he was killed, so Christ knows who else is mixed up with them.'

'But why would they kill Fuentes and his family?'

'Remember when we saw his car arrive? He was looking round as if he was searching for an address. I think he was expecting to meet someone.'

'You're just speculating.'

'They set him up,' Galíndez went on. 'When he arrived, those men on the roof were waiting to open fire. At the same time, the special forces went into the *pensión* to take out Sancho and Señor Espartero.'

'But why would they do that?'

'I think the Fuentes family were killed to cover up the attack on the *pensión*,' Galíndez said. 'Sancho's death was completely overshadowed by it.'

'But no one knew Sancho was at the *pensión* except us.'

Galíndez started putting on her shoulder holster. 'Mendez knew. And possibly Capitán Fuentes, since he had that *Centinela* ring in his pocket.'

Isabel's face was tense. 'So what do we do now?'

'We'll do what you suggested: go to the university and stay out of sight. When it gets dark, we'll go to Guzmán's *comisaría* and take a look at this Western Vault.'

'No, Ana. I'm not going anywhere unless you call your uncle and ask for backup.'

'I'll do it on my own then.'

'And I'll report you to the *guardia* for your repeated misuse of prescription drugs.'

Galíndez scowled. 'You wouldn't.'

'I care about you, Ana, so I'm not going to let you risk your life if there's no need.'

'OK, you win,' Galíndez sighed as she took out her phone and called Ramiro's number. His voice boomed out from the answering machine, telling the caller that this was a private phone, that time was money and that all messages should be short and succinct.

'There,' Galíndez said as she finished her message. 'Now we can go to the university and wait until we hear from him. Happy now?'

'I wouldn't say happy,' Isabel smiled, 'but I do feel better. How about you?'

'Good to go.' Galíndez nodded. 'I'll just pop to the bathroom before we go.'

'It's that cold beer,' Isabel laughed as Galíndez closed the bathroom door.

Inside, Galíndez locked the door and then gulped down her last two painkillers.

Isabel was looking out the window when she came out of the bathroom.

'Let's get going, shall we?' Galíndez said, suddenly energised as she went to the door.

They went downstairs into the street. The traffic was backed up in a thick line, with fractious drivers passing their enforced confinement by shouting insults and blasting their horns at the slightest provocation.

From a doorway across the road, Mendez watched them get into Galíndez's car. As the car swung out into the heavy traffic, provoking a dissonant protest of horns, Mendez returned to the side street where her own vehicle was parked. Unlike Galíndez and Isabel, she walked slowly. There was no need to hurry: the moment Galíndez started her engine, the tracker would tell Mendez exactly where she was.

CHAPTER 23

MADRID, OCTOBER 1982, CALLE DEL TRIBULETE

The narrow street was packed, and Guzmán was forced to push his way through the bustling crowd outside the Molino Rojo. He had visited the place so many times in the past to paw the burlesque dancers and rob their pimps, he could have found his way around blindfolded. Overcoming a nostalgic inclination to go in for a quick look, he carried on down the road, looking for Señor Pedraza's address.

As he passed the old cigarette factory, memories surfaced as he paused to look up at the wall of the building ahead. The bullet hole was still there, a wild shot fired at him one winter's night when he spirited a woman away to safety. But back then he was dangerous company and Alicia Martinez had ended up in the Almudena Cemetery like so many others.

His dark thoughts dispersed as he found the building he was looking for. Shabby bricks and peeling paintwork, grimy curtains behind streaked windows. Grim accommodation for someone who was supposed to be a genius.

Guzmán went into the reeking entrance hall and found the name on the mailbox. Señor Pedraza lived on the third floor. He climbed the stairs, followed the landing to Pedraza's door and pounded on it. A tremulous voice behind the ramshackle door inquired who was calling.

'Señor Benavides sent me,' Guzmán said, quietly.

The chain rattled and the door creaked open. Guzmán had been expecting a genius, but Señor Pedraza didn't meet his expectations. Thick glasses, wild, badly cut hair, worn patches on the elbows of his jacket. A waistcoat buttoned incorrectly. The look of a mad man on a day off from the asylum. 'Will the gentleman come in?'

Guzmán slammed the door behind him. On the table he saw the familiar shape of the encryption machine in its leather case.

'You said you've a message from Señor Benavides?'

'That's correct,' Guzmán said, extemporising. 'You're in great danger.'

The eyes behind the thick lenses widened. 'But why?'

Guzmán pointed to the papers on the table. 'That code belongs to a criminal gang and they're looking for it.' He paused, letting the news sink in. 'They're looking for you as well.'

'Oh dear.' Pedraza stood stock-still, frozen with fear.

'Don't worry,' Guzmán said, amiably. 'I'm going to take the code into safekeeping. As for you, you're off to Cordoba for a week or two.'

'Cordoba?'

'Yes,' Guzmán said, giving him an irritated look. 'It's in Spain, remember?'

'I don't know anyone there.'

'I'm sure you don't know many people in Madrid either,' Guzmán growled, gathering up the various components of the code and putting them into the case. 'What did you make of the code, by the way?'

'Incredible. I don't know who created it but it's very impressive.'

'I understand it's German.'

Pedraza nodded eagerly. 'That would account for its precision. Those Nazis, eh? But there's something else as well, almost a kind of poetry in the way it's arranged.'

Guzmán decided to nip this conversation in the bud since Pedraza was never going to see the code again. He took five thousand peseta notes from his pockets and offered them to the little man. 'This is to get you to Cordoba.' He handed Pedraza another piece of paper. 'And here's the address. Stay there until you're contacted by Señor Benavides.'

Pedraza took off his spectacles and wiped them with a soiled handkerchief. 'This is all most unexpected, I must say.'

'Don't worry, I'll come with you to the station. I want to be sure you get your train.'

'Who are these people who're looking for me?' Pedraza asked, hurriedly cramming some of his clothes into a battered old valise.

'Some far-right group, I understand.'

'But I'm not a left-winger,' Pedraza gasped. 'I always supported Franco.'

'This isn't about politics.' Guzmán went to the window and drew back the dirty muslin curtain as he scanned the street below. 'These people believe the code is anti-Catholic.' He saw Pedraza about to protest and cut in. 'We have to hurry. I want to get this code into a safe place as soon as possible. And you, of course.'

Pedraza carried on packing. When he had finished, the ancient suitcase bulged with his crumpled laundry and it took Guzmán's assistance before he could fasten the worn clasps. Even then, it seemed unlikely the case would survive the journey to Cordoba.

'Hurry up, you've a train to catch,' Guzmán said, irritated now.

Pedraza stayed silent.

When Guzmán turned to look at him, the little mathematician was staring at his bookshelves, his eyes glistening with tears. 'My books,' he whispered. 'I don't know which ones to take.'

'You're not taking any,' Guzmán said, taking a firm grip on his arm. 'I'll have them sent on to you.' He pushed Pedraza out onto the landing and marched him towards the stairs.

As they hurried down the creaking staircase, Guzmán couldn't help thinking that it would have been much easier just to kill him. He almost had when Pedraza opened the door but then the man's words of praise for the code had tempered the decision. In any case, once he was in Cordoba, this half-blind mathematician would never find his way to the end of the street, let alone back to Madrid. He would be fine: a mathematician could beg as well as the next man.

Their feet clattered on the tiles as they crossed the entrance hall. Guzmán stopped at the door, listening to the sounds of evening revellers on the street. Sick of the cloying smell in the hall, he opened the door a little. Groups of young men and women bustled past, singing the song that had plagued the World Cup that summer. Something about birds coupled with a dance that involved flapping their arms while forming a circle. A futile and moronic waste of time, he thought. A few years earlier it would have been illegal, he was certain.

As the crowd bustled off down the street, Guzmán pushed the mathematician ahead of him, looking back to check if they were being followed. The pavement across the road was less crowded, enabling him to see the entrances of the apartments across the street. Lights were on in the hallways, highlighting dark shapes as people came out for their evening walk.

As he turned his gaze in the other direction, he saw a figure standing in a doorway, ten metres away. A figure in a white suit, his arm extended as if pronouncing judgment.

Guzmán reached for the Browning, shouting to Pedraza to run. He might as well have told the little man to fly. Pedraza's first instinct was to try to return to the safety of his apartment and his books. He scuttled towards the door in a blind panic, pursued by the insane mechanical stutter of the Uzi as it traced a line of bullets along the wall, raising a cloud of powdered brick that pursued the fleeing mathematician and then cut across him, folding him like a rag doll as he fell to the pavement.

Guzmán opened fire, the empty shell cases rattling on the cobbles like coins. Screams from the people in the street as they started to flee. Dull echoes from the high buildings around him. Guzmán fired again and a window behind the Italian shattered, spilling glass shards onto the pavement. And then the rattle of the Uzi was abruptly silenced as the clip emptied. As Guzmán started across the street towards him, the Italian turned and dashed through the crowd cowering on the pavement, sending panicked onlookers diving for cover as they tried to get away from him.

Guzmán held the Browning two-handed, trying to track the

Italian as he weaved through the crowd, holding the Uzi above his head. A sensible tactic, Guzmán knew, since the sight of the weapon provoked another desperate scramble that blocked Guzmán's line of fire as the Italian disappeared into the throng milling over the street near the Molino Rojo. Within moments, he had disappeared into the crowd.

Guzmán reloaded the Browning and then turned back to check on Pedraza.

The mathematician was lying face down in the gutter. At his side, an elderly woman dressed in black knelt by the body. She took off her rosary and began to pray. 'Do you know his name, señor?'

'Not a clue.'

He heard sirens. Hurriedly, he looked round for the leather case containing the code machine, keen to get away before the police arrived to complicate things.

The case was nowhere to be seen.

He knelt by the side of the praying woman and rolled Pedraza onto his back to make sure the case wasn't hidden under his body. It was not, and he got to his feet, glowering at the gawping spectators around him. There was no point looking any further: the leather case and his code books were gone. He left the devout old woman still praying over the unfortunate Señor Pedraza. There was only one thing to do in a situation like this and that was find a policeman. The irony of that was not lost on him.

MADRID, OCTOBER 1982, CALLE DEL AMPARO

Spots of rain were starting to fall as the uniformed policeman escorted Guzmán from the police station and led him down a side street into Calle Amparo. 'The warehouse is just down there, sir,' he said, pointing. 'He's the most notorious criminal fence in the area.'

'If he's so well known, how come you haven't got him in a cell?' Guzmán scoffed.

'Sebastian Uribe's a sly one, sir.'

Guzmán frowned, deep in thought. 'I knew an Alberto Uribe, back in the day.'

'That was the father,' the officer said. 'His son's almost as big a villain as he was.'

'And you've never managed to pin anything on him?'

The policeman rubbed his thumb and index finger together. 'Greasing someone's palm with cash solves most problems round here.'

Guzmán suspected the man was speaking from experience. 'I'll take it from here.'

Guzmán waited until the policeman's heavy footsteps faded and then made his way down the street. Feral echoes shimmered through the shadows and a strong odour of cess drifted up from the drains. He remembered these streets from when he was younger. It had been bleak then. A liminal world where people lived on the margin between poverty and depravity, their lives punctuated by the violence that always accompanies such conditions. It had suited Guzmán well.

A hundred metres further on, he arrived at a ramshackle warehouse, set in a cobbled yard off the main street. Large double doors, wet and glistening in the rain. Above the entrance, a sign: SEBASTIAN URIBE LTD. AUCTIONEER.

He went to the wicket gate set in the side of one of the doors and hammered on it.

A suspicious voice inquired who was there.

'A customer,' Guzmán said, lowering his voice. 'I'm looking for something I lost earlier this evening.'

'Get lost.'

'I'm also a police officer.' He took a pack of cigarettes from his pocket and put one in his mouth. 'We can do business now or I'll come back with a truckload of uniformed cops and take this place apart.' He lit the cigarette. 'And everyone in it, starting with you.'

He heard a sudden muffled conversation on the other side of the gate. The sound of bolts sliding. The wicket gate opened a few centimetres and a cadaverous face peered out. 'Business, you said?'

'Exactly.' Guzmán nodded. 'I'm looking for some lost property.'

An indifferent shrug. 'You'd better come in.'

Guzmán stepped into the loading bay of the warehouse. Flickering oil lamps threw a greasy light over the clutter around him. He saw racks of clothes, motorcycles and boxes, piles of them, big shipping crates and smaller items wrapped in oilcloth. In the hearth, a small coal fire was burning, nuancing the room with erratic shadow.

'This place looks like a museum,' Guzmán said.

'You'll find everything you could wish for here, señor.' A sharp voice, beyond the ring of pallid firelight.

Guzmán peered towards the speaker. As his eyes adjusted to the darkness, he saw a large man sitting behind a desk. A wide, well-fed face, cruel, glinting eyes. His pinstriped suit seemed incongruous in these sordid surroundings. Behind him, Guzmán saw the obscure outlines of more stacked crates.

'You'd be Señor Uribe, I take it?' Guzmán asked, walking towards him.

Uribe held up a hand. 'Not too close, my friend.' He gestured to one of the men who hurried forward with a chair and placed it in front of the desk.

'Have a seat,' Uribe said. A harsh, smoky voice. 'You're a police-man, I understand?'

Guzmán shook his head. 'Not for the purpose of this visit.'

'You seem familiar.'

'I knew your father.'

A sudden creaking of wood as Uribe leaned back, adjusting his great bulk in the chair. 'A lot of people knew Alberto Uribe. He was well respected.'

That was not strictly true, since Guzmán could recall watching his *sargento* kick Señor Uribe senseless in the cells below the *comisaría* on several occasions. He decided not to share that memory.

'I'm looking for some property that was stolen in Calle Tribulete earlier this evening,' Guzmán said, provoking a muffled giggle from one of Uribe's men.

Uribe leaned forward, clasping his hands on the desk. 'Is this property valuable?'

Guzmán nodded. 'It has sentimental value.'

'Value is value,' Uribe said. Casually, he took a cigar from an inside pocket, bit off the end and spat it onto the floor. 'Cuban,' he said as he lit it, exhaling a mouthful of smoke.

It was indeed Cuban, Guzmán knew from the aroma. He had started the conversation not liking Uribe, but his failure to offer him a cigar like the one now clutched in the fat man's mouth was downright insulting. 'The contents were in a leather case.'

'I may be able to help.' When Uribe smiled, the lamplight glittered on a gold tooth. 'Assuming you can pay.'

Guzmán reached into his jacket and took out his wallet, or more accurately, the late Señor Benavides' wallet. He flicked through the thick wad of banknotes, making sure Uribe saw it and then tucked the wallet back in his jacket. 'Let me see the goods.'

Uribe made a brusque gesture to one of the men hovering in the shadows. As the man scuttled away into the dim recesses of the loading bay, Guzmán took the opportunity to count the others. There were four, five when the other one returned. And Uribe, of course.

'We couldn't understand what exactly it was,' Uribe said. He met Guzmán's gaze, his demeanour slightly more pleasant now he'd seen the colour of his money.

'I invent things,' Guzmán said. 'It's one of my inventions.'

'What does it do?'

'Profit and loss calculations,' Guzmán said with a sudden improvised authority. 'Ideal for small businesses.'

Uribe's flabby face displayed no interest. He sat, his big hands still resting on the table until his man returned with the leather case.

'Everything's still in there, I hope?'

'Of course,' Uribe said. 'We didn't know what to do with it anyway.'

'Can I ask who supplied it to you? Just out of interest.'

Uribe laughed. 'María the black widow. If someone faints or slips on the cobbles, she's always on hand, wailing and offering up a Hail Mary for them while her daughter robs anyone within reach.'

Guzmán looked at the case lying on Uribe's desk. 'How much?'

The fat man's face set with professional interest. 'Let's say half a million pesetas.'

'Let's say your mother's a whore,' Guzmán said. 'I could just as easily arrest you.'

Uribe grinned. 'I've got five lads there who say you're not leaving with that case unless you come up with the money.' He took another long drag on his cigar. 'And don't think you'll be coming back with a bunch of coppers for it either, because I'm protected. You must have heard of Eduardo Ricci?'

Guzmán took a deep breath. He needed to think of this as a business transaction, he told himself. Throttling this fat toad of a man would only complicate things. Even so, the thought that the fat fuck didn't know Ricci was dead pleased him immensely.

'Half a million.' Guzmán smiled, reaching into his jacket.

Uribe slouched back, taking another satisfied pull on the cigar. Then his eyes widened. 'What the hell?'

The shot briefly echoed round the darkened warehouse. Uribe slumped back, his weight upending the chair as he toppled to the floor in a crumpled heap.

Guzmán pointed the pistol towards the stunned men. 'There are twelve bullets left in this pistol,' he said, cheerfully. 'Whether I use them or not is up to you.'

'Don't want any trouble, officer,' the skull-faced man said.

'That's sensible.' Guzmán nodded. 'Maybe you should take over, now Señor Uribe's indisposed?' He picked up the leather case. 'Show me out, will you?'

As Guzmán stepped out of the wicket gate, the door slammed behind him and the bolts rattled into place. Inside the warehouse, he heard an argument starting. With luck they would have killed one another before morning.

He strolled down Calle Sombrerete. Near the Plaza de Lavapiés, a taxi had pulled up by the kerb. Guzmán gave the driver an address and climbed in.

'End of a late night out, señor?' the driver asked.

Guzmán shook his head. 'It's only just begun.'

MADRID, OCTOBER 1982, CALLE FERNÁN CABALLERO

The taxi dropped Guzmán at the end of the street. The road was quiet, apart from a babble of voices coming from a bar on the corner. He soon found the address he was looking for: an old weathered door with a sign offering repairs to all manner of electrical appliances. He knocked twice. After a moment, he heard the sound of hurried footsteps and then a key turned, and then another. Finally, the door opened.

'Christ, you've got more locks on that door than the Bank of Spain,' Guzmán said, pushing past Julio. In front of him, he saw a steep flight of stairs descending into darkness.

Julio followed him down the worn stairs. The air was thick with damp, a familiar smell: it reminded Guzmán of the cells beneath Calle Robles.

At the bottom of the stairs, Julio pressed a switch and a dull light glowed in the ceiling. Ahead, Guzmán saw a sturdy wooden door.

'In there,' Julio said.

Guzmán pushed the door and went into a small cellar. A single bulb in the ceiling illuminated the stains splattered over the mildewed wall. In one corner, he saw a pile of tools and chains.

'You'll never guess what used to happen here,' Julio chuckled.

Guzmán lit a cigarette and blew smoke into the pale light. 'The question is, does she?'

Paloma Ibañez's eyes widened as the two men turned to look at her. Uncomfortable under their gaze, she tried to move, though since she was securely bound to a heavy wooden chair, there was little chance of that. An uncomfortable experience for her, Guzmán was sure, though it was hard to know for certain, since Julio had gagged her.

Guzmán pulled the gag from her mouth.

'Do you know who I am?' Paloma said, outraged.

'Of course I do,' Guzmán said, untying her wrists. 'Do you know who I am?'

Paloma was too busy rubbing the circulation back into her wrists to answer for a moment. 'I have no idea, but I tell you this, you're in trouble unless you release me at once.'

'My name's Guzmán,' he said. 'Your friend Javier Benavides told you all about me at your meeting at the Torre de España.' He watched her eyes widen. 'What? Didn't you think anyone might be spying on you?'

Paloma gave him a furious stare. 'Things have changed since you were last in Madrid, *Comandante*. Let me go now and I'll overlook this unfortunate incident.'

Guzmán took a thoughtful drag on his cigarette. 'Some things haven't changed.'

'Oh no?' Paloma sneered. 'Like what?'

'Principles,' Guzmán said. 'Principles like avenging murdered friends, for example.'

Paloma swallowed, hard. 'What are you talking about?'

'You hired the Italian. He killed a friend of mine and her father. That makes you responsible.'

'It wasn't entirely my decision,' Paloma said. 'Javier was the one who gave him permission to come after you. I don't know anything about the other people.'

'Javier's dead,' said Guzmán. 'I killed him, Ricci and several of his lackeys. That leaves you.'

'Don't forget I'm protected. If you hurt me, the *Centinelas* will come after you.'

'Know what?' Guzmán said. 'No one is fucking protected, señorita. Least of all you.'

'I am.' Paloma's voice cracked with emotion. 'They said so.'

Guzmán turned to Julio. 'Did you get them?'

'Yeah.' Julio took a thick brown envelope from his coat. 'The old man said you owe him plenty for this.'

'He always says that.' Guzmán smiled, spilling the contents of the envelope onto the filthy tabletop.

Paloma stared at the wad of documents lying on the table. 'What are those?'

'These are copies of your bank statements, showing various withdrawals you've made over the last two years. There are receipts for cars and antique furniture, designer clothes and holidays, all drawn against the *Centinelas'* private account.'

Paloma frowned. 'They must be forgeries.'

'Of course they are,' Guzmán agreed. 'Done by one of the best in the business. They show you've been skimming money from your employers.' He picked up one sheet and brandished it in her face. 'You even made a contribution to the PSOE's election campaign.'

Paloma stared wide-eyed at the paper. 'But I hate the Socialists.'

'I'm sure they feel the same way,' Guzmán smiled and leaned closer, 'but what's General Alvaro going to say when my courier delivers these papers to him? "Oh, Paloma would never do such a terrible thing?" Or is he going to send someone along to put a bullet in your head as a reminder of what happens to people who betray the *Centinelas*?'

Her face grew pale. 'They'd kill me.'

'I expect so,' Guzmán said. 'Still, those who live by the sword, eh, señorita?'

'You've got to stop that courier. I'll pay you.'

'I never thought I'd say this, but you haven't got enough money.'

Nervously, Paloma ran a hand through her hair. 'What can I do to stop you delivering those papers to General Alvaro?'

'Leave Spain,' Guzmán said. 'There's a fake passport here. I suggest you use it.'

'Leave the country?' Paloma spluttered. 'You can't be serious?'

'The girl at the *pensión* was eighteen,' Guzmán said. 'Her father was in a wheelchair. They got caught in someone else's war. Since you and Benavides call the shots on behalf of the *Centinelas*, it makes sense to kill you as well as Javier. The only reason I haven't is because Daniela wouldn't have wanted me to. She thought the war was over.'

Paloma swallowed, hard. 'But the war is over, *Comandante*.'

'There's always a war,' Guzmán said, shaking his head. 'Leave Spain, or you're the next casualty.' He smiled. 'And the funny thing is, I won't be the one to kill you. Your colleagues will do it for me.'

'But where would I go?' Paloma asked, though her expression suggested she was already considering the possibilities.

'You're a lawyer, you work it out. If I were you, I'd empty my bank account the moment the banks open this morning and then get a plane to somewhere warm. I'm sure you'll do well wherever you go.'

'All right, I'll do it,' Paloma said, mopping her brow with a handkerchief. 'I just need to collect a few things from home.'

'No, Julio will take you to the bank and then the airport. You can buy clothes there.'

'And you promise not to give Alvaro those documents?'

'Of course not. I don't trust you an inch. My courier will deliver them at nine thirty this morning. You've got just enough time to get your money and drive to the airport. Julio will make sure you're on a plane.'

Her shoulders slumped. A long resigned sigh. 'Just as you say.'

'Where will you go?' Guzmán asked. 'Merely out of interest.'

'Argentina,' Paloma said, without hesitation.

'What, gauchos and the rolling plains?'

'Not at all,' Paloma said. 'The country's run by a dictator. There should be plenty of opportunities for someone like me.'

'I think you're right,' Guzmán said.

Villanueva watched the afternoon shadows lengthening. By the church hall, men were unloading crates of bottled water and hampers of food for the villagers. Many protested, asking why they could not return to their homes. Surely they would be safe enough there? Their protests were cursorily dismissed. No one wanted to tell them that the real reason for their isolation was to prevent them contacting the press.

Villanueva saw Guzmán coming towards him, accompanied by a tall, bald-headed man.

'This is Brigadier General Gutiérrez,' Guzmán explained. 'He's in overall command of this operation.' From his tone, Villanueva sensed Guzmán was not entirely pleased at that.

'There are eighteen children in that bus, is that correct?' Gutiérrez asked.

Villanueva nodded. 'Ten boys and eight girls. Where are they now?'

Gutiérrez pointed up at the headland. 'Somewhere up there. He says he's filled the bus with explosives and we've no reason to disbelieve him: he's done these things before. If we send in the police and guardia, *he'll kill them all.'*

'So what do we do?'

'He wants the money delivered in large-denomination notes,' Gutiérrez said. 'But we can't trust him to keep his part of the bargain so whoever delivers the money will have to kill him and that psychotic woman accompanying him.'

'It has to be done soon,' Guzmán cut in. 'What we didn't tell the villagers is that Santorini spent time in an asylum: he's half crazy.

341

And he's particularly violent towards women. If he thinks we're trying to trick him, he's likely to kill the girls first.'

'You'll have to give the Italian the money,' Villanueva said, his face pale. 'My sergeant's daughter is on that bus, you can't risk the lives of those children.'

'I spoke with Franco half an hour ago,' Gutiérrez said. 'He was very clear. There's no chance of those prisoners being released from prison, today or any other day.'

CHAPTER 24

MADRID 2010, UNIVERSIDAD COMPLUTENSE, DEPARTAMENTO
DE HISTORIA CONTEMPORÁNEA

Galíndez slowed as they approached the campus. In the distance, across the tan lawns near the faculty building, she saw the fountain, a stream of diamonds and ice fire in the afternoon sun.

'This was a good idea,' she said as she turned onto the slip road. 'It'll be hard to find us in a campus teeming with thousands of students.'

'Let's hope so.' Isabel was interrupted as Galíndez pulled up in front of a wooden barrier blocking the road leading into the campus. A handwritten sign was fixed to the centre of the barrier:

CLOSED DUE TO A GENERAL STRIKE OF STAFF
AND STUDENTS AGAINST GOVERNMENT CUTS.
JOIN THE DEMONSTRATION AT 3.30 THIS AFTERNOON
IN THE PLAZA de ESPAÑA!

'I don't believe it,' Isabel groaned. 'That means practically the whole campus is empty. You must have run over a black cat on the way here.'

'It doesn't matter,' Galíndez said. 'If there's no one on campus, why would they think of looking for us here? I'll park the car out of sight and then we can hide in our office until it's dark. Then we'll go to the *comisaría.*'

They spent a few minutes searching for somewhere to hide the car. Finally, Isabel saw the ideal spot behind a row of large garbage bins at the rear of the departmental car park.

As they made their way towards the faculty building, the silence reverberated with the sound of their footsteps. At this time, the grass was usually littered with students, sprawling amid the scattered detritus of campus life: books, newspapers, and discarded pizza boxes. Usually a radio would be playing, the bass notes reverberating around the campus buildings. Today, there was only the background hum of the city and the soft progression of their footsteps. A sense of isolation.

As they went down the stairs to their basement office, Galíndez stopped and put a finger to her lips. Below, they heard a soft deep voice. Isabel put a restraining hand on Galíndez's arm as she started to reach for her pistol. 'It's OK, Ana, that's Madame D'Nour.'

Sure enough, when they reached the bottom of the stairs Madame D'Nour was sweeping the floor outside the Research Unit. She looked up as she heard their footsteps and beamed. '*Bonsoir, mesdemoiselles.* Look at you: two pretty girls and not a man in sight, no wonder you look so unhappy.' Her deep laugh echoed down the corridor. 'You spend too much time down here like little moles when you should be up in the sunshine. At this rate you'll never meet the right man.'

'I'm sure you're right, Madame D'Nour,' Galíndez said as she unlocked the door.

'I'll say a prayer for you, Mademoiselle Ana.' Madame D'Nour gave her a dazzling smile. 'You need to find a man before that frown line gets any deeper. Men don't like a sulky woman.' She turned to Isabel. 'And you, Mademoiselle Izzy, with those hips, you should have a family of five by now.'

'I'll bear that in mind,' Isabel said, hurrying into the office.

Galíndez slipped off her shoulder holster and put it on a work surface near the sink. She touched her brow with the tip of a finger. 'Have I really got—'

'No, forget it. And no comments about my hips either. She doesn't mean any harm. She just wants us to be happy.'

Galíndez raised a hand to her temple. 'God, that hurts.'

Alarmed, Isabel hurried to help her into a chair. 'What's the matter?'

'It's nothing,' Galíndez said, though her face said otherwise.

'You're not having a seizure, are you?' Isabel asked, alarmed.

'Don't worry, it's passing.' Galíndez suddenly flinched. She saw Isabel's concerned look. 'It's OK, that bundle of papers is digging into my side.' She reached inside her jacket. 'Might as well have a look at the rest of these while we're here.'

'Lay them out on the table. I'll make us a coffee.' As Isabel filled the kettle, she saw Galíndez's pistol lying in its shoulder holster on the work surface. 'Sorry, I can't work with a bloody big pistol lying about, it's intimidating. I'll put it in your bag, OK?'

'Whatever,' Galíndez murmured, distracted as she began separating the dusty sheets of paper. None was on old parchment like the map of the vaults. These seemed to have been torn from an exercise book. Bold, angry writing, the ink faded but still legible. She shivered as she realised where she'd seen the writing before.

October 26th 1982

Dear General Ortiz,

If anything happens to me, I trust you'll know what to do with the files I'm putting in the Western Vault. You'll see the location on the map I've enclosed. These files heap everlasting shit on both Franco and the Centinelas. If something happens to me, I leave it to you to do what you think is best with them.

Cordially yours,

Leo Guzmán

Galíndez stared at the note, deep in thought. She looked up, startled, as Isabel put a cup of coffee on her desk.

'Did I make you jump, Ana?'

'Take a look at this, Izzy: this note is from Guzmán to General Ortiz, telling him to use the files he's left to damage Franco and the *Centinelas* if anything happens to him.'

Isabel frowned. 'That doesn't make sense. According to Sancho, Guzmán kidnapped you because he was helping the *Centinelas*.'

'Maybe he had other ideas,' Galíndez said. 'Look at the date on this letter. He hid these files in the vault back in 1982.'

'So why ask you about the Western Vault if he knew all along?'

'No idea.' Galíndez started to examine some of the other papers. 'These are the names of generals and politicians who worked in Franco's regime. Each name has a number alongside it.' She bent forward, examining the numbers more closely. 'They look like file references. And here's Guzmán's name, with a reference to Alicante. Christ, Izzy, there might be a whole catalogue of his crimes in that vault.' Her dark eyes glistened with excitement as she looked at her watch. 'Only another two hours till sunset. Once it's dark, we'll sneak in there and grab the files.'

CHAPTER 25

MADRID, OCTOBER 1982, CEMENTERIO DE NUESTRA SEÑORA
DE LA ALMUDENA

A heavy sky, thick grey autumnal clouds. A long, snaking line of black limousines edging into the heart of the sprawling cemetery, its vast rows of memorials shadowed in early-morning gloom. A silent grey rain fell as men in mourning suits hurried from the cars to the graveside; hard-faced men, accustomed to the rituals of death, here to honour one who knew those rituals better than most.

By the side of the grave, beyond the muddy pile of excavated soil, the firing party waited in their dress uniforms, expressionless as the priest accompanied the pallbearers to the graveside. More than a few mourners smiled discreetly at the notion of a religious send-off for their departed colleague. Certainly it was hard to think of anyone less disposed towards religion than the man in the oak coffin now being borne to his final rest on the shoulders of several burly troopers of the *guardia civil.*

'No flowers,' Corporal Ochoa observed, looking at the coffin. 'Just a flag.'

Brigadier General Gutiérrez nodded. 'Highly appropriate, I'd say, Corporal. When did you ever see him with flowers?'

Ochoa shrugged. 'Come to think of it, I never saw him with a flag either.'

The mourners fell silent as the committal began. The priest seemed in a hurry, rattling out the familiar words as though he had more pressing business elsewhere.

Ochoa had attended so many funerals they no longer had the

power to move him. This was how it all ended: in a wooden box, surrounded by a crowd of people whose opinions of the deceased were mixed at best.

'As Jesus Christ was raised from the dead, we too are called to follow him through death to the glory where God will be all in all.'

Gutiérrez sighed as the priest finished the blessing. He was already late for one meeting. At this rate, he'd miss the next one as well.

The firing party stepped forward, aiming into the leaden sky. A sudden, barked order. Three volleys, crisp and precise, the stammering echoes unfolding over the cemetery. And then the mournful notes of the 'Last Post' rising into the soft grey rain. Finally, the familiar military song of farewell: 'Death is Not the End'.

Whoever wrote that song didn't know much about death, Ochoa thought.

Gutiérrez recoiled as someone came up behind him and poked him in the back with a big, meaty finger.

'Did I miss much?' Guzmán asked.

'You nearly gave me a heart attack coming up behind me like that, *Comandante*. Where've you been?'

'I had to find a new hotel.' Guzmán lowered his voice as he glanced round at the mourners lining up to throw a handful of earth onto the coffin as they said their last goodbye. 'How come they're burying him so quickly? A man like General Ortiz deserves a full military funeral.'

'It was in his will, apparently,' Gutiérrez said. 'No fuss and an immediate burial.'

'So what the fuck happened?'

Languidly, Gutiérrez raised an eyebrow. 'Your sources must be slipping, *Comandante*.'

'Most of my sources are senile these days,' Guzmán snorted. 'I overheard someone talking about a heart attack, is that right?'

Gutiérrez lowered his voice. 'Suicide,' he muttered. 'Shot himself last night.'

'A man like Ortiz? He would never kill himself, he's a good

Catholic – apart from his affair and a few massacres in the Civil War.' Guzmán looked round, furiously. 'If you ask me, this was the work of the *Centinelas.*'

'Maybe the passage of time was getting to him,' Gutiérrez said, sadly. 'None of us are getting any younger.'

'Thanks for the reminder,' Guzmán said. 'Look, there's Ramiro Junior.'

'He's junior no longer, is he? I'll go and give him my condolences.' Gutiérrez staggered off across the soaking grass.

'That'll be a great fucking comfort, no doubt,' Guzmán growled.

'He was a good man, the general,' Ochoa said, wiping rain from his spectacles.

'He was,' Guzmán agreed, recalling that General Ortiz had been so good, he'd promised to put Guzmán's secret papers in his safe.

He waited until Gutiérrez finished talking to Ramiro and then went over and slapped the young man on the back, almost pitching him into the grave on top of his father's coffin. 'I can't tell you how sorry I am. What happened?'

'It's all a blur,' Ramiro said. 'I cleaned his pistol for him as I always did and then I went out to meet Miguel Galíndez.' He brushed his hand over his face. 'When I came back, an ambulance had just arrived and the maid was hysterical. If I'd been there, maybe I could have stopped him.'

Guzmán was no longer listening. His thoughts were focused on the papers he'd entrusted to General Ortiz. 'Which uniform was he wearing?'

Ramiro gave him a confused look. 'I'm not sure.'

'It's a simple enough question,' Guzmán said, suddenly aggressive.

'His usual weekday uniform, as I recall, *Comandante.*'

'Have you kept it?'

'Of course not, we buried him in it.'

That was the same uniform the general was wearing when Guzmán gave him the papers. He looked down into the grave. The coffin was covered with a thin layer of soil.

'He won't be down there long,' Ramiro said, noticing the attention Guzmán was paying to the coffin. 'Once the mourners have gone, we're going to inter him in the family crypt. The workmen are waiting over there.'

That was it, then, Guzmán realised. There was no chance of the general's coffin being left unattended long enough for him to retrieve those papers. Restraining a violent urge to punch Ramiro, he gave him another manly slap of consolation on the arm and left him to his grief.

As he trudged back to Gutiérrez and Ochoa, someone called his name. Guzmán turned and saw Carmen Galíndez coming towards him, dressed in black, her high heels sinking into the wet soil as she walked. She was no longer the radiant woman he'd met in the bar León. Now, she was pale-faced, her hair wet and bedraggled, her eyes red from crying.

'Señorita Galíndez,' Guzmán said. 'Are you all right?'

'Of course I'm not.' Carmen rubbed tears from her eyes. She glowered at Ramiro who was still at the graveside, accepting the condolences of his father's colleagues. 'Do you know that little shit planned to bury him without even telling me? He always thought his father was betraying the memory of his sainted mother by being with me.'

'The general thought the world of you,' Guzmán said. 'He told me so.' He'd also told Guzmán exactly what Carmen was like in bed, though Guzmán kept that to himself.

She took a deep breath, trying to calm herself. 'Has Ramiro told you what happened?'

'Just a few details. It's a tragedy.' Guzmán thought again about the documents he'd entrusted to General Ortiz that were now about to be interred with him.

'There's more to it than Ramiro says,' Carmen said. 'Doesn't it strike you as odd how quickly the general's been buried?'

'He says his father didn't want a full military funeral.'

'Ramiro's a liar.' She pressed a hand to her mouth, too proud to weep.

'He has an alibi for the evening,' Guzmán said, 'before you jump to any conclusions.'

'What good are conclusions now?' Carmen said, bitterly. 'He's gone.'

'If it's any consolation, he'd never have married you.' Her expression suggested she took little comfort from that, Guzmán noticed.

'*Adios, Comandante.*'

He watched her walk away, admiring the sway of her hips beneath the black dress.

As he rejoined Ochoa and Gutiérrez, he saw their expressions. 'What?'

'Just a little bet with the brigadier general,' said Ochoa.

'The corporal was wondering if you'd asked General Ortiz's mistress out for dinner.' Gutiérrez said. 'Naturally I bet against it.'

Guzmán ran a hand over his hair, exasperated. 'This is terrible.'

'Sorry, sir, I meant no disrespect.'

'I don't mean your fucking bet, Corporal. I'm thinking about Ortiz. We've lost our main ally against the *Centinelas*.'

'Very true,' Gutiérrez agreed. 'Now he's gone, they've got more chance of infiltrating the *guardia civil*, especially when you consider who's taken charge.'

Guzmán glared belligerently at him. 'Who is it?'

'General Amadeo. He's taking over until they make a permanent appointment.'

'Amadeo's a traitor,' Guzmán spluttered. 'I saw him chair the *Centinelas'* meeting at the Torre de España. He's part of their central council.'

'Nothing we can do.' Gutiérrez shrugged. 'The *guardia* is outside our jurisdiction.'

'So what do we do now?'

'I suggest you get on with completing this mission, *Comandante*. That way, you get your money and I destroy the *Centinelas*.' His face suddenly tightened as he remembered something. 'By the way, I'm still waiting for your code.'

'That's right,' Guzmán said. 'You are.'

'It's not a normal business transaction,' Gutiérrez said, scowling. 'I can't wait for ever. And frankly, *Comandante*, you know the rules. You have to sell something like that in-house. It's technically the property of the state. We can't allow anyone else to have it.'

'And I don't allow anyone to threaten me,' Guzmán said quietly. 'Least of all in a fucking graveyard.'

'You know perfectly well what I meant,' Gutiérrez said. 'No offence.' He waved a bony hand towards one of the limousines lined up along the drive. 'That's my car over there.'

Guzmán frowned. 'How come you've got four drivers?'

'One driver. The rest are bodyguards. If General Ortiz didn't commit suicide, then I'm inclined to agree with you that he was killed by the *Centinelas*. And if they can kill a man of his reputation, they could just as easily get me.'

'Or me,' Guzmán grunted.

'Well, yes, I suppose so.'

They picked their way across the muddy grass to the car. As Gutiérrez approached, one of the men in dark suits stepped forward and handed him a slip of paper. He read it and turned to Guzmán. 'Apparently, there's been a shooting. A massacre, in fact. Shall we take a look?'

Guzmán took a last look in the direction of the general's grave. The workmen were already hauling out the coffin, ready to take it – and Guzmán's papers – to the family crypt. There was no use dwelling on it further, and Guzmán got into the limousine, wondering how many funerals he'd attended here. More than most, he was sure.

MADRID, OCTOBER 1982, BAR SAN NICOLÁS, CALLE DRACENA

An anonymous bar on the ground floor of a newly built apartment block, flanked by a ladies' hairdresser and an optician. Towels and various items of clothing hung limply from the balconies above. Further along the pavement, a few spectators were watching the brown-uniformed *policía nacionales* clustered outside the bar.

Across the road, a policeman was taking a statement from a shopkeeper, yawning as he wrote in his notebook. Something had happened here, there was no doubt of that. The bar's window was shattered, only a few jagged pieces of glass remained and even those had bullet holes in them.

Holding up his ID, Guzmán pushed past the uniformed police into the bar. Their commander came bustling over, demanding to know who was interfering with his case.

'State Security,' Guzmán said, pointing to Gutiérrez. 'Ask the brigadier general if you've any more questions.'

There was no further discussion and he went inside. Gutiérrez and Ochoa followed, standing behind him as he looked over the scene of carnage.

The room was narrow with a few small tables and chairs along one wall and a small zinc-topped bar on the other. At the end of the bar was a flight of stairs leading to a small dining room. Behind the bar were shelves full of bottles, or, more accurately, the remains of bottles, since most were now shattered, their contents dripping onto the linoleum floor.

It would have been a tight squeeze for customers to manoeuvre between the bar and the tables at the best of times, Guzmán could tell. As with many of these small bars, getting to the toilet or the dining room at the back would have been a slow process when the place was crowded. Probably, that was why the dead were heaped together among the overturned tables and chairs. Not one had got as far as the stairs.

Ochoa began examining the bodies. Guzmán saw him reach into one of the dead men's pockets and bring out a card. 'What's that, Corporal?'

'A membership card.' Ochoa peered at the details through his thick glasses. '"Catholic Action Force".' He shrugged. 'New one to me. I've never heard of them.'

Guzmán went to the stairs and knelt, turning one of the dead men onto his back. 'This one's a priest.'

'Any identity on him, sir?'

'Well, he's wearing a dog collar and there's a crucifix hanging round his neck.' Guzmán reached down and ran a hand over the priest's thigh. 'He's also wearing one of those spiked things round his thigh, the ones the Opus Dei use.'

'A cilice.' Ochoa nodded.

'I might have known you'd be familiar with something designed to inflict misery, Corporal,' Guzmán muttered. He rummaged in the priest's pockets and took out his wallet. From his expression as he opened it, Ochoa deduced there was no money in there.

'What do you make of it, *Comandante*?' Gutiérrez asked.

'They've all been shot in the back.' Guzmán picked up a shell casing from the floor, and put it in his pocket. 'You may as well let Forensics loose on them.' He walked back to the door and went outside.

While Gutiérrez spoke to the police commander, Ochoa joined Guzmán on the pavement. They stood by the car, smoking.

'What do you think, Corporal?' Guzmán's tone didn't suggest he cared all that much.

Ochoa shrugged. 'The gunman came in, the customers tried to run to the stairs at the back and he shot them down before they could escape.'

Gutiérrez had finished his conversation with the commander and was now coming towards them, accompanied by Capitán Utrera.

'That's what I thought at first,' Guzmán said to Ochoa.

'So what do you think now, sir?'

'I think you should get the door for the brigadier general, Corporal,' Guzmán said, as Gutiérrez joined them. 'Where are your manners?'

MADRID, OCTOBER 1982, BIBLIOTECA MILITAR,
CALLE MÁRTIRES DE ALCALÁ

As they went down the stairs of the military library, Gutiérrez paused, resting a hand on the wall until he regained his breath.

Guzmán waited a couple of steps further down, growing ever more impatient. Higher up the stairs, Capitán Utrera and Corporal Ochoa waited in silence.

'It's the dust,' Gutiérrez panted.

'What did you expect in a military archive?' Guzmán snorted. 'You should have stayed in the car.'

'I'll be fine,' Gutiérrez said. 'I want to show you this myself.'

At the bottom of the stairs, he pointed to a nondescript door in the far wall. He took out a large key and gave it to Guzmán. 'If you'd do the honours, *Comandante*? I hurt my wrist last time I turned the key in the lock.'

Guzmán snatched the key from him and shoved it into the ornate lock. Metal grated on metal and then the door creaked open. As he peered into the darkness, he heard Ochoa and Utrera shuffling closer to get a better look.

Guzmán fumbled around on the wall inside the door, cursing until his hand closed on an old wooden switch, dangling from a length of wire. A soft, waxy light slowly infused the shadows, illuminating rows of shelving that ran the length of the room. The shelves and the aisles between them were crowded with boxes and crates. Stacks of papers bound with string piled up in corners. Guzmán recognised some of the boxes the squad had retrieved from the railway tunnel.

'You'd never make a librarian.' Guzmán chuckled. 'What a mess.'

'Doesn't matter, it's all here.' Gutiérrez's voice was hoarse from coughing. 'These are the most incriminating files.' In the pallid light, his face was cadaverous. He was not long for this world, Guzmán thought, not for the first time.

'We'll need to get this material loaded as quickly as possible, tomorrow,' Gutiérrez said. 'Then all that remains is for you to drive it to Toledo.'

'So which material do we take?'

Gutiérrez led him a few paces into the archive, out of earshot of the others. Even then, he lowered his voice. 'The most important files are stacked in the front rows. It's the material that affects us and our competitors.'

'You mean the *Centinelas*?'

Gutiérrez winced. 'Don't say that name. We don't know who we can trust.'

'If you'd give me the money I'm owed, I'd trust you a whole lot better.'

'We've had our differences, Guzmán, but we really need to trust each other now.'

'Why break the habit of a lifetime? Give me the fucking money.'

Gutiérrez gave a long, whistling sigh. 'I've got a bankers' draft here.' He put a hand inside his jacket and took out a narrow envelope. 'You can use this at any bank in Spain.'

Guzmán took the envelope and put it into his pocket. 'That wasn't too painful, was it?'

'It's a very large sum. Your pay-off and the money for sole owner-ship of the code.' Gutiérrez's tone suggested the money had been removed from his personal bank account. Naturally it had not.

'So it should be,' said Guzmán. 'Now, you were telling me about Toledo?'

'I was, before you interrupted. Once you deliver those files in Toledo, I've got a specialist team waiting to read them and make copies of all the documents that implicate the *Centinelas'* leadership in war crimes and atrocities. They'll also make sure nothing remains of any files that mention our past activities. By tomorrow night, no one will ever know what we did for Franco. Apart from us, of course.'

'And the dead.' Guzmán smiled.

'Who cares about the dead, *Comandante*?' Gutiérrez shrugged. 'Certainly not you.'

'And what happens once your team have done their work?'

Gutiérrez leaned closer. 'By next week, all the incriminating evidence on the *Centinelas* will have been copied and sent to journalists throughout Spain.'

'And you're sure that will be enough to damage them?'

Gutiérrez nodded. 'There's enough in those files to make your hair curl.'

Guzmán looked at him, amused. 'Shame it's too late for it to work for you.'

'Very droll. Now, if you'll excuse me, I've got a meeting in twenty minutes.'

They went back up the stairs of the old seminary and out into the afternoon sun. Capitán Utrera went to the car to open the door for Gutiérrez. Once he was inside, Utrera gestured for Guzmán and Ochoa to follow.

Guzmán grabbed Ochoa's arm as he tried to get into the car. 'We'll walk.'

'Suit yourself,' Gutiérrez said. 'Good luck for tomorrow. I'll talk to you once you've reached Toledo.' He gave a nod and the driver accelerated up the street.

'Why are we walking?' Ochoa asked.

'There are things we need to discuss,' Guzmán said, glowering at him. 'And don't start moaning. I'm already in a bad mood. And frankly, Corporal, I blame you.'

'It's not my fault if you're in a bad mood, sir.'

'I didn't say it was your fault. I just said that I blame you,' Guzmán sighed. 'Listen: there's a chance I may not be joining you tomorrow.'

Ochoa's expression changed. 'That's not like you.'

'Something's come up.' Guzmán took out his cigarettes and offered one to Ochoa. He used his Zippo to give him a light before lighting his own. 'I'm thinking of packing it all in and going somewhere quiet.'

Ochoa's pale blue eyes flickered. 'A woman, is it?'

'How did you know?'

'I didn't. You just told me.'

'I might end up going on my own, I don't know. But I do know I want out.' He waited for Ochoa to say something. Annoyingly, he said nothing.

'I suppose you think it's a dereliction of duty, Corporal?'

Ochoa shook his head. 'Who am I to criticise you?'

'Exactly what I was thinking. Anyway, if I'm not there tomorrow, you're in charge.'

'Will there be a bonus?'

'I expect they'll have a special one arranged just for you, Corporal. I've never known a man who attracts money like you. You'll be so rich in your retirement, you won't live long enough to spend it all.'

'Doesn't matter, sir. I put most of my money away for my kids.'

'You do realise your children could almost be grandparents by now?'

Ochoa looked away, uncomfortable. 'They're still my children, *Comandante*.'

'And you're still going to keep searching for them once you've retired?'

'Of course. I'll have more time then.'

'What if you don't find them?'

Ochoa shrugged. 'I'll keep looking until I do.'

Guzmán sighed. 'Have you ever read *Don Quixote*?'

'Not me, sir. I don't like big books.'

After that, they walked in silence until they came to a crossroad. Guzmán held out his hand. 'Good luck, Corporal.'

'We've had some good times, haven't we, sir?' Ochoa said as they shook hands.

Guzmán thought about it. 'Not really.' He turned and walked away.

'Is there any chance we might see you tomorrow, sir?' Ochoa called.

Guzmán was walking fast and if he replied, Ochoa didn't hear it.

MADRID, OCTOBER 1982,
HOTEL SUIZA, CALLE SAN ONOFRE

When he got back to the hotel, Guzmán checked with the desk clerk. There was no mail and no one had telephoned. He went up to his room and changed. Then he took a bottle of Carlos Primero from the wardrobe and poured himself a large glass. Outside, the narrow street bustled with people. He leaned on the railing of the balcony to watch the passers-by, sipping his brandy as he guessed their occupations and destinations.

Not so long ago, he would have been watching for any demeanour that suggested guilt of some kind. Now, he watched with a critical eye, despising the wide, padded shoulders of the jackets, the long hair – some men seemed to be sporting perms – and, even more annoying, men wearing running shoes with their suits.

He took out his Ducados and lit one. At five to five, he took off his jacket. At five o'clock, there was a knock at the door.

'I'm late,' Lourdes said, pushing past him into the room. She put down her shopping by the nightstand and turned, her arms outstretched as he came towards her. 'Did you have a good day, Leo?'

'I'll tell you later,' Guzmán said.

MADRID, OCTOBER 1982, GUARDIA CIVIL HEADQUARTERS

Miguel Galíndez slicked back his hair as he left the building. He was in need of a drink after another day spent collecting yet more dusty files. Still, a few beers in the Café León would wash the taste of dust from his mouth. He walked quickly across the parade ground, his boots crunching on the hard surface. Spotlights around the walls threw white light over him as he walked. The air was chill, another sign of autumn turning to winter. Not that Miguel cared. He knew how to keep warm in even the worst of winters. It was just a question of finding somewhere where you couldn't be seen skiving. His favourite trick was to pretend to be following up a lead on some crime or other and then spend most of the day in a bar.

Whores were good too: interviewing them about crimes they couldn't possibly have committed required the interviews to take place somewhere warm. It wasn't like they could complain, even when he availed himself of their services and then refused to pay.

There was ever only one loser in such a confrontation and it was always the whores. Once they'd had a beating from Miguel, they knew better than to argue the next time he came calling.

Miguel said goodnight to the sentries at the gate and went out into the street. Traffic was light and there were few passers-by. As he walked along the pavement, a man stepped out from behind a parked car.

'Teniente Galíndez?' An unrecognisable accent. 'Could I have a word?'

Miguel scowled, suspecting he was about to ask for money. 'I don't have the time.'

'Don't be like that, *signor*.'

Something in the man's voice made Miguel look at him more closely. He was shorter than him and older too, with close-cropped grey hair and beard.

'Or what?' Miguel laughed.

The man smiled. 'Or I'll spread you all over the pavement.' By way of emphasis, he took a small pistol from his belt. 'You really ought to listen to what I've got to say.'

If Miguel had been braver, he might have run the moment the man approached him. It was too late for that now. 'Go ahead.'

'Very sensible.' The man pulled a plastic bag from his pocket.

'What are those, your holiday snaps?'

The man took several black-and-white photographs from the bag. 'Miraculous things, Polaroid cameras, don't you think?'

'I wouldn't know,' Galíndez muttered as he stared at the first photograph.

He was not laughing now.

MADRID, OCTOBER 1982, HOTEL SUIZA, CALLE SAN ONOFRE

Lourdes stood at the window, looking out at the shadowed street. The lights of the hairdresser's shop glowed on the wet cobbles. 'I love watching it get dark.'

Guzmán went to the window and stood behind her, resting his hands on her shoulders. The light was almost gone and he saw their faces, pale reflections in the glass.

'It's a shame we can't choose the life we live,' Lourdes said softly. She turned away and started to pick up her clothes from the floor.

Guzmán sat on the bed, watching as she dressed with small, careful movements. 'What sort of life would you choose?'

'Things would be nicer for a start,' she said, reaching for her skirt. 'People would be nicer, that is.'

She picked up her silver necklace and fastened it in front of the mirror.

'That necklace suits you,' Guzmán said, without looking. It was cheap, like the rest of her jewellery. He would buy her better things when they reached Alicante.

'It belonged to my aunt.' She frowned. 'It would be nice to have one with my initials on it but that was...'

'Too expensive?' he cut in. She nodded, embarassed, so he changed the subject. 'So where would you live if you could choose a different life?'

'Somewhere down south where it's warm.' Dressed now, she bent to look in the mirror on the dressing table, teasing her hair with a brush. 'You could choose where,' she said, satisfied with her coiffure. 'You know the south better than me.'

She was prompting him for the story again. He obliged.

'There's a place near Alicante.' Guzmán took out his cigarettes and offered her a Ducado. She shook her head. 'Llanto del Moro,' he continued. 'It's a little village. There's a hotel on the cliff top overlooking the sea.' His voice trailed away as he saw it, the dark swell of the ocean, the rustling of trees in the ocean breeze. Other memories too, of course, though of a time long past. He shared those with no one.

'Don't stop.' She sat on the bed to put on her shoes. 'It sounds lovely.'

'It can be.' Guzmán nodded.

Lourdes got up, admiring herself in the mirror. 'How do I look?'

'Very pretty and very respectable.'

A shy smile. 'Respectable? After what we just did?'

'Absolutely.' He put on his watch, glancing at the time. 'We could be there in under nine hours by train.'

Outside, he heard people shouting. Somewhere on an upper floor, the mechanical rumble of the lift as it started to descend.

'You really mean it, Leo?' Her face was pale. 'Even though it's a sin?'

'It's not a sin to be happy.'

Ever the good Catholic, she struggled with that idea for a moment or two.

It had been a long shot anyway, he thought.

'All right,' Lourdes said, nervously. 'If you're sure?'

'I'm very sure,' Guzmán said. 'Have you got time for a drink before you go?'

A quick shake of her head. 'He expects dinner on the table the moment he gets home.'

He picked up his jacket and put it on the chair. Once she was gone, he would put on the shoulder holster. 'So we'll go then?'

'Do you really want me?' Her brown eyes glinted as she pressed against him, surprising him with the sudden fury of her kisses.

'We'll meet early tomorrow morning and get the train,' he said, imagining it. Choosing a new life. A different life.

Her face fell. 'Tomorrow's our busiest day of the week. The laundry has to be labelled and bagged up for delivery. Señora Bartolomè can't manage all that on her own and I can't let her down.'

'Who's she?' Guzmán growled.

'The owner of the laundry. She's been so nice, I can't just walk out on her. I'll take my suitcase in with me and meet you after work. Tell her it's a holiday or something.'

'Say you're going somewhere up north,' Guzmán said, through force of professional habit. It was always best to deceive people even when there was no real need. 'Meet me at Atocha Station beneath the clock. Would six thirty suit you?'

'I'll be there.' A last brief kiss before she slipped out into the corridor.

Guzmán closed the door. By the nightstand, he saw her shopping bag and ran out with it into the corridor. 'You forgot these,' he shouted as the lift door opened.

She took the bags from him, muttering about her stupidity. Things were always her fault, he'd noticed. Maybe that would change once they were far away from this city of guilt and secrets. Once she was happy.

Back in his room, he heard the slow abrasive sound of the winch mechanism as the lift descended. He went to the window and watched as she left the hotel, heading towards Calle de Valverde. A cold rain was falling and the street glistened with the light from the shops as she headed for the Metro.

Behind her, two men detached themselves from the shadowed doorway of a bodega across the road, walking slowly and casually behind her. So slowly and casually that there was no mistaking the fact that they were following her. Guzmán snatched up the Browning and ran to the door.

The end of the street where it met Calle de Valverde was crowded with weary shoppers and dull-faced workers, all heading in different directions. Guzmán walked fast, dodging through the crowd, shoving people out of the way when necessary. Ahead, he saw the heads of the two men as they tailed Lourdes towards the Gran Via. He quickened his pace, dodging less and shoving more. In the sea of heads bobbing towards the main road, he could just make out her dark hair and the upturned collar of her poplin raincoat. He cursed himself for his lack of caution. If the *Centinelas* could find him without difficulty, the same was true for anyone else he associated with.

Lourdes took a right turn at the Gran Via, towards the Metro. Guzmán abandoned any pretence at civility and began to run, pushing aside anyone in his way. He could guess what the two men ahead had in mind. Somewhere along the road, before Lourdes reached the Metro station, a car would pull up at the kerb, she would be bundled in and they would drive off at speed, leaving onlookers bemused, probably thinking the men were the police – if they thought anything at all.

But Guzmán also had a plan: get up close and drop the men with head shots before they made their move. In the ensuing panic he would get Lourdes into the Metro, jump on a train and take things from there.

Close now, he saw the men's arms swinging, as if out for a brisk walk. Cheap, unstructured suits made of absurdly soft material. Things he despised. That would make it even easier to pull the trigger on them. He reached into his raincoat for the Browning. Felt the familiar adrenalin rush that preceded killing. That he expected. The men's next move he did not. As he bore down on them, drawing the pistol, the lights changed and the two men hurried across the road through the stalled traffic and went off down Calle de la Abada.

Suspecting a trick, Guzmán spun round, just in time to see Lourdes go down the steps into the Metro. There was no sign she was being followed. He took a deep breath. Perhaps the men's interest had merely been in watching her arse as she walked ahead of them. Perhaps they hadn't noticed her at all. He was being paranoid.

He stopped for a moment and returned the pistol to his pocket. The rain was getting heavier and he turned up the collar of his coat as he returned to the hotel, feeling the adrenalin ebb from his body. He was slipping: the two men had been only a moment away from death. This close to the election, with the city braced for acts of violence aimed at disrupting the democratic process, it would have been difficult even for him to explain why he'd shot them.

Back in his hotel room, he lifted the mattress to take out the leather bag containing the code equipment. He took the bag over to a small table near the balcony and arranged the material on it before fetching the brown cardboard file from its hiding place under the wardrobe. There was one other thing he needed before he began work and that was the bottle of Carlos Primero in the drawer of the nightstand.

He filled a glass and then sat, staring at the file malevolently as he sipped his brandy. Almost eighteen years had passed since this operation and in all that time the events logged in this dusty red file with its faded label had never been disclosed to him. A file like so many others he'd seen over the years: a few pages of flat, dispassionate prose setting out the details of a particular operation. A bland account with no reference to blood or screaming, the harsh crackle of gunfire or the sibilant whine of bullets. He stared at the file, hesitating to open it.

Brigada Especial: Top Secret
(Restricted Access)
Report on the incident at Llanto del Moro, Alicante
September 25th 1965
Classification: Top Secret [Permanent]

There was nothing this file could tell him that he did not already know. He'd been there, for Christ's sake. It made no sense to delve into the memory of what happened: at best, it would annoy him. And at worst? He had no idea what that might be.

A gust of wind sent rain rattling against the window. Far off, a church bell tolled the hour. He took a cigarette from the packet and lit it, staring at the file again. It was time to know the truth, whatever that was. It was not a question that had exercised him much before.

He opened the report and looked down at the jumble of letters and figures on the first page. It was a military code from one of the many branches of the security services. He smiled, remembering how the Nazis had complained about the Spanish inefficiency of having so many competing intelligence agencies. They never really understood that Franco's security services trusted no one, not even their own colleagues. If you had spies, you needed more spies to spy on them. That was obvious to the Spanish: it was why they'd invented the Inquisition.

No matter what code had been used, Guzmán was confident he

could decrypt it. The necessary tools were all here. It was just a matter of selecting the right tool for the job. *Like golf*, he'd said once to Admiral Carrero Blanco, by way of a joke. Not that the admiral had laughed, the Jesuit bastard.

He took a last swig of brandy and then set to work deciphering the report. After that, he heard nothing but the scratching of his pen.

He was still working as he heard the deep notes of the church bell toll four. He stared bleary-eyed at the file lying in a corona of light from the lamp, its pages now annotated with angry scribbles and vexed comments. And next to it, a few pages in his broad impatient handwriting, reconstructing the original contents of the report. Checked and rechecked several times now. Even so, he felt a great temptation to start again, focus on details he might have missed, nuances he might have overlooked. But there was no point. No matter how many times he read this report, the deciphered version always came out the same. The problem was nothing to do with translation. It was far greater than that.

Because now, he knew everything. And all of it was bad. He reached for the Carlos Primero and poured a hefty measure. Somewhere down the corridor a door opened and he stiffened, suddenly alert. As a precaution, he drew the Browning and put it on the table.

All his life, he had stuck to Franco's unassailable principle. *Trust no one.* That way, everyone was suspect. And yet despite that ingrained belief, he'd arrived back in Madrid believing that things had changed enough to make such perennial mistrust unnecessary. That had been stupid. It was the logic of a dead man.

He lit a cigarette, taking in the implications of it all. He'd been wrong. That was not something he would normally admit to, even to himself. But now he knew the truth, something had to be done, something that would provide a seismic response the equal of what he had just discovered. Something to repay the lies and deceit that had blurred his memory with false thoughts for eighteen years. But his memory was clear now and it would have its revenge for this deception. That had always been his way.

He rummaged in his pocket for a scrap of paper and dialled the number on it.

The sarge's son was as outraged as might be expected at four fifteen in the morning.

'I've got a job for you,' Guzmán said. 'Have you got your tools?'

A menacing snigger. 'They're in my van. Who do you want me to kill?'

'No one. It's just a little job but you need to do it now, while it's dark.'

'Hang on, I'll get a pencil.' A sudden agitated scuffle. The sound of things being thrown around the room. 'OK, boss, fire away.'

'I want you to go to the *comisaría* on Calle Robles,' Guzmán said. 'So listen carefully, because I want this done right.'

CHAPTER 26

MADRID, UNIVERSIDAD COMPLUTENSE

I can't sit about doing nothing for another three hours,' Isabel groaned. 'I'm going upstairs to do a bit of work. It'll pass the time.'

'Do you want me to come with you?' Galíndez asked.

Isabel shrugged. 'The outside doors are locked. I think we're safe in here.'

After Isabel had gone, Galíndez stayed at her desk, listening to the dull noises from the pipes in the ceiling, thinking about the haul of files waiting in Guzmán's old *comisaría*. There were some who said it was time to forget the past but Galíndez wasn't one of them. She thought again about the scar down her side, about being tortured by Franco's favourite assassin, years after the *caudillo* and his regime were supposed to have passed into history. How could she forget the past when it posed such an immediate threat?

It was time to even the score, strike back against those remnants of the dictatorship, the *Centinelas*, a group who long ago learned that power could be exercised from behind the scenes as well as by the use of the iron hand. *Steering not rowing*. A process of subtle control, pulling strings, carefully reminding those who benefited from their patronage that debts must always be paid in full, that as long as such debts were honoured there was no need for violence. But when there was, the *Centinelas* returned to their old ways with the deadly reminder of the bomb and the bullet or the faked accidents. Things they deployed to silence the most problematic individuals, those who posed an intolerable challenge to their power. People like her.

But there were others as well, like Capitán Fuentes and his family. She had no idea what Fuentes had done to offend the *Centinelas* but she was certain the family had been killed on their orders. She had a chill recollection of sitting in her black cowl in the refectory of the monastery, listening to the man on the podium: *You pay with your dead*: the *Centinelas*' punishment for treachery, killing not just the traitor but three generations of the family. She'd been wrong, she realised, when she suggested to Isabel that Capitán Fuentes and his family were killed to draw attention from the murder of Sancho and Espartero. It was more likely Fuentes had done something the *Centinelas* thought worthy of their most drastic punishment.

She sighed, twisting a lock of her hair as if somehow it would release the truth. But no matter how much thought she gave it, she kept returning to the same suspects. Besides Galíndez, only Mendez had known Sancho was holed up in the *pensión*. And since Mendez had worked with Capitán Fuentes for years, it was possible she also knew he was a *Centinela*. Or worse, maybe she was one as well. That made her even more of a threat because Mendez knew the layout and the workings of HQ intimately. God, she was on first-name terms with practically everyone in the building.

And there was one person Mendez knew better than any: the girl who'd studied martial arts at a dojo in Lavapiés so kids at school would stop bullying her. The girl whose father died a hero in a terrorist blast: Ana María Galíndez.

She let go of the lock of hair, tired by her circular thoughts. It was time to take a break, take her mind off things for a while. She went out into the corridor.

From a door further along, she heard singing. A moment later, Madame D'Nour emerged from an office, pulling a large plastic sack, her hair tied up in a multicoloured scarf.

'*Muy buenas*, Madame D'Nour. That's another lovely song.'

The cleaner gave her a brilliant smile. 'It's a song about a girl who loves someone and doesn't know how to tell them, Mademoiselle Ana.'

Galíndez gave her a shy smile, thinking of Isabel. That was what she would do, she decided: go and tell Isabel how she felt.

Madame D'Nour pushed open the door to Galíndez's office, still singing. There was not much to do today, she could see. The coffee mugs were lined up by the sink, all washed. That was *Mademoiselle* Isabel's doing, she guessed. Mademoiselle Ana might be pretty, but she needed to learn how to tidy up if she ever hoped to keep a man. She saw their desks: Isabel's was arranged neatly, her pens placed side by side; Galíndez's was strewn with notes, broken pencils and pieces of orange peel. With a sigh, Madame D'Nour set to work, tidying and dusting, singing loudly as she worked. So loud that at first she didn't hear the door open. As she turned, she saw the figure in the doorway, outlined against the light of the setting sun.

'You scared me, sister,' she said. 'Can I help you?'

Galíndez had just reached the top of the stairs when she heard the cry. She turned and went back down the stairs. As she neared her office, she saw Madame D'Nour's plastic sack lying on the floor, surrounded by waste paper. The door was open though the lights were off. Her broom lay on the floor just inside the darkened office.

Tentatively, Galíndez stood in the doorway. Though the room was in darkness, there was still enough light to see Madame D'Nour's body lying behind the door, the floor glinting with her blood. Galíndez knelt and checked in vain for a pulse.

From the deep shadow that obscured the detail of the office, she heard a slow, tentative footstep. Instinctively, she reached for the Glock and felt only her empty holster, suddenly remembering that Isabel had moved the pistol.

Galíndez turned and started to run. She took the stairs two at a time, focused only on warning Isabel. As she reached the floor above, the overhead lights went out, plunging the long corridor into darkness. That left at least seventy metres between her and the office where Isabel was working.

Behind her, she heard footsteps on the stairs and she ran faster, shouting as she ran: 'Isabel, they're here, get out of the building. Open the emergency doors and run. Fuck's sake, Izzy, get out now.'

She ran, gasping for air, her canvas bag bouncing against her side. At the end of the corridor, she saw Isabel come out of her office, silhouetted against the dull light from the windows.

Galíndez shouted again, her voice harsh and unfamiliar, the words coalescing into one long sentence fused by fear: 'Izzy, open the fucking doors, get to the car, for God's sake, run.'

A metallic crash as Isabel kicked the handle of the emergency exit, the dusk light spilling in as the doors flew open. Isabel running out through the exit. Above the sound of her tortured breathing, Isabel's words came back to her. *I can't work with a bloody big pistol lying about. I'll put it in your bag.*

Without slowing, Galíndez shoved her hand into the canvas bag, scrabbling through the contents as she ran: phone, lipstick, a packet of tights. And then her hand closed on the Glock.

Twenty metres to go. The ragged sound of her pursuer's breath behind her as she turned, firing blind without seeing her target, illuminating the corridor with the sudden white flash, hearing a cry of pain as the attacker reeled back into the darkness.

Galíndez charged through the emergency doors, almost losing her balance on the smooth stone ramp. Ahead, she saw Isabel, her long legs pumping as she sprinted towards the line of garbage bins that hid their car. Sudden moments of clumsy panic as they scrambled inside. Galíndez gunned the engine and the tyres squealed as she accelerated away from the faculty building.

For a fleeting moment, she saw a figure standing in the emergency exit, someone dressed in black, the detail lost in shadow. Then she turned her eyes back to the road, looking for the turn off to Vallecas. It was a journey she had made before. On that occasion she nearly died. She had never expected to return.

ALICANTE, 25 OCTOBER 1965, LLANTO DEL MORO

The village was never a noisy place, but now, as the sun went down, it was silent.

The doors of the church hall were open to let in the sea breeze. Inside, Villanueva heard sporadic weeping and a few voices raised in protest at this enforced confinement. Since armed guards surrounded the building, the protests did not last long. A while later, the local priest was brought in to offer spiritual assistance. Villanueva doubted that would be of much use. The last time the priest had offered assistance to a large group of people had been in the war, when the members of the village's Communist party were shot before being thrown into the dried-up well on the edge of town. Where they still lay, he recalled.

As he passed his comisaría, *he heard raised voices coming from the rear of the building. After a furtive glance to see if anyone was watching, he slipped down the side of the* comisaría *to stand beneath the open window of his office.*

'Guzmán can't go up there alone,' Carrero Blanco said. 'It's suicide. I can't believe you're even contemplating such a thing.'

'Men like Guzmán are dispensable. If he pulls it off, he's a hero, if he dies in the attempt, we give him a medal.' Gutiérrez lowered his voice. 'For God's sake, no one is going to save those children from that madman and the harpy he's got with him. We need to end the situation and then make sure the censors keep press coverage to an absolute minimum. At least the tragedy will prompt Franco to consider implementing the new security service I proposed.'

'Frankly, you disgust me,' Carrero Blanco said. 'You want to let Guzmán and eighteen children die to further your own career?'

'I might be in charge of the new unit, but you'd have overall command. It would enhance your prestige immensely.'

'I've already given you my answer,' Carrero Blanco said. 'Fetch Guzmán, at once.'

'That's not possible,' Gutiérrez said. 'He set off half an hour ago. He's taken the case of fake banknotes with him.'

Villanueva did not wait to hear Carrero Blanco's reply.

As he passed the priest's house, the door was open. Quietly, he slipped inside. The telephone was on a small table inside the door, alongside a crucifix sporting a particularly agonised Christ. Villanueva dialled his brother's number. One of the chambermaids answered and he heard the chatter from the dining room for a few moments before his brother came to the phone.

Their conversation over, Villanueva made his way out of the village, following paths he'd known since childhood as he headed for the sloping track leading up to the headland.

CHAPTER 27

MADRID, OCTOBER 1982, CALLE DE RONCESVALLES, MADRID

D awn was still some way off as Guzmán left the hotel. After hours of sitting hunched over his code, the cold morning air was refreshing. Somewhere in the darkness, he heard revellers enjoying what remained of their night out. Probably they were staying up until the polls opened so they could vote before returning home to sleep off the night's excess. He hadn't even considered voting. There were more pressing things to worry about now, the most pressing of which was how to survive the day in a city where any number of people wanted him dead.

Ahead, he saw the lights of a bar and went in for a brandy.

The bar was small. He saw a small stage with an ancient microphone on an upright stand, a few cheap tables and chairs around the stage. At the base of the stage, a worn-out piano. Two dull-eyed gypsies were sitting on stools in a corner, their guitars propped against the wall. Both were dead drunk.

'Quite a place you've got here,' Guzmán said.

The barman stared at him with bloodshot eyes. He stayed awake only long enough to serve him and then laid his head on his folded arms and slept. Guzmán went and sat by the window to avoid the barman's troubled snores.

He glanced at the gypsies from time to time, resisting an urge to go over and pick a fight with them. Bored, he looked out into the darkness, thinking once more about the change the election would bring. It was not a comfortable experience.

He had always opposed change. When something worked, it was best not to go against it. For a long time he'd thought that of

Franco's regime, although it was stretching the truth to say it worked. It had worked for some: mostly for Franco, and then in lesser degrees for a whole pyramid of subordinates, not least Guzmán, though deep down, he had always suspected the dictatorship might eventually crumble under the weight of its own hypocrisy and incompetence.

Despite that, he had also hoped the dictatorship would last for his lifetime. That would have been most convenient. But the dour structure Franco built had already been fatally eroded over the years, not by armed resistance or guerrilla warfare but by foreign music and films, men with long hair and women wearing bikinis on the beach. People no longer defined themselves in terms of which side their fathers fought on in the war, but looked further afield to other countries, craving the freedom and democracy that had eluded Spain for so long.

Despite Guzmán's scorn for the regime, it had been good to him. It had given him the opportunity to learn during his long years at Calle Robles. Beneath that old police station, the dungeons of the Inquisition hid secrets in its dark recesses unknown even to Franco's spies. Guzmán had visited that darkness and, on occasion, had asked for its help and received it, though he also learned that if a man asked for such help and his call was answered, afterwards, the darkness remained with him. For some, that was a curse. For Guzmán, it had been a blessing because it gave him power, an invaluable currency in a country where those who lacked it went hungry.

But things were about to change. And the change would begin around six thirty. While Ochoa and the squad were in Toledo, delivering the files, Guzmán would meet Lourdes at the station and board a train heading south, leaving the city and its shadows behind, where they belonged.

He got to his feet, glowering at the two musicians as he went outside. When he looked up at the church clock, he realised he would have an entire day to pass before he met Lourdes. A whole day staying out of trouble. Naturally, there were art galleries and museums, where he could lose himself among the crowds of tourists. But he hated such places with a passion and the people who visited them even more. He needed to give the matter more thought. Before he could do that, he paused, sniffing the morning air. A pleasing odour, the smell of frying. Someone was cooking *churros*.

Suddenly cheered, he let his nose guide him along a dark cobbled alley. At the far end he saw a stall outside a café. A man was placing the lines of batter into deep, hot fat and then covering them with sugar and salt when they were done. Unable to resist, Guzmán bought a bag. They tasted of salt and fat and sugar and the hot batter burned his mouth as he ate them in big, greedy mouthfuls.

Lost in memory, he strolled, munching happily as he peered into shop windows, savouring the sweet-salt batter. Some people cooked *churros* just right and when they did, there was nothing finer on a cold night. Or any other night, come to think of it.

His thoughts were interrupted as he saw a flickering light in the window of a shop a few doors away. Indolent with *churros*, he went over, wondering what kind of shop opened at four thirty in the morning as he stared in through the smeared glass. The window was almost empty, but for a shelf covered with a piece of ragged velvet. On the shelf, a small lantern burned alongside a glass ball with a handwritten card next to it:

Juanita, Genuine Gypsy from Cadiz
– Fortunes told – Tarot and palm readings – Love potions
– Husbands and Wives found – Luck restored.
Exorcisms by appointment only.
No refunds.

Guzmán finished the last *churro* and tossed the paper bag into the gutter. He wiped his mouth with the back of his hand and entered the shop. The room was small and draped with dark cloths embroidered with the moon and the stars in silver thread.

The thick smell of paraffin from a lantern gave the room a ghastly pallor. As his eyes grew accustomed to the gloom, he saw a woman sitting in the shadows. He was expecting a wizened crone, but this gypsy was not old. Caught between the shadows and the vacillating lamplight, her face had the terrible beauty of a classical statue.

'Can I help you?' Her voice was deep and rasping. Too many cigarettes and too much singing, he imagined.

'I'd like my palm read,' Guzmán said, still smacking his lips from the *churros*.

'You've been here before.' A statement, not a question.

'I have. But I didn't see you.'

'Who knows who they talk to when they consult a gypsy?'

'I do,' Guzmán said belligerently. 'The one I saw was about ninety. You aren't.'

She tossed her long hair from her face. 'Appearances are deceptive.'

'Gypsies are deceptive,' Guzmán growled. 'Just read my palm and cut this nonsense.'

'Come nearer, I don't bite.'

He pulled his chair towards her, savouring her perfume. An odour of smoke and roses. A fragrance he always associated with gypsies, though invariably dead ones.

'So, what is it? Unlucky in love?' The woman took his hand in hers, tracing the lines on his palm with her nail.

'Bad things are happening,' he said. 'I want to know how they'll turn out.'

The gypsy sighed. 'Don't we all.' She bent closer. 'I see a woman. Is there a woman in your life?'

'That possibility exists,' Guzmán said, deciding to make her work for her money.

'I see her clearly, dark hair and big brown eyes.' She looked up at him. 'There's an air of sorrow hanging over her.'

'She's been unhappy,' he agreed. 'But things are getting better.'

'You're wrong. There's no happiness for her, not with you.'

Guzmán glowered, suddenly uncomfortable. 'Why not?'

She frowned. 'No matter how hard she tries, she can't find you.'

He pulled his hand away. 'What the fuck are you talking about? She knows exactly where to find me.'

'Soon she will. But that's when her torment will really begin. You can't save her.'

He felt the gypsy's hand grow cold. When he glanced at her face, her eyes shone with a strange light. 'Can you see her?'

'I can hear her talking, she's frightened.' She put her hands to her ears, as if in pain. 'Can't you hear them?'

He shook his head. 'What's she saying?'

The gypsy's eyes rolled back in their sockets and her mouth sagged open. Then she spoke, though the voice he heard was not hers. *'Please, don't let me burn.'*

'You're making this up.' Guzmán jumped to his feet. 'This is the last time I visit a gypsy.' He threw a hundred-peseta note onto the table and stamped out into the street.

The gypsy stayed at the table, watching the lamplight play over the walls as his footsteps faded away down the road.

'You're right about that,' she said.

MADRID, 28 OCTOBER 1982, CALLE DE PEDRO UNANUE, LAVADERO EXPRÉS

Guzmán found a café a few doors away from the laundry and ordered coffee. The day was getting warm and he took off his jacket and hung it on the back of his seat. Sitting at the end of the counter, if he leaned slightly, he could see Lourdes, a vague shape through the misted glass of the laundry.

He looked at his watch. It was eight fifteen. Ochoa was probably getting ready to brief the men about now. He doubted Ochoa would do it as well as him, though he would try. He was always fucking trying.

'Leo?'

He looked up from his thoughts.

Lourdes was wearing a plain brown overall, her face glistened from the heat of the laundry. 'I can't stay,' she whispered, taking the seat next to him. 'We're so busy, it's crazy in there.'

'At least have a coffee.' Guzmán looked round for the barman. 'He must be in the kitchen, I'll get him.'

She started to say something but he was already marching down the bar towards the kitchen. She heard the tinny sound of a transistor radio as he opened the door and shouted to them to bring a coffee, at once. She tensed. If she was going to do this, she had better do it now. Quickly, she took an envelope from her overall and put it into his jacket pocket.

'Lazy bastard,' Guzmán growled when he came back. 'He's making it now.'

'I can't stay, Leo. I'd better get back or the laundry won't be ready for delivery.'

'So, six thirty at Atocha Station, then?'

'Yes.' She hurried away.

The barman brought the coffee and Guzmán drank it, thinking about Lourdes. She was a hard worker, that woman. She cared about her work, that was very clear. Christ, she'd been so worried about getting the laundry ready for delivery she was shaking like a leaf.

He finished the coffee and slapped a few coins on the bar.

Outside, he set off at a brisk pace only to slow as he realised he still had nine hours to kill until he met her at the station. He thought about that for a moment. Then he sighed and went back in the other direction in search of a cab.

A man could always find something to do if he put his mind to it.

CHAPTER 28

MADRID 2010, COMISARÍA, CALLE DE ROBLES

A street silent in darkness. Deep nuanced shadow broken by pallid street lights. Music and laughter from a nearby bar. The sinister outline of the *comisaría*, dark and threatening, its detail lost in night shadow. Across the road, a parked car. Inside, two women arguing in furtive whispers.

'Just who are you going to give that USB stick to?' Isabel asked.

Galíndez sighed. 'I think I should hand it over to the CNI.'

'You think the *Centinelas* don't have contacts in the Secret Service?'

'I don't know. But the CNI are our only hope unless we go on the run.' She tried to smile. 'Like Thelma and Louise in that movie, remember?'

'Yes, and look what happened to them,' Isabel muttered. 'Look, let's go in, get the files and leave. After that, you call the CNI and we take the files straight to them.'

'You're right.' Galíndez paused. 'There's something I want to say to you.'

'OK.' Isabel shrugged. 'Go ahead.'

Galíndez took a deep breath and then drew the Glock to check the action. 'I'll tell you later, let's get this over with first.'

As Isabel climbed out of the car, she saw Galíndez reach into the back and take out a carry case. 'What have you got there?'

'My camera,' Galíndez said. 'I want to get a few pictures of this Western Vault.'

They hurried across the cobbled street to the dark bulk of the *comisaría*.

Above the doorway was an old sign bearing the faded colours of the flag and the words *Policía Armada*. Fixed to the doors was a more recent notice:

Policía Nacional
Dangerous Building
Permanently Closed
Keep Out

'They've put a padlock and chain on the door,' Isabel whispered. 'We'll never get in.'

'We'll see about that.' Galíndez put down her bag and took out a hefty-looking bolt cutter. Moments later, the chain and the heavy padlock clattered onto the step. She gestured to the door. 'After you, Señorita Morente.'

Isabel put a hand on the door and pushed. The door swung inwards and she stepped inside, aiming her flashlight into the darkness. Galíndez stood next to her, watching as the brilliant beams revealed the reception hall in all its grim detail.

She saw the faded map on the wall, the ancient desk at the far end of the lobby. Beyond that, a pair of swing doors that opened into the narrow corridor where Guzmán's office was located. 'This way,' she muttered, heading for the swing doors.

Over a year had passed since she was last in this hideous old building. Now, in the narrow claustrophobic passageway, that visit seemed much more recent.

As they passed Guzmán's office, she looked away, unable to bring herself to look. Then curiosity overcame her and she stared into the wreckage of Guzmán's lair.

Little remained intact. The doorway was now a ragged, gaping hole. Inside, she saw piles of shattered bricks, wooden slats nailed haphazardly over a space where the window had once been. The floor was littered with pieces of charred furniture and splintered joists dangling precariously from the sagging ceiling. Galíndez turned away, suddenly uncomfortable. There were too many memories here.

They moved on past the ruined mess room and down a short flight of stairs into the low, arched passageway where the masters of the *comisaría* once kept their prisoners. On either side of the passage were cells, the doors open, their damp walls twinkling green under the beam of the torches.

'We found a name scratched on the wall of one of these cells,' Galíndez whispered, unable to bring herself to speak louder. 'A woman called Alicia Martinez.'

'Who was she?' Isabel asked.

'One of Guzmán's prisoners, I guess, brought here to be tortured or killed.' She shone the flashlight upwards, lighting up the low stone ceiling. 'See those carvings?'

Isabel's eyes followed the beam. 'Holy Mother of God.'

The lintel swarmed with carvings. Small, delicate, time-worn filigrees of menace and hate: bodies being torn apart, impalings, hangings, corpses with no heads, skulls with eyes being gouged out. Spectacular, impossibly violent rape, insanely bloody slaughter.

'I'm surprised you could bear to come back here, Ana.'

Galíndez attempted a smile. 'So am I.'

At the end of the corridor, they stopped to examine the ancient iron-banded door.

'This is impossible,' Galíndez said. 'I saw photographs that were taken after the explosion. This door was badly damaged.'

'They must have put in a new one,' Isabel said. 'To keep trespassers out, maybe?'

'Maybe.' Galíndez knelt and ran a hand over the thick iron bands. 'Look at this lock, there's no key: I'm not sure we'll be able to get in.' Angrily, she hit the door with her hand, and stared as it swung open.

'That's odd,' Isabel whispered, staring into the darkness.

'Isn't it just?' Galíndez raised the torch, illuminating a small stone balcony inside the door. At one side of the balcony, a stone spiral staircase twisted down into the shadows.

Galíndez moved to the top of the staircase and shone the

flashlight down over the stone steps, seeing only darkness beyond the limits of the pale beam. Cold dank air rose from below as they made their way down the stairs. She felt a sudden momentary vertigo and put a hand against the wall to steady herself, feeling smooth, damp stone, worn by centuries of dripping water. Below, in the darkness, she heard soft whispers.

'Are you OK?' Isabel said, aware of Galíndez's silence.

'I'm fine.' A lie was always more comforting than truth.

At the bottom of the stairs, Galíndez pointed out the great arched ceiling above them, ribbed and skeletal like some underground church. Isabel gasped as she saw carvings leering out from the stonework, depicting the slaughter and savagery of some hellish massacre. It was easy to see the antiquity of these malevolent runes, the stone so worn by time it seemed almost transparent in the beam of the light. Above the carvings, a single sentence in large letters following the curve of the roof.

VERITAS PER POENA

'What does that say?' Isabel asked. 'I never studied Latin.'

'The truth through pain.' Galíndez frowned as she heard a sound in the distance. 'Can you hear that? It sounds like a river.'

'It can't be,' Isabel said. 'There are no rivers near this place.'

Galíndez took another look at the parchment map. 'There should be a doorway somewhere here.' She played the light over the stone wall. 'There it is.'

They were forced to stoop as they went through the opening into a narrow, rough-hewn tunnel. The sound of water grew louder, almost overpowering their voices as the tunnel opened onto a patch of damp rock.

'Jesus Christ, what the hell is this place?' Isabel shouted, moving towards the edge of the path to get a better look.

Galíndez pulled her back. 'Be careful, Izzy.' She pointed the flashlight in the direction Isabel had been heading. A metre below, a torrent of dark water cascaded from a crevice in the sheer stone wall to their right, surging past in a great muscular tide before thundering into a rocky chasm further downstream.

'Where the hell does that come from?' Galíndez said.

'And where does it go?' Isabel wiped spray from her face. 'It's not on any map of Madrid I've ever seen.'

They followed the path to a small chamber carved out of the rock. The inside of the chamber resembled a small chapel, like those of country monasteries. Crudely cut stone ledges lined the walls and Galíndez stopped, intrigued as she shone the torch over a carefully arranged line of objects, furred with cobwebs and dust. 'Wristwatches,' she said, examining them.

'What was that?' Isabel's voice was strained. 'Jesus, I hope it's not rats.'

'You know, it's strange,' Galíndez said. 'I haven't seen one rat yet. You'd think there'd be lots.'

'I wouldn't be here if there were,' Isabel muttered.

Galíndez heard something snap beneath her feet, dry and brittle. She shone the flashlight onto the ground. 'Jesus, look at this. These are human bones.' She stooped to look closer and whistled in surprise. 'It looks like someone was torn apart.'

'How much further to this Western Vault?' Isabel asked, unhappily.

Galíndez glanced at the map, and pointed at the far wall. 'We need to go through that opening over there. Ready to take a look at what Guzmán's hidden down here?'

'Definitely,' Isabel agreed, though she stepped back to let Galíndez lead the way.

Galíndez paused at the end of the passage, in front of a wooden door. When she spoke, her voice was taut with excitement. 'This is it: the Western Vault.'

She reached for the big iron doorknob, fashioned in the shape of a scowling ogre, and turned it. As the door opened, a sudden draught of fetid air rushed past them from the darkened vault. Isabel gagged and turned away. As the air cleared, Galíndez peered inside, her eyes following the erratic trajectory of their flashlights.

Puzzled, she held her hand under the beam of her flashlight. 'This lock's been oiled recently.'

'Never mind that, Ana,' Isabel whispered. 'Look.'

Ahead of them was a narrow vault, its arched roof some ten metres high. On the far wall was an ancient fireplace, the mantel cracked and broken. There were things piled in the fireplace, covered by what looked like a dirty sheet. That was of no interest to Galíndez now as she stared at the files, boxes and papers scattered around the vault.

'Guzmán's files,' Galíndez said, raising the camera.

Their flashlights revealed a sloping stone chute, rising up into the shadows. 'That was the line we saw on the map,' Galíndez said. 'The Inquisition must have used it to drop supplies down to the prisoners.'

Isabel picked up a file and wiped dust and cobwebs from its cover as she read the label. '"Top Secret. Details of an Operation to Assassinate Ramfis Trujillo, Son of the Dominican Dictator, 27th December 1969. Authorised by Generalisimo Franco and Admiral Carrero Blanco."'

'Christ,' Galíndez said. 'Guzmán's note to General Ortiz said these files had all the shit on the regime. Looks like he was right.'

'You wanted to uncover his secrets and you've done exactly that,' Isabel said, staring at the profusion of files and boxes rising up towards the back of the vault. 'How are we going to get them out?'

'Why don't you keep watch at the end of the passage for a few minutes while I take a quick look through those files? If anyone comes, shout and I'll come running.'

Isabel gave her a dubious look. 'I don't think we should split up.'

'I'll only be a few minutes, then we're out of here, I promise.'

Isabel tapped her watch. 'Ten minutes, OK?' Without waiting for a reply, she went out into the passage.

Once Isabel had gone, Galíndez went to the litter of documents, trying to evaluate their importance from the titles. Going through the dusty papers was hard work and her growing anger was aggravated as she tripped and went sprawling into a jumbled mass of paper, raising a thick cloud of dust that settled over her hair and clothes. Cursing, she wiped a string of cobwebs from her face and looked round for her camera.

Something flashed across her vision. At first she thought it was a shaft of light from a window. But there were no windows here. Then a barb of pain lanced through her temple and she knew exactly what was happening. These were warning signs, the precursors of her seizures. She started to get to her feet, putting one hand on the papers ahead of her for support. There was no support and her hand sank into something brittle, like a pile of dry wood, though it was not wood, she realised, as she extracted her hand from the ribcage of the body in front of her.

A man's body, what was left of it. Lying face down, arms outstretched. A man wearing a suit, made of what appeared to be fine tweed, though the pattern was obscured by dust and much of the material had crumbled away. In this dry atmosphere, the corpse had mummified, leaving a thin parchment-like layer of skin. Her forensic training had taught her the need for caution in such situations. But there was no time for that now and she worked quickly, lifting the jacket and running her fingers over the crumbling silk lining as she started to search his pockets.

Her fingers touched leather straps: the man was wearing a shoulder holster. Carefully, she ran her hand under the broken ribcage, fumbling until she located the pistol and pulled it from its holster, using her fingertip to smooth away the dust covering the maker's name engraved on the weapon.

BROWNING HI-POWER.

She turned the pistol in her hands. The dark metal was slick with oil. When she worked the action, she heard a round go into the chamber. She put on the safety and pushed the pistol into the belt of her jeans.

This must be another of Guzmán's victims, she guessed,

wondering why he had been brought here to die. She decided it was best not to dwell on that, but her curiosity was aroused now and so she continued searching the man's pockets. Inside one was a crocodile-skin wallet containing a wad of faded thousand-peseta notes. A laminated card bearing the owner's name was wedged at the front of the banknotes. As she read it, she felt a chill crawl over her skin.

Comandante Leopoldo Guzmán
Brigada Especial
13 Calle de Robles
Vallecas, Madrid

It was him.

All this time, she'd been searching for a dead man.

She slipped the ID card into her shirt pocket and rummaged through Guzmán's other pockets. Inside one, she found a folded envelope with something hard inside. Clearly Guzmán had never read the contents of the envelope, since the seal was unbroken. On the envelope, she saw his name in faded ink, written in a hand that seemed almost familiar: *Leo.*

Galíndez pushed her finger under the seal and tore it open. Inside was a folded piece of notepaper and below it, something heavier, wrapped in tissue. She unfolded the notepaper and read the few lines below his name.

29th October, 1982

Dearest Leo,

I'm not coming with you to Alicante. I really can't, though God knows I want to. But it's a mortal sin and I can't come with you knowing that. Funny, isn't it? I can't go against the church and yet all those times we made love it never seemed wrong. The fickle will, my priest called it in one of his sermons. I know you're not one for religion but it means a lot to me despite the fact that I've committed a sin. Worse than that, I lied to you.

I'm not called Lourdes, I'm afraid. Please forgive me for not telling you my name sooner, I was terrified Miguel would find out. He's a brute, unlike you. Even so, the marriage vows say till death us do part so I'll stay with him though it will always be you I love.

I hope you'll think of me now and again, when you're on the beach in Alicante looking at all those Swedish girls.

Yours always, my love,

Amaranta

Galíndez unfolded the tissue. Nestling inside was a silver chain. At its centre, three silver initials. She blinked as she remembered seeing this chain in a photo of her parents, the silver initials sparkling against her mother's tanned skin. *Amaranta María Galíndez.* A woman who'd named her daughter so she'd have the same initials as her.

A sudden pain pulsed behind her eyes. *My mother knew Guzmán.* Knew him very well, it seemed. So well, that the possible result of that relationship burned in her mind. She did the maths, trying to dispel the appalling possibility. Though the time frame made it possible, the words of her mother's letter made it hideously probable.

Her stomach knotted as she tried to grasp the inevitable. *Please God, no. He can't be my father.*

She leaned forward and retched, her body straining as if trying to expel the dark secret it had harboured for so long. But all that left her mouth were incoherent denials only she could hear.

Still shaking, she examined the body, trying to be her usual professional self, cool and detached. It was hard to say how long his body had been here, or what had killed him, but she knew one thing: the man who'd tortured her in the cellar with Sancho had not been Guzmán.

There was no time to ponder that now and Galíndez tensed, ready to make a move. As she began to get up, she saw Guzmán's outstretched arm, the claw-like hand resting on the red cardboard cover of a file, as if trying to drag it towards him. She reached over his body for the file and read the title:

Brigada Especial: Top Secret
(Restricted Access)
Report on the incident at Llanto del Moro, Alicante
September 25th 1965
Classification: Top Secret [Permanent]

Galíndez left the file where it was and retrieved her camera. Brushing off dust and stray cobwebs from the lens, she took several photos of the body. When she looked down at the view screen to check the images, her hands were shaking. She flipped from one image to the next, blinking in surprise as the dark pictures of the desiccated remains of Franco's favourite assassin changed to a colour picture of a beaming Uncle Ramiro.

She enlarged the picture, taking comfort in the familiar detail of her uncle and his office, recalling the day she'd taken it, when Ramiro signed the authorisation for her investigation into Guzmán's activities. And now, she thought bitterly, she'd found him.

Her gaze returned to the photo of Ramiro. It was good, the detail much sharper than she'd expected. His ruddy cheeks, the avuncular moustache, his blue twinkling eyes. Every detail reproduced with needle-sharp clarity, even the green pen he'd used to sign the form. She remembered him rummaging impatiently through his drawer, tossing aside the contents as he searched for that pen, a pen that had been carried by three generations of the Ortiz family through their various wars. The pen that bore the name of his great-grandfather's house at military school.

She adjusted the focus until Ramiro's hand almost filled the screen and rotated the image to read the word on the side of the pen. A sudden chill as she stared at the word picked out in silver letters.

Xerxes.

She returned the picture to its normal size and orientation. Uncle Ramiro signing the paper. To his right, a jumbled heap of office paraphernalia. Normal things. Things that happened a lifetime ago when he was Uncle Ramiro and not the leader of a ruthless criminal organisation. Now, in this new, adrenalin-soaked reality, only one thing was clear: she needed to find Isabel and get the hell out of here.

The spasm of pain caught her unawares, a pain so sharp it soaked her body in cold sweat. The file fell from her hand as she staggered towards the door, trying to ignore the pain and the lights swirling across her vision. And then, as she fumbled with the handle of the door, she heard the distant echoes of someone shouting in pain.

It was Isabel.

ALICANTE, 25 OCTOBER 1965

The brooding sky darkened into night and the sea gleamed with the last rays of the dying sun. Ahead, the sharp contours of the headland became a silhouette. An old sign pointed inland along a steep track hemmed in by rocky outcrops. Taking a torch from his pocket, he shone the light up the slope, its pale beam roving over the rocks and dark branches. The signal the Italian had asked for.

He heard the dull sound of waves in the distance. And above that, the muffled throb of an engine, the crunch of tyres on parched soil. As the bus approached, he lifted the heavy briefcase into the beam of its headlights. Inside the case was the money the Italian had demanded, though the bills were counterfeit, hurriedly delivered to the village that afternoon. In the darkness they would appear real enough. At least, he hoped so.

As he walked towards the bus, he saw children's faces at the windows, pale orbs in the weak interior lights. The front door opened, revealing the driver, his hands resting on the wheel, his face pale and drawn. A woman stepped down onto the platform, a battered ticket machine hanging round her neck. He recognised her from the photographs sent by HQ. 'Do you want a return ticket, señor?' A mocking tone.

Guzmán moved fast. As he drew the Browning, the woman realised what was about to happen and threw herself back into the aisle, shouting a warning as Guzmán opened fire. The woman moved fast, unfortunately for the driver, and he died instantly. Guzmán ran forward and jumped up onto the platform, leaning in to get a shot off at the woman. Along the narrow aisle, the children cowered in their seats. Behind them, he glimpsed a man standing near the rear of the bus. Grey, close-cropped hair, a close-trimmed beard.

The first explosion threw Guzmán back onto the platform, clutching at a wound in his leg from a piece of flying metal. The children screamed as a cloud of thick smoke rolled through the bus. And then two more explosions ripped through the vehicle, one after the other.

The screaming stopped.

Guzmán jumped down onto the track, keeping the pistol raised towards the shattered windows of the bus as he backed away, ready to take a shot the moment the terrorists showed themselves.

A sudden noise from the rear of the bus. He spun round, firing as the Italian came through the rear exit, followed by the woman, machine pistols in their hands.

Guzmán traded shots with them as he backed away, trying to reach the cover of the trees. As the first bullets struck home, he sank to his knees, keeping the Browning aimed, though things were suddenly blurred. Sweat ran down his face, blood soaked his shirt. Cursing, he looked up as the Italian started to approach him.

'Throw down your weapons.' Villanueva emerged from the darkened trees aiming his .38. Behind him, Guzmán saw another man, holding a shotgun. He was standing too close, presenting a target.

The Italian swung the machine pistol towards them and Villanueva fired once before the hail of bullets sent him falling into the parched grass. The woman kept her weapon low, firing in a long burst, as the man with the shotgun fell in broken motion to the ground. A brittle silence. Night sounds, distant and faint. The sound of Villanueva groaning.

Guzmán lay on his back, grunting at the radiant pain of his wounds.

The track was illuminated by the oily flames from the burning vehicle. The man with the shotgun was dead. Villanueva lay nearby, moaning in pain. A couple of metres away, the Italian was struggling as he pulled something from the bushes. At first, it was hard to see what he was doing. Then, as the wind fanned the flames, the sudden glare illuminated the outline of a motorcycle. The Italian had brought his means of escape with him.

Guzmán tried to sit up though his body defied him. He saw the Browning, lying on the baked soil, near his right hand. When he flexed his fingers, his hand ignored him.

As the woman walked towards Villanueva, Guzmán saw her take a handgun from her belt, her arm straightening as she aimed. The sudden gruff bark of the shot. Villanueva's scream as the bullet hit him in the leg. Guzmán reached again for the pistol, sweat stinging his eyes, his fingers slick with congealing blood as they closed on the Browning.

The woman gave Villanueva a savage smile as she aimed the pistol at him again. Behind her, the Italian called to her for help, saying he was hurt. As she turned to him, Guzmán sat up, aimed and fired. The bullet took off the top of her head, dropping her to the ground. As he fell back, Guzmán heard the roar of the bike's engine as it raced away up the track.

A sudden calm now. He lay on the hard ground, shivering in the night air. Above him, something moved in the dark sky. A small light, slowly beginning to expand into a series of concentric circles, turning slowly above him, shimmering and imprecise.

It was the view of a drowning man, the circles turning faster as they rose through the darkness towards the surface and the light. But it was not the circles that were rising, Guzmán realised. He was sinking into the darkness. Far above, a voice was shouting to him to live, that help was on the way. Then, slowly, Villanueva's voice faded into darkness.

CHAPTER 29

Ochoa led the squad across the parade ground to the squadroom. An orderly brought in a pot of coffee and they sat round the table, blowing on their drinks to cool them. Tense faces, no one making eye contact. No one in a hurry to speak.

'When's the boss going to get here, Corporal?' Quique's words were muffled by the large sandwich he was eating.

Ochoa shrugged. 'He's got a meeting with the top brass. He might not make it.'

'You mean we're going to carry out the operation on our own?' Ramiro's unease was contagious. Boots shuffled on the tiled floor. A rapid exchange of anxious glances.

Ochoa gave them what he hoped was a stern look. 'It's not a problem: I'll take command if the boss can't make it.'

Quique took another bite of his sandwich. 'I'm not worried, Corporal.'

'Maybe you should be, kid,' Ochoa said. 'Worrying keeps you alive.'

'It can't be that dangerous,' Galíndez cut in. 'We're only delivering a bunch of files.'

'I hope you've made a will, Galíndez?' Ochoa saw a wave of fear suddenly pass over Miguel's face and smiled. 'You're looking pale, *amigo*, but don't worry, that'll change when the shooting starts.'

'Shooting?' Galíndez muttered. 'I thought the boss said it would be easy.'

'The boss would say that if we were up against a division of

Russian tanks. There's only one thing that's guaranteed in this job: when things get rough, you're on your own. No one's going to hold your hand. That fat guy didn't choke himself to death in the archive the other day, did he? The boss knew what had to be done and he did it. He took responsibility. That's what you need to do today, all of you.'

Suddenly cowed, the men fell silent, remembering how the fat man died. For a moment, the only sound in the room was made by Fuentes as he stripped down his pistol and began reassembling it for the fifth time.

Ochoa checked his watch. 'It's nine o'clock. Looks like the boss isn't going to make it, so I'll start the briefing. You don't need to make notes.'

Behind him, the door opened and Ochoa turned, hoping it was Guzmán.

'Sorry I'm late, Corporal.' The sarge's son looked as if he had been dragged behind a car. His clothes were filthy, his boots scuffed and unpolished. 'Had a job to do for the boss last night.' He slumped into a seat. 'Don't let me interrupt.'

'We'll be in two trucks today,' said Ochoa. 'I'll be in the first with Quique and Julio. Fuentes, you, Ortiz and Galíndez will be in the second truck. Our first stop is the military library on Mártires de Alcalá. When we get there, put all the files in the second truck.'

Quique raised his hand. 'Why, Corporal?'

'Because if we hit trouble, the second truck takes another route while we cover them.'

'Brilliant,' Quique cut in. 'That means we'll be right in the middle of the action.'

Ochoa looked at him, almost amused. 'And that's a good thing, is it, Private?'

'It's how you get medals,' Quique said, finishing his sandwich.

The others didn't share his enthusiasm, Ochoa noted. 'Any questions?'

'I've got one,' a deep voice behind him. 'How come you're not in the fucking truck?'

Guzmán sauntered into the room, brushing *churro* crumbs from his coat. 'My train doesn't leave for eight hours, so I thought I'd give you a hand.'

'I was just briefing them, sir,' Ochoa said. 'They're looking forward to some action.'

A long, uncomfortable silence. 'Yes, I can see they're champing at the bit.' Guzmán fixed Quique with a steely gaze. 'Are you eating, Private Vidal?'

Quique nodded, his cheeks bulging. 'Just a chorizo sandwich my Mamá made for me.'

Guzmán sighed. 'Fuck's sake, stop him a week's pocket money, Corporal.' He cast his eye over the other men. 'You look a bit strange, Galíndez.'

'It's flu, I think, sir. The wife says I ought to see a doctor.'

'Really?' Guzmán asked with assumed empathy. 'Just before the battle of Belchite, one of my men had the flu. Made him completely unfit for duty, he said.'

'That's how I feel, sir. Sick as a dog. I'd probably be better home in bed.'

'I shot him in the head,' Guzmán added. 'No one else felt ill after that.'

Galíndez licked his lips nervously. 'It'll pass, I expect.'

'It had better,' said Guzmán. 'Because if you don't pull your weight, I'll use you as a sandbag when the shooting starts.' He went to the door. 'I'll see you outside directly, Corporal. It's time we got moving.' The door slammed behind him.

Ochoa picked up his weapon and went after Guzmán. Aware of the silence, he turned in the doorway and glanced back at the squad.

For the rest of his life, Ochoa would remember the men as they were now: pale-faced, sitting stock-still in a nervous tableau around the table. Ramiro looking out of the window, Galíndez staring at the floor, Quique fiddling with the strap of his shoulder holster.

Then, from outside, he heard Guzmán's voice, loud and authoritative, telling them to get a fucking move on.

MADRID, OCTOBER 1982, BIBLIOTECA MILITAR,
CALLE MÁRTIRES DE ALCALÁ

'That's the last box,' Guzmán grunted as Quique and Fuentes came running from the door of the seminary, carrying a large crate of files. He watched as they shoved the files into the back of the truck with the others.

As he waited for further instructions, Quique began examining the levers by the tailboard. 'Sir? What's this lever for?'

Guzmán frowned. 'Don't touch that, kid, this is a dump truck. The driver raises the platform and when it's tilted, you pull that lever to let the cargo slide out. In this case, the cargo is about half a ton of files, so don't touch any of those controls.' He went round the side of the truck and pulled himself up into the cab. 'That kid's like a monkey,' he said to Ochoa, 'he meddles with everything. Good job we're not using grenades or he'd be pulling out the pins to see what happens.'

Gutiérrez came out of the ancient building and slowly made his way across the road to the truck. 'I could have got more men to help carry the boxes if you'd asked, *Comandante*.'

Guzmán leaned out of the window. 'You could have arranged a brass band as well, so the entire fucking city would know what we're doing.'

'It was only a thought.' Gutiérrez handed a map to Guzmán. 'Here's your route.'

'I know how to get to Toledo,' Guzmán snapped. 'It isn't complicated.'

'I've planned this route specially,' Gutiérrez said. 'There are units stationed at regular intervals along the way, ready to help out if you're attacked.'

'Very sensible,' Guzmán said. 'Now stand away so we don't run you over.'

'Call me when you've got the material locked away in Toledo.'

'Naturally.' Guzmán watched Gutiérrez limp back to the seminary entrance, almost bowled over as Quique came running out with a final box of documents. The lad dashed over and hauled himself up into the cab. 'Shall I sit in the middle again, sir?'

'No, you can sit by the window today,' Guzmán said. 'I want to talk to the corporal.' He put the map on the top of the dash, in front of Ochoa. 'Gutiérrez's put armed units along this route, so follow the directions he's marked out.'

Julio came shambling towards the truck.

'Get in the back,' Guzmán ordered, 'and keep an eye out for anyone following us.'

Ochoa turned the key and the engine spluttered into life. The gears meshed noisily as he eased the truck away from the kerb and headed towards Calle Princesa. 'So I follow these roads marked in red ink?'

Guzmán nodded. 'That's all you have to do, Corporal.'

'Not the route I'd have picked,' Ochoa said, frowning.

'Just drive.' Guzmán took a packet of Ducados from his pocket and lit one.

'I reckon they won't try anything in the city,' Ochoa said. 'Once we get into the countryside, that's when they'll make their move, I reckon.'

'Then we've got something to look forward to,' Guzmán said, slowly exhaling smoke. 'Can you see the other truck behind us?'

'Yes, they're sticking close, just as you told them.'

'Let's hope they remember everything I told them.' He glanced at Quique. 'You're quiet, kid.'

'Just thinking, *jefe.*'

'About seeing some action?'

'About General Ortiz's girlfriend. She's going to be lonely without him.'

Guzmán and Ochoa exchanged a look.

'Why don't you ask her out, kid?'

'Not me, sir. I heard her give you the brush-off the other night. She's scary.'

The truck slowed in heavy traffic near the Plaza de España. 'Go down Calle del Reloj,' Guzmán said, pointing.

Ochoa slowed and turned into the narrow street. On either side, tall apartments rose above them and he felt the steering wheel judder as the truck bounced over the cobbles. In his mirror, he saw Fuentes and Ramiro through the windscreen of their truck as they followed him into the warren of streets, their faces pale circles in the darkened cab.

'I read the file on Alicante last night,' Guzmán said quietly.

'That was top secret, wasn't it?'

'I wasn't asking you for permission, Corporal.'

'No, sir.'

'Gutiérrez set me up,' Guzmán growled. 'He called off the backup so the Italian would kill me.'

Ochoa gripped the wheel tighter. 'Why would he want you dead?'

'He thought if I was killed by a foreign terrorist, it would shock Franco into reforming the *Brigada Especial* into a more powerful organisation with him in charge.' Angrily, he reached into his pocket for a cigarette. 'If that small-town cop hadn't pitched in, I'd have been dead.'

Ochoa said nothing.

'Are you listening?' Guzmán asked.

'I was just thinking about those kids, sir.'

'I might have known you wouldn't be concerned about me.'

'You survived,' said Ochoa. 'Eighteen children died.'

'That wasn't my fault.'

'You were the best he had.'

'I still am, Corporal.'

'Seems a bit of an odd way to deal with you, though. Not very efficient.'

'I didn't realise how much my survival disappointed you.'

'He could have had you killed any time, if he wanted. Why do it like that?'

Guzmán sighed. 'Perhaps he had it planned for years or perhaps it was a fucking birthday present, I don't know.' He twisted round and peered into the back of the truck. 'What's that noise?'

'It's me, sir.' The sarge's son rose from behind the seat. In one hand he held a long Moorish dagger, in his other was a small whetstone. He grinned, showing a line of dark, ragged teeth. 'I always sharpen this before battle.'

Guzmán gave him an approving nod. 'Carry on.'

'So what now, sir? Are you going to kill Gutiérrez?'

'I haven't made up my mind, Corporal.'

'It's nearly eighteen years ago. Maybe he changed his mind about you since then?'

'I don't care if he's fallen for my manly charms. It's the principle of the thing.'

'It certainly makes him hard to trust, boss.'

'That's an understatement.' Guzmán glanced at the map. 'Turn left.'

Ochoa twisted the wheel. 'It doesn't make sense to try and kill you and then just let it go, as if it were nothing.'

'He's a tricky one.' Guzmán scowled. 'He learned his trade in Germany during the war.' His tone suggested that wasn't a compliment. 'He was there, 1939 to '44, learning interrogation techniques. Naturally, he got out before the Russians and *Yanquis* arrived.' He stubbed out the cigarette in the overflowing ashtray on the dash. 'You know he's dying?'

'I do now.'

'Radiotherapy, I heard,' Guzmán said, cheered by the thought. 'The *Centinelas* know all about it, so when he goes, they'll try and infiltrate the *Brigada* like they have the police.'

'Perhaps he's sorry he played such a long game now.'

'Hard to say. Some men want statues to preserve their memory, Gutiérrez wants a new security service. Even while the cancer's eating him up, he's still pursuing his ambition.' Guzmán turned his back on Quique and lowered his voice. 'The Italian's in Madrid. It was him who bombed Gutiérrez's warehouse.'

Ochoa raised an eyebrow, so discreetly Guzmán thought at first he was ignoring him. 'Is he here to disrupt the elections?'

'I thought so. It seemed the sort of thing the right-wingers would do: hire an insane terrorist to commit a few atrocities that could be blamed on Communists or trade unionists.'

'You mean those dead guys in the café were trying to hire the Italian?'

'They did hire him.' Guzmán nodded. 'At least they thought so. What they didn't realise was that he had a different agenda.'

'Which was what?'

'Killing me, Corporal.'

'So how come he killed the men in the café?'

Guzmán shrugged. 'They were of use when he arrived but after that, they were just potential witnesses, and the Italian never leaves witnesses if he can help it.'

Ochoa nodded, taking it in. 'He killed that priest as well. Was there anything in his wallet, by the way?'

'The wallet?' Guzmán gave Ochoa a look so charged with violent intent, the corporal almost ran down a nun standing on the edge of the pavement. 'If I've ever given you the impression that I thought you were a useless miserable bastard, Corporal, I only meant half of it.' He reached into his jacket and rummaged through his pockets. 'Here it is.' He took out the worn leather wallet and opened it. 'Five hundred pesetas.' He scoffed, putting the money into his top pocket. 'Nothing worse than a cheap priest.'

'Anything else, boss?'

Guzmán shook the contents of the wallet into his lap. He picked up a small piece of paper and examined it. 'An airline ticket from Milan to Madrid, one way.'

'So the priest hired the Italian?'

'That makes sense. No one would take any notice of a priest, Spain's awash with the bastards.' He frowned as he saw a small piece of white card. The name and address in small bold black letters. 'This looks like someone's business card.'

A long silence followed, broken only by the sonorous rumble of the engine and the rattling of the truck as it jolted over the cobbles. Ochoa darted a glance at Guzmán and looked away quickly.

'The fucking bastard.' Guzmán held out the card in the palm of his hand. Ochoa looked at it and turned his eyes back to the road.

> Brigadier General L. Gutiérrez
> Brigada Especial
> 14 Calle del Doce de Octubre, Madrid

'I don't fucking believe it.' Guzmán turned the card over and Ochoa heard a sudden intake of breath as he read the handwritten note on the back.

> *Guzmán is staying at the Pensión Paraíso,*
> *10 C/del Carmen*

'So that's how the Italian knew.' Guzmán struggled to control himself. 'He lured me to the Bar Navarra and then, when he failed to kill me, he killed Daniela and her father.'

'Why kill them, boss?'

'Because he's a fucking madman who hates me for what I did to his girlfriend,' Guzmán said, waving the business card angrily. 'And because Gutiérrez gave him the address of their *pensión*.'

'It's worse than you thought,' Ochoa said, even more sombre than usual.

'Much worse. Gutiérrez set me up just as he did at Alicante.' Guzmán took out his cigarettes and lit one. 'This is all part of the same plan. That bald fuck's been waiting years for the right time and now it's come. He thinks he's finally going to get his big new organisation from a bunch of vegetarian socialists and fuck people like me who've done his dirty work all these years.'

'But if he's still following that plan, that means he'll try to kill you again.'

Guzmán looked out of the window at the sheer buildings towering above them. Countless windows, each one a potential hiding place for a sniper. 'You're right. And it's going to be sooner rather than later. You can guess why he gave us this cockeyed route.'

'We're in trouble.'

Julio's ravaged voice came from behind them. 'Trouble?' He was smiling.

Guzmán sank back in the battered leather seat, thinking hard. There was much to think about, but worst of all was the realisation that he and the Italian shared a common characteristic. One that made them perfect for Gutiérrez's plan.

They were both disposable.

sabel closed the door to the Western Vault and walked slowly down the passage. She was far from happy. Nothing Ana had told her about Guzmán's old *comisaría* had prepared her for this chamber of horrors. An underground river and the bones of someone who'd been ripped apart? All Isabel had wanted to do was to write a book about Ana's hunt for Guzmán. And look where it had got her: standing here, alone in the dungeons of the Inquisition while Ana indulged her obsessional pursuit of Guzmán's secrets. She would have plenty to say to her once she'd finished in that vault.

Isabel's thoughts were interrupted by a noise further down the passageway. She froze, wondering if she'd been mistaken. Another rustle in the shadows: she was not mistaken. Taking a deep breath, she tried to calm herself. There was no one down here but Galíndez and her. She was just frightening herself. It was probably just a rat. She'd soon scare that away. She started down the passage, gripping the flashlight.

A metre along the passage, she saw the low arch of an ancient doorway. It was probably best to wait for Ana, she thought, check it out together. But that idea rankled. She wasn't a child, in need of a nanny, she'd been a top radio journalist, for God's sake. Would be again, hopefully. Suddenly confident, she stood in the doorway, shining the flashlight into the shadows, revealing stone columns draped in candyfloss spider webs. There was nothing of interest and she turned, deciding to go back and find Ana. Behind her, she heard scuffling. That damn rat again. The fierce beam of the torch would see it off. As she stepped through the doorway, she remembered what Galíndez said as they walked by the strange river. There were no rats down here.

A hand clamped over her mouth, dragging her backwards. The flashlight fell from her hand, clattering on the flagstones. As she struggled, a violent shove sent her to the floor. Before she could get up, a sudden blinding light shone into her eyes, forcing her to raise a hand to shield them.

'Nice to see you again,' Mendez said. In her hand was a retractable baton. Isabel heard a sibilant metallic hiss as she pushed the release button and extended the baton.

'I'm looking for Ana,' Mendez said, 'and I'd like you to bring her to me.'

'No chance. I'm not helping you,' Isabel said.

Mendez came towards her. 'You just make a bit of noise and she'll come running.'

Isabel watched as the baton rose. Then she bellowed in pain as the blow hit her shoulder. Mendez swung the baton once more, catching Isabel on the thigh as she scrambled to her feet. Before Mendez could hit her again, Isabel turned and ran into the darkness. Behind her, she heard Mendez shouting to her to come back. Isabel turned a corner and after that, all she heard was the sound of her echoing footsteps.

Galíndez clutched the wall, feeling her legs starting to fold under her. Her previous seizures had begun this way and all had ended in a blackout. She needed to find Isabel before she passed out. She stumbled to the door and fumbled clumsily with the latch. Finally, the door opened and she staggered out into the passage.

For a moment, Isabel's cries echoed along the stone passageway and Galíndez heard the sound of someone running, their footsteps fading into silence.

She stumbled forward, supporting herself with a hand on the wall until she reached the end of the passage. From a door a few metres away, a pool of light spilled out over the stone floor. 'Izzy?' A sudden blinding flash pulsed across her vision. 'Isabel?' She turned into the doorway and saw the flashlight on the floor. 'Izzy, where are you?'

'She's not here.' Mendez was standing behind her, holding the baton. 'Behave yourself and I'll take you to her.'

'I'm having one of my attacks,' Galíndez whispered. 'Help me.'

Mendez gripped her arm, tight. 'There's no helping you now, Ana.'

Galíndez leaned against her for support, her legs buckling drunkenly. 'You've got to get me to a phone. I need to call the CNI and have Uncle Ramiro arrested.'

'I know what you need.' Mendez stopped and pushed Galíndez against the wall, holding her by her lapels. 'You need target practice, Ana. You could have dropped me with one shot at the university if you hadn't panicked.'

The sound of the river grew louder as Mendez bundled her down the passage to the chapel. There was more light now: several oil lamps had been lit in niches in the rocks and the rough-hewn window of the chapel, throwing strange geometries of light over the stone walls around them. Intent on staying on her feet, Galíndez was only dimly aware as Mendez stepped behind her and kicked her behind the knee, sending her falling to the ground.

'Isabel will be here soon,' Mendez said. When Galíndez failed to answer, Mendez slapped her across the face, hard. The sound of the blow echoed off the walls, blending into the roar of the river. Mendez dragged Galíndez to her knees and then gripped her hair, forcing her to face the stone chapel. 'Look.'

Galíndez looked, though grey lights danced across her vision, blurring the figure emerging from the chapel, moving backwards with a strange, hesitant gait.

It was Isabel, silhouetted against the flickering light of the oil lamps. Confused, Galíndez stared at the dark line extending from Isabel's face. And then, as Isabel turned towards her and the angle of the light changed, Galíndez understood.

The dark shape in front of Isabel's face was an arm, the hand gripping a pistol, its barrel in her mouth. Galíndez heard her swallowing in small frightened gulps. Isabel took another couple of steps, guided by the gun barrel, her arms fluttering at her sides, helpless. The glow of Mendez's flashlight danced over her, highlighting the figure in black holding the gun. The chill air turned to ice.

'*Buenas noches*, Ana María.'

'Uncle Ramiro.' She tried to stand but her legs failed to obey.

'You look like you've seen a ghost,' Ramiro said, keeping the gun in Isabel's mouth. 'Better behave yourself or I'll blow your friend's brains out.'

Galíndez obeyed her uncle, though this was not Uncle Ramiro as she knew him. He was a far darker version, big and powerful in his black combat gear. His face had lost all of the ruddy humour it had when she took his photo, and his eyes shone with glassy malice.

Isabel made a gurgling sound and Galíndez saw a silver string of saliva hanging from her mouth, spilling down her sweater as Ramiro lifted the pistol, forcing her to raise her head, moving it left, then right, following the movements obediently, trying not to do anything to make him pull the trigger.

'Not as confident as she was on the radio, is she?' His voice was flat, cruel. 'That's the trouble when women get above themselves. They always come down hard in the end.'

He took the pistol from Isabel's mouth and gestured towards a stone table carved from a large rock near the river. 'Get up on there.'

Isabel went to the table, and sat on it, her hands nervous and uncertain.

'Lie on it,' Ramiro said.

Isabel obeyed, though her body did not and her limbs jerked and trembled with fear.

Ramiro loomed over her. She flinched as he ran an exploratory hand over her.

Galíndez raised her head. 'Leave her alone.'

'I told you to behave yourself,' Ramiro snapped. 'But then, it's been a long time since you obeyed orders, hasn't it, Ana?'

Galíndez stayed on her knees, trying to blink away the lights whirling before her eyes.

'Did you really think you could get away with this?' Ramiro's face twisted with rage. 'All this time and you still haven't learned to keep your nose out of things that don't concern you. Christ, I kept letting you go on secondment to chase Guzmán. You could have stayed in that little room at the university, poking about in the past to your heart's content and I would have kept the funds coming. You could have been happy. You might even have learned something.'

Galíndez struggled to speak. 'I learned one thing.'

'Really?' Ramiro scoffed. 'What was that?'

'Your father didn't commit suicide. He was shot in the back of the head.'

His eyes narrowed. 'How the fuck did you find that out?'

Galíndez lowered her head and shook it slowly, trying to clear her mind.

'She broke into your family crypt,' Isabel said.

Ramiro glared at her, his eyes bulging. 'She did what?'

'She wanted DNA samples to see if Lucia Estrella was your natural daughter.'

'Ana took samples from her corpse?' Ramiro's face was incandescent.

'From all the bodies.'

'You monstrous bitch,' Ramiro shouted at Galíndez. 'Where are those samples now?'

'At HQ,' Galíndez muttered. 'In the lab.'

'Sweet Jesus, they'll have to be destroyed,' Ramiro spat. 'Got that, *Sargento*?'

'Yes, sir,' Mendez said. 'I'll see to it as soon as I get back to HQ.'

Ramiro turned back to Isabel. 'Do you know what the results show?'

She watched him, warily. 'Not yet.'

He grinned, though there was no humour in his smile. 'It won't hurt to tell you, I suppose, not now.'

'Feel free,' Isabel said, keeping her eyes on Galíndez.

'Estrella wasn't my natural daughter,' said Ramiro. 'I bought her from a hospital. Happened all the time back then. The staff took her away after she was born and told the parents she'd died.'

'And baby Ramiro was stolen as well, I expect?' Isabel couldn't keep the scorn from her voice.

'Don't jump to conclusions, Señorita Morente. Baby Ramiro was Estrella's child.'

'She was only twelve,' Isabel gasped. 'Who was the father?'

'Me.' Ramiro shot a scornful look at Galíndez. 'You wanted to know who your family were, Ana. Well now you know.'

'She knows what you are,' Isabel said, starting to get up.

Ramiro gave her a backhanded slap that snapped her head back in a sudden spray of dark hair. She fell back on the stone table, dazed.

'*Sargento*?' Ramiro said, glaring at Mendez. 'It's about time you did something useful. Come over here and take Señorita Morente's clothes off.'

Mendez frowned. 'Why, General?'

'Because I just told you to.' Ramiro's face darkened. 'You might need to hold her down as well. The unwilling ones are always the best, my father used to say. God knows he had enough experience of that in the Civil War.'

Isabel raised herself on her elbow and looked over at Galíndez. Her heart sank as she saw her eyes rolling as she fought to stay conscious.

'I gave you an order, *Sargento*,' Ramiro bellowed. 'Do it or I'll send you back to the Dominican Republic and you can spend the rest of your days picking coconuts off the beach.'

'Isabel?' Galíndez spluttered, still on her knees.

'God, look at her, what a mess,' Ramiro sneered. 'Pathetic, like her father.'

Galíndez raised her head, staring through the blizzard of lights flashing across her vision. 'My father was a hero,' she whispered. 'Everyone says so.'

'Miguel Galíndez was a drunk, a coward and a liar,' Ramiro said. 'I hated him almost as much as I hate you.'

Galíndez blinked, trying to focus. She was losing it.

'He was a loser in every respect,' Ramiro said. 'Don't you remember?'

Galíndez heard Ramiro's voice, though it was becoming faint. She heard another voice now: *Here, Ana. I got you this doll. Off you go and play.*

'Miguel was a rotten bastard,' Ramiro continued. 'He cheated at cards, he cheated at everything, really. Above all, he cheated on your *mamá*.'

A grey mist was rising, swamping her thoughts and feelings, though she felt less pain now. That was good. Maybe she could sleep soon, let it all pass.

'Ana?' Isabel called, seeing the change in her.

Through the mist, Galíndez heard Ramiro slap her.

You like the doll, don't you, Ana?

'You want to know about Miguel?' Ramiro asked. 'He was a shit. But even in death, he had a lucky streak: after we atomised him with that car bomb, the press turned him into a martyr. Not a week goes by without someone reminding me what a hero he was, even though they never knew him. There's no justice in this world.'

Galíndez slumped forward, her arms around her body, hugging herself tight, feeling the cold stone floor pressing against her forehead. As long as she stayed quiet and didn't move, no one could hurt her now. Just stay still, ignore the voices echoing around her.

And there were new voices now. Voices lost in time.

Mamá, why is Papá shouting?

Go to bed, niña, don't make him angry.

'Why did you hate Miguel so much?' Isabel asked, playing for time. Though time to do what, she wasn't sure.

'He was useless. By the time we got rid of him, the bastard was drunk most of the day,' Ramiro said. 'Out of pity, we still used him for the odd assassination which we blamed on ETA. But even that got too much for him.'

'So you murdered him?' Isabel's head snapped backwards as Ramiro hit her again.

'It was no more than a thug like him deserved.'

'He was obeying your orders.'

'True, though there was nothing he wouldn't do for the price of a drink. He'd argue for a while, but in the end, he always did what I told him.'

Galíndez listened to their voices floating above her, light and inconsequential. Just Isabel and Ramiro talking. Grown-up conversations, the background of her childhood.

The sound of the door when Papá *came home. The smell of sweat and cigarettes, the creaking of his leather belt and holster. The sound of a bottle opening. Liquid pouring into a glass. Her mother's voice, shouting, downstairs. No, Miguel, no more, for the love of God.*

'You corrupted him.' Isabel's voice was low.

'Let's say I brought him round to my way of thinking. Not that it was difficult.'

'But why?'

'Power,' Ramiro said. 'My father was a powerful man: people obeyed his orders or he gave them a kicking, me in particular. I soon learned power was something to savour.'

Galíndez felt herself cast adrift from the world, moving slowly away from their echoing voices. Other voices remained, though. The voices in her head.

Shouting. Mamá *crying. The front door opening, then slamming shut. The tic-tac of* Mamá's *heels on the pavement. Downstairs, men's voices.*

'You left something out.' Isabel wiped her nose on her sleeve. Saw blood on it.

Ramiro laughed. 'Did I? What was that?'

'What you did to Ana.'

The door to the living room opening. Stay quiet. Don't breathe.

Quiet, keep quiet, stay under the duvet where no one can find you.
'How do you know?' Ramiro pointed at Galíndez. 'She doesn't.'
The door handle turning.
Somewhere above her, Isabel's soft voice, the words laden with pain.
Wake up, Ana.
Galíndez hugged herself tighter, clasping her sides, her fingers digging into her flesh, her right hand pressed against the scar on her side, her body starting to sway.
It's time to play, Ana María.
Rocking gently, rhythmically. *Make it go away. Please, make it go away.*
Ana, wake up. It's Papá.
'She has nightmares.' Isabel wiped something from her eye. 'And when she does, she talks in her sleep.' Her voice trembled with anger. 'How could you do that?'
'Because I could.' Ramiro laughed. 'Power means never having to say you're sorry.'
It's a new game tonight, Ana. Look who's here, it's Uncle Ramiro.
'It wasn't just once, was it?'
A harsh laugh. 'Power's like that. You always want more. Power is why you're sitting there waiting for me to kill you. Because I have it and you don't.'
'Christ, what kind of man are you? You abused her and then murdered her father.'
Ramiro shrugged it away. 'After her mother's suicide, I wanted Ana to live with us but her Aunt Carmen wouldn't have it, the interfering bitch. If Ana had lived with Teresa and me, she would have been a different person. A normal person.'
Afterwards, the smell of whisky. A present left on the pillow. Be careful what you say, Ana. This is our secret. If you tell, they'll take Mamá *and* Papá *away and you'll be alone.*
Memories surfacing from the darkness, a hail of ice in her heart. She had never told anyone. Even so, someone took *Mamá and Papá* anyway.

'Let Ana go. I'll do what you want.' Isabel's voice was tight with fear and anger.

'You don't have any say in it,' Ramiro snarled. 'If I want you, I'll have you.'

He's hurting Isabel. Keep rocking, make it go away.

Galíndez's fingers dug into her sides as she rocked, feeling the warmth of her flesh, holding herself tight, tracing the scar down her side, her hand moving over her hip. A sudden jolt as she felt the hard contour of Guzmán's Browning, lodged in the waistband of her jeans.

'I gave you an order, *Sargento*,' Ramiro said. 'Get Señorita Morente's clothes off.'

Mendez shook her head. 'I'm not helping you rape her.'

'You're forgetting that you took an oath of obedience, *Sargento*.' Ramiro's voice was thick and threatening. 'Do what you're told or I swear to God I'll have you and your entire family shipped back to the Dominican Republic in coffins.'

'Anything's better than doing what you're asking,' Mendez said. 'Long ago, you told me the *Centinelas* were honourable. From what I just heard, you're far from it.'

'Stop bellyaching,' Ramiro said, 'and do as you're told or you and your family will end up like Fuentes' did.'

A sudden silence. 'No. I've had enough.'

Ramiro shot her. The echoes hammered around the walls of the cavern as Mendez staggered against the stone wall and slid down it, clutching her belly, blood welling through her fingers.

'I ought to kill you,' Ramiro said, glaring at Isabel. 'But I'll give you a chance.' He indicated Galíndez with a flick of his head. 'I'll let you both go if you tell me where that sword is.'

Isabel frowned. 'What sword?'

'Guzmán's sword,' Ramiro yelled. 'Don't treat me like an idiot, I know she found it, so where the fuck is it?'

'She gave it to Cryptography so they could analyse the verse on it,' Isabel lied.

Ramiro's face twisted with anger. 'She gave it to the Cryptography

Unit? For God's sake, they'll make copies and share it with other agencies. Those bastards are probably writing conference papers about it right this minute.'

Out of the corner of her eye, Isabel saw Mendez trying to drag herself along the wall.

'You're all dead,' Ramiro said, shaking his head. 'I'll have to sort the rest out later.'

Galíndez looked up, wincing as a storm of unwanted memories surfaced with unbearable clarity. As she struggled to her feet, she saw Isabel lying on the stone table, her face bruised from Ramiro's blows. And slumped against the wall, Mendez, clutching her belly. Their eyes met.

'It's over, General,' Mendez groaned, clawing at the wall with bloody hands as she dragged herself to her feet.

'Not until I've thrown you in that river, *Sargento*,' Ramiro snarled. 'I never forgive disobedience.'

'Ramiro.' A clear voice, harsh and authoritative.

Ramiro turned. Galíndez was on her feet now, her face smeared with dirt, the Browning held in a two-handed grip. In the half light, it seemed as if her eyes were entirely black.

Ramiro started to speak, though his words were sheared off by the percussive blast of the pistol. A look of surprise as he clutched his chest, struggling to stay on his feet as he began lumbering towards the river and the path back to safety.

Galíndez went after him, purposeful and unhurried. He heard her footsteps and turned, standing with his back to the low stone wall. Below the wall, the endless tide of black water surged past, smashing its way into the chasm downstream.

Ramiro clasped his hands over the wound. For a moment, Galíndez saw a sudden splinter of light reflected from the gold ring on his finger.

A voice behind her. 'Get out of my way, Ana María.'

Mendez staggered past her, the baton in her right hand.

'Good work, *Sargento*,' Ramiro grunted. 'Deal with them and I'll promote you.'

'Fuck you, General.' Mendez swung the baton at his head. She was weak from loss of blood and Ramiro easily knocked the blow aside and seized her arm, twisting her round to face Galíndez, holding her in front of him with an arm around her throat.

'Put the gun down.' A cruel smile. 'You don't want me to hurt the *sargento*, do you?'

Galíndez stood, frozen with indecision. She kept the pistol aimed for a moment and then started to lower it.

'Don't kill me, I don't want to die,' Mendez shouted. Without warning, she sagged against Ramiro's arm, forcing him off balance as he tried to keep her shielding him.

With Ramiro off guard, Mendez smashed her head backwards, hitting him full in the face, sending him toppling over the low wall into the river. Galíndez saw a pale hand clutch the wall and heard his desperate breathing as he struggled to hang on. Suddenly, both hands gripped the wall and Ramiro reared up out of the water, locking his arms around Mendez's legs, trying to haul himself back onto the bank. Before Galíndez could reach her, Mendez stopped resisting and let herself fall backwards, taking Ramiro with her into the surging current. Galíndez watched helplessly as they were swept by the raging current into the foaming crevice in the rock. A sudden abrupt cry of fear, suddenly terminated. After that, there was only the incessant roar of the water.

Galíndez stumbled against the wall of the cavern, gasping for breath. Isabel ran to help her. 'Ana, are you OK?'

'I'm alive,' Galíndez said, blank-faced.

Somewhere along the path, they heard sounds, sharp and repetitive. Echoes in the darkness, footsteps coming towards them. A tall figure emerged from the shadows. A man wearing a long dark raincoat and hat.

Galíndez stared, her mouth open.

Guzmán had returned.

CHAPTER 31

MADRID, OCTOBER 1982, CALLE RELOJ

uentes sighed as he watched the brake lights of the truck ahead. 'I don't know why we had to come this way, it's taking for ever.' 'I hope Guzmán knows what he's doing,' Galíndez said, leaning over from the back.

'Don't you ever stop complaining?' Ramiro snapped. 'It's a piece of cake. We just drop off these files and the job's done.'

'So why all that talk about wills and shooting? He's expecting trouble.'

'At least he's on our side,' said Fuentes. 'That gives us an edge.'

'My father said he was the best.' Ramiro opened a pack of cigarettes and offered them round. 'He said in the middle of a battle, the best place to be was standing next to Guzmán.'

Miguel leaned over for a light. 'Because you had a better chance of surviving?'

'No,' Ramiro laughed. 'Because they were more likely to give you a decent burial.'

'That's a great comfort.'

'He knows what he's doing,' Ramiro said. 'He said he had a plan, didn't he?'

'Yeah, but the boss is a war hero: his plan might be to fight to the death.'

Ramiro shook his head. 'I just hope he's got a better plan than that.'

'There's a square ahead,' Guzmán said. 'Pull over and we'll work out a new route.'

416

Ochoa slowed and pulled up by the kerb. The square was plain and dull, surrounded by apartment buildings. He saw a small church on the far side and near it a tiny bar with a tailor's shop on the corner.

The exit from the square was surrounded by wooden barriers, piles of muddy soil alongside them. By the barriers, a workman was holding a green-and-red sign on a long handle. As he saw the two trucks, he turned the sign to STOP.

'Seems quiet enough,' Guzmán said. 'Apart from those two cars by that bar.'

Ochoa looked across the square. A blue Rover was parked on the pavement in front of the bar. Tinted windows hid the occupants. Two or three metres away was a black Toyota.

'What do you think, Corporal?'

Ochoa's voice was bitter. 'Gutiérrez drew up the route.'

'I could go over there, boss. Take a look who's in the car,' Quique said.

Guzmán thought about it. 'All right, but be careful. Walk over to the church and go inside for a moment.'

Quique nodded. 'I'll light a candle for my *abuela*.'

'Light it quickly then and don't stop to say a prayer for her.' Guzmán reached over and lifted the side of the kid's jacket. He sighed. 'Do you know you've got the wrong fucking holster for that weapon, Private? No wonder you've been fiddling with it. Take it off and stick the pistol in your belt.' He waited while Quique obeyed his order. 'If anyone in that car pulls out a weapon, just draw and squeeze the trigger, got that? Give them the whole magazine, that'll keep them quiet until we get there.'

'Got it, boss.'

'Right, now wander over to the church and when you come out, walk back without letting them see you're watching.'

As Quique climbed down from the cab, Julio leaned over the seat, treating Guzmán to a blast of his rancid breath. 'I could pop out the back and have a chat with that workman, boss. If anything kicks off with the kid, I'll be there to help him.'

'Let him get across the square first, then do it.' Guzmán nodded. 'Ochoa, in a couple of minutes go over to the other truck and warn them there might be trouble. I want them ready if anything starts.'

'As the *comandante* says,' Ochoa said, suddenly formal.

They watched the kid stroll across the square, casual and relaxed, looking up at the rooftops as if he had all the time in the world. 'I'd like to have a son like him,' Ochoa said. 'He's keen and he's brave. I think he'd have done well in the war.'

'Inventive too,' Guzmán laughed. 'I like his idea of lighting a candle for Grandma.' They continued watching as Quique walked past the parked car and under the portico of the church. Behind him, Guzmán heard a soft movement as the sarge's son moved towards the back of the truck.

'Take it easy, Julio,' Guzmán called.

'*Viva la muerte.*' The sarge's son opened the tarpaulin at the back of the truck and climbed down without making a sound. A moment later, Guzmán saw him walking towards the roadworks on the corner.

'"Long live death"?' Ochoa grunted. 'They're half crazy, those legionnaires.'

'Just like his father,' Guzmán muttered. He suddenly tensed and leaned forward, to get a better look at what was happening across the square. 'The kid's gone into the church.'

Inside the church, Quique waited for his eyes to adjust after the abrupt transition from daylight to almost total darkness. Soft whispers echoed around the altar where a few spluttering candles illuminated the crucified Christ in all his gory detail. Quique went to the font, dipped his fingers in the holy water and crossed himself. Then he went to the altar and put twenty pesetas in the box before taking one of the large candles from the box labelled *100 pesetas*. Twenty was all he had till payday and he was hardly going to give his grandmother a cheap candle. He lit the candle from the flame of one of the others and placed it on the altar.

After a quick Hail Mary, Quique wiped his eyes before he went back outside. He could imagine what the *comandante* might say about one of his officers blubbing. He was not going to be the butt of anyone's jokes, especially if they related to his late grandmother.

As he opened the door, blinking in the daylight, he saw the Rover, still parked outside the bar. For the first time he noticed the NO PARKING sign behind the car. An idea suddenly came to him, and he felt his chest swell with pride.

'He's coming out of the church,' Guzmán said as Ochoa climbed back into the cab after giving Fuentes and the others their instructions. 'The time it's taken, I think he must have had the priest say a requiem mass.'

'He's doing what you told him,' Ochoa said, sliding into the driver's seat.

'No he's not.' Guzmán leaned forward, staring across the square. 'I don't fucking believe this.'

Quique's footsteps seemed very loud as he approached the car. As he got closer, he saw his reflection in the Rover's tinted windows. A *guardia civil* must exude authority, that was what they'd told him in training, and he pushed back his shoulders in what he hoped was a suitably authoritative posture. In the Rover, he saw vague signs of movement. A sudden buzz as the rear window slid down. A harsh face stared out, wild eyes, thick stubble.

'Is this your car, señor?' Quique asked.

The workmen were shovelling clay and soil onto the pavement as Julio strolled towards them, giving them the benefit of his slightly deranged smile. They were making a mess of it too, he observed. A couple of legionnaires could easily have done that job in a morning. Across the square, he saw the kid going into the church.

The man with the STOP/GO sign was standing next to the

hole, watching the others. Clearly he was the foreman since he was doing nothing. 'Can I help you, señor?'

'I was wondering how long these roadworks are going to be here,' Julio said. 'Me and my pals back there,' he gestured at the trucks parked in the corner of the square, 'we've got to bring up a big load in a couple of days' time.' He looked dubiously at the hole in the ground. 'If that hole's still going to be here, we'll need to take another route.'

The foreman put the sign down, resting it against the rough wooden fencing that kept pedestrians away from the hole. 'We're nearly done,' he said, wiping sweat from his face. 'We'll be finished tomorrow so you'll be fine the day after.'

'That's all I need to know,' Julio said, looking again at the hole. Shallow, badly dug, no sign of pipes or cables. Certainly no reason to have four men working on it. By the wall, he saw an array of tools, all clean as the day they left the store. Several were nothing like the tools of municipal workmen at all.

'Something the matter?' The foreman's voice was less friendly now. Julio felt the other men tense. One was edging warily towards a canvas bundle on the pavement. As he did, the foreman started to reach inside his shirt.

'There's the kid,' Fuentes whispered as he and Ramiro sheltered behind Ochoa's truck. Behind them, Galíndez was standing with his back pressed to the wall, out of sight to anyone in the square, useless as backup if anything kicked off.

Ramiro peered around the tarpaulin flap. 'Julio's talking to the workmen. Why's he doing that?'

'Don't ask me,' Fuentes said. 'What's the kid up to?'

'Looks like he's going over to that Rover.'

'Is this my car?' The man stared at Quique. 'Whose fucking car do you think it is?'

'You're illegally parked.' Quique tried to make his voice sound more authoritative. 'Can't you read?' He gave a brief nod towards the sign on the pavement.

'I can read just fine, *chico*. Now piss off home and fuck your mother.'

Quique's mouth was dry. 'Illegally parked,' he repeated. There was movement in the car, muttered exchanges. The man in the window continued staring.

'That's it.' Quique took a step towards the car. '*Guardia civil*: you're under arrest.'

'I'm under arrest?' The man grinned. Quique heard laughter from inside the car. It was time to be assertive, he realised. Take responsibility, just as the *comandante* had told them. He took hold of his lapel and pulled back his jacket, revealing the Star 400 semi-automatic tucked in his belt.

'Why is he talking to them?' Ochoa said. 'You told him to take a quick look.'

'I don't know what the fuck he's doing,' Guzmán growled.

'He's drawn his pistol,' Ochoa said. Across the square, they heard the sharp sound of metal on stone. 'Christ, he's dropped it.'

As Quique tried to pull the pistol from his belt, something snagged. Flustered, he pulled harder and the pistol suddenly jerked free, slipping from his clammy fingers onto the cobbles. As he bent to retrieve his weapon, the man in the car leaned through the window and shot him. The brittle echo of the shot hammered around the square, sending pigeons scattering across the red-tiled roofs.

'He's shot the kid.' Before Guzmán could stop him, Ochoa jumped down from the cab and started running across the square.

'For fuck's sake.' Guzmán kicked open the door, keeping the Browning levelled as he followed Ochoa.

Men were getting out of the Rover. Guzmán counted four, three carrying machine pistols, one with an automatic rifle. Instinctively, he dropped to one knee and began firing to cover Ochoa. As he did, one of the men fired a short burst from a machine pistol, sending a stream of bullets ricocheting off the cobbles as Ochoa ran towards them, screaming for the kid to get up and make a run for it.

For a moment, Ochoa stayed on his feet, holding the Uzi in one hand, clutching a wound in his side with the other. Then he pulled the trigger and the square echoed to the Uzi's metallic stutter as a hail of bullets tore through the Rover and the men standing near it. Bodies rolled on the ground, punctured tyres wheezed air. It took only seconds for Ochoa to empty the entire clip. As he reached into his jacket for another, he caught a glimpse of a man outside the bar, raising a pistol. In the brief moment before the bullet struck, Ochoa felt a sudden, bitter disappointment. He had never been lucky.

As Ochoa fell to the cobbles, Guzmán raised the Browning and the square echoed to the thick, percussive blast as the man tumbled back across the pavement and fell against the bar's front window. Guzmán's next shot hit him in the chest, knocking him through the shattered glass into the bar, provoking a chorus of shouts and screams from inside.

As Guzmán dashed forward, he heard the sharp whip crack of a shot and the seething hiss of a bullet as it passed his head. He swung round, realising the shot had come from the Toyota. Another bullet from the Toyota ricocheted off the cobbles, forcing him back. He tugged a magazine from his pocket and slapped it into the Browning. On his right, Guzmán saw Julio, clutching his belly as he staggered towards the Toyota. Behind him, the bodies of the workmen were sprawled around the fake roadworks.

'We're with you, *Comandante*.' Guzmán glanced back and saw Ramiro and Fuentes approaching him, their pistols drawn.

'Shoot at those bastards,' Guzmán called. They opened fire at once, forcing the men in the Toyota to take cover. Guzmán ran forward, grabbed Ochoa by his lapels and dragged him away across the cobbles. There was a lot of blood. Some pain as well, judging from the corporal's shouts.

'I'm dying,' Ochoa moaned. 'Get a priest and let me die in peace, you bastard.'

Guzmán grunted as he dragged Ochoa to the truck, leaving a long smear of blood over the cobbles. 'Me, me, me. It's always the same with you, Corporal.'

A bullet whined past, uncomfortably close. Guzmán let go of Ochoa and fired a couple of shots at the gunman. As Ramiro and Fuentes opened up on the Toyota, Guzmán looked with grim pleasure at the steam rising from the engine, the shattered windscreen, and above all, the twitching bodies on the ground by the car.

'Get me an ambulance,' Ochoa gasped. 'And call my wife.'

Guzmán dragged him behind the truck. 'Firstly, Corporal, addressing me as a bastard is a breach of military regulations.' He stopped talking as Ochoa's eyes closed. Angrily, he reached down and lifted one of the corporal's eyelids, causing Ochoa to bellow with pain. 'I knew you were faking.'

'Leave me,' Ochoa moaned. 'Get the kid to a hospital.'

'I will, don't worry.' Guzmán paused to reload the Browning and then stepped out from behind the truck, cursing Ramiro and Fuentes who were now lying on the ground, pinned down by the men in the Toyota. Guzmán started towards them, firing as he went, slow steady shots, keeping the men in the car occupied. To their right, he saw Julio moving unsteadily in their direction, the blade of the kris glittering in his hand.

Sudden movement behind Julio. One of the workmen was dragging himself on his knees from the roadworks, raising his pistol. Guzmán started to shout a warning but his words were lost as the shot echoed around the square. Julio stumbled to his knees, his face a grey mask of pain. Guzmán took aim and dropped the phoney workman with a body shot, sending him crashing through the wooden barrier into the badly excavated hole beyond.

The men in the Toyota had had enough. As the driver started to reverse, Guzmán opened fire, the soft-nosed bullets tearing into the car, showering the cobbles with shards of glass and metal. And then to his right, a blur of shabby clothes as Julio leaped up and sprinted towards the Toyota, the kris in his hand, no longer worrying about holding in the bloody intestines protruding from his belly as he hurled himself through the open window of the car, screaming the battle cry of the Foreign Legion, '*Viva la muerte.*'

Guzmán ran towards the Toyota as it trembled and quivered on what was left of its suspension. There was much screaming, though none of it from Julio. Inside the vehicle, he saw a tangle of flailing limbs and then even that limited view was lost to him as a sudden spurt of arterial blood turned the inside of the windscreen crimson. As he reached the car, the vehicle shuddered as a single shot rang out, followed by a silence broken only by the hissing of steam and the steady drip of fuel beneath the vehicle.

As Guzmán watched, the driver's door slowly opened and a bloody hand gripped the roof as a man pulled himself from the car, clutching at the door to keep himself on his feet. His face was bloody and his clothes appeared to have been shredded by a wild animal. He stared at Guzmán wide-eyed, as if unable to comprehend the horror of what had just taken place inside the vehicle. Guzmán saw he'd lost an ear. That was the least of his worries.

'I surrender,' the man gasped.

Guzmán's eyes narrowed as he raised the Browning. 'No you don't.' The bullet sent the man flying onto the pavement. Streaks of his brain ran down the shattered café window.

Guzmán went to the car and peered inside. Julio lay amid the corpses of his enemies, the kris still clutched in his right hand. In his left was a ragged, bloody ear.

People were coming out of the bar now, an array of frightened faces. Only one man dared to approach him. 'Shall we call the police, señor?'

'No need: I'm a police officer.' Guzmán was distracted by a groan from one of the men lying alongside the Rover. A yard away, Quique lay on his back, looking up at the sky, his fair hair framed by a halo of blood.

Guzmán gave the wounded man a savage kick in the ribs. 'Did that hurt?'

It took a moment for the man to spit the words out through his cracked lips. 'Yes.'

Guzmán shot him in the chest and the body arched upwards with the force of the blast. That was more than enough for the small crowd, who retreated into the dubious safety of the bar. Far off, he heard sirens.

He walked slowly across the square, reloading the Browning as he went. Gutiérrez had betrayed him again. And again, Guzmán had survived. No doubt the brigadier general thought that, by now, the files were in the hands of the men whose bodies littered the square and that Guzmán and the squad had been wiped out. He would have to learn the lesson Guzmán learned long ago: life was full of disappointment.

There was no question of completing the operation now. He'd been stupid to go through with it this far. The sensible option would have been to grab Lourdes and catch the train south yesterday. And yet something had stopped him: his sense of duty. His belief that once a man started a job, it must be finished. When he was younger, he would have called that stupidity.

Stupidity or not, there was still that one abiding principle that overrode all else as far as he was concerned: *Never let an injury or slight go unpunished.* And determining the most appropriate form of revenge was easy: it was a merely a question of discovering what someone wanted most and then taking it from them. And what Gutiérrez wanted most was the collection of files in the truck. So now, instead of Gutiérrez choosing which files would be preserved or destroyed, Guzmán would let the whole fucking world read them. Let them know what Franco, Guzmán and Gutiérrez had done. He had never entertained such a thought before, but he thought it now: *let people know the truth.* Not because they deserved to and not because it was their right, but because it would fuck up Gutiérrez's career, permanently.

He looked at his watch. There was plenty of time yet before his meeting with Lourdes at the station. Time to do what he had to and then go to Atocha and have a last drink in the decrepit station bar before she arrived. And then head south, to Alicante.

As he came back across the square, Ramiro and Fuentes were leaning against the truck. Ramiro was nursing a slight wound on his arm. Guzmán saw blood, though not enough to evoke sympathy. 'Where's Galíndez?'

Ramiro shrugged. 'He said he was going to get help.'

'He ran away?'

Ramiro paused for a moment. 'Yes, sir.'

'Get a field dressing from the truck and fix Ochoa up until the ambulance gets here,' Guzmán said. 'Once he's taken care of, go over to those babbling peasants in the bar and take statements. When the police arrive, tell them you stumbled across a robbery and intervened. That's all you know. If you're lucky, you'll get a medal.' He slapped Ramiro on the arm, making him wince.

Ramiro climbed into the truck to get the first-aid kit, leaving Guzmán and Fuentes alone.

'We've got a job to finish,' Guzmán said. 'When people ask you about it later, you've got a faulty memory, understand?'

'As you say, sir.' Fuentes nodded.

'Right. You're driving.' Guzmán hauled himself up into the cab. Fuentes ran round to the driver's side and got behind the wheel.

Guzmán lit a Ducado and inhaled deeply. 'We haven't got all day, Fuentes.'

Fuentes started the engine and turned the truck across towards the exit, slowing as they drove over the dead men lying in the mud of the roadworks. 'Where are we going, sir?'

'Vallecas,' Guzmán said, leaning through the open window. 'The old *comisaría* on Calle Robles.' He settled back, aware of the ringing in his ears for the first time. 'And get a move on, I've got a train to catch.'

Cowering behind a parked car near the roadworks, Miguel Galíndez held his breath, waiting until the truck turned a corner and disappeared from sight before he started running.

Villanueva stood outside his brother's hotel, watching as Guzmán's white Ford came to a stop by the gate. Guzmán took his time getting out. Villanueva thought it best not to offer assistance.

'How can you drive with one arm in a sling?' he asked.

'The same way you walk with that crutch stuffed under your arm: with difficulty.' Guzmán took out his cigarettes and offered one to Villanueva. They stood in silence smoking, watching the grey waves break on the beach below.

'They tell me I won't walk without a stick again,' Villanueva said.

'That's too bad. What will you do?'

Villanueva indicated the hotel behind him with a nod of his head. 'My brother wasn't married so I've inherited this place. I think I can make a go of it.'

'Your brother was a brave man,' Guzmán said, exhaling smoke.

Villanueva sighed. 'I didn't know those people were so heavily armed.'

'I would have died if you hadn't raised the alarm,' Guzmán said.

'It's what you do when you're in the police, isn't it, look out for one another?'

'In your police, maybe.' Guzmán looked at his watch. 'I have to go. It's a long drive.'

'I've invited the women to come here.' Villanueva's voice was distant. 'Each year, on the anniversary of...' his voice cracked, 'of what happened. They can stay overnight, comfort one another.' He saw Guzmán take something from his pocket. 'What's that?'

'Money.' Guzmán held up a large roll of banknotes. He peeled off a number of high-denomination bills and handed them to Villanueva.

'Get them a bouquet of flowers each year when they come. Women like flowers, don't they?'

Villanueva nodded. 'I'll tell the ladies you've sent them.'

Guzmán opened the door of his car. 'I wouldn't. They blame me for what happened.'

There was no more to be said now and so they said nothing. A brief handshake told Villanueva they would not meet again.

Guzmán started the car. As he went down the narrow street, heads turned away and he heard cat-calls through the open window. And in the mirror, he saw their eyes, burning into him as he accelerated onto the main road, leaving the village and its dead behind him.

CHAPTER 32

Galíndez stared at the pistol in the man's hand. 'What are you doing here?'

'You know him?' Isabel asked.

'He's the one who tortured me. He said he was Guzmán.'

'You were very brave, señorita,' the man said, still aiming the pistol at her. 'Though it was a waste of time, since you knew so little. Drop your weapon, would you?'

The Browning clattered onto the ground.

Galíndez's eyes narrowed. 'You're going to prison, whoever you really are. Kidnapping's a serious offence.'

'Indeed it is, though I'm afraid the charges won't stick. I'm afraid you're going to be disappointed, as you so often are.'

'All right,' Galíndez said. 'Disappoint me.'

He gave a languid sigh. 'Needs must.'

As the old man raised his left hand, she saw the Taser. Heard the sudden noise as the barb penetrated Isabel's shirt and hit flesh. Isabel fell to the ground, jerking as the electrical charge turned her world into a stuttering series of broken images. When her eyes opened, she was lying on her back, convulsed with pain, helpless as he towered above her, keeping his pistol pointed at Galíndez.

'Perhaps I should introduce myself? Brigadier General Gutiérrez.' He doffed the fedora with a mocking gesture, revealing his bald head. 'Head of the *Brigada Especial*.'

'You can't be,' Galíndez said. 'The *Brigada* was disbanded in 1983.'

He gave her a patient smile. 'Not really. We just made it a little more clandestine.'

'So what are you doing here?'

'Something I should have done a long time ago,' Gutiérrez said. His laugh was dry and humourless. 'Stay where you are, and do keep your hands where I can see them.' He waved the pistol at Isabel. 'Perhaps you should help your friend to get up, Dr Galíndez?'

'What happens now?' Galíndez asked as she helped Isabel to her feet.

'You could start by telling me where Guzmán's sword is. I know you have it.'

'I did have it,' Galíndez nodded. 'But Sargento Mendez stole it, and since she fell into the river with General Ortiz a few minutes ago, I have no idea where it is.'

He sighed. 'That sword holds the key to Guzmán's code. I've been looking for it for some time.'

Galíndez shrugged. 'I can't help you.'

'No, you can't,' Gutiérrez said. 'But there's still something that needs to done in the Western Vault.' He gestured with the pistol. 'You know the way, I believe?'

Isabel clung to Galíndez, still groggy. 'Why do you need us?'

'A matter of housekeeping, señorita. I never leave any loose ends after an operation.'

'What loose ends?' Galíndez asked. 'Ramiro's dead and Mendez died with him.'

Gutiérrez laughed. 'Actually, I was referring to you, Dr Galíndez.'

CHAPTER 33

MADRID, OCTOBER 1982, CALLE RELOJ

S weat poured down his face, stinging his eyes as he ran, the desperate rhythm of his boots on the cobbles rebounding in mocking echoes around the high walls on either side.

It seemed to Miguel Galíndez that his heart would burst if he ran a step further. But the fear of being shot was even more terrifying and he kept running.

The moment the shooting started, Miguel had decided enough was enough. Even though Ochoa and Guzmán had both said there might be trouble, he had not expected it to be so sudden or so brutal. He could only thank God that Guzmán sent the kid to scout out the square and not him. By now, the others were probably all dead. At least he hoped so. That way, he could spin whatever story he liked about events in the square. But there would be time for that later. Right now, he needed to get away. And the further the better.

Gasping for breath, he decided to duck down a narrow side road. Anyone following would never expect a fugitive to head that way, he was sure.

The leg came out of nowhere, extending just as Miguel passed a small passage running along the side of a building. He fell forward on the pavement, skinning his hands, though it was not scraped palms he was concerned about as he rolled onto his back, lifting his hands into the air as he saw the pistol aimed at him. 'Don't shoot.'

The man stood over him, pointing the Beretta. Lazily, he stroked his grey beard with his free hand. 'You know, there's a certain smell comes off cowards like you. I really don't know why I bother helping you.'

'You haven't helped me with anything,' Galíndez whined.

A soft mocking smile. 'I told you your wife was playing around.'

'Oh yes, thanks a lot.'

The Italian took an envelope from his jacket pocket. 'Here's a few more photos for you. I knew you'd want to see them: the two of them going into a hotel, another where your wife is closing the curtains of his room. A nice one of them dancing together. "*Historia de un amor*" is her favourite song, I believe?'

Galíndez scowled. 'How would I know?' He looked at one of the photos and cursed.

'A real man would want revenge,' the Italian scoffed. 'But then, I've heard you have other, much younger interests?'

Galíndez gave him a furtive look. 'It's Ramiro who's into that stuff.'

'Don't waste my time with pathetic excuses.' The pistol came closer. 'What you do is your business. Except when it's mine as well.'

'Well it isn't,' Galíndez said, petulantly.

'Where did Guzmán go in that truck?'

For a moment, Galíndez thought about lying. But only for a moment. 'The old *comisaría* on Calle Robles.'

'You know where that is?'

'Of course.'

'Take me there, now. In return, I'll give you the chance to take revenge on Guzmán.'

Galíndez laughed. 'I've heard stories about him. He's not a pushover.'

'There'll be no comeback: no one will even know what you've done. You'll get him at a vulnerable moment. One shot, two maybe and he's history.'

Galíndez gave him a cunning look. 'Can you guarantee that?'

'I can, *signor*.'

'And what if I say no?'

The Italian shrugged. 'I'll blow your head off.'

MADRID, 28 OCTOBER 1982,
POLICÍA NACIONAL, CALLE ROBLES

The buildings became increasingly familiar as they neared Calle Robles.

'You did well today, Fuentes,' Guzmán said. 'I did wonder if you had it in you.'

'First time I've fired a shot that wasn't on the firing range, boss.'

'There's always a first time.' Guzmán turned on the radio. 'Let's see if there's any news of the election.'

An excited voice cut across the crackle and hiss of the radio. 'Large numbers now voting… queues at polling stations… exit polls predict a significant victory for the PSOE…'

Guzmán switched off the radio. 'Sounds like the Socialists are going to win.'

'I know it sounds strange, boss, but I think it might be a good thing if they do.'

'You know what? I think you're right,' Guzmán said. 'Maybe it's time for a change.'

'That's Calle Robles coming up isn't it, boss?' Fuentes said, slowing. 'The street with the pharmacy on the corner?'

Guzmán ordered him to pull over and they sat for a few moments, with the engine idling. A cloud of greasy exhaust fumes rose from the back of the vehicle.

'We're not going to Toledo,' Guzmán said.

'Aren't we?' A note of surprise in Fuentes' voice.

'The plan was to destroy evidence that would incriminate certain people who worked for the regime.'

'I'd figured that out, sir.'

'That material is far too important to be destroyed,' Guzmán went on. 'So we're going to put it somewhere safe. After that, I want you to forget about it until the result of the election is settled. After that, it's up to you who you tell about it.'

'Begging the *comandante*'s pardon, but I'd rather not have that responsibility.'

'You're the only person I can trust,' Guzmán said, making it sound like a threat.

'But where will you be, sir?'

'I'll be long gone.' Guzmán took out his cigarettes and lit one. 'If I was you, I'd wait for a while and let the new government get settled in. Then let them know where the files are. Tip them off anonymously, if you want.'

Fuentes' face set with concentration as he thought about it. 'All right, I'll do it.'

Guzmán clicked his Zippo into flame and lit the cigarette. 'Good man. The *comisaría* is on the left about a hundred metres further on. You'll see a big church nearby that looks like it was designed by a drunk.'

Fuentes pulled up outside the *comisaría* and waited as Guzmán jumped down and went to the big iron-banded entrance to read a tattered notice pinned on one of the doors.

'Perfect,' Guzmán said as he returned to the truck. 'It's been closed down. Now, while I get things ready, I want you to reverse towards that metal plate in the wall.'

As Fuentes began manoeuvring the truck, Guzmán examined the iron plate. Julio had obeyed his instructions to the letter: each of the nuts holding the plate in place had been carefully loosened, though not so much that the plate would come away from the wall and attract attention. He was a good lad, Julio, Guzmán thought. The sarge would have been proud. Probably, anyway. No one really knew what went on in the old sarge's head. He had not been a man given to introspection or kindness. Or loyalty, now that he thought about it.

The nuts were easy to remove and as the plate started to come loose, Fuentes jumped down from the truck to assist. The iron plate was about two metres long and the height of a tall man. It weighed a lot and Guzmán struggled as they wrestled the plate to one side, its ancient hinges creaking in protest.

Fuentes leaned forward to look down into the gaping hole they had uncovered. At his feet, a sloping stone chute descended steeply into the darkness. Twinkling clouds of dust rose up into the afternoon light, accompanied by ancient smells of damp and decay.

'Is there a cellar down there, boss?'

'A dungeon,' Guzmán said. 'There's room in there for all these documents.'

Fuentes looked again at the steep drop. 'How do we get them down?'

'Why do you think we've got this dumpster? Back it up another metre and then pull the red lever by the steering column. The files will slide out and fall into the chute.'

Fuentes went back to the truck and reversed, keeping an eye on Guzmán's signals in his mirror.

'Stop right there,' Guzmán called. 'Any nearer and you'll push me in.' He edged back around the truck and went to the cab. 'Once the files start sliding into the chute, don't stop for anything. If anyone tries to get in the way, I'll deal with them.'

'Fine by me, boss,' Fuentes said, glancing nervously down the street.

Guzmán looked at his watch. 'It's nearly three. You may find the church bell a bit strange if you've never heard it before. It's like someone took hold of your heart and squeezed.' He turned to the back of the truck and worked his way along the edge of the chute, resting a hand on the back of the vehicle to steady himself as he unfastened the catch on the rear panel.

Somewhere near, he heard a squeal of tyres. Maybe it was the autumn air, or maybe it was because he was standing on the edge of a sheer drop, but the air seemed suddenly cold. The tyres squealed again, closer now. 'Raise the bed of the truck,' he called.

The engine growled as the flat bed of the truck started to rise, though only for a minute: from somewhere in the mechanism, they heard a harsh grinding noise. A smell of burning grease.

'Pull the lever harder,' Guzmán shouted.

The truck bed juddered and then ground to a halt. Fuentes tried again and this time, the bed raised about half a metre. That was progress at least, Guzmán thought, though the angle was still not steep enough to tip the files into the chute. He reached up, trying to find the bolts on the flap of the truck.

Further down the road, near the pharmacy, a car squealed around the corner and pulled to an abrupt stop sixty metres away. The door opened and a man got out.

'It's stuck, boss,' Fuentes yelled.

'Keep trying,' Guzmán said, watching Miguel Galíndez running towards them.

'What the fuck do you want?' Guzmán asked, as Galíndez reached the truck. He was sweating heavily and his dark, unshaven face gleamed in the afternoon light.

'Some Italian's coming after you, boss,' Galíndez panted. 'He turned up at the square asking questions.'

'Why didn't you arrest him?' Guzmán snapped.

'He pulled a gun, boss. He knew you were coming here and wanted to know why.'

'What did you tell him?' Guzmán heard Fuentes trying to raise the truck bed again.

'I ran off,' Galíndez said, sheepishly. 'The others had gone to hospital with the corporal. I just panicked. Once I'd got away from him, I thought I'd better come and let you know he was on his way.'

Guzmán looked past Galíndez down the street. 'I think he's just arrived.'

A hundred metres away, a car pulled up and Guzmán saw two heavily built men get out of the car. Hired muscle, by the look of it, though too flabby to be on a par with the Italian. Then he saw him. Still recognisable after seventeen years, the clipped grey hair, the linen suit. The fucking Italian bastard.

The Church of Our Lady of All Sorrow sounded the hour, sending visceral bass notes swirling down the narrow street. Guzmán raised the Browning and fired, sending the Italian scrambling for cover. One of the men with him fired back and his shot whined over Guzmán's head towards the church.

'Go round the front of the truck and open up on them,' Guzmán told Galíndez. As Miguel slunk away down the side of the vehicle,

Guzmán fired a couple of rounds that ricocheted off the dusty pavement, forcing the Italian to shelter in one of the alcoves set in the ancient wall of the *comisaría*.

Behind him, Guzmán heard the metallic scream of the engine as Fuentes tried to bully the truck into tilting. 'It still won't shift, *Comandante*.'

Crouching at the back of the vehicle, Guzmán loosed off another round before he glanced up at the lifting mechanism. The bed was still only slightly tilted and he called to Fuentes to give it more power.

A sudden flat crack. The bee-whine of the bullet, uncomfortably close. Guzmán spun round and saw the Italian slip back into an alcove at the side of the *comisaría*.

An excited shout from the cab. 'It's moving, boss.'

Guzmán darted a glance behind him and saw the truck bed starting to tilt, sending the boxes of documents tumbling against the rear panel. 'Open it up, Fuentes.'

The bullet hit him in his side, sending him staggering towards the dark entrance to the chute. Warm blood, pain spreading fast, like a woodland fire. He took a step forward and saw one of the big goons lumbering towards him. Guzmán's first shot hit the man just below his chin and he grunted with satisfaction as he saw him thrashing on the ground for a few moments before he died.

The truck bed was still angled downwards though none of the files had yet come out of the rear flap.

'What the fuck's happening?' Guzmán called. The effort brought blood to his mouth and he hawked and spat onto the cobbles.

'The bolt on the panel needs to be unfastened.' Fuentes drew his service pistol and fired a shot that sent the Italian scampering back into cover. Behind the truck, Guzmán pulled his handkerchief from his pocket and pushed it under his shirt to stem the bleeding.

'Keep them busy,' he growled as he sidled along the edge of the chute.

There were two bolts on either side of the rear panel. Guzmán grabbed the first one and tried to pull it open. Normally, the effort would have meant nothing, now, he felt like the crucified Christ in the macabre church up the street.

Fuentes kicked open the cab door and jumped down onto the cobbles. For a moment, Guzmán thought he was about to flee. Then he heard the shots as Fuentes opened fire, driving the Italian back along the wall of the *comisaría*.

A rapid flurry of shots tore into the side of the truck as the Italian and his remaining goon returned fire. If Galíndez started shooting now, those two would be pinned down.

'Get back in the fucking truck, Fuentes,' Guzmán shouted, keeping the pistol aimed into the street. As he heard the cab door slam, Guzmán shoved the Browning into its holster and then jumped, clutching at the panel with his left hand and hanging from it, his legs swinging above the black opening below. 'Tilt the fucking truck.' The truck's engine throbbed as Fuentes raised the bed, tilting it to its extreme angle, its contents falling haphazardly against the rear panel. Ignoring the pain, Guzmán drew the Browning and smashed the butt into the rusty bolt. A slight grating sound as something moved. Something red slid into the gap beneath the rear panel. He saw the dusty cover and the typewritten heading. The report on Alicante. Guzmán gave the bolt another savage blow with his pistol butt.

'I wouldn't bother if I was you.' Galíndez was standing behind him.

'I told you to stay up front,' Guzmán shouted. Turning his back, he brought the Browning crashing against the bolt, knocking it open.

The flap flew open as an avalanche of dusty papers slithered from the rear of the truck and spilled into the chute for a few moments before coming to a halt as the rear flap jammed on a large box. Guzmán went towards the flap. 'Give me a hand,' he shouted to Galíndez. As he reached the back of the truck, he saw the Alicante file lying near the rear wheel. He reached down and picked it up, suddenly aware of Galíndez's silence.

As Guzmán started to turn, Galíndez shot him in the back.

Guzmán staggered, trying to stay on his feet as another batch of files slid from the back of the truck and plunged into the chute, taking him with them.

Galíndez stared into the dark mouth of the chute like a man waking from a dream. Shots rattled off the bodywork of the truck. Clearly the petrol tank had been hit: the air was thick with the smell of petrol.

'Christ's sake, Miguel,' Fuentes shouted. 'Back me up.'

Galíndez ran to the vehicle and opened the cab door. 'Let's get out of here.'

'They'll gun us down if we try to run.' Fuentes looked round desperately, trying to think of a way out, coughing at the thick stench of petrol. He looked down and saw the dark pool growing under the cab. 'Run for it, it's going to burn,' he called to Galíndez, firing a couple of wild shots at the Italian's surviving gunman. The man raised his machine pistol and raked the truck with bullets, forcing Fuentes to scramble across the seat and jump to the ground, following Galíndez down the road to take shelter in the shuttered doorway of an ironmonger's shop.

As they watched, the gunman climbed into the cab of the truck and revved the engine.

Fuentes took a clip of ammunition from his belt and slapped it into his pistol.

'Let him go, for Christ's sake,' Galíndez said.

'Fuck you, Miguel.' As the truck slowly moved forward, Fuentes moved out from the doorway and fired at the engine block, sending a shower of sparks flying from the grille. A sheet of dirty flame rose over the sides of the truck and Fuentes fired again, this time aiming more carefully.

The petrol tank exploded in a vivid ball of fire, engulfing the vehicle in flames. The gunman leaped from the burning vehicle, raising his hands as Fuentes came towards him through the oily smoke, holding the pistol in a two-handed grip.

A single shot, the sound of its blast resonating around the buildings of the narrow street as the gunman pitched forward onto the ground. Flames from the spilled fuel licked around his body. Fuentes and Galíndez ignored him, too busy watching the Italian as he approached through the smoke, holding the machine pistol.

'Is it done?' he asked, looking at Galíndez.

Galíndez nodded. 'It is.'

He stared at them for a moment. 'Can you close that chute?'

Galíndez nodded.

'I'll watch to make sure you do,' the Italian said. He laughed to himself, as if at some private joke. 'You two had better prepare your story,' he said, glancing at the burning truck. 'It's best if the world thinks all those files went up in smoke.' He gestured at the entrance to the chute. 'Forget the documents that went down there. No one will go looking.'

'What do we say about the *comandante* if anyone asks?' said Fuentes.

The Italian shrugged. 'You know nothing, so you say nothing. That's not hard, is it?'

'I can do that,' Galíndez said, suddenly sensing things were working in his favour.

'You'd better.' The Italian smiled. 'Because I can find you wherever you are, Galíndez, if I want to.' He gave Fuentes a cold look. 'You too.'

'Close the chute, you said?' Fuentes coughed as a cloud of black smoke wafted over them. 'And then we forget about what happened?'

'That's all it takes.' The Italian turned and walked away to his car.

As the Italian drove off, Fuentes went to the mouth of the chute and called Guzmán's name into the darkness several times. There was no reply, only the sound of the flames consuming the truck. He waited a moment longer and then went over to the iron plate and called to Galíndez to help him close it before tightening the bolts. When it was done, he lit a cigarette and stood back to watch the truck burn itself out.

'What now?' Galíndez asked.

Fuentes gave him a dark look. 'Get out of here, Miguel, and forget what happened, that's what I'm going to do. While you're at it, you'd better apply for a transfer to another unit. That will be best for all of us.'

He turned and walked up the road just as the first fire engine came round the corner and made its way towards the wreckage of the blazing vehicle.

MADRID, 29 OCTOBER 1982, BRIGADA ESPECIAL HEADQUARTERS,
14 CALLE DEL DOCE DE OCTUBRE, MADRID

Gutiérrez stood in the window watching a man get out of a taxi on the other side of the road. Slim, greying cropped hair and beard. A pale blue linen suit. The taxi driver took out a Luis Vuitton travel bag from the boot, accepting the passenger's tip without comment. The man waited on the pavement until the taxi had driven away. Then he crossed the road and came up the steps.

As Gutiérrez heard the footsteps coming on the stairs, he turned and sent the three armed men standing behind him back into the depths of the building.

A knock on the door. A single knock. Confident.

As he opened the door, Gutiérrez took a long look at the man outside. '*Buongiorno*.'

'It's *arrivederci*, Brigadier General.' The Italian smiled. 'Another job over, even if it did take seventeen years to get him.'

Gutiérrez nodded. 'Some things take time to resolve. Like feuds, for instance.'

'Like feuds,' the Italian agreed. 'Though I confess I'd almost given up on this one. That was why your initial approach surprised me.'

'I knew you'd take the job, though I was surprised you turned down the money.'

'Between Guzmán and me, it was personal. I didn't kill him for the money. That would be an insult to our profession.'

MARK OLDFIELD

'Honour amongst thieves, Signor Santorini?'

'Perhaps so, Brigadier General. Speaking of which, I apologise for the destruction of the files. Guzmán's last shot, you might say. Still, at least they were all burned.'

'Indeed,' Gutiérrez agreed. 'It's a relief that the new government will never see them.'

'And I imagine you and the *Centinelas* are satisfied with my services?'

'Of course. We're very grateful. No doubt they'll express their gratitude in due course.'

'What about Miguel Galíndez? He knows more than is healthy for him.'

'Leave him to me. We'll promote him, that will keep him quiet for now. Maybe we'll advance his career for the next year or so. And then, after a while...'

Santorini narrowed his eyes. 'After a while?'

'When he least expects it, I'll do the business,' Gutiérrez said. 'I owe Guzmán that.'

'When it comes down to it, it's all business, *signor*. Did you get me a car?'

Gutiérrez handed him a key on a leather fob. 'That Porsche 911 parked over there. The documents are on the seat.'

Santorini weighed the key in his hand. 'Let's see how fast it gets me back to Italy.'

'It's a long drive.'

'You haven't seen my driving.' Santorini chuckled as he picked up his suitcase. 'I'll be off. I want to spend the night in Nice.'

'*Buen viaje.*'

Santorini paused. 'You know, I heard you were sick? You look well enough to me.'

'Just an allergy. I start gasping and wheezing if I forget to take my medication.' Gutiérrez took a packet of Peter Stuyvesant from his pocket and lit one. He exhaled a cloud of smoke. 'Have a safe journey.'

Santorini went across the road to the car and stowed his case in the back. The engine purred into life and the car pulled away from the kerb, smooth and unhurried. The Porsche slowed as the lights changed at the junction with Avenida de Menéndez Pelayo. Across the busy road, the trees in the Retiro were bright with autumn colours.

Gutiérrez reached into his pocket and took out a small metal box. As the traffic lights started to change, he pressed his index finger on a button mounted in the centre of the box.

The Porsche exploded in a dirty ball of flame, sending clouds of dark smoke up into the bright morning. Gutiérrez turned and went back inside the building. Another terrorist atrocity in Madrid. The perils of modern life.

He went downstairs and pushed open the conference-room door. A man was sitting at the table browsing through a pile of papers. He looked up as Gutiérrez came in. An instantly recognisable face, thick, dark hair in need of a barber. 'Was that an explosion I heard, Brigadier General?'

Gutiérrez shrugged. 'An accident of some sort, I expect. Sorry to have kept you waiting, especially today of all days.'

'I'd prefer you not to do that now I'm prime minister.'

'Congratulations on your victory, by the way. The polling stations were packed, I'm told.'

'Democracy in action,' the man agreed, pushing his papers into a file.

'So what was it you wanted to see me about?'

Spain's new prime minister wasted no time in getting to the point. 'Once we're in power, Brigadier General, we're going to have to do something about terrorism. ETA in particular. It will be a dirty war, though it's one we must win. Which means I'm going to need advice from someone who knows how to handle such things discreetly.'

'I could be of use,' Gutiérrez replied, almost coy, 'though the department's been run down, I'm afraid. After Franco died, our funding has been cut year after year. I don't know how we've kept going.'

The man opened his briefcase and shoved the file into it. 'Funds can be restored very easily, Brigadier General. I don't see any problems there. I'll have my people address it once we've settled in. It'll be business as usual for you.' He pushed back his chair and got to his feet. 'Any questions?'

'None whatsoever,' Gutiérrez said, extending his hand. 'Business as usual, then.'

CHAPTER 34

MADRID, OCTOBER 2010,
POLICÍA NACIONAL, CALLE ROBLES

Still dazed from the effect of the Taser, Isabel clung to Galíndez as they walked. Behind them, the old man kept his distance, keeping the pistol on them, holding a lantern in his other hand.

'Inside,' Gutiérrez said as they came to the door of the Western Vault.

Galíndez pushed open the door. The heap of files was still there, though shrouded in darkness. Strange shapes from a lantern played along the walls. In the shadows by the fireplace, two men were piling things inside the chimney.

The men came over to Gutiérrez. 'It's all ready, Brigadier General.'

'You can go,' Gutiérrez said. 'I can handle these two.'

The door slammed as the men left.

'Didn't you ever wonder what had happened to Guzmán?' Galíndez asked.

Gutiérrez shrugged. 'I was pretty sure he was killed, though there was never any conclusive proof. Only one person might have known but he refused to say anything.'

'Who was that?'

'A *capitán* in the *guardia*, someone called Fuentes. He was with Guzmán at the end, though for some reason he denied knowing anything about what had happened to him. He kept quiet about the files down here as well. When Ramiro finally found out about his deception he had him and his family killed.'

'You pay with your dead.' Galíndez's voice was flat.

He nodded. 'That's what the *Centinelas* say, you're correct.'

She narrowed her eyes, calculating her chances. He was too far away for her to make a move without being shot. 'So you still don't know for sure what happened to Guzmán?'

'The man I hired to kill him said he'd done the job and I had no reason to disbelieve him,' Gutiérrez said. 'But you could never be sure with Guzmán. He was like a cat, he had nine lives.'

She glanced at the huge fireplace where the two men had been working. The hearth was crowded with plastic containers, piled up into the chimney. 'What are those?'

'Those containers are full of highly flammable liquids,' Gutiérrez said, as if it was obvious. 'There's a detonator attached to them. When it goes off, the flames will shoot up through the building and set fire to its timbers. Within a short space of time, the entire building will collapse.'

'Why do you want to destroy the building?'

'To make sure all these files are finally destroyed, young lady. The material in them is toxic, I need to be sure that future historians can't draw on any of it.'

'You've had thirty years to destroy them. Why do it now?'

'Because I thought they'd been destroyed when Guzmán's truck exploded. None of us knew about this labyrinth underneath the *comisaría* – except Guzmán of course, and he couldn't tell.' He gave her a malicious smile. 'Perversely, it was only when I became aware of your investigation into his activities the other year that I began to realise what might have happened – as did Ramiro, of course. He just sat back and let you do the work for him.'

'But what difference can it make now?' Galíndez persisted.

He sighed. 'Because I want people to remember what happened in the war in a certain way. History is memory, señorita, and memory has a strange way of taking vengeance if left unchecked. No state can tolerate a high level of truth about its past. Secrets are best kept that way and this *comisaría* contains more secrets than I care to think about. It's best if it's destroyed.'

'And you're the person who decides what the State's interest are?' Galíndez scoffed.

'Since you ask, yes. There are things in those files that could harm me.' He smiled, revealing an array of yellow teeth. 'My connection with the *Centinelas*, for one.'

'What connection?' Galíndez asked, surprised.

'Who do you think's going to take over as head of the *Centinelas* now Ramiro's gone?'

She stared at him, slowly realising. 'You? But the *Centinelas* were your enemies.'

'Ramiro was my enemy, but he's dead now. Very soon, I'll be the new Xerxes. With my connections, I can make the *Centinelas* even more powerful. We can shape this country the way it should have been shaped years ago.' He saw Galíndez's expression. 'I'm surprised at your naivety, señorita. Just think of it as a corporate merger, though perhaps a little more violent.' He gestured towards the fireplace with his pistol. 'Time's getting on, I'm afraid. Move over there please, Señorita Morente.'

Isabel shot a desperate glance at Galíndez as she walked over to the fireplace.

'On your knees,' Gutiérrez said.

Reluctantly, Isabel knelt. Gutiérrez handed her a pair of hand-cuffs. 'One around your wrist, that's right, now put it through the rail and cuff the other hand.'

Isabel did as she was told. Cuffed to the heavy iron rail, she could hardly lift her head.

Gutiérrez took a step back, keeping them both covered with the pistol. 'Don't worry, ladies, I'll allow you to leave before the detonator goes off.'

Galíndez doubted that. 'Do you want to know what happened to Guzmán?' she asked softly, talking a step towards him.

He raised the pistol, pointing it at her chest. 'Stay where you are, Dr Galíndez. Don't insult my intelligence by sneaking towards me like that.'

'Guzmán's body is over there,' Galíndez said, pointing over

at the scattered files. 'I found it earlier. He still had his ID card on him.'

Gutiérrez stared at her. 'You're sure it's him?'

'I'm certain. He was wearing a tweed suit and he still had the Browning.'

A heavy sigh. 'There was part of me that would have liked him to survive. But I'd tried to get rid of him once before. If I'd tried again and failed, he would have come after me.'

'His hand was on a file, as if he'd been trying to open it.'

Gutiérrez's eyes locked on her. 'What file?'

'Something about Alicante.' Galíndez pointed into the shadows. 'It's over there.'

Gutiérrez faltered for a moment, perplexed. 'Go and get it.'

She stayed where she was. 'And what do I get in return?'

'I'll put a bullet into your friend's head if you don't.'

In the fireplace, Galíndez saw the small winking light of the detonator. At this rate, she would have to attack him and risk being shot.

He saw her watching him. 'Hurry, Dr Galíndez. The detonator will go off in about six minutes and you don't want to be in here when it does.' He went over to the fireplace and rested the oil lamp on the mantel, filling the chamber with sinister shadows.

Galíndez worked her way through the clutter of files to the spot where Guzmán lay amid the lethal paperwork of Franco's regime. Behind her, she heard Isabel asking Gutiérrez questions, trying to keep him talking.

She knelt and rummaged through Guzmán's pockets. A sudden thought: maybe he'd strapped a pistol to his leg like undercover cops did? She ran a hand over the tweed-covered leg, feeling only dry, fragile bone. A sudden sense of resignation: there was nothing for it. She would have to disarm Gutiérrez and then stop the detonator going off. How she would do that, she had no idea.

As she prepared to get up, she examined Guzmán's other leg for a hidden firearm. A moment of bitter disappointment. No pistol there either. But there was something strange. She felt the outlines of the femur, tibia and fibula but there was something else, something hard, not connected to the other bones. Careful not to attract Gutiérrez's attention, she tore open the faded tweed, her eyes widening as she saw the trench knife nestling in its soft leather sheath.

She glanced back to where Gutiérrez was standing guard over Isabel. Quickly, she slipped the knife from its sheath and then retrieved the Alicante file, putting the knife underneath it.

Gutiérrez saw her coming back and raised the pistol. Then he saw the red cover on the report she was carrying. 'Is that the file?'

'See for yourself.' She offered the file to him, slowly, holding it just out of reach.

He stepped forward, lowering the pistol as he reached for the file. As his fingers closed on the red cardboard folder, Galíndez thrust the knife into the side of his neck. He cried out in pain as he fell to the ground, clutching his throat, trying to stem the bleeding.

'Ana, the timer,' Isabel called. 'Get out, save yourself.'

Galíndez picked up Gutiérrez's pistol and went over to the fireplace.

'Shoot me, Ana,' Isabel shouted. 'Please, don't let me burn.'

'Close your eyes.' Galíndez pressed the muzzle of the pistol against the chain between the metal cuffs. The blast of the pistol made Isabel cry out. Stunned, she lifted her hands away from the rail, the shattered chain dangling loose from the cuffs.

Galíndez dropped the pistol and dragged her to her feet. 'Run, Izzy, for fuck's sake.'

Isabel reached the door first and began fumbling with the latch. It was a job that needed strength and Galíndez pushed her aside and gave the latch a savage kick, knocking it open. As she wrenched open the door, she heard the brittle crack of a shot and felt the sting of powdered stone on her face as the bullet hit the wall above her head.

'Run.' Galíndez shoved Isabel out into the corridor. A sudden noise behind her: Gutiérrez staggering after them, clutching the pistol. As she turned to run Isabel stumbled and fell, tripping Galíndez and sending her sprawling on the stone floor alongside her.

'You're too late, ladies.' Gutiérrez said.

Galíndez rolled onto her side and looked back into the vault. A sudden nightmare vision: Gutiérrez reeling towards the door, his face and neck covered in blood, the dark suit streaked with dust and cobwebs, holding the pistol two-handed as he came.

The vault suddenly glowed with virulent light as the detonator went off. A sudden deep gasp as the liquids in the containers ignited, quickly followed by the gruff bass swell of an explosion that drenched the vault in a liquid fire setting ablaze the great mounds of paper and cardboard.

Gutiérrez kept coming, his clothes burning, his hands charred as they gripped the pistol. His mouth hung open as he took careful aim at Galíndez. She heard Isabel scream, though she kept her eyes on Gutiérrez as she braced for the shot.

Behind him, a deafening banshee howl as a sudden blast of fiery air surged through the ancient vaults engulfing him in flames as the blast slammed the door shut.

For a few moments, Galíndez heard weak blows drumming against the door. Then they stopped and the only sound she heard was the muffled roar of the fire raging inside the vault. She grabbed Isabel's hand and pulled her to her feet. 'Let's go. We need to get out before the fire spreads up into the *comisaría.*'

Running now, they went back past the river, retracing their steps along the ancient passageways and up the spiral staircase into the passage that housed the cells, choking in the acrid smoke now billowing through the *comisaría*. The building trembled as the flames from the vault channelled upwards, igniting the desiccated rafters and joists of the antiquated building.

They dashed past Guzmán's old office, dodging a flurry of scorching embers as the ceiling collapsed in an avalanche of burning timber. Galíndez pushed Isabel through the swing doors and their footsteps echoed across the tiles of the old reception hall and out onto the cobbles. A suffocating wave of sound swept over them. The ancient bell of Our Lady of all Sorrow was sounding the hour.

Exhausted, Galíndez helped Isabel to the pavement across the street and they fell against the wall, holding one another as the fire raged through the *comisaría* in an inexorable storm of destruction. Ceilings and walls collapsed, sending furious showers of glowing sparks into the night sky, the few windows left unbroken now shattering in the intense heat.

Far off, sirens wailed. Along the street, a small crowd was gathering outside the bar.

'I found Guzmán's secrets,' Galíndez said, watching the incendiary fury of the blaze. 'And now they're gone. All of them.' She ran a hand through her hair. 'There's some water in the car. I'll get it.' Unsteadily, she went up the street to her car.

Isabel heard her sudden brittle laugh above the sound of the fire and hurried to join her. 'What is it, Ana?'

Galíndez took a piece of paper from under her wiper blade. 'I've got a ticket.' As she opened the paper, her laughter stopped.

Isabel saw her expression. 'What does it say?'

'It's written by Mendez,' Galíndez said. 'It says there's a problem with the boot.'

Cautiously, she went round to the back of the car and knelt, checking for signs of a booby trap. Finally, she reached for the catch. A sharp noise as the boot opened. She stood, staring inside until Isabel could bear the silence no longer.

'Christ's sake, Ana, what is it?'

Galíndez lifted something from the boot, letting the baleful light of the fire play over it, making the engravings on the blade dance to the hypnotic rhythm of the flames. Slowly, she sank down onto the kerb and they sat in silence, listening to the sirens growing louder on the M-30.

As Galíndez looked down the darkened street, its cobbles glowing with the hellish light of the blaze, she noticed someone watching her from a doorway. Her eyes flickered away, diverted by the death throes of the *comisaría* as it finally collapsed, disappearing in a deluge of flame and smoke into the ancient vaults of the Inquisition.

When she looked again, the man was gone.

CHAPTER 35

MADRID, 1982, POLICÍA NACIONAL, CALLE ROBLES

For a long time, he lay amid the vast sprawl of documents, taking stock of his injuries. It was not promising. With great effort, he struggled to sit up, managing to prop his back against a cluster of heavy boxes. His shirt was wet, he noticed, probably from the water dripping from the roof. But when he touched the dampness with his hand, he recognised at once the thick viscous quality of blood.

A vague sense of disappointment. So this was it, the final chapter of a life he'd stolen from another, long ago. There were things he needed to do, places he'd planned to visit. They no longer mattered, even if he lived; what more could he expect other than a decline in his formidable abilities, a sad life tormented by the bitter awareness that the country was changing despite him and not because of him?

He felt the Browning, nestled under his left arm. As long as that was with him, he was not alone. He rummaged through his pockets and found a cigarette and his lighter. When he lit the cigarette, the lighter flame briefly illuminated the vault and the scale of the heaped documents around him. Earlier, he had heard Fuentes calling his name though he had not replied. If they came looking for him, they would find the documents and Guzmán was not prepared to fuck up another mission. Alicante had been one too many.

He heard the metallic clang as Fuentes replaced the iron cover over the mouth to the chute. He was a good lad, that one. Guzmán had no doubt Fuentes would keep the location of this place secret.

453

Revealing it would put him in danger and he seemed too sensible for that.

The pain was getting worse and his face was bathed in sweat. Briefly, he entertained the notion of taking out the Browning and ending it. Do it sooner rather than later. What did it matter to a man like him? What was life anyway but a rambling interlude before the iron certainty of death? A fleeting moment when happiness seemed almost possible, a flurry of transient pleasures and flimsy achievements. Death was the only true certainty. Find death and you would find truth. And yet, he thought, leaning back against the boxes, there was no need to seek death. When it was ready, it would come for him.

A sudden thought. Where was the Alicante file? He remembered carrying it with him on the truck, hidden beneath his shirt. When he felt for it, his hands encountered only wet, torn cotton. He raised the Zippo again, throwing an uncertain halo of light around him. A metre or so away, the file lay on top of a profusion of loose papers. When he reached for it, the pain was intense. Slowly, he eased himself to the ground and started to crawl, wincing at every movement. There was a strange hissing in his ears, and he lay still, one hand reaching for the file as he shuddered under the waves of pain caused by his exertions. There was nothing to do now but wait. Despite what others might have thought, he had always been a patient man when the situation required it.

For a long time or no time at all, he lay, waiting in the silence and the dark.

And then, nearby, the sound of a door opening. A sudden blast of wintry air. Slowly, he looked up. The old sarge was standing in the doorway. Behind him, Guzmán saw the shadowed city, white with falling snow. The sarge's breath came in ragged clouds of mist as he beckoned to Guzmán.

It was time.

He had not waited long.

Once again, the women return. Older now, the years of sorrow etched deep on faces that resemble those of the crucified Christ in the nearby church where tomorrow a few of them will take mass. Most will not. Faith is so often a casualty of these events. That and truth, of course.

Each year they gather on this date, their numbers diminished by the inevitable attrition of age and sickness. But those who can will make their way once more to this isolated hotel, noting its slow decline without comment, perhaps sensing the deterioration of the building mirrors their own.

The women keep to themselves in the small garden, quietly watching grey waves break along the shoreline below. The past still lies across their lives, a dark monument to cruelty, its presence raw and immediate. No amount of talk can alter that and so they say little. Perhaps there is comfort in the silence, a hope that someone might say something that would, in some unimaginable way, alleviate their inexhaustible grief. No one ever does.

At the end of the second day, as taxis arrive outside, their engines grumbling in the heat, the hotel manager, Señor Villanueva, appears on the terrace, stooping as if he bears the accumulated weight of the women's pain. This year, he is obliged to walk with the aid of a walking frame and it takes some time to get down the steps to lay the bouquet of flowers on their table as he always has. The women wait in silence until he is back inside the hotel. Then they rise, take the flowers and throw them to the ground before trampling them into a fragrant mulch as they always have ever since that day, fifty years ago, when Señor Villanueva told them who had sent them the flowers.

Each year they come, these women, and each year they are fewer. One day soon, there will be none.